In the voice of the bees...

Human beings exist connected each to each but believe that they are not. Honeybees dwell in the full realization of that connection and have done so for eons. The unity we embody is a reflection of the kingdom-wide Unity that dwells in us all.

This we offer you. Come sit. Be with us. Drink in the Unity as you would fresh rain.

—Jacqueline Freeman, *Song of Increase*

THE BEEKEEPER'S QUESTION

Love and Honey, War and Reckoning
A Novel of WWII

christina baldwin

2024 © Christina Baldwin
All rights reserved.

The characters do not represent actual persons, living or dead.
All opinions expressed are those of the characters and
should not be confused with the author's.

Cover design: Olive Elizabeth Black
Text design: Beth Farrell
Butte cover photo: Rebecca Dougherty
Author photos: Susan Scott

Sea Script Company
Seattle, Washington
www.seascriptcompany.com
contact@seascriptcompany.com

ISBN: 979-8-9916718-0-4

First Printing September 2024

No part of this book—text or images—may be reproduced or utilized in any form or by any means, electronic or mechanical, including photocopying and recording, or by any information storage and retrieval system without permission in writing from the author.

Printed in the United States

SEA SCRIPT COMPANY
BOOK PUBLISHING

Author's Note

This is a work of fiction. Though the story is imbued with aspects of my family heritage, the characters do not intend to represent actual persons, living or dead. I have borrowed the homestead and occupation of my grandfather to set the stage for this fictional story. The town is a fictionalized locale embedded in the landscape of west central Montana. At the beginning of the twentieth century, there was an Indian boarding school in the area. Incidents related to the school and portrayed in the story are fictional, though the horrors of Euro-American treatment of Native Peoples are heartbreakingly real.

Characters' conversations, prejudices, language use, relationships and events are portrayed in the context of the story and the years 1942-1943. I have done extensive research to maintain accuracy regarding historical events and their impact on rural America during World War Two.

This story stands on the traditional territory of the Blackfoot Confederacy. I am profoundly grateful for the education and support of a tribal cultural advisor who has reviewed my presentation of Blackfeet characters and situations. Bundle keepers in the tribe have asked that acknowledgment be made to the people of the Blackfeet Nation (*Amskapi Piikuni*), generations past, present, and future. I bow to their generosity of spirit. I pray this story educates and awakens white readers and that Native readers feel respected, even in the hindrance of my cultural blinders. All inaccuracies or misrepresentations are mine. Some aspects of tribal knowledge have been deliberately fictionalized out of respect for the sacred nature of these teachings.

The invitation of fiction is to increase readers' capacity to imagine lives widely divergent from our own. Writing fiction requires the author to slip skins and trust imaginal sources. Writing fiction is an act of co-creation between the author's original plot and emerging engagement with those who answer the call of story. As characters took their voices and places, I have done my best to shape their stories without getting too much in their way. May this alchemy hum through these pages.

*For the generations behind us, within us, before us,
may we honor the stories that preserve,
strengthen, and imagine.*

A festoon of bees

Christina Baldwin books and eBooks available at:
Amazon.com

To contact Christina:
christinabaldwin.com

Facebook

Part One
The Irish Girl & The Beekeeper's Son

1
The Irish Girl

AUTUMN 1941: *Armies of the Third Reich occupy most of the countries of Europe. Japanese forces occupy island nations of the Pacific. No one stops them.*

FLAILING AT BLANKETS, STIFLING A SCREAM, the Irish girl woke, gasping from a shadowed dream. She pushed her ghostly pursuers back to the nether regions of night and gathered herself for another day. Before she rose to tasks of monotonous servitude, dressed in the black uniform (she washed), the starched apron (she ironed) and sensible laced heels (she polished), she recited her morning mantra. "My name is Maire MacDonnell. I am a grown woman, gainfully employed, in Philadelphia, America. The Atlantic Ocean guards me from the bully who woulda ruined me life." An Ulster Protestant, she made no sign of the cross but nervously pressed her pounding heart. "Dear Lord, busy though Ye be, watch over me today." She inhaled a calming breath and oriented herself in the small attic room.

Tuesday: Ladies' Luncheon. The Missus would be aflutter.

"And faeries," her Nana's voice vibrated in her mind, "Dinna forget the wee." Maire ran her fingers through a tangle of dark auburn curls and swung her feet to floor. She didn't believe in the wee folk. Not since they had abandoned her to the mean hands of Broin Mulvaney that horrible day in the hedgerow. Her tenth birthday.

After he ruined her, Broin always caught Maire alone, pressing her against a knobby wall, the backside of a cottage, even the tombstones she tended in the Methodist graveyard. For him, no one to see; for her, no one to help. "Coming for you, girl," he hissed. "You turn sixteen, you mine." He pinched her cheeks, forced a kiss, grabbed her wherever he pleased. "You be wantin' it when you finally get it." He would grind his big boy hips to her little girl bones, a hard sausage under his trousers. Broin Mulvaney was half an orphan whose father beat him for every offense until the day Broin broke a chair over his Da's head and battered him near to death. The old man was a simpleton after that. The boy, burly and raging, good with a knife, fists the size of cobblestones eager to fight. No one stopped him. "I'm saving some'thun real special for ya weddin' night." And then he'd pin her arms, lean so close spit hit her face, "Fuck anyone else, and I'll kill the both of yeh."

Fearing she might accidentally do the thing that would make Broin kill her, Maire pestered her brother, George, "What does it mean, that word 'fuck'?"

George laughed weirdly, his voice half-boy, half-man. "Fuck is when a bloke puts his bod up your twat." He swallowed hard, "Juss be a good girl. Don't let anyone do it." She still had no idea.

When Maire was twelve, Nana took sick and after an agonizing winter was lowered into the churchyard, another grave for the girl to tend. That sorrowing day, she stood wrapped against the rain in a long grey shawl that nearly touched the ground off her small shoulders. "My arms are always 'round you." Nana had barely finished knotting the fringe before the faeries carried her away. "A gift for your wedding night," she had whispered, pressing the heirloom into Maire's arms. Maire prayed it would protect her from the fuck.

The Beekeeper's Question

When she was sixteen and a week, her father stumbled home from the pub bragging he'd traded her to Broin for three sheep. "We raised a pint. You be his wife."

Maire jolted from half-sleep, pulling her night shift around her shoulders. "Broin's a bully, Da. Let me hire out in Ballymena, find work and a kinder man."

Her father had leaned over her, swaying with drink. "Broin may be rough, but he makes the world give'em what he wants. He wants you."

Maire pushed tangled curls from her eyes and held her ground. "No. I say no, Da." It was the first time Paddy MacDonnell hit her instead of her mother, so she guessed she was a woman now, but she would not be Broin Mulvaney's woman.

"You all I got to bargain, girl," he slumped onto his cot. "Get a yes out'n her, Ailish." His wife slipped off his worn boots, slid a pillow under his head. "We need sheep."

Ailish MacDonnell turned and cradled her daughter's face in bony hands. "Ah, me gal, I canna bear to see you live me same life." Maire nuzzled the rare and tender gesture. "Nana said to mind the spark in you. I shoulda done better." Ailish glanced at her snoring husband. "I know where they hidin' passage money fer George." Her fingertips shushed Maire's lips. "Take it 'fore the boys come back or yer da comes 'round."

Tears spurted from Maire's eyes, "I dinna know anythin' about the big world, Ma."

Her mother was firm. "Ballymena cain't hide yah after now. Get to Belfast. Book yerself to somewhere." When her mother wrapped her in Nana's shawl, Maire knew her life in Cullybackey was done. "You stood for yerself. Yer smart. You can handle the world, *mo chroi*." Ailish pressed a worn leather pouch into Maire's trembling hands and pushed her out the door. "Find your way. Trust the Lord. Send me word you live."

A well-dressed woman sat in the immigrant boardinghouse parlor to interview for a girl. Maire inhaled courage and stepped over the threshold carrying a tea tray. "My name is Maire MacDonnell." She nervously rattled off the sum total of herself. "I have my visa. No diseases. Legal age. Protestant. Northern Ireland." She dipped a curtsy, subtle enough for the lady to notice, but not so deep that Maire felt subservient. "I was applying to service when the opportunity arose for travel to America." She briefly met the woman's gaze and handed her the cup and saucer with a steady hand, scrubbed fingernails.

"Where did you learn such fine speech, Mary?" The lady was fine-boned, skin white as the cup in her gloved hands, maybe ten years older than Maire herself.

"I am educated to the eighth form and had good teachers."

"The lilt is charming. The tea graciously served. Can you manage household chores?" The lady tilted her head, straight brown bob under a modest hat.

"The only girl in my family, Ma'am. I do laundry, cleaning, can raise a garden plot."

Maire watched the woman conjure images of a thatched cottage with smiling leprechauns wishing their plucky daughter farewell. "Well then, my name is Eleanor Annenberg. My husband, Roger, is in the shipping business in Philadelphia. I can offer you room and board and $4.00 a week. Wednesday afternoons free." There was something frail about her, Maire thought, as though she'd once been ill and survived but never completely recovered. "Do you accept, Mary?"

"Moo-rah, my name," she whispered, then more loudly, "Yes, Ma'am."

Eleanor extended her hand, "Welcome to the household, Mary." They caught the 3:00 p.m. train from Penn Station. At 7:00 p.m., she who would be called Mary, was dressed in a black uniform and white apron, serving Mr. and Mrs. Annenberg their evening meal. At 8:00 p.m., she was eating late with the cook, nodding at Regina's instructions. By 9:00 p.m., Maire had unpacked her few belongings into an attic bedroom, washed in a real bathroom, laid down between real sheets in an alcove with electric lights and her own small window that framed a half-moon. It was the greatest luxury she'd ever known and the loneliest she had ever felt.

Maire folded her hands over the sheet. "Thank'ee God for bringin' me safe to shore. Ease Mum's heart. Pray Pa don't beat her hard nor George be too hepped up. Cover me trail that Broin never finds me. Amen." She forgot to pray for no nightmares.

Near four years on, Maire knew the brand of perfume that wafted off Eleanor's shoulders and what it cost at Gimbals. She ironed her mistress's dresses, starched the master's shirts. She knew how much cream they took in their coffee, how much jam on their toast. She cleaned their chamber and toilet, untangled sheets after their sex and washed the disappointment of another month's blood from Eleanor's nightclothes.

First Tuesdays, the ladies rotated from house to house for elegant luncheons that set each matron into a tizzy of perfection. "Mind the crusts, and don't butter the bread until you hear their voices. I don't want soggy sandwiches."

"We do it right. Don't you worry, Missus." For Regina, the trial was in the kitchen; for Maire, in the serving.

"Your Irish girl is charming," Mrs. Potter remarked when Maire's back was turned to the sideboard. "Those curls, trim waist, ever make you nervous, Eleanor?" Her cup clinked lightly on the saucer. "Myself, I like Negroes in the house. My Elsie is plain, but I never worry about her inciting mischief." Maire felt an appraising glance slide up her spine. It made her shiver. The Mister made her shiver, too, but he never touched her. Instead, he granted her access to their library and engaged in little tests about her reading as though constantly amazed that someone of her class was capable of comprehension.

christina baldwin

Most nights, Maire read to utter exhaustion. With volumes piled under the bed, tucked against her torso, flopped open on her belly, she crowded out her hauntings with story and knowledge. Twice a year, going through the Cullybackey postmistress, Maire sent home remittance and her mother sent back news. Broin had gone to prison, sentenced for battery. George had gone to Australia. Gordy worked in Belfast. Her father worked in a boot factory in Ballymena. Except for nights of surprise that jolted her rudely awake, her private terror subsided as the world's terror escalated. Nazi armies marched over Europe. People huddled in the park under cardboard and canvas. She was lucky to be Annenberg's Irish girl.

Autumn 1941, with the Selective Training and Service Act drafting young men, Army recruits streamed into the city on weekend leave from Fort Dix and Fort Monmouth, New Jersey. "There are Saturday night dances at the Armory," she kept her voice neutral, "Chaperoned. Other people's girls are going."

Mister flapped his newspaper, "I expect you to comport yourself as befits our reputation." Missus gave her a green dress, matching pumps, and a smile.

Hand on the doorknob, Maire prayed to the spirit of her grandmother. "Help me, Nana. I need a man to make me own life."

Late September, Glen Miller's "In the Mood" blaring from a phonograph and speakers, she sat in the far corner of the hall perusing the young men who were perusing her. A recruit in Army khaki stood silhouetted in the doorway. He ran his fingers over a military cut of brown hair. Their eyes met. An internal buzzing stirred through her. The air seemed to fill with high-pitched humming. She thought she smelled honey. The harshly lit room turned warm and golden. She heard her Nana's voice, "Trust the fey."

2
The Beekeeper's Son

AUTUMN 1941-JANUARY 1942: *Britain stands alone against the Nazis. Churchill pleads for American entry. Congress remains isolationist. Roosevelt plans for the inevitability of war.*

FORT MONMOUTH, NEW JERSEY, was not anything like Pigeon River, Montana. Franklin Cooper was far from home and that was the point—to get away. He'd tried a year of college but came home declaring, "I'm just wasting money, Pa, until I know what I want." He worked as a gandy dancer for the Northern Pacific, set semaphores, learned Morse code, and telegraphy. The job gave him an eye to the wider world, a glimpse of city life when he overnighted with his brother in Seattle, but the work itself didn't satisfy. By default, he endured another summer as the only remaining son in his father's Cooper & Sons honey business, work Leo Cooper found rewarding but only made Franklin more restless.

When they talked, elbows resting on hive lid or kitchen table, they veered away from familial deaths and departures into discussions of politics, religion, social issues. To prepare sermons in his double role as the local preacher, Reverend Leo Cooper read *TIME* and *LIFE* and *Zion's Herald*. "Beyond the banks of Pigeon River," he intoned from the pulpit, "the world faces a crisis that will determine the fate of the modern era." Franklin slouched in the back pew cleaning his fingernails with a pencil point from the offering box. "This conflagration may seem far away, but in the next few years we will face an historical destiny that tests humanity's character and faith." Franklin jerked to attention. His father's prophecy rang in his bones. A week later, he hitched into Great Falls to an Army recruiting station. He didn't wait to be drafted. He didn't apply for agricultural deferment. He didn't ask his father's approval. If war was destiny, Franklin Cooper would step into the fray, not wait to be dragged off the back of the honey truck when things got desperate. The Army would be his path to manhood.

Beekeeping wasn't on the list of the Army General Classification Test, so he mentioned his familiarity with railroad telegraphs and found himself at Fort Monmouth, New Jersey, U.S. Army Signal Corps. In three weeks of basic training, PVT F. Cooper learned to shoot an M1 Garand rifle, handle a 16-inch steel bayonet, and toss MK 2 fragmentation grenades with a clear understanding of how long four seconds is.

Lying in the dusky barracks, shadowed by spotlights that glared across the yards, recruits and draftees traded bravado like baseball cards. "War coming or we wouldn't be here... Not our fathers' war, no trenches... Jerries stomping over Europe, we'll be chasing Nazi asses with tanks and telephones. Third Reich won't last a thousand days once we're in... Japs just as nervy. We better watch both coasts... What's America waiting for? Let's get'em, get it over... I got a gal at home... Me too."

The DI yelled through the open door, "Shut yer traps, scumbags or you'll pull extra duty." Someone tapped F-U-D-I in Morse code on a bunk rail; waited for his buddies to decode it: *fuck you drill sergeant.* Snorted laughter, then snoring. Soon the DI would torment new recruits, and Franklin would advance into training with field telephones, portable switchboards, miles of wire, transmitters, generators, and radios. Under the banter, these guys were smart. Boys from Ohio, New York, Texas, California... and him. So, it wasn't only his almost-a-doctor-brother Boyd who had brains. He lay there grateful for years of dinner conversations, newspapers and magazines, parental quizzes on current events. He missed his father, even though their conversation had sputtered to a halt, and they didn't know how to restart it. The guys ragged him. "There's girls and dances at the Armory in Philly. Do you good."

Franklin stood in the doorway watching a gawky blond in Navy blues thread his way toward a young woman with auburn hair, wearing a bright green dress. She looked like Christmas. He caught her eye. She smiled. He wanted to see that smile again. He ran his fingers over his cropped hair and loped across the room, intercepting the sailor. "Sorry Navy," he reached for the girl's hand, "This one's an Army gal. Right Miss?" She blushed. He pulled her gently to standing and led her onto the dance floor. "My name's Franklin," he said. "Not much a dancer but we can fake it a few minutes." He dipped and didn't drop her.

"A noble rescue is a good beginning," she smiled again. "My name is Maire."

He backed up, looking her over. "Well, Miss Moo-rah, sounds like you come from further East than Philly." He stepped on her foot.

She winced. "Northern Ireland. The Protestant part. Methodist actually—no drinking, no cards, no dancing."

He burst out laughing, "You're Methodist?" Her spine stiffened under his hand.

"My da is just Irish, but my ma is devout."

"No offense," he said quickly. "It's just that *I'm* Methodist. I mean my pa is devout; me, well, everything is assumed." He gestured toward two chairs at the side of the room. "Can this preacher's boy buy you a soda pop?" He dashed to the bar and returned with two bottles of Coca Cola; she hadn't moved.

christina baldwin

A good sign. "Pigeon River, Montana is a bump-in-the-road. Everybody I knew, I knew all my life. I had to get out of there, see something of the world."

Maire smiled, "Cullybackey, County Antrim is a wee bump too. I... I had to leave. Been here since '37, hired as a housemaid."

He leaned toward her, elbows on his knees, "So, we are both adventurers." He hoped he guessed right. "I enlisted to take on something big. History is happening." He took a long swig of Coke, looked her in the eye, "Don't you think so, Maire?"

She met his appraising gaze. "Have you ever read Arnold Toynbee?"

He whistled. "You mean, *The Breakdown of Civilizations*, Oxford University guy?" She nodded. "Does it count that my father quotes him at the dinner table?"

They met again the next Saturday. And the next. He listed the books she referenced, began looking for a library near the base. He mimicked the lilt in her voice with his western twang, said her name, rolling the 'r' self-consciously. "Moorrrah... it sounds like water with reeds and little fishes nibbling at your toes." She unraveled tales from the big house. "Bet they love you treating them like landed gentry with that accent and all. They ought to come West, they want land. We got it—dirt and rocks, Big Sky, a few good rivers, and miles of ditch." He'd showed her his calloused hands, flexed his muscles, wrapped her fingers around the bulge of his bicep. "This is what it means to be 'landed,' in America, and you can forget the 'gentry' part." The matrons tapped their shoulders with a yardstick, "Six inches of separation." Six inches that filled with electrical storm.

And then a larger storm: December 7, 1941.

"A date that will live in infamy." The President addressed Congress with deliberate cadence, letting the gravity of the situation sink into a continent of ears. "As Commander-in-Chief of the Army and Navy, I have directed that all measures be taken for our defense. No matter how long it will take us, the American

The Beekeeper's Question

people, in their righteous might, shall win through to absolute victory." The U.S. declared war on Japan. Three days later, Germany declared war on the U.S. History happening for sure.

The awkward scene at the farmhouse table the day Franklin told his father he'd enlisted faded behind his new experiences. He'd crossed the continent, gotten assigned to Signal Corps, made new buddies. Now he had a girl. If this was destiny, well things were going swell. "I'll be stateside for months, Maire. Rumor says my unit is going to Texas for advance training. It's warm there, even in winter. We could give each other a lifeline to get through." They'd been walking along the banks of the Schuylkill, ducked into a diner for soup and coffee. He held her hands across the tabletop. "I've never met anyone like you, I want to know you. I want you to know me. It's like we've been looking for each other, don't you think?" He searched her face. "These are risky times. Will you take a risk on me?" He got down on his knee. His heart racing in his chest, he held his breath, extended his hand.

A surprised look, a pause, a smile. She inhaled, "Yes." Franklin exhaled. The waitress rang a spoon on a glass, everyone cheered. December 15, 1941. They'd known each other eleven weeks and four days.

Franklin shoveled coal into mansion basements, made extra cash to buy a wedding band, 14-carat. On Christmas Eve, a free Wednesday, when the justice of the peace asked, "Do you take this woman to be your lawfully wedded wife?" he saluted, "Yessir." The U.S. Army gave him a forty-eight-hour leave. Roger Annenberg gave them twenty-four hours at the Rittenhouse Hotel. Eleanor gave her a satin nightgown and matching bedjacket. When she stepped out of the bathroom tears welled in his eyes. "You're breathtaking, Moy, my darling girl." She walked shyly into his embrace. He tipped her lips to his, ran his trembling hands over the sheen of satin. They eased down onto the sheets.

Franklin commandeered a Jeep and cut the back highways across Jersey, showed up every chance he could. Slipping into the kitchen entrance, he charmed Regina out of dinner leftovers on his way to the attic. New Year's Eve, after the rise and fall of making love, he proclaimed, "We're going to be really good together, don't you think?"

She tightened her hold on him, "Promise me you'll get through. Don't get hasty to fight. I'm counting on you to be broody, *mo chroí*."

"You make me sound like an old hen." He lit a cigarette, even though the Missus didn't approve of him smoking in the attic, and the Methodists didn't approve of him smoking at all.

She traced his jawline with her fingernail. It made him hard. "Broody is a man who swallows his first word and speaks his second. Broody is a man who chooses when and how to prove himself, because war dinna give you a second chance."

"Well, I'll have to think about that…"

"That's what I mean, you *think*. A necessary thing out there, darling."

"If I like this thinking stuff, I won't be content on the family homestead." He stared out the dormer window. "Country preaching can't support a family, so my father manages colonies of bees placed around the valley. Named the honey business Cooper & Sons, but he didn't consult the sons. My oldest brother Boyd escaped to university in Seattle. My other brother Jesse ran off to be a cowboy. I enlisted." Franklin blew smoke toward the rafters. "We got differences, but my pa's a decent man." He inhaled a long drag. "If things fall apart, you go there, Moy. He'll take you in, and I'll know where to find you." Maire lay her head on the rise and fall of his chest. Franklin's hand tapped Morse code on her shoulder blades.

In the aftermath of Pearl Harbor, Roger Annenberg and his associates positioned themselves for profit as the shipping industry flipped into high military production. Maire poured coffee and emptied ashtrays, overhearing library discussions fueled with French cognac and Cuban cigars. The Mister's benevolence toward his maid and her soldier boy played well amongst these men. Maire tolerated their glances. She and Franklin had their own plans, and the Annenbergs didn't know about Texas. They would move together into a community of the newly enlisted and newly married—soldiers in training, wives working off base, potluck suppers and card games, nights at the movies.

January 14, 1942, Franklin got papers for detached assignment to the 34th Infantry Division with orders to report for deployment into European operations. He sputtered in shock, protested to his superior officers. Maire cried. They had twenty-four hours.

"I canna stay here the whole war," she confessed into the tangle of sheets and limbs as they lay alongside one another one last night in their attic nest.

Franklin stroked her back. "The war will change things, Moy, you watch," he traced the knuckles of her spine sending shivers that turned to heat between her thighs. "A war needs everything all at once. America got to mobilize like never seen before and when the men are gone, women will have new opportunities."

She ran her hands over his cheek bones, through his hair, across his muscled shoulders. "I hardly know anything about America except this household. And we've had so little time. Promise me you won't forget us?"

"Not a chance!" He smiled into her worried face. She felt him go hard. She felt herself go wet.

The next morning, they walked as slowly as possible toward the train station and the moment of parting. "You *are* going to write me."

"Long as you remember I'm most charming in person."

She stared at him, memorizing the cut of his chin, his prominent but shapely nose, blue eyes deep-set and often lively as if self-amused. He was charming in person. "I just write APO and it finds you?"

"Armies move. Trust the code to follow the unit and the man."

"Trust each other." She squeezed his hand.

At 30th Street Station, she buried her face in his jacket, nervously twisting the brass buttons bright on olive-green wool. Franklin heaved his duffel onboard and jumped up behind it. His hand reached through an open window. Maire's hand reached from the platform. The hiss of brakes releasing. Rail cars jerking. Fingers slipping. His hand waving among dozens of finger-tipped branches reaching from the train. He was a soldier. She was his wife. It was their war.

3
Riding West

MAY 1942: *German forces battle British troops for control of North Africa. Northern Ireland is billeting thousands of U.S. troops. Generals debate strategies for gaining a toehold in Europe.*

HILLS SPROUTING IMPOSSIBLE SHADES OF GREEN rolled to the unbroken horizon. Cows and calves, a blur of birds. The *Empire Builder*, double locomotives pulling fifty freight cars and two passenger cabins, heaved pastel tongues of vapor into the vast panorama of Dakota/ Montana borderlands. Maire was nearly two thousand miles from Cherry Street and still riding west across a continent as wide as the Atlantic. Echoes of her desperate flight out of Ulster ricocheted in her mind. Then. Now. There. Here. Girl. Woman. She'd never taken holidays. Never traveled further from the big house than sixty miles when the neighbor's chauffeur had driven her to Atlantic City to touch the sea and she'd blackened his eye for touching her. Swaying in the rhythm of the train, her hands clutched a tweed valise containing a second housedress, two blouses, and a pair of jeans all purchased from Goodwill. Its zippered pocket held a thin bundle of Franklin's letters she'd nearly memorized. Wife. Alone.

January 30, '42 letter #1 and two weeks since I kissed your lovely lips.

Dear Maire (Moy-darling)

We were six days crossing the Atlantic. I stood on the deck for hours, thinking of you being only sixteen and headed the other direction. Day four they announce we're headed to Northern Ireland. Docking in Belfast. Guess you know where that is.

We are living in tents while we build an Army base. It's freezing! It's raining! We're putting up Quonset huts in a muddy field in County Antrim. My hands are cut from handling sheet metal. The troops will practice maneuvers until High Command decides how to liberate Europe. I'll keep watch for anyone named MacDonnell and introduce myself. It's not a big place. What's the name of that town? Love, Franklin

PS: Miss our cozy bed and the warm fire of you.

Maire, too, missed their cozy bed. Her protective wall of books all hard corners after their precious weeks of passion and bare-skinned tangle. Her nightmares of pursuit now complicated by panic. She'd read the headlines: **First U.S. Troops. Belfast, Northern Ireland. Assisting the Allies.** What if Franklin stumbled into the secret terrors of her childhood and the real demon, with real fists, and real rage? She had mailed her letter imploring "Where are you?" a day before Franklin's letter revealed his whereabouts. The news was shocking. He was there; she was here. She dreamed of mailbags tossed in ship's holds, love letters torpedoed into the Atlantic. Their mismatched communication made her nauseous. Her hands trembled as she set down morning toast and coffee. Mister harrumphed behind his newspaper. Missus took the plate from her hand. "You best figure how to live with this, Mary. It's going to be a long war."

February 18, 1942, #2

I got your letters #1 and 2 and the photo of us. I miss you too. Days are a blur of training in every weather.

we got enough huts up to eat and sleep inside, but rain on metal is deafening. Everybody trying to adjust.
   My old signal unit did go to Texas. We were so close to having more time! I can see the 34th needed radio men, just wish it wasn't me. Pouring rain. Gray skies. Chilling damp. Fog. Sheep. You know! Still looking for some MacDonnells.
Love, Franklin

When Maire wrote her mother in January, she had signed the letter, "Mrs. Franklin Cooper." The thought of them meeting, a tiny thrill. When her mother wrote back that Broin was out of prison and meaner than ever, the thought terrified her. She scribbled Franklin an urgent caution and prayed her words made it safely across the war-ravaged ocean that separated them. She stacked volumes of *Encyclopædia Britannica* along the hollows of her bed, sat curled in lamplight trying to squeeze their promises into a line of ink. Nothing kept her nightmares at bay. She woke grunting in fear, afraid to go back to sleep. Sometimes even Franklin seemed a dream.

The train had edged through urban underbellies—Pittsburgh, Cleveland, Toledo. Maire and other civilians slumped over their luggage, napping while freight was loaded off and on, war production taking precedence over personal journeys. A woman with three raggedy children handed her a cellophane sleeve of saltines. "This'll get you through," she said, "you're done the worst of it. Just nibbles and water and don't drink anything that ain't poured from a pitcher." Her Appalachian drawl hinted an ancestor's Ulster lilt.

March 8, 1942 my letter #3
Dear Moy,
   Sorry to hear you've been sickly. Wish my Auntie Doc was around—she'd fix you right up. 'A kiss on your sweet brow—and other places.

We're stationed outside a village called Cullybackey. A buddy met a guy named MacDonnell at the pub. Is it a common name? Maybe a relative? Not much to report, training to field telephones and radios waiting for something to happen. Maybe sunshine? St. Patrick's Day? Spring? How's everything there? Love, Frank

How is everything? Maire dusted furiously through the mansion. *You're standing in my backyard! If you meet Broin, Irish weather will not be your biggest problem!* She rewrote her urgent letter. *Stay away. Be careful.* She broke a dish. Regina frowned. She woke in a sweat, clutching volume 17 of *Britannica*. Her worst dream yet—Broin and Franklin rolling in a bloody tumble of fists and knives. She ran to the toilet and vomited her fear.

March 27, 1942
Hi Moy, I got a smudged-up letter from you—looks like it had a rough crossing, but at least it wasn't torpedoed! Says you don't want me to find your family. Okay, I'll duck and cover. There's so much fun stuff to do on the base (haha)—training all day then card games, dice, poker... not very Methodist! Guess I'll start reading. The library here is an ammo box of girlie magazines, Bibles, and Zane Grey novels. Looking for some brainy guy to lend me a history book. Hope you feel top-notch by the time you read this. Love, F.

She felt top-notch at his reassurance, though her stomach remained unsettled most mornings. Before serving breakfast, she dry-heaved in the utility sink. Regina gave her a sharp look, "When did you last bleed, girl?"

As the Empire Builder left Union Station, Maire claimed a window seat. The train rolled north along Lake Michigan, stopped in Milwaukee, cut through Wisconsin to St. Paul, Minneapolis, and then west across Minnesota farm fields. At the Dakota border, landscape flattened under towering clouds. By Minot, the air in the passenger car was stale with half-eaten lunches and the tang of sweat. Lingering tobacco smoke clung to the uniforms of a dozen servicemen who lurched down the aisle after boisterous rendezvous between the cars. Wrapped in Nana's shawl, shivering in its waning comfort, Maire nibbled crackers and reread another letter.

> Dear Maire, April 15, 1942
> I got letter #6. Holy smokes! I didn't mean to leave you in such a pinch. I know I'm responsible. I just don't know how to help you from far away. If Annenbergs won't let you stay, go to Montana. My dad will adjust. I'll adjust, too.
> Love, Franklin

The Missus had found her in the kitchen and announced, "I've arranged for you to see my physician next Wednesday, Mary."

"I'm feeling better, Ma'am."

"But that's not the issue, is it?" The color drained from Maire's face.

A week later, the Mister summoned her to the library, pacing as he talked. "I understand that besides your impulsive marriage, you are now pregnant." Maire pressed against a row of books. "I'm sure you know that Eleanor desires to be in your predicament, but for reasons the doctor cannot determine, has been unable to conceive." Maire blushed fiercely. "You are intelligent and healthy, the young man seemed the same."

"Franklin, sir, his name."

Mister brushed a speck off his lapel. "At best, you won't see him again until war's end, which is going to be years. You are in no position to raise a child. We are. Assuming you carry this pregnancy to term and the doctor determines the baby is normal, we propose to assume all legal relationship to it. You may remain in our employ for the duration, but the child is never to know." He gestured toward a crystal carafe; she poured him a snifter of cognac. "You have several days to decide."

Swaying with the motion of the train, Maire dozed with chin propped on hand and elbow propped on windowsill. In the nightmares that had ceased when Franklin arrived and returned when Franklin left, she was always running over uneven ground, afraid of falling in the river Main. The wind of rage howled at her back, she daren't turn round. Broin's growl, "...anyone else and I'll kill the both of yeh." Even the river hissed, "You no match for the world, Cullybackey girl! Give yourself to me."

"No, I won't give up!" She dreamt in gasps and moans, body twitching.

Reaching across the aisle, a farmwife slapped Maire's knee with a copy of Good Housekeeping. "Wake up, Miss."

Maire's elbow slid off the sill. Her hand slid off her chin. Her forehead hit the greasy pane of the train window with a crack. She cried out and blushed under the scrutiny of fellow travelers, pulled the shawl over her head. Maire hated the dreams. Hated waking with her heart pounding, her thoughts careening down alleys of panic. She never got caught. She never got away. Her father, her brother, her bully man, a slow fade of terror. Maire poked her fingers at matted curls, dug a saltine from her pocket. Then. Now. There. Here. The train wheels mocked her. Alone. Away. Alone. Away.

Daylight up, the conductor pointed out the window, "Eastern Montana, nation's breadbasket." He scratched his ample belly through the blue of his uniform, punched another hole in her ticket. "When we get to Havre, you disembark, change for Great Falls and the spurs. Pigeon River, end of the line." Maire winced to have her destination revealed. "Reckon we'll need every grain of wheat to win this war. You got a man in it?" Maire nodded. "I made it through the war before this'un. Only a scratch, though I seen awful. Wish the same for him." He handed back the crumpled ticket. "Don't look out there too long, make you dizzy."

He was right, she was dizzy. She pulled out *The Joy of Cooking* Regina had given her. What would folks eat at the end of the line? How to kill a lobster, skin a squirrel, cook a woodchuck. How to make creamy sauces to bestow vegetables with fancy names. And for desserts—meringues, angel food, lemon curd. Finally, ten pages for cooking potatoes, a few words about oatmeal, a recipe for biscuits. The farmer and his wife were staring at her. She loosed her hair to hide her profile.

April 25, 1942
Dear Maire,
    I am not mad at you. Protection was my job and I let you down. Are you still pregnant? My mother lost more babies than she carried. Are you considering adoption? I would have to sign papers. Are you going to Pigeon River? I should write Pa. These are probably stupid guy questions. You have to get through the war, too, just like me. Whatever you do is okay with me. I want you happy.
Franklin
    PS: Some Irish around here are plumb crazy. So glad I got a good one.

She cashed out her savings and bought a one-way ticket, washed, ironed, and handed in her uniforms. "I'm sorry, Missus."

"Keep the courting frock, Mary. You've been a good girl." Their eyes no longer met.

On the morning she left, Regina pulled Maire into the kitchen. "Montana is real, isn't it? You're not going onto the street."

"It's real," she'd assured the cook. "Franklin wrote. His father is a preacher man, charitable toward strangers. I'm sure we'll get along." Mile after clicketty-clacketty, rail-rocking mile, she prayed this was the truth. Then. Now. There. Here. Alone. Away. Alone.

4
County Antrim

APRIL 1942: *One-third of the convoys shipping troops and cargo to Britain are torpedoed and sunk. Jews are rounded up and forced to wear the yellow Star of David. Nobody stops them.*

NAVIGATING HIS NEW WILLYS through heavy fog, Franklin's driver, Corporal Tommy Thompson, ran a litany of complaint, "Can we just get into the war, through the war, and over the war? Is that too much to ask, Bee Man?"

The 34th Infantry was largely composed of Iowa National Guard. Some were graduated schoolboys trying to impress local girls whose smudged photos lay under their pillows far from the Nishnabotna River and fields of home. Most were farmers, businessmen, laborers, and tradesmen, weekend patriots who stewarded the rural landscape of America. Thomas Milford Thompson was a bow-legged, twenty-eight-year-old potato farmer from Montgomery County, married, three little kids. The Army needed a baseline of military men, so it pulled the National Guard out of the corn state. The 34th needed signal men, so it pulled Franklin from his unit and his bride. He was supposed to be stateside driving Maire around a Texas countryside blossoming with bluebells. Instead, he was hunched under the canvas awning of the Jeep, chilled and grumpy.

April 1, 1942—#5
Dear Franklin,
    I wish the mails would deliver our letters in order, so we don't misunderstand each other. I got your letter #3, but when you wrote, it seems you hadn't got my letter #3. I asked you <u>not to find my family</u>. I said to please not tell anyone in Cullybackey that you know me.
    I didn't do anything bad, but you could step into trouble, and with the Irish, things can go wrong in unexpected ways. We are standing at the edge of a real grownup life. We just got to get through the war to claim it. Being nervous makes me sick. I'll get better. Just stay away from the locals. Love, Maire

Her urgent request had rattled him. Well, families were a motley crew. His too. He'd avoid any local MacDonnells best he could. It was their other predicament that washed over him in waves of empathetic nausea.

April 10, 1942 #6
Dear Franklin,
    The Missus' doctor said I'm pregnant. I nearly fell off the table. Pregnant, like a baby? Yes, he said. I haven't bled since you left, but I thought it was nerves. I got on the streetcar and cried all the way home. Regina and the Missus were waiting in the kitchen. Suddenly it was the two of them knowing it all, and me just a misfortunate girl. I had to remind myself we are married. I am not bad. This is just a surprise. The Missus is talking to the Mister, see if they keep me on. Please don't be mad. We would have had a baby someday, just not so soon. Love, Maire

He got stiff when he thought about planting his seed, but now their pleasure was overlaid with fear at what a baby would mean. His plans had been going so well. Then deployment orders. Then a torn rubber. What the hell.

> April 15, 1942 #7
> Dear Franklin, I don't even know if you got my letter saying I'm pregnant, and now Mister and Missus offered to adopt our baby. They say I can stay on and work for them, but the child will be theirs. On one level it solves my problem, but on another level, it creates a life of secrecy for the baby and for us. I don't know what it feels like to be a mother, but I don't think selling my firstborn is a good start. I'm pretty sure you don't want your child to grow up hoity-toity, but I don't know what you *do* want. Or what I want, either. I'm hanging onto one thing—that you and I are meant to be together, and we will figure this out. I love you, Maire

They were overdue, hurrying back to base. The road angled sharply. A flock of dirty white sheep emerged in the dirty white fog. Before Tommy could brake, they were surrounded by bleating ghostly bodies. One white-faced ewe stopped dead ahead, crumpled as the Jeep hit her and nearly overturned the vehicle as the front right tire rolled over her body. And there they were in the middle of some cloud with bells and baahing and no shepherd. They dragged the ewe from under the chassis, her eyes glassy, ribcage crushed. Thompson pulled his officer issue M1911 and shot her in the back of the head.

Franklin jumped. "Jesus, Tommy! Could'a been an accident, anyone could'a hit her, but now she's got a U.S. Army bullet in her brain." He hoped Thompson, technically his NCO, and privately his buddy, didn't notice his shaking.

"Farmer ethics," Thompson holstered the revolver. "Don't let an animal suffer. This is somebody's livelihood. We got to make it right."

The two men stood looking down on their disaster. The rest of the herd stalled in the road around them. "Hallo!" Franklin shouted. Baaaah. Baaaah. The only reply.

"Got to bleed her." Thompson snapped open a five-inch Buck knife and bent over the carcass.

"That Army issue?"

"I'm a farmer and a hunter, I carry a blade." He slit the ewe's neck on both sides. "My dad's. He gave it to me for luck." A geyser of blood shot onto the roadway. Franklin swayed. "Get a grip, Cooper. You're a farm boy."

"I'm a beekeeper! We don't shoot 'em or slice 'em." While the ewe bled out, Thompson felt her belly and made a cesarean cut, pulled out a lamb, cleared the birth-slime from its head, stuck his pinky up each nostril, blew breath into the tiny creature. "You must've been one hell of a pig farmer."

Thompson looked him over. "Pigs easier to cut, but piglets more work. Some local girl can play mommy."

"And now?"

"Load her up, find the town, find the shepherd." Franklin hefted half the ewe's weight into the Jeep's hatch. "It's not a sheep anymore, Bee Man, it's meat. You better toughen up. Target practice, plunging bayonets, we're not training for Sunday school. Here, take the lamb."

"I don't want to hold the baby!" Franklin winced. He hadn't yet told Thompson.

April 20, 1942
Dear Franklin, #8

Regina thinks I should let the Annenberg's adopt the baby then leave and get on with my life. Yikes. I don't know how to find a job, where to go. Every consideration seems overwhelming. I'm crying, hardly sleeping, throwing up, scared I'll lose the baby, scared I won't. Praying for a sign. The Missus keeps staring at my tummy waiting my answer. Write me. Help me. Love me. Maire

The lamb was shaking, and the umbilical cord hung from its tiny belly. "I hope he doesn't think I'm his mamma." Franklin managed a weak smile.

"Nah," Thompson snorted a laugh, "He thinks you're Jesus Christ."

Down the road, the swing arm sign of a pub emerged from the fog. They pulled in front and Thompson placed the holstered semi-automatic carefully under his seat. "No need to alarm the natives," he said and strode toward the pub door. "Evening gentlemen, Corporal Tommy Thompson, Private First-Class Franklin Cooper, U.S. Army." A dozen men in various stages of drink stared at the sight of them, one spattered with blood and the other carrying a newborn lamb. "We've had an unfortunate accident involving our Jeep and a local sheep. We are farm men ourselves and want to make right by the owner."

An older man, wiry and graying, recovered the power of speech. "You kilt one of uz sheep?" Thompson nodded. "Whad'ya do wid her?"

"Bled her, took the lamb. She's good for meat."

"Well doncha have this all figgered out." His tone was not friendly. "Guess we better looksee." He pushed up from the table, "Dinna touch me pint." He scanned the back corner, "Coming Mulvaney? She's probably your'n." A large burly man rose out of the shadows. He was taller and bigger than either Franklin or Thompson, biceps that bulged out of a tight shirt, greasy pants, uncut bush of red hair and a crooked nose, trophy from a previous fight. Something about him made Franklin's stomach turn.

Mulvaney flipped the dead weight of the ewe as though it was near to nothing. "Aye, that's me smit," he gestured at the colored mark painted across the ewe's rump. "Who cut her? You're good with a knife." The lamb bleated in Frank's arms. "You gonna nurse it yourself?"

"We thought maybe some town girl...," Franklin tried to look military.

Mulvaney snorted. "Most my flock lambed weeks ago. This laggard, orphaned, never catch up." Franklin tightened his hold on the innocent creature.

"Whad'ya think, Paddy," Mulvaney fingered the fleece, "I'll settle five quid for me loss."

Thompson nodded. "Okay, but we don't have the money on us."

The big man's temper exploded, "Bloody hell! How'm I s'posed to deal, you got empty pockets?"

Thompson raised his voice in return, "You carry five quid on you, Mr. Mulvaney?"

Mulvaney turned to the older man, "Heh, MacDonnell, you lend these boyos a cash?"

Thompson's head whipped around, "Isn't your gal Moorah from 'round here Frank? Name of MacDonnell?" Franklin froze, caught in the moment he'd promised to avoid.

"Fuck NO!" An animal roar came out of Mulvaney. He grabbed the lamb so hard its neck snapped. Little black eyes blinked dark. Mulvaney flung the body into the roadway and lunged. "Maire MacDonnell be mine!"

The drill sergeant's commands rang in Franklin's mind, "Hold your stance, man to man. Go down and you're dead." But there was nothing between himself and the enraged Irishman, no gun to fire, no point to plunge. Mulvaney's fist a piston aimed for his face. The combat phrase, "one punch homicide," filled Franklin's mind. He feinted left. The punch took wind, but Mulvaney snagged his arm and flipped him like a sheep for shearing. His shoulder wrenched. Hobnailed boots kicked his kidneys. A rib snapped. Dirt stifled his scream. He had just failed basic training.

Overhead Paddy MacDonnell was shouting, "Broin, for crissakes, dinna kill a bloody soldier. You be in the clinker fer the rest of yur days!"

The Beekeeper's Question

Franklin writhed under blows and bellows. Suddenly Mulvaney's body froze mid-fight. Thompson had flicked his knife, twisted Mulvaney's arm into a Half Nelson, and was pressing the blade alongside the big man's throat hard enough to cut skin. Blood pearled off the point. Thompson's voice, more menacing than he'd ever imagined the Iowa farmer could muster, commandeered the situation. "I'll bleed you out, you make one move, Mr. Mulvaney." Franklin rolled away from under Mulvaney's raised boot and struggled onto his knees. He could hear everyone's breathing—his own pain-wracked shallows, MacDonnell's hyperventilating, Mulvaney's fueled panting, and Thompson's long, slow intake and outflow, the way a rock might breathe. The fighter eased his foot to ground. The stare he gave Franklin would have been a death blow.

Franklin grabbed the Jeep rail and hauled himself up. He'd been in boyhood scuffles but never hurt like this. This was practice for real war. He had to override his body's desire to curl into shock, had to breathe through piercing pain, hold focus, keep thinking. He reached for the Colt, and just outside the circumference of possible lunging, thumbed off the safety. A soft click. "You're covered," he told Thompson. He aimed at Mulvaney's chest. Practice. For real war.

Thompson's voice low and controlled, "Okay then. Mr. Mulvaney, you are going to walk slowly back inside and finish your beer." Franklin's finger twitched on the trigger. Voices shouted from the doorway. The Irishman's blood drooled into his shirt collar. He gave the slightest nod to Thompson who eased back but kept the knife ready to plunge. Franklin followed every move steadying the pistol in his hand.

Mulvaney flexed his fists. "You live another day, soldier boy." His buddies reached for him.

Thompson wasn't done. "You're not the war we come to fight, Irish. We make report. We pay your quid. You don't make trouble. We don't file charges." The men in the doorway nodded, MacDonnell nodded.

Mulvaney turned and spit. "I'll kill ye if'n it's true." His eyes were radiating malice. "I kin get cash for America. Get her back."

Franklin kept the gun aimed at the threatening hulk in the pub door while MacDonnell and Thompson slid the dead ewe onto the road edge. Tommy wiped his blade on the pelt. The old man kicked the lamb to the gutter, spoke low, "Broin Mulvaney purdy much gets what he wants 'round here. I promised him me daughter and she ran away. Shamed him. He dinna forget." His face became unreadable. "Best not renege on that quid."

Thompson gunned the engine. Franklin eased into the passenger seat, trying not to breathe. Beyond the radius of one streetlamp the evening had turned a blanketing dusk. "Holy smokes, Cooper, what was that all about?"

"No idea," he grunted. "Take it easy on the bumps."

"Guess you just got toughened up."

"Guess I just met Maire's old man… and old boyfriend." He could hardly speak for the pain. His mind was reeling. "This is a world war," he stuttered, "what are those odds?"

27 April 1942 #9
Dear Franklin,
　　Last night my Nana came in a dream. She told me, "Trust what happens in your life. Trust the man. Trust the child. Listen. Leave. Find. Believe." It is the first peace in my heart since you left. I'm clear now. Love, Maire

Franklin peed blood for a week. Medics taped his ribs. He didn't breathe deep for a month. His shoulder screamed to heft equipment. His war had begun. He learned what every soldier learns: There's things you don't write home.

5
Arrival

MAY 15, 1942: *Japanese troops clear an airfield on Guadalcanal threatening Australia. American troops begin a counter-invasion. Over 7000 Allied combatants will die in this battle.*

IN LEO COOPER'S MIND, A DAY IN MAY was perfect creation—countryside covered in wildflowers, fruit trees and dandelions blossoming, warm enough for bees to fly. Working alone among his hives boxes, Leo the beekeeper made only a small denim dot in the vast landscape. This place needed him, and he needed the bees. Hands on hips, he stretched his spine, creaking from the necessary bends of positioning honey supers. Come August, each super would weigh fifty pounds, frames full of honey and beeswax, and the familiar complaints of his oldering body would sing as loudly as last Sunday's hymn. *"This is my Father's world..."* a refrain of inner hum that matched the bees. *"I rest me in the thought..."* His dear Charlotte would have joined in on the piano, made him sound good. A tear moistened his two-day stubble. He acknowledged his solitude and the toll of heavy labor. His body reckoned how much weight he'd hefted over the years, both spiritual and physical. He would need help to bring in the honey crop and help to steady his congregation through the war. Leo the pastor lifted his eyes to the hills and hoped the Lord was paying attention.

He pondered next Sunday's sermon and how to stitch faith into a world swiftly tearing apart.

The bees drifted around him. "Counting on you little gals. Remind me there is sweetness at the end of the day." Their industrious *hmmm* filled his mind. "*...All Nature sings and around me rings, the music of the spheres.*" He whistled for Franklin's dog and started up the truck.

"This is it, Missus," the conductor loosened his uniform buttons, "Pigeon River, Montana, end of the line." He stepped onto a wooden platform and extended a hand. The train had shuddered to a halt alongside several tall structures of slatted wood with tin roofs and huge metal necks. He noticed her gaze, "Those're grain silos. Springtime, trains carry in what the farmers and ranchers need. Harvesttime, trains carry it all away." He pointed down the road. "That-a-way is the General Store and Post Office. Aim for the flagpole. Woman named Gertrude can direct you."

Maire stepped onto Montana soil. Tears of disappointment stung her eyes. She scorned her naïve imaginings that she and Franklin would arrive here together, a two-person victory parade to impress his father. She was here. Now. Alone.

The rail line ran at the north edge of town near a square of buildings Franklin had described as "the old Fort" and which, by the playground equipment, she remembered had also been a school. Keeping her eye on the flagpole, she walked by simple houses stuck like toys in the dirt under the immensity of sky—painted shutters, faded siding, pansies planted in an old tire, cats sprawled on dust. She walked by a garage and gas pumps with the legs of the mechanic sticking from under a truck. A single-story brick bank looked more like a cookie jar than a financial institution. She prayed Franklin was right about his father's sense of charity. He hadn't met the train.

The Beekeeper's Question

30 April 1942
Dear Franklin,

    When I told Missus she couldn't have the baby, she told me I couldn't stay. She would have loved our child, but the Mister not. I'll miss her. In ways we never spoke, we watched over one another. I bought a train ticket to Montana. I wrote your father. I am doing the best I can. Don't be mad. Maire

    The highway bisecting the town made an odd trinity in which the store and saloon faced the Methodist church across two lanes of asphalt. Twenty feet of wood-planked sidewalk defined the storefront, and a wind-frayed flag designated its dual purpose as a government building. Maire stared at the church spire and potholed parking lot. An iron fence marked the perimeter of the final resting places for Franklin's mother, his little sister, and other previous residents of the valley. Somewhere nearby was a corner lot with a honey house, a warehouse, a small barn, and the home where Franklin had grown up.

April 29, 1942
Dear Maire,

    Everything is so unsettled. Hitler is sitting on most of Europe and I'm not even in the war yet. Victory will take a while. The baby could be years old before I see you again. I'm still adjusting to being a married man, let alone a father. I'll stand by whatever you decide. I'm as confused as you are, from the man's point of view, of course. I'm doing the best I can. Don't be mad. Franklin

    A shopkeeper bell signaled Maire's entrance. A middle-aged woman in a floral housedress looked up from the cashier counter, brown roots growing out from her blonde hairdo, surprise in her eyes. "Help you, Miss?"

"I'm looking for Reverend Cooper."

The woman gave her a thorough glance over. "He expecting you?"

"Yes," though she wasn't exactly sure.

"Just off the train?" Maire nodded. "Well, you walked this far you can walk the rest. Go past the church 'til the street comes to a tee. Cooper's a little brown house. Honey sign on a warehouse door. He has mail. And he ordered a pound of flour. Maybe help you say hello."

Maire took the flour bag and a smudged envelope—her letter of introduction. So, he didn't yet know she was coming. She crossed the highway with Gertrude's stare heating her back. A phone rang in the house on the right and a face poked through curtains. A phone rang in a house on the left and a young mother with a baby in arms waved from the door. "Reverend's not home. Folks usually wait on the porch." She wore a paisley housedress with a pink sweater, brown hair in a simple victory roll. "I mean, being a preacher, strangers come by."

Maire's arms ached with the weight of her luggage. "I'm not just coming by. I married his son, Franklin." Her belly fluttered.

"Oh my, I hadn't heard…" She shifted the baby on her hip. "My name's Hazel Pocket."

"Glad to meet you," she almost curtsied, "I'm Maire Cooper."

"Well, as you're family, best wait in the kitchen. I'll come over tomorrow, say hello." Hazel pointed across the street, *Cooper & Sons, Beeline Honey*, brown planked building, peeling paint. She stepped into Franklin's life.

Rounding the house to the back entryway, Maire finally set down her load. She leaned against the doorjamb, shaky, thirsty, hungry, and afraid. Franklin had said he announced their marriage. She thought his father might have spread the news. Except for the telephone ringing through the wall of the kitchen, the house squatted in stillness. Maire stood a long time with her hand on the knob. Here. Now.

> May 10, 1942 #8—I think
> Dear Franklin,
>   I got your letter saying maybe let them adopt. I hope you got my letter saying I told them no. I'm choosing to let this surprise change my life. I'm scared. I need help. I wrote your father. I'm leaving. Write to me in Pigeon River. I am counting on you. Please keep loving me. Maire

She used the Reverend's absence to wash the sour from her armpits, change into her only other dress and tidy her hair. She set down the flour, found eggs, some milk about to curdle: *Joy of Cooking*, page 632.

The biscuits were in the oven when a flatbed farm truck pulled into the yard. The truck, originally dark blue, was streaked with rust, dust, and good use with low wooden rails along the bed. It was loaded with bee boxes and an odd jumble of equipment pushed up against the cab. The engine coughed into silence. A graying man, somewhat shorter than his son, jumped to ground with strength and stride. He slapped at mud-splattered jeans and unbuttoned a denim jacket, didn't look up until he stepped into the mudroom, saw the luggage, and smelled the biscuits. "What the...?!" Franklin's black and tan farmyard dog rushed past him barking.

"Hellooo Preacher Boy," Maire squatted, and the dog skidded to a halt, head cocked. Leo stopped in the doorway. She had to breathe to speak, "Hello, Reverend." Her lips were trembling. "I'm Mrs. Cooper, your daughter-in-law. I believe Franklin wrote you of our marriage at Christmastide." His eyes flashed disbelief. "I wondered if you mighta met the train but when I stopped at the store my letter of introduction was just arrived… so I see you weren't expecting me." If she stopped talking she would start shaking too hard to continue. "I'm not here to inconvenience you. I've housekeeping skills and Franklin's Army dosh. He said to come if I had need."

Maybe she'd feel better standing. The old man reached to steady her. "You got a name?"

"Maire MacDonnell, sir."

He brushed off the word with a little frown. "Please don't call me, sir. And your accent?"

"Scots-Irish."

"Religion?"

"Methodist." He registered surprise. "The church was there, so that's what we were," she said.

Leo scratched his head. "Some folks in the valley might say the same. How'd you get here?" His eyes were like Franklin's, sky blue, but going quickly overcast.

"By ship out of Belfast in '37, workin' in Philadelphia where Franklin and I met."

"I mean, how did you get *here*—to Pigeon River, in my house, making biscuits in my wife's apron?" They stood eye to eye across the narrow gap of linoleum. The dog pivoted from one face to the other.

"Oh. Four days on the train." Her voice quavered. There. Here. Now.

"You stopped at the store." She nodded. "And talked to Gertrude?" She nodded again. Leo Cooper's face turned into a profound frown.

"I needed directions, sir. No one met me."

"No one, if you mean me, knew you were coming." His voice was raspy and smooth at the same time. A man who spent the sabbath preaching into the hollow of the church. A man who spent the week soothing his throat with honey.

"I wrote—" she handed him the letter.

"—a letter I had not yet received." He ran a fingernail around the stamp, examined the postmark that verified its origin... and hers. "Shall I read this now, or will you tell me why you're here?"

"I'm your son's wife. We planned to live stateside, then he got reassigned to a battalion headed to Northern Ireland. We thought we'd been careful but after he left I, well, (she felt her face hot) I'm carrying his babe. My employers had a complicated reaction. And Franklin told me... Don't you know this, sir? He said he had let you know."

Leo grimaced at the "sir," but she couldn't help it. The old man reached for the Bible resting on a small shelf over a sturdy wooden table. He pulled a postcard out of the New Testament. A photo of the Liberty Bell. Liberty had been crossed out and there were two interlocked circles, like Franklin had traced a couple of dimes and the date they had visited the justice of the peace. 12-24-41.

> Giving up my liberty... though Army says I'm not at liberty per se. War for real, Pa. Don't' expect me back for a while. Take care of yourself and I'll try to do the same. Franklin.

She handed the card from the son back to the father. "T'is all you know?" she whispered the question.

Leo nodded. "I wasn't even sure what it meant."

Maire swallowed waves of anger and sorrow, looked Leo Cooper in the eye. "The Women's Christian Temperance Union supervised dances for the troops. The Missus gave me a dress and allowed me to go."

"The 'Missus'?"

"I was a maid." The dog settled between them, a pile of matted fur, ears curled forward like a collie. "Franklin is charming, handsome, wants to make something of himself..." Her teeth were chattering with tension, "That he's full of bravado heading into war is not so strange in the world out there."

"What do you know about war, Miss MacDonnell?"

"Mrs. Cooper," she corrected him. "I'm Irish. It's a bloody land." She pulled biscuits from the oven and slid them onto a chipped serving platter. "Best when hot."

The dog's tail thwacked the linoleum. "You met my son at a dance hall in…" "October 4th." She twirled her wedding band.

"And you married him on Christmas Eve?"

"I'm a decent girl, Reverend." The platter of biscuits shook in her hand. "I saw something in Franklin, and he saw something in me. We decided to risk loving each other. Is that so awful?"

Leo's eyes were black clouds in a blue rim. "I presume you have papers?"

His question felt like a slap from the father on top of the slap from the son. "Dinna you believe me?"

"I've been here thirty years, Miss. You are not the first strange woman to get off the train. So, yes, I'm asking to see papers."

Maire felt her Irish rising. "Franklin and I had to stand six inches apart. Church ladies measured the space with rulers. He told me about this place, you and the bees, his gone away brothers, his sister and ma dying." She gulped for air. "I'm your daughter-in-law, Reverend Cooper. I'm carrying your grandchild. Franklin said you'd have the charity to take me in."

The dog stopped wagging his tail. Leo finally spoke, "You don't know what I've seen out here on society's ragged edge."

"Everywhere is a ragged edge now. Nazi armies goose-stepping through towns like this. Bombs dropping on folks like us." She swiped angrily at tears. "Your son and I have a deal—he'll do his best to live. I'll do me best to save his pay. We'll write." The old man harrumphed. "Who knows, sir, you might even find me useful in this busted-up family."

"Stop calling me, sir! And we are not a busted-up family!" Leo's eyes flashed. "I'm the local preacher. I hold a moral standard for this community. By now Gertie has informed half my congregation that an unaccompanied woman delivered herself to my house from the afternoon train."

They were each breathing hard. Maire took a deep breath. "Forgive me, sir. I'm over tired and overwrought." She smeared tears off her cheeks. "Biscuits are chilling. Might we sit?"

The question hung in fragrant space. "Of course, Miss... Mrs. Cooper." Leo pulled out a chair for her and set down a crock of butter and a jar of translucent amber—Cooper & Sons honey. He bit into the steaming bread. "Oh my."

She folded her hands in her lap. "I have my A4 Immigration Visa, our marriage certificate, and a letter of recommendation from Mrs. Eleanor Annenberg." Her hands trembled. "I'm not delicate or demanding. I have $225 stuffed in a sock to deposit in that wee bank. If you don't want me working here, I'll..."

Leo swiped crumbs from his stubbled chin. "Whoa, young lady, I'm just thinking how to make this proper." The dog resumed wagging his tail.

She dribbled honey awkwardly on her biscuit. "Do you know where Franklin is?" Leo stared at her. "He's a signal corpsman stationed in the very county where I was born. There, my people are letting young men who talk funny and have no papers run through their sheep paddies with their boots and Jeeps." She felt breathless with strain. "Here, you are being asked to put up one foreigner with a legitimate claim. Surely the people of Pigeon River can accommodate that." His eyes turned blue again.

"It's just you took me by surprise." Leo went to the old-fashioned wooden box phone attached to the kitchen wall and cranked it. "Three shorts for the doctor; two longs, the preacher." He put his finger to his lips, "And anyone else curious." She could hear a faint "Hello" through the earpiece. "Jereldene, could I offer you supper? I have an Irish stew." He smiled at his clever code. She was here. Now. Beginning.

6
Into Good Hands

MAY 15, 1942: *A bill creating the Women's Auxiliary Army Corps is signed into law.*

LEO ATE ANOTHER BISCUIT before leaving to fetch Doc. "I'll set you up to make supper while I'm gone." He opened the door to the cellar, turned slightly and informed the girl, "There's a light bulb, but you have to take the first step in darkness. Reach for a string with a clothespin tied on the end." The stairs creaked where they always creaked, and the packed dirt floor was uneven in all the places his foot expected. He descended into cool moisture and earth smell.

Year-round, the cellar remained a consistent fifty-five degrees, a room hollowed into the first layer of earth, same depth as a grave. He often felt close to Charlotte down here. They'd worked the space together, caching her annual labor of garden produce in jeweled rows of quart jars. He had proudly tamped the walls, keeping the corners square. They'd even made love down here once, she protesting that she wasn't a pretty sight, he saying he didn't care. They allowed the mood to take them while the older boys ran toy trucks across the parlor overhead and Frankie slept in his crib. Leaning against the coal bin, panting and quick, she had grabbed his shoulders to steady herself and sometimes he still felt the ghost of that grasp. His thrust, her groan. "Well, Reverend Cooper, that should inspire quite a sermon." Her laugh. Gracie conceived.

During the cancer autumn, their sweet years gone, Charlotte had compulsively filled every shelf, laying away provisions for when she could no longer feed and tend. Sometimes Leo came down here, before and after her death, and sat on the pickle barrel to weep, biting down hard on the bunched-up cloth of his shirtsleeve. And in recent years, his husbandly grief calmed but his fatherly grief riled, he put his hand on the wall of dirt and talked to her. More of his family lay underground than walked in daylight—his wife, his daughter, three babies who barely drew breath, the girl who left them Jesse—all resting in the arms of God. He wanted comfort. He wanted guidance. He wanted it again right now.

The churchwomen kept him stocked, but the near-empty shelves were evidence of a long winter. It seemed the Irish girl could cook, biscuits anyway. He reached for a quart of green beans, a jar of stewed beef, felt in the sandbox for potatoes and not-too-shriveled carrots. He gave himself a little shake and headed up the stairs.

Leo eased the Chevy sedan out of the yard, not wanting to kick up dust that would turn into gossip before he even got to Doc's. Ralph Pocket was leaning on his yard fence sucking a bottle of Coca Cola. Waved. Ralph and Hazel, known each other since grade-school. No surprise when they got hitched. Hazel's folks had sold their place, headed to California, but Hazel stayed, made do, lived with Ralph's folks, now a baby. Country life, how it's supposed to be.

When he drove over the graveled hump in the road between their homes, the town disappeared from his rearview mirror and Doc's place came into view—a planked cabin with her barn and buggy and the old gelding grazing out back. Torgerson's beef cattle dotted the low hills beyond the ditch. Sivertsen's tractor left a trail of roiling field dust in the early evening light. The empty landscape and hugeness of sky released a familiar sensation in Leo's belly, sometimes comforting, sometimes terrifying. He'd gotten through Charlotte. Shored up his control, worked hard, worked the boys, watched in disbelief as one by one they left the valley. Left him. Leo pulled into Doc's yard, trying to pull himself together.

Weathered and wise, vibrant mid-seventies, Dr. Jereldene Jesperson remained an imposing figure in valley life. She carried an unadorned beauty lit by a ready smile. She walked toward Leo, tucking shirttails into her overalls. He leaned against the fender, pulled reading glasses from his shirt pocket. "There's a young woman in my kitchen who says she's Franklin's wife." Leo watched surprise flash across Doc's face. "She and this letter arrived together." He read aloud.

> May 5, 1942
> Dear Sir,
> As you know from your son, we are rightfully married as of Christmas, and he is now stationed in Europe. Through unfortunate circumstances, I must leave my employment in Philadelphia. I have been assured by Franklin that you could be made favorable to my presence in the village of Pigeon River for the duration of the war. Upon arrival, I will enumerate my skills and we can discuss suitable arrangements. I will arrive by train mid-May. I understand travel of this distance may be disrupted by the war effort, so please forgive that I cannot give you an exact date nor await your reply before departing the East. I present myself trusting in your Christian charity and our kinship.
> Most sincerely,
> Maire MacDonnell Cooper

Doc let out a whistle. Leo stared at the page. "I can't believe this is happening. They met in a dance hall. She's an Irish housemaid with an accent but not Catholic, thank God. And… she's pregnant. Says it's Franklin's."

Doc rested her hand on Leo's arm. "She sounds earnest and surprisingly educated. Let's assume she's telling the truth."

Something crumbled inside him. "She's wearing Charlotte's apron. She called us a busted-up family. All my sons are gone, Jereldene, where did I go wrong?"

The sun slanted around them. "I don't think that's the question for this moment, my friend." Doc walked around to the passenger door. "Introduce me. We'll figure it out."

Jereldene Jesperson had arrived in the valley on a hot August day in 1910 after learning such a place existed from a letter posted on the bulletin board at Starling Medical School, her alma mater. She was a spinster nearing midlife, educated beyond a woman's expected role. Her father had been a doctor and she, his only child, had been given advantages that should have gone to a son. The sole female in her medical school class, the good old boys of Columbus, Ohio, including former colleagues of the late Jerald Jesperson, thwarted her hopes of assuming her father's practice. The medical board assigned her duty at the penitentiary, where she treated gangrenous toes, stab wounds, broken bones, and internal injuries; oversaw cases of syphilis, tuberculosis, whooping cough, and other communicable diseases. True to her Hippocratic Oath, she refused to further abandon men already largely abandoned. She developed a capacity to do medicine in almost any circumstance and to handle herself in an all-male environment. She was not, however, able to break through the stonewall of male doctors and often felt her skills and interests were as captive as the lives of her patients. The letter intrigued her.

christina baldwin

To Whom It May Concern:

    We are writing on behalf of a pioneering community of hardy souls located in the state of Montana, 35 miles northwest of the city of Great Falls. While there are doctors and a hospital in the city, the community requires a local physician skilled in general practice, willing to relocate, and to provide medical care to a population of hardworking men, women, and children. Land is available for homestead and local menfolk are willing to construct suitable housing and a clinical office. This is rolling hill country with clean air and a Rocky Mountain vista. If interested, please send vitae to: Reverend and Mrs. Leo Cooper, Pigeon River, Montana.

She took it off the wall and brought it home.

Dear Reverend and Mrs. Cooper:

    I received my degree from Starling Medical School in 1903, and am board-certified in general practice. I anticipated taking on the practice of my father, also a physician. His death and my mother's ill health and eventual demise disrupted this plan, but I do have experience providing medical care to a largely working-class population.

    I am unmarried and available to reconsider where and how I want to live and practice. I wish to serve a community in genuine need and am intrigued by the idea of relocation in the setting you describe. Please advise if you wish to proceed with introductions and references. Sincerely,

J. Jesperson, MD

The Beekeeper's Question

Jereldene went from the post office to the library and researched the state of Montana. Why not go where she would be the only doctor and people would have to accept her? Why not explore the Wild West before it disappeared? After several exchanges, the minister and his wife extended an invitation and, except for the hour sitting by her parents' graves, it was easy to bid Columbus farewell. She sold the family home and shipped the best of her father's equipment to General Delivery, Pigeon River. On a stayover day in Chicago, she happened upon a shop promising to "outfit the lady of adventure" and bought what she hoped was appropriate attire. She dined on oysters and champagne, spent a night on satin sheets at The Palmer House, then boarded the train heading into the western settlement.

The reverend's jaw had dropped when she introduced herself, but Charlotte extended a welcoming hand. "Why how marvelous that you are a lady doctor. Valley women need you, and the men will adjust. Won't they Leo?" Charlotte shared Leo's height, with similar blue eyes, and brown hair pulled back at the neck. She wore a lightweight summer frock buttoned to the collar, long sleeves buttoned at the wrists, and buttons down the length of the skirt that came almost to her ankles and, in concession to the environs, sensible shoes. Jereldene was similarly dressed and happy to have guessed well. After a few minutes, Leo managed to close his mouth and doff his hat. He'd been less than gracious the next several days, held her diploma to the light to look for the watermark and probed her background in ways that made her defensive. Doc could easily imagine the scene that had just played out in his kitchen.

An auburn-haired young woman stood at the stove stirring a pot. Doc registered first impressions: pretty face, sturdy on her feet, calloused hands and, judging by the thickening at her waist, seventeen, maybe eighteen weeks gravid. "I'm Jereldene

Jesperson, though like everyone else around here, you'll probably call me Doc." She extended her hand. "We read the letter, dear."

"I made stew," Maire spoke in a warbled tone. "I'll not be a bother."

"Please sit down." Doc guided the young woman to a chair. "You wrote a forthright letter, so here's a forthright response. Franklin chose you, and as Franklin's family, we choose you." Leo harrumphed and Doc shot him a stern glance. Doc served three bowls. Leo set out more biscuits. Doc entertained with anecdotes and local introductions. Leo talked about weather and beekeeping. Maire shared her astonishment at the size and scope of the nation she had crossed. After a while, Doc gave Leo an appraising look. "Your daughter-in-law is exhausted. Is the bed made up in Franklin's room?"

"Bathroom is an outhouse," Leo said. "Been meaning to get modern plumbing, but it was just Franklin and me, and then just me, and I haven't got round to it. Good well water coming in the sink, hot and cold."

It wasn't exactly a "Yes," but it would do for the night. Maire used the outhouse. Doc moved luggage down the hall, called out, "Door on the right."

"This is him," she whispered. Franklin's clothes hung in the closet and filled the chest of drawers. A lucky rabbit's foot, coins and keys on the dresser top, and a framed photograph taken when all the Coopers had been alive together. Maire unlatched the suitcase and undressed with her back turned, filling in details. "Franklin knew Morse Code so the Army put him in the Signal Corps. Then he got transfer orders and sailed away." Tears leaked down the young wife's face. "I last bled just before our wedding night. We were careful, you know, rubbers. Well, mostly." She blushed fiercely.

"It's okay, dear. I'm used to these conversations." Doc turned down the sheets. "Once upon a time, we all got off the train," she said gently. "Pigeon River will become familiar and friendly.

The land's beauty will emerge." Maire slipped into bed. "You would have been fertile again just before Franklin left, so that's when. Sleep now. Chamber pot if you need it."

"Thank you," Maire touched Doc's hand, "I don't know what would have happened… "

"Leo's a good man. He and I, well, we've come through a lot together. As for you, emotions, dizziness, heart palpitations, all part of being pregnant."

"And dreams?" the prone girl whispered, "Bad dreams? Sometimes." Her eyes searched Doc's face.

"A woman's body chemistry gets out of sorts growing a baby. Wake yourself up, roll over, get a drink of water. You are a brave young woman marrying Franklin, coming here. Everything will be all right." Doc turned and closed the door.

Leo lowered the roll top over the pigeon holes and nooks of his old desk and swiveled in his chair. His eyes were broody. "Why must I always inherit Franklin's half-considered projects, Jere? What do I know about young women? I'm the father of boys."

Doc leaned against the doorjamb. "No, Leo, you are the father of men. Men fall in love. They marry. They make babies. This is that moment." Doc reached for the wall calendar and began counting weeks. "You have become a father-in-law. Middle October, all goes well, you will become a grandfather. I told her to rest tomorrow. You take a lunch and go sit by some bees. That'll settle you."

"And when I get off my patootie and come home?"

"We're a team. We'll figure it out." Doc squeezed his shoulder, feeling his clavicle bonier than in younger years. "I'll walk back, I need the moonlight. And Leo, look at her not through the eyes of surprise and inconvenience, but with the heart of the man you are."

1
Make Yourself at Home

MAY 16, 1942: *The United States 1st Armored Division joins the 34th Infantry Division in Northern Ireland, doubling the number of American troops training at the edge of Europe.*

IT WAS LATE MORNING WHEN MAIRE WANDERED OUT and back from the outhouse. The last biscuit and a couple of hard-boiled eggs had been left on the table along with a handwritten note: *Gone to see the bees. Told Hazel to wait a day. Make yourself at home. Leo.* His name soft as butter on the palette.

The house, she knew from Franklin's stories, had been built in the summer of 1908. A time when railroads transported flatcars of brick and mortar, planks of oak, pine, and fir to foster settlement. The station master kept track of billings and payments. Indians were incarcerated on reservations, the bison slaughtered, and tribal ways of life destroyed. The Homestead Act parceled out the landscape while the Corps of Engineers harnessed the rushing rivers of the West. Like thousands of others, Leo and Charlotte packed up their life dreams and rode to the end of the line. Cooper's farmhouse was a square box that had been expanded to add a porch, wire in electricity, upgrade to the coal furnace that squatted like a cold black bear in the center of the house.

Wrapped in her shawl, Maire stood in the open arch between kitchen and dining room. Along the outer wall, a long wooden table was covered with a bed sheet and stacked with ledger books, charts of bee yards, office trays overflowing with papers. She hovered over the piles, touched nothing. The door to Leo's study was closed.

In the parlor, window shades were drawn along the east side. The room was furnished with a sofa, an end table and reading lamp, a rocking chair with a large wicker basket alongside. Charlotte's place, she thought. Charlotte's piano, too, silted with a sheen of dust. There was an amateurish painting of a bugling elk on the back wall and a full bookshelf with family photos on top. The only sign of habitation was the worn seat of an overstuffed chair placed for listening to the radio in its Bentwood chest and a garnish of dog fur on the floral maroon rug. Leo's place and the dog's.

The parlor door exited to a long porch that faced the gravel road and a vista of strange barren humps and boxy squares rising out of the valley floor and towering over the farmland. Butte country, Franklin had called it. Crops greened where irrigation ditches stretched alongside country roads. Above the ditch, a wilder mix of prairie grass webbed with nearly invisible strings of barbed wire fencing. Cattle spotted the rolling tablelands where one butte and another stood sentinel. Maire pressed her nose to the door screen and recited the map Franklin had penciled onto a diner placemat. Southeast along the river was Great Falls. Through the gap and south was Helena and over the mountains, a longer drive to Missoula. North was Glacier National Park and the Blackfeet Reservation. "And that's about as far as anyone ever goes," he'd said. Except the Cooper boys.

The stairwell smelled of memories and she guessed it was not a place Reverend Cooper frequented. Six steps up was a landing just big enough to hold a narrow chair and lady's secretary desk. She lifted the lid, leaving fingerprints on a film of dust. Stationery, ink, a fountain pen with a dried nib. "Hello, Missus Charlotte," she whispered.

The view from the landing's little window overlooked the garden and barn, an empty livestock pen, stacks of hive boxes. A squarish butte dominated the horizon. Tangled together in sheets of a different attic, Franklin had described this scene to her. How he did his schoolwork sitting at the turn of the stairs, trying to keep his mother's melancholy at bay. His tenderhearted stories had made her fall in love with him. Surely his heart would be equally tender to her.

The hurt she had stifled reading his cryptic postcard rose in her now. Two circles, a date. He hadn't made even the tiniest space for her to step into this house. "How could you not even say my name to your father?" She kicked at the stair where the wraith of the tender boy looked up with woeful eyes. She didn't care. Her voice banged in the stairwell. "Ya said it, Franklin. Dinna deny it. My day off switched to Friday after Thanksgiving, we were walking in Swarthmore. Rain turning to snow. You talking ideas for after the war. I recited *Invictus*, *"I am the master of my fate, I am the captain of my soul."* You laughed. You kissed me. You said you loved me. I've hung my life on that promise, Franklin Cooper. Now, I'm having your baby 'cause you didn't have a rubber the last night! I've had to leave everything I knew, begging charity from a man who dinna even know I exist! Do you have any idea how hard that is?" The woeful boy stared at his shoes. Maire spun on the landing. "You said you had written him. You lied." She stuffed the hem of the shawl in her mouth to stifle angry sobs.

Maybe he was ashamed of her.

Maybe he was right.

They had waited that day, but barely. He'd unbuttoned her coat and his and they stood together, cocooning their bodies' warmth against the raw November wind in a park gazebo amid old newspapers and dried leaves. She'd let him have tastes of her: the inside of her mouth, the lobes of her ears, the nape of her neck. Then he reached down the neck of her sweater searching inside her brassiere. Fingertips touching her nipples made her almost explode. She ground her hips into his trousers and felt him erect, his heart pulsing so hard she could count the beat of it through layers of cloth. She flailed about for willpower. "Wait," she had gasped, "we have to wait."

"Why? Why not now, Maire?" His lips were all over her. He eased her down on a bench, out of view, "I have a rubber." His voice hot in her ear.

She had summoned the halting point from deep inside herself. "Not here. Not like this." Maire MacDonnell had a plan and it was not, after all these years, to let herself be taken without guarantee. Fragments of fear blew like dried leaves at the edge of her passion. She commanded her body to hold out for the promise of future security. "I am a good girl, Franklin Cooper," her voice was breathy, "and you canna just have me." She wrested herself to sitting, tucking her blouse into her slacks, buttoning her sweater, hands shaking as she fumbled with her coat.

Franklin leaned back, surprised, but stopped, watched as she put her clothes to rights. "Maybe we should get married then, Moy." He was panting and smiling. "Just do it. What the heck, there's a war on. If I make it through, with your brains and my charm, we can make a good life. If I don't... well, you'll have enough money to stop being a maid for the hoity-toities."

She looked up from the bench, searching his eyes. "Dinna ask me, Franklin Cooper, less you mean it." They had buttoned each other up and caught the local train back to the city. A week later, Pearl Harbor. Two weeks later, a real proposal.

The ghost boy slid to the side as she stomped up the stairs. The door at the top opened to a dormer room—two iron bedframes, two dressers. The bigger boys had slept here. Over one bed, a faded clipping from the *Great Falls Tribune*, "Pigeon River Boys Take State Debate." Boyd, the studious son, she thought. Over the other bed, a movie poster *Hopalong Cassidy Returns*. Jesse, the runaway cowboy.

Two high windows were positioned across from each other to catch a summer breeze. An ornate metal grate in the floor, now boarded over with plywood, allowed heat to circulate from the furnace below. At the back of the bedroom, a small door opened into narrow storage space walled off under timbered eaves. She eased in and surveyed the contents.

Boxes of discarded boyhood treasures, a chair in need of caning, head and foot boards of a crib, the mattress wrapped in newspaper and tied against dust with fraying twine. A trunk of women's things: sweaters, housedresses, sensible shoes. A square white box marked in careful handwriting, Grace Jereldene, 1923-1931. Three cigar boxes, one marked Franklin. His boyhood tumbled into her lap. A small tin of baby teeth. School report cards. A drawing of stick figures and a spiky sun next to a blue cloud. School photos. His brown hair, thick and unruly. Slicked up, slicked down. He was in fifth grade when Gracie died; in eighth grade when his mother died. Eyes vacant, a hollowed-out boy. His graduation photo was downstairs—defiant, straight at the camera. *See me!* it shouted. Did she? Yes. No. Maybe. Well, he had to see her, too.

Leo was standing at the table looking over paperwork as she emerged from the stairwell. "I didn't touch anything."

"I appreciate that," he gestured at his piles, "I got two enterprises going here—bee business and God's business. Did you sleep well?"

"Yes. Thank you."

"The house hasn't had a woman's touch since Charlotte died. I suppose you noticed."

"Yes, sir." He grimaced. "After you were in bed, Doc and I had a conversation. It can be complicated, fathers and sons." They stood with the table between them. She met his gaze.

"There's things a parent wants for his child, and sometimes the child doesn't want those things for himself."

"What did you want for Franklin then, sir?"

He didn't answer right away. "I wanted him to want this life. I wanted him to stay home." Leo reached under some papers and handed her a second postcard, a photo of Belfast harbor.

Dear Pa, In the Army, but not in the war. Currently deployed with infantry division stuck in North Ireland doing maneuvers in sheep pastures. Don't much like holding patterns, as you know. Miss my miss. It rains here <u>all the time</u>. Franklin

"So, you *did* know!"

"Well, you weren't in my imagination," Leo stuttered, "so I dismissed *the miss* part as merely cryptic. It never occurred to me he'd just up and marry like that..."

"Like *that*? Meaning *like me*?" Maire shook inside the cocoon of her shawl.

"No, well, I never met a maid before... You seem like a smart girl..." Maire didn't care if her gaze was making him squirm. "But why Franklin?"

"Are you asking me? Or asking him?"

Leo scratched his head. "I don't know, Mary. All I should say now is, I'm sorry."

Maire blinked. "I'm sorry, too, not about Franklin, but that I am such a surprise." She handed back the postcard and tucked her chin into the fold of the shawl, its soft grey threads the only thing that held the whole of her life.

Leo's eyes stayed blue. "Did you open the trunk? You can wear Charlotte's clothes. Doc said you don't have many things."

"Maybe I'll trade the dancing dress for house dresses. Put the green velvet away for when he returns."

"God willing," said Leo. "Want a cup of tea?"

Spoonfuls of honey clinked against crockery. "I could get some chickens and you start up the garden again." He searched her face. "I'm not quite sure how to do this, Mary. After Charlotte died, I swept the house, learned to cook. It wasn't pretty, but it kept us going."

Maire put down her spoon. "You were your own maid, then, sir."

"I did woman's work. Had to. The ladies of the Tuesday Club, Charlotte's friends, brought baked goods and the boys hunted game. Doc tried to nurture us through. Boyd was already gone to Seattle studying. Then Jesse ran away—do you know this? Did Franklin tell you?"

Maire shook her head—yes, no. "Our stories jumbled out in pieces, between dances, wandering the city on my day off. Sometimes we rode the train to outlying towns just to get to the country. Franklin says he wanted away from here, but this place is in his bones. That's why I came—well, and I had no place else to go."

"No family in Ireland?"

"My parents be alive but it's complicated. Like Franklin, I got two older brothers. One in Australia, one in Belfast." Maire stared out the window. The roofline of the honey warehouse, a rusty fence, and the church steeple pricked the sky. "No one in Cullybackey could ever imagine this much space."

Leo stared too. "We're not the wild west anymore. Farmers and ranchers. Fences and water rights. Most folks don't think about what came before us."

"Red men on horseback, like in the movies?"

"Blackfeet live on a reservation ninety miles north. Most live off the pittance the government provides. Every now and then a few young men come down for field work. Frank would bale hay with them."

Maire sipped her tea. "I read *The Last of the Mohicans*, by James Fenimore Cooper. Any relation?"

Leo shook his head. "And how did you come by this book?"

"There was a library in the house. My employers let me read from it."

"What else have you read?"

"Collected plays of William Shakespeare, most of Charles Dickens, Louisa May Alcott. *Gone with the Wind, Uncle Tom's Cabin; The Seven Pillars of Wisdom*, by T. E. Lawrence; Mark Twain, John Steinbeck's *Grapes of Wrath* and his new one, *East of Eden*. Missus liked novels. Mister liked history and social analysis. So, I read Toynbee, Franklin said you're a fan. And I often fell asleep perusing the 14th edition of the *Encyclopaedia Britannica*."

Leo whistled. "You better be careful, Mrs. Mary, or you'll end up a schoolteacher." He carried his dishes to the sink. The turn of his back seemed friendly.

She took a breath, "About my name..." In this new life, if he was not "sir," she would not be "Mary." Her voice trembled. "People assume every Irish girl is named Mary. I got used to it. But Irish got an Old Tongue mixed in with English. M-a-i-r-e, we say Moorah." She rolled the 'r' slightly, the flutter a comfort on her tongue. "When Franklin called me by my real name, I knew he was the one."

Leo practiced. "Moorah, it is, then." He sipped tea. "I'll tell Doc... and Gertie."

The fetus that would change her life forever and bind her to this man, this family, this place, twitched in her belly.

May 20, 1942 #10

Dear Franklin,

I'm in Pigeon River since last week. My letter of introduction did not arrive in advance, so your father was quite surprised. And I was equally surprised to learn he did not even know of me. It's not right that I had to start from nothing but two postcards. You didn't even say my name or claim our marriage.

I tell myself you just never thought I'd end up here or that you intended to introduce us in person, but I am your wife, you should have made a place for me. I tell myself you love me. I tell myself I love you. I tell myself we made a good choice, and we will find our way after the war. I tell myself that having the baby will help us. Does saying make it true? Please don't abandon me. I will not abandon you. Maire

PS Doctor Jesperson came over and helped us through the first night.

PPS: I felt our baby move!

8
The Lessons of the Bees

EARLY JUNE 1942: *U-Boats sink 834,000 tons of supplies and war materials in the worst convoy losses of the war. Rommel's Army surrounds the British in North Africa.*

"VEGETABLES FOR VICTORY!" Leo turned over beds. Maire weeded 'til her fingers bled. It took a week to restore the garden, and now with shoveling done, Leo was eager to hand Maire's tutelage over to Hazel. "You can be friends. She'll help you know the womenfolk." That was his plan. He wrote Franklin.

> *Sunday, June 8, 1942, 78°, partly cloudy. 37 souls in church.*
> *Dear Franklin,*
>   *I am sure you know your wife arrived here mid-May. Maire is helpful and I'm adjusting. It's impressive how she's educated herself, and I'm glad to hear she is inspiring you toward the same. I'm sorry you two didn't have more time to influence one another and I pray that time will come. Cross-pollination is the greatest mystery in a marriage. I see why you were smitten, and I encourage you to carefully tend the commitment you made to her and the child she carries.*
>   *Clover is popping. Not sure how I'll manage honey harvest this year. Not sure where Boyd is, what with*

doctors needed in the war. He hasn't written. Maybe Jesse will show up. Maybe I'll find an industrious drifter.

I pray for you, my son, your protection, our victory.
Your father, Leo
PS: Doc sends her love.

Chores done, garden readied, Leo sipped a cup of Postum, accommodating himself to the taste of roasted wheat bran and molasses, imagining his missing cups of coffee in the hands of weary soldiers. Monday was his day of solitude in the company of bees. He stared out the window into morning light. The panes had been cleaned to sparkling. Maire entered the kitchen dressed in overalls, a chambray shirt, and work boots, a bandana tying back her hair. She twirled for his inspection. "Hazel hemmed the pant legs, and there's room for my baby belly. Might I come along to see the bees?"

He regarded her over the lip of his cup. "I've never had a woman in the yards." The very idea shocked him. "You should stay here, plant something." Bee yards were hallowed ground, marked only by his own boots and patterns of work and reverie. How could this immigrant girl possibly understand?

Maire pulled herself to full height. "I'm reading *ABC and XYZ of Bee Culture*. It's fascinating."

"It's 900 pages in small print." Leo gave the girl another look. "And I don't know as the bees'll accept a woman handling them…"

"From what I read, except for a few lazy drones, all bees are female. I think the little ladies and I will get on just fine." She jammed her hands deep in the pockets of his son's overalls, tapped her foot in his dead wife's work boots, and stared him down.

The Postum soured on the back of his tongue. One day out there should refocus her contentment toward house and garden. "It's not all hum and honey," he warned her, "Best tie up those cuffs."

Twenty minutes later, the dog jumped onto the flatbed and Maire slid into the passenger seat. Leo headed north up the highway. He cut across field tracks and a farm bridge, the river still brown with spring run-off, and snaked up a rutted road toward the bench. When the truck surfaced over the ridge they were suddenly alone with the western vista. Wheatgrass, tall enough to be caught in the wind, shivered like green skin over the rolling land. Mountains erupted along the horizon, slanted heaves of rock face, sugared with snowfields.

"On the train," Maire whispered, "the view kind of hypnotized me."

"Grass madness," Leo nodded. "Charlotte always felt she might disappear into the expanse. I planted the yard with cottonwoods and fir trees to hold her in." A merchant's daughter from Minneapolis, Charlotte had been raised for a fancier parlor than the Cooper homestead. She loved him. She followed him. But late at night, Leo would wake to the haunting largo of *Clair de Lune* and know she was roaming an unspoken melancholy. He waited until the last chord. Sometimes she wept in his embrace. Sometimes she pulled away. Sometimes Leo heard strains of Debussy in the underbuzz of bees.

"My condolences, sir." Maire's soft voice startled his reverie.

Leo cleared his throat, "You aren't going to call me sir, remember?" He pointed at a far-off cluster of grazing animals, distinctive white rumps shining in the morning sun. "Pronghorn."

"Oh my, is this where the deer and the antelope play?"

"Yup, home on the range." He gestured into the view, "I could drive these honey roads in my sleep."

Maire laughed. "That's what Franklin said!"

Leo swallowed hard. "When he talked about this, did he sound like he loved it?"

"Folks be attached to where they come from, even if it was hard." She sighed. "What are we looking for?"

christina baldwin

"See that darker green?" Leo pointed north, "That's alfalfa fields and the irrigation ditch. There's a cluster of stacked white boxes." Maire squinted. "Bee yard. On my chart, it's CR-17 named for Creek Road and the number of hives." The truck lurched over crusted-up tracks. "Laid these ruts myself tucking in the bees. Rain-turning-to-snow, ground freezing, Franklin gone; I was late. After harvest, beekeepers make sure to leave the hive enough to get through to next blossoms." Maire nodded. "Today we'll see how they're doing. Should be a lot of bees as there's a lot of work. We will stack empty supers, set them up with room for honey production. Alfalfa bloom will run a month, then farmers cut for hay, the plants regenerate, and another cut middle August. Meanwhile, there's wild clover, hairy vetch, wildflowers. Best honey anywhere." Leo parked and the dog jumped down to run perimeter, barking, spinning, lifting his leg. "Marking territory," Leo said, "making sure any varmints know he's keeping an eye on things."

Maire was pulling on the gloves and bee bonnet he handed her. She tucked her pants cuffs into the boot tops. "Can I move? Will they sting me?"

"They don't want to sting you. You're not a flower so, basically, uninteresting." Leo opened his toolbox and pulled out a small metal canister the size of a coffee can with a leather bellows attached to one side and a spout on top. "This is the smoker." He opened the hinged top of the can and put in shredded newspaper and a few wood shavings. He lit a match curled in the palm of his hand and held a small twist of paper to the tiny flame. "Old sermon notes," he smiled. "Once it's going, I drop it onto the newspaper and wood chips and blow gently. It's catching now." Leo tipped the canister so Maire could peer inside.

The Beekeeper's Question

"Now we need smoke." He reached into a small bag and pulled out frayed strings of burlap and a crumbled disk of dried cow pie which he dropped onto the tiny fire a few bits at a time. "The bellows are attached at the base to force air through the smoldering fuel." He squeezed the vee of the leather bellows. A thin, grey plume of smoke wafted out of the cone tip. He handed it to Maire, bellows first. "Well, Mrs. Cooper, shall we meet some bees?"

Thousands of tiny, blurred bodies careened into the warming day. Maire kept shaking her head, trying to clear her hearing and focus her sight. The bee bonnet slipped around on her hair. Leo's instructions became a droning backdrop of words amongst a higher pitched *hmmm*. "Don't let it go out... not too hard, tend the quality of the smoke." Her body felt slightly electrified as though she was a conduit between earth and sky.

Leo pointed to a thin slit at the bottom of the hive. "Just above the baseboard is the entrance." He scraped a crust of wax with the metal blade he called a hive tool. "In winter, we want the opening narrow to keep out cold and intruders, and in summer we want it wide to handle the traffic."

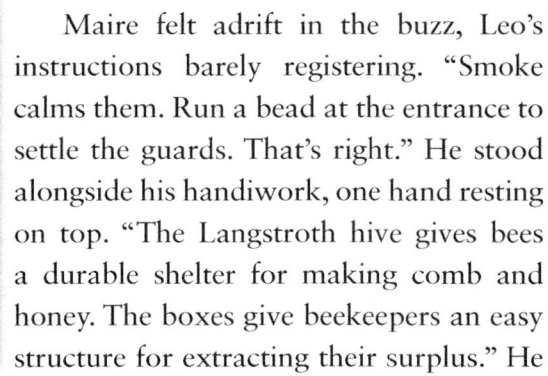

Maire felt adrift in the buzz, Leo's instructions barely registering. "Smoke calms them. Run a bead at the entrance to settle the guards. That's right." He stood alongside his handiwork, one hand resting on top. "The Langstroth hive gives bees a durable shelter for making comb and honey. The boxes give beekeepers an easy structure for extracting their surplus." He patted the small rectangular tower. "The boys and I constructed these hives ourselves."

A memory seemed to buzz alive in Maire's mind: a room that smelled of beeswax, a hanging bulb, a plank table. Leo younger. Franklin and his brothers piecing together sticks of wood. The room was cold, and the boys puffed visible breaths pretending to smoke cigarettes while their father pretended disapproval. A woman brought cocoa. There. Then. The smoker shook in Maire's hand. Here. Now.

Leo kept talking, "This bottom box serves as kitchen, nursery, living room, and bedroom, bees all nested together." He seemed so at ease; she wanted that. "Life in the brood chamber revolves around the queen. If the queen is well, the hive is well. Except for one mating flight she spends her entire life in the dark, laying eggs, fed and fussed over, positioned gently over the prepared brood cells. Right now, building up the colony for summer, she's laying 1500 eggs a day, more than her body weight."

Maire felt Leo's lessons depositing themselves into the comb of her mind. "And twenty-one days later the egg has grown to flying insect. Some workers stay and nurse the queen. Some feed pollen to the larvae and cap the cells of the pupae. Most of them, tens of thousands of hive mates, fly for miles and visit hundreds of blossoms a day. They communicate the location of nectar by dancing. They extrude wax from slits in their abdomens to construct the comb. And if the hive is threatened, they defend it with their lives." Leo lifted the hive lid. "We're going to check how they're doing, then add empty supers and frames for honey production."

Maire peered in. "It's all wooden slats." Leo pried loose a frame from the brood box and raised a tray of comb crawling with golden striped insects. Behind the veil, something kept buzzing in Maire's chest. "They're so beautiful!" She tried to pick one bee and follow her path across the comb. She lost track. Or maybe she didn't. She couldn't tell.

Leo pointed at the center of the frame, "There's the queen. She's longer, bigger." The bellows of the smoker breathed. Maire breathed. "Since everything looks healthy, we're going to slip in the queen excluder, a mesh screen sized so only workers can move around the whole hive. We don't want her majesty laying brood in with the honey. Then we'll stack empty supers on top. These are our honey factories. We close everything up, move to the next hive, do it again." Maire nodded. "A beekeeper is constantly cycling between yards," he cautioned. "I tend hundreds of hives, and keeping a million workers happy is a big job."

CR-17 took them an hour—checking queens and workers, placing excluders, stacking supers. They moved up Creek Road yard by yard. The dog was a muddy mess and rode with his body wedged in the crease of the truck's fender, face in the wind. At noon they leaned against the truck grill staring west, eating cold chicken and saltines, gulping water out of Mason jars. Maire pulled off the bee bonnet and shook her hair free. "Bee life is so organized."

"Perfection of order," Leo sucked a chicken bone, "Everything in a hive runs on an instinctual purity of pattern."

"No shirking, bossing, or laws?" she asked. Leo shook his head. "No stockpiling honey so the drones may gorge while the workers starve?" He shook his head again.

"There *is* death in the hive," he admitted. "Only one queen rules, workers exhaust themselves in summer frenzy, drones mate and die. Like the sex drive, self-defense is essential to preserving communal life. If the wasp comes to steal honey, guard bees defend the hive, but there is no wanton violence, no rape of innocents, no horrors of war. Bees do not hate."

"You are describing a world without evil." Tears sprang into Maire's eyes and a buzzing question filled her mind. "If the hive is a more benevolent society, why don't *humans* live as *bees* live?"

Leo's face flushed. "*That* is my beekeeper's question! I have spent years peering into their society like a curious god trying to translate what works for beekind into something that works for mankind."

She felt smoked and dreamy. "Why then are *we* the keepers of the bees? Shouldn't the bees be the keepers of us?" Maire grasped Leo's hands, amazed at her presumption. The buzz intensified until her whole body felt consumed by the *hmmm*. A barrier dropped between them. She saw in him the young husband and father, building the house, the church, the honey business. She saw Jesus in his hive-white robe, hands dripping with honeycomb, imploring humanity to discern the sacred pattern. In turn, she let Leo see Irish hedgerows and herself a girl escaped from chores. She let him see her years of service and reading by lamplight, waiting, waiting. She showed him Franklin moving across the dancehall as focused as a drone drawn to the virgin queen. Then she blinked. He blinked. They were again two giants standing among the floating golden bodies of *Apis mellifera*. She dropped his hands, suddenly shy. "Forgive me, sir. It's just, the bees wake something in me." She searched his face for comprehension.

At the end of the day, Leo had to admit he was impressed. The workload seemed to enliven the girl, and he pondered that honeyed moment when she first proclaimed her attachment to the bees. They worked bare-handed, settling equipment onto the truck bed while stray bees crawled around the honey-scented supers and scavenged wax from encrusted boards. "Yow!" Maire let out a surprised cry, "I'm stung!"

Leo took his thumbnail and plucked the stinger and venom sac from the back of her hand. "A bee's stinger has a barb like a fishhook. The bee plunges it into your skin and when she lifts her abdomen, the stinger remains, disemboweling her." Tears welled in Maire's eyes. "Does it hurt that much?" He was suddenly alarmed.

"No… but she died."

Leo watched the skin redden. "This is normal. Over time, you get less reaction." He smiled reassuringly. "You can't be a beekeeper and worry about stings, Maire. And you can't fret over individual bees. We step on them, pinch them, scatter them. The bees that tend the hive through winter don't live to fly in spring. Generation upon generation, they push tiny carcasses out of the entrance or fly off to die alone." He looked for flushing at her neck. "The queen is the only individual, everyone else is just a living function of the hive."

"They don't have emotions?"

"Emotions are mental. Reactions are physical." Without warning, Leo pinched the sting site and Maire jerked back her hand. "That's reaction," he explained. "But wondering if I meant to hurt you and why, then connecting this pain to previous hurt, that's emotion." He caressed her palm in apology.

Maire nearly whispered, "Do you think Franklin meant to hurt me by not speaking of our marriage?"

Leo looked deep into the young woman's eyes. "I think he meant to hurt *me*." He released her hand. "Three weeks ago, I thought your arrival an unwelcome disturbance. This morning, I tried to dissuade you from coming with me. Yet here you are, with sore muscles and sunburn, beeswax under your fingernails, and a sting on your hand. Do you still want to be a beekeeper?"

"You said I have the beekeeper's question. Isn't that a sign?"

"That was *my* question," Leo spoke tenderly. "It took me years to understand what I sought from the bees. To know yourself, Maire, is to discover what question resides deepest in your heart."

Her eyes took on light, "When I met Franklin, I called him a broody man. I din't have words for it, sir, but I think he's gone to war to find his question."

"War is a dangerous quest." Leo stared over her shoulder into the landscape. "I prayed my sons would find their questions here. But Boyd would only study bees under a microscope, Jesse deserted me, and Franklin enlisted." He gestured at the hives around them. "Beekeeping is heavy lifting and long hours on hot days. There's delivering sugar syrup when the world is freezing. There's disease and disaster and the occasional bear." Leo sighed. "But there is also horizon and solitude. Holding one's place in Creation, decoding the pattern. Maybe *you* are the one who can find your question here."

Maire sucked the bee sting. "Women's work is also heavy lifting and long hours, usually without the bear." She smiled. "If you will have me, sir, I am your apprentice. If the bees will have me, I am their guardian. And if the question will have me, I am its seeker."

"Good. We'll start, then." Leo realized he'd been holding his breath. "And Jere promised grilled cheese sandwiches if we came by." He whistled to the dog and started up the engine, their bargain struck.

9
The Long Reach

END OF JUNE 1942: *Rommel retakes the Libyan supply port of Tobruk from British forces, keeping much of North Africa in Axis control.*

ESPECIALLY IN SUMMER, Doc liked to converse her way around town. She leaned over fences, petted wandering dogs, greeted children in their yards and old folks on their porches. When she ambled by Cooper's, she noticed the rooms had been dusted, scrubbed, and tidied, curtains starched, and windows shined. She waved at the bent backs of Maire and Hazel, working rows of garden vegetables. She finally put her thoughts together and wrote Franklin.

June 27, 1942
Dearest boy,

We are growing quite fond of that girl you married. Maire's fast learning the ways of country living, and folks are happy to have someone new around. I know she is writing you the details. As your auntie, just let me say you made a good choice in a hard time. Though the separation and pregnancy came fast, I pray you will hold onto each other with love through the years. Right now, your marriage is a long rope. You each got to keep tugging your end, letting the other one know you are there. Letters are rope. Words are touch. That's my whole advice. I miss you. Be careful. Win the war. Come home safe. Everything else we'll figure out. Love, Auntie Doc

She waved at Maire weeding radishes. "I'm headed to Gertie's," she called.

"Please check for post." Maire pushed back damp curls. "Come back for lunch."

After soup and cold cuts, Doc had barely got her hands in dishwater when an anguished howl careened through the house. She found Maire on a porch rocker, bent awkwardly over her thickened waist. The freshly delivered Army stationery was crumpled in her hands. The young woman's body vibrated with panic. Doc gently pulled Maire's shoulders back and wrapped her in a strong embrace. "What's happened, dearie?"

"He promised to stay away. He promised...oh my God, oh my God...what if Broin kills him? What if he comes for me?" Maire shook in Doc's grasp, eyes unfocused, wringing her hands, gasping breaths. Doc had held shock before. Memories raced through her mind: the coal miner's woman, the farmer with charred legs, Charlotte on the day Gracie died, the vacant faces of Indian children when the Fort had been a residential school. The darkened closet; she stopped her thoughts.

Doc breathed as she wanted the girl to breathe, "Take a breath, dearie, slow and deep." Maire hiccoughed. "Exhale 1-2-3-4. Pause empty. Inhale 1-2-3-4. Pause full. Again, again." When she felt tension easing, Doc released her hug, pulled up a chair, held out her hands. "You got a load of fear in you, girl." The young woman's eyes were as wild as sky when a storm has passed but thunder still rumbles in the distance. "Talk to me."

"Frank got in a fight," Maire's voice was wobbly, "in Cullybackey, where I come from, in the local pub, with my father and the man he sold me to." She handed over the letter.

The Beekeeper's Question

June 16, 1942—lost count, but I know what day it is!
Dear Maire,

Now that you're safe and settled about the baby, I got to tell you something. Middle of April, driving maneuvers, Thompson and I hit a sheep in the road. Tommy decided we had to fess up to the locals, so we found the nearest pub. The sheep belonged to a man named ~~Briaoin~~ Mulvaney. He had a friend, an old guy named MacDonnell. In the heat of the moment, my buddy said that I had married a girl from here named MacDonnell. Suddenly Mulvaney went crazy, jumped me, beat me up, threatened to kill me. Thompson pulled a knife and held him back. We paid for the sheep and figured it done. I didn't mean to find them. It wasn't my fault.

But then Mulvaney got hired by the Army. Supply chief says he's a master at finding things that don't officially exist. I told Andy to watch out, the man comes with a hell of a temper. Last Saturday night, someone broke into the Quonset barracks, went through stuff, stole things. Thompson and I were questioned again about the pub incident.

Upshot is I'm getting transferred into Belfast to calm things down. I'm sorry to get your history riled up, Moy. I got more understanding why you left here. I wish you had told me, but you probably didn't think I'd land in your old life any more than I thought you'd land in mine. I'm healed up. Love, Frank

Story began spilling from Maire as the shaking subsided. "He beat his own father near to death. Well, Mr. Mulvaney might of deserved it, but still, so much rage." Doc kept her face calm. "He hurt me. In my privates. In front of my brothers. Said I belonged to him. He bothered me. I was always scairt what he'd do next, the whole town scairt of him, not just me. When I turned sixteen, Broin offered my da some bred ewes in trade for me." Doc's mind was swirling with the long reach of terror. "I said no. Pa hit me. Ma gave me passage money they were saving for my brother. I walked into the night, got to Belfast, got on a ship, got to New York where the Missus found me, and I worked for her until Franklin found me, and then I came here and found you." Maire gulped for air. "That's my whole life." She was crying again. "Mrs. Reid, the postmistress helps Ma and me trade letters January and June. At the end of 1937, Broin went to prison for assault and burglary. I relaxed. Last June, Ma wrote he was back and talking that he's coming to America to get me. Ma said I best marry someone soon. I found as good a man as I could, Doc. A man who smelled like honey. A man from far away." Maire was shaking again. "But out of the whole world, in a war as big as this, Franklin ends up walking smack into my old life."

Doc grunted to standing and paced the length of the porch and back. She felt Maire's unspoken pleading: Say something, do something, know something. "First off, this news is weeks old. Franklin is already safe in the big city. As for this character Brian…"

"Broin…" Maire winced to speak the name.

"For all his talk, he's still in Calleybuck."

"Cullybackey, along the river Main."

"Yes, where he's a big bully in a small town. If he leaves Cullybackey, he's nobody. A man like that counts on people fearing him because they heard how bad he is. He's got no power if he's got no reputation for power."

Maire took a ragged breath. "Sometimes I dream my da is beating me. Sometimes my brother is chasing me. The worst is when it's him, sneaking through dark hallways, finding me. When I met Franklin, my nightmares stopped. I wrote Ma I am safe. I signed my new name. Then the nightmare on the train…"

Maire wrapped her arms around the bulge of her growing baby. "He used to threaten that if I… if I, you know, had sex with anyone else... He will kill Franklin if he figures to get away with it. If he gets to America and has got the city address, he'll terrify the Missus."

"Did you ever tell the Missus about Pigeon River?" Shake of the head. "She can't reveal what she doesn't know." Doc felt perspiration prickle at her hairline. "Influential people don't stand for intimidation, Maire. They call the police. The police take notice. A lowlife man bumps into the law at every turn. He's already been to prison; he'll be in prison again. He's far away. Travel is nearly impossible. If he ever did get on a ship, customs will stop him. Law will stop him. This is America."

"I want to believe you, Doc, but I know his evil ways." The girl was still pale and trembling. "He always came on me when I was scairt."

"His only power is the fear he stirs in you. You've been courageous every step of the way, Maire. Pigeon River is your hideaway. I am part of your safety net. And Leo..."

"No, please, only us women. The Reverend is just considering me more help than hinder. And I din't tell Franklin because I din't want him to think me tainted." She tightened her hold on her belly. "Rev Leo says everybody got an essential question in them that drives their life. What if my question is a curse?"

Doc took Maire's hands in hers. "You have so much light and curiosity and courage in you, Maire. Look there for your question. Let me take your fear."

"Can you take it?" Her earnest look near broke Doc's heart.

"Alongside my house there's a slanted door that goes into the ground, like for a cellar." Maire nodded. "Well, I don't have a cellar. Under the door is a sand box designed to keep potatoes." Maire's eyes went round. "Doctoring isn't only illness and injury, sometimes people's stories need healing as much as their bodies. When I come home with a load of secrets and fears, I open that door and slip the new fright in amongst the old. I say a little prayer, get myself up, and carry on."

"You will do that for me?"

"Yes, but that's only half of it. How will *you* let go of fear?"

A light flickered in the young woman's eyes. "Bees," said Maire. "Bees turn bitter into sweet, nectar into honey. With the bees, I feel safe." Maire led Doc into the parlor. "When I dusted Mrs. Charlotte's piano, I found a chart. The notes are letters repeated over and over." Maire eased onto the bench, raised the lid, and laid out a scroll of the scales that slipped behind the keyboard. "Listen." She pressed the note D-above-middle-C. Then she pressed all the adjacent notes creating a blurred sound. "It's the bees, Doc. I found their buzz. Din you think that's something?" She pressed the sustain pedal and a throbbing buzzing sound reverberated in the room. Maire's dissonant chord sounded more Bartok than Debussy, but as it summoned solace and safety, a resonating harmony emerged from the mash of notes.

Doc bent down and spoke directly into Maire's ear, "Whenever you are afraid, call the bees. Let them help you see your way."

Maire leaned into the sound, fingers tense. "And if he comes, I will sting him like the guard bees sting whatever tries to rob the hive. Sting him to death. Bury him in wax."

"And no harm shall come," Doc spoke the benediction.

Jereldene Jespersen, before she became just "Doc," knew the price a woman paid to step outside accepted roles. The cost of her education had been made horribly clear to her late one evening studying alone in the anatomy lab; an evening it turned out she was not alone. And not her father's stature, nor the family's standing, could prevent her humiliation when her professor pushed her into a closet and took what he felt entitled to take. There was rage in that closet, mixed with the blood of her virginity, the leak of semen down her thighs. Long after he was gone, she pried open the closet door and stumbled through midnight streets to her father's home. She would not betray one doctor to another, but two years later, walking across the stage in front of the faculty, sheepskin diploma in hand, she had turned her head and spit on his shoes. If Maire wanted this secret held woman to woman, she had confided in the right woman.

10
A One-Man War

JUNE & JULY 1942: *The Germans control Tobruk. The Italians control the Mediterranean. The Japanese control Guadalcanal.*

MONDAY MORNING, AFTER THE WEEKEND BREAK-IN, Franklin was summoned for questioning. He slicked back his hair, tucked the slack of his shirttails deep into his uniform trousers. "Private First Class Franklin Cooper, Signal Corps reporting, sir." Similar hut, desks instead of bunks.

The captain looked up. Thin lips, thinning hair, a small cloud of cigarette smoke drifting above his thin shoulders hunched over a thin stack of papers on his desk. "At ease. Take a seat. Lucky Strike?" Franklin accepted the smoke. "We have a problem with your name on it." The captain reached across the battlefield of the grey metal desk with his official Army insignia lighter. Franklin lit up, exhaled toward the ceiling. "This report from your encounter with civilians in a local pub last April says that you and Corporal Thompson had a vehicular collision. With a sheep."

"It was late afternoon, sir. Dense fog and…"

"I just reread your report, Cooper."

"Yessir." The captain flipped through papers filled out in Thompson's handwriting.

"Says you ran over one female sheep and drove the carcass to a nearby pub where you identified the sheep's owner as Brian Mulvaney, currently employed by Sergeant Anderson as local procurement assistant."

"Broin Mulvaney. Yessir, so I heard, sir."

"And did you pay Mr. Mulvaney the sum of five pounds to settle the debt?"

"Thompson took the cash, sir. It didn't seem prudent for me to return."

"Why exactly is that Cooper, in your own words…"

"During our exchange at the pub, Mr. Mulvaney picked a helluva fight, sir, turned on me after some remark Thompson made." Franklin's armpits greased with nervous sweat. "I was down, sir. We drew arms in self-defense. Mulvaney backed off and I haven't seen him since. Anderson told me he's working around the base."

"And the remark that set off the fight…" The captain lit another Lucky.

"There was an older man in the vicinity of the Jeep named MacDonnell, and Thompson remarked that is the maiden name of my wife."

"You married a local?" The captain glanced at his file, "I don't have paperwork."

"She emigrated from here in '36. We married stateside, sir, before I shipped out. Now, she's there and I'm here."

"I see. And the relationship of Mulvaney to your wife?" The captain blew smoke into Franklin's face.

"She inferred there had been trouble when she left. She was just sixteen, sir." Franklin inhaled, sucking in the questions that had haunted him in the weeks since the fight. Midnight hours when he wondered if he knew who Maire really was; wondered if he'd been stupid to tie the knot, and now a baby. Then a letter would arrive, and her earnest sorting of her dilemma restored his affections.

He remembered Thompson's counsel after they'd each read letters from home. "The strength of a marriage depends on two people taking each other at their word." Tommy sniffed his letter for traces of perfume. "My wife says our farm's running fine with the help of two high school kids. I believe her. I say driving a Jeep is one of the safest jobs in a war zone. She believes me." He had slapped Franklin's knee, "That's my advice, young groom, pour honey on the truth and keep going."

Franklin didn't like the look on the captain's face. "My wife, sir, may have come from a poor local family, but she is an enterprising woman of fine character. Whatever drove her from County Antrim as a girl, well, that's her business and my good fortune. Mulvaney is a brawler and a sneak thief, and recently out of prison."

The captain drummed his fingers on the incident report. "The U.S. Army is quite accustomed to making use of questionable characters. He is, of course, a prime suspect in the burglary of your quarters. Report says cash was stolen and personal effects. Such as…"

Franklin willed himself not to squirm. "Resale items mostly, Thompson had a personal knife, canteens, insignia. Letters had been rifled through." Franklin was sweating harder now as he remembered the hiss and spittle of Broin's threat, "I'll kill ye Cooper if'n I find it's true."

The captain ground his cigarette into a full ashtray. "I've drawn up orders assigning you to Belfast. You will process arriving personnel until further notice."

"I'm Signal Corps, sir."

"You're a soldier, Cooper. You serve under my command. Dismissed."

"Yessir." Franklin pushed back his chair, saluted. "And Mulvaney, sir?"

"Do not engage." The captain tossed the empty cigarette pack toward a bin. Missed. "I'm doing you a favor, Cooper."

The Beekeeper's Question

"Yessir." Franklin saluted, turned, and stepped squinting into daylight.

Guys had teased them that at least the Jeep had seen action, dented fender, dried blood. Franklin was in the field with his unit practicing laying wire for the field phone when Thompson drove up. "Hey, Bee Man, ready for the next situation?" Franklin hefted equipment and jumped into the passenger seat. "Local woman came round selling sheep cheese, God that stuff's awful, and asking who knows the men from the pub fight. Skittish as a barn cat. I tell her I'll get you. She set up this rendezvous. You sure you know what kind of a family you married into?"

Franklin ran his hand through his hair. "Pretty sure I do *not* know. Also, sure the women aren't the problem." His laugh sounded more like a croak.

"She's waiting in the Methodist church. You'll feel right at home." Thompson pulled onto the lane. "You got ten minutes. I'll swing back. Be ready." Thompson rolled the Jeep to a bare halt, Franklin jumped out and sprinted between the hedgerows that cut through the lawn and cemetery to the front door.

The hinges creaked. Old. Damp. Historical. Franklin's eyes took long seconds to adjust. A woman stepped into view. He saw the resemblance immediately. "Me name is Ailish MacDonnell," she reached for his hand with both of hers and searched his face. "You the man married me daughter?" She was smaller than Maire, weathered, hair turning grey. Her shoulders were permanently stooped, and she looked up at him from a slightly cockeyed angle.

Franklin nodded. "Since Christmas, ma'am."

"She wrote me. But it's dangerous," her eyes were darting side to side. "When Maire turned sixteen, her father promised her to the man who beat you. When she dinna agree, he hit her." Franklin felt his heart ratchet up. "Tell me you are a kinder man."

Her hands felt like chicken bones in his palms. "We're beekeepers, Ma'am. I would never hit a woman."

Ailish continued in a shaking voice. "I helped her get away." She looked around as though she expected her husband and Mulvaney to jump from the pews. "It was months afore I even knew she'd made it to somewhere."

"I'm so sorry, Mrs. MacDonnell." It seemed a lame response. "And Mulvaney?"

"Broin isna like other people. Once he's set on somethin', yah canna turn him aside. Maire said no to 'im and the whole town knew." She dropped her voice. "Scorned by a girl he thought was easy taking. He was ragin' to follow her but went to prison instead. First thing out, he come at me, gonna make me say where she is. I stood me ground, I did." Franklin froze in the intensity of her eyes. "When yer buddy said you was her husband, he'd a kilt yah right then, or any day since. He thinks he's smarter now, schemin' to git money, git passage, go git her."

Franklin's mind was reeling. "What does Maire know?"

"I tole her he went to prison. Last year I tole her he was out and to find herself a good man." Ailish MacDonnell looked him over with piercing blue eyes, "She found you."

Franklin looked into the woman's earnest face. "I hardly know what to think, Mrs. MacDonnell. We married on good faith, but she hid this."

"Maire risked everthin' to make herself a better life. She's a true heart and a brave girl!" the mother said. "I were so proud, her being a maid, but not a servant. You know what I mean? And readin' all those books. She was holdin' out for just the right man. When she wrote in January, she was genuine happy."

"We were both happy," he responded. "But to have a man like that chasing her…" he searched Ailish's face.

"Broin is the devil's brother." She looked around the empty church as though it had ears, "You be careful, he'll like to get you outta the way." She smiled as though she had just delivered kindly advice, not a death threat. "I'm feared he mighta pinched the address for the big house."

"She's already gone from there." Ailish jerked in surprise. "She's with my father, who is a Methodist minister, and my aunt, who is a doctor. She's in Montana."

Ailish stepped back, "Dinna say me where." Tension flashed through her. "Broin tellin' ever'body he gonna hire on a merchant ship."

"Not a great time to cross the Atlantic." Now Franklin glanced around the church. "She would want me to tell you, there's a baby coming." Franklin watched the news sink into the woman's eyes.

She did not speak for a moment. "Ah, be good she'll have someone, then." She bit her lip. "May the fightin' go easy on yah, young man. May 't all come to victory. Tell her I'm glad. Tell her I'm well. Tell her that Mrs. Reid died and nah to write anymore." She scrutinized him one more time, "As for Broin…" she spit to one side, a cursing gesture, "May the war get him first."

Franklin felt a rush of protectiveness. "I'll do my best to take care of her, Mrs. MacDonnell. She gets my pay. She has a local friend teaching her to garden. My father is teaching her to tend bees. There's fresh air, sunshine, good people."

Thompson honked from the Jeep. "God bless you both. Be careful." She turned into the musty shadows of the church.

Franklin let himself out of the creaking door and sprinted down the walkway, ducking as though under fire. Thompson sped away. It took several miles for Franklin's thoughts to swirl into coherence. "I got three things to say," he announced, "First off, Mulvaney is truly dangerous. The U.S. Army should not be letting him in our perimeter. Secondly, my wife is an amazing survivor and I'm lucky to have her. And three, if her mother comes round again, just buy her cheese."

christina baldwin

> Sunday June 21, 1942—calling this #10 and starting the count again
> ~~Dear Maire, I met your mother. She's a nice lady.~~
> ~~Dear Maire, I understand you better now.~~
> ~~Dear Maire, why didn't you tell me why you had to leave here?~~
> Dear Maire,
> I know we each got things that happened to us, hard to talk about, but someday, please tell me about leaving Cullybackey.
> I transferred to Belfast. You know it's not dangerous if I'm behind a desk! I'm getting used to the idea that we are really married and going to have a baby. Hope you are feelin' okay and getting settled. I am safe where I am. You are safe where you are. So far, so good. Your man,
> Franklin
> PS: There's a huge city library, send me a reading list.
> PPS: Don't ask me how I know, but a lady named Mrs. Reid died.

Intrigue gave him a stomachache, but at least he was back to believing Maire loved him. Like Thompson said, he would take her at her word and offer her his word and they would stand in that honeyed truth. He licked the envelope.

Belfast was a city still in shock as it went about its daily business. It had been an undefended seaport, considered out of range of the Luftwaffe, until four nights in April and May 1941 when a quarter of the city was destroyed. A thousand citizens were killed, and twenty-thousand refugees scattered into the countryside. Franklin wandered down blocks of ruined buildings seeing firsthand what bombs do. "Get out there and create some good will," his sergeant ordered. He and other GIs worked alongside locals, putting the city back together brick by brick. He was glad to roll up his sleeves after hours of paperwork.

Evenings stretched light 'til 11:00 p.m. He got a library card and began following Maire's routine: work, read, sleep, rise, repeat. He stayed watchful, avoided pubs and crowds.

> July 15, 1942, #13
> Dear Franklin,
>
> I was true scared when you wrote about the fight. I'm glad you are in the city and harder to find, and that I'm in the country harder to find. That man hurt me as a girl, and he would have hurt me all my life. Like you said, we each have things that happened and shaped us. I was terrified to leave County Antrim, but I got away. The Mister and Missus worked me hard but let me read. I raised hopes for myself and met you. I'm still raising my hopes—or at least raising bees! Hazel and I are overcome with vegetables and the ladies are teaching me to preserve.
>
> love, Maire.
>
> PS: Sorry to hear about Mrs. Reid. Ma said she was going blind, so I haven't writ since January. Now I don't know what to do.
>
> PPS: I don't think I'll feel truly safe until B. is dead and you are home.

Northern Ireland was busting at the seams with uniformed Yankees. Franklin kept the ledgers, verified orders, organized transports. Twice a week he was assigned hospital detail to account for both civilian and military patients rescued from torpedoed ships and cold water. Men barely stuck together—emergency surgeries, bones set, wounds stitched. The worst cases transferred to England into military hospitals. And then what? Franklin didn't want to ever find out. After a day like that, he'd raise a Guinness even though he thought it bitter. Bitter was just the right taste.

He grew enthralled by European culture, the history of his skin. He mouthed words like Renaissance, Reformation, colonialism, monarchy, Parliament. He poured over tomes of art and architecture, discovered the Sistine Chapel, the Colosseum, treasures of the Louvre. There was enough in one library to study for a lifetime!

July 30, 1942
Dear Maire,
    I am busy as a bee! From my desk, I help guys get to their units, handle medical transfers, or just maintain a bit of order while organizing thousands of men. It's like radio communication without the radio.
    I got a library card. I understand how books kept you going all those years. I have thoughts I didn't know were in me. I talk to Malcolm the librarian, and he recommends the next book. Sometimes I want the Army to let me stay here pushing paperwork. But when I hear what's happening under Hitler's boot, I want to fight for people like you and me, Moy. Ordinary folks trying to hold our little bit of the world together. I'll do my part. Then we'll figure out our life together. Your broody man.
    PS: A book mobile comes out from Great Falls Library. You can request titles.
    PPS: Haven't heard from Mulvaney. He's bound to screw up soon and get himself back in jail.

Thompson ran supplies and paperwork between the city and country bases and made Franklin part of his official business. It was good to have a buddy. They knew it. "Remind me, why are we sitting here?" Thompson was enjoying his one-for-the-road Guinness.

"Reinforce the Brits now that Churchill and Roosevelt are such sweethearts." Franklin was downing a Smithwick's.

"Nazi army is marching into the Soviet Union." Thompson licked foam off his upper lip. "How much territory does Hitler need?"

"Does the word megalomaniac mean anything to you?" Franklin lowered his voice, "Delusional mental illness, obsessed with power, convinced of personal greatness, proclivity for violence, no regard for human cost."

"You studying psychology now?" Thompson poked Franklin and laughed.

"One book. But I started thinking I had every symptom, so I stopped." Franklin shrugged.

"So, if Hitler is a megalomaniac, is Mulvaney a minimaniac?"

"Any sightings?" Franklin was curious. He had to be curious.

Early August, Thompson pulled Franklin into their usual corner in the pub. "Sad news for your wife, and maybe not what it seems." He handed Franklin a news clipping.

LOCAL WOMAN DROWNS

The body of Cullybackey resident, Ailish (nee Donnelly) MacDonnell, age 49, was recovered from the River Main Friday last. Her husband, Mr. Patrick MacDonnell had reported his wife missing on 15 July. No search was instigated as her disappearance was considered a private matter. The corpse had been in the river several days before retrieval near the bend at Galgorm Manor. Bruises consistent with floating through the weirs were present on the body. Ruled death by drowning, accident or suicide, unknown. During questioning, Mr. MacDonnell informed authorities that his wife could not swim and did not "seem the sort to end it, though she been acting strange of late." Mrs. MacDonnell was buried alongside her parents in Cullybackey Methodist

```
Church. She is also survived by sons George and
Gordon, and daughter Maire.
```

Franklin started to sweat. "Couple weeks ago, she came by. How do these people know where we are when we're not telling 'em?" Franklin shook a cigarette out of the pack. "Said she was visiting her son, asked me to post a letter to Maire. I been holding it, since I haven't told Maire I'd met her mom." He took a long drag.

Thompson sucked his Guinness. "Whad'ya think? Accident, suicide? A push from Broin?"

"Geez, Tommy, I only knew the woman twenty minutes max."

"We took more care to make right by that sheep than the authorities are doing for this family." Thompson sounded disgusted.

"What family? Paddy just tidying up the file. Pretty sure the Belfast boy is a poof, so he doesn't want any attention from the Royal Ulster Constabulary. Other brother went to Australia, no forwarding address. And Maire's hiding in my bedroom, making breakfast for my father, and hearing tales of my ill-spent youth from old school chums." Franklin blew smoke out his nostrils.

"Jesus-H-excuse-my-French!" Tommy's favorite curse, "MacDonnell and Mulvaney already hooked up running penny-ante schemes shagging the U.S. Army." Thompson downed the pint. "Can we puleeze get outta here, fight some real Nazis, get this over with!"

"It ain't Iowa, Tommy. MPs can't get enough on Mulvaney to turn him in, and the RUC isn't exactly the FBI." Franklin folded the scrap of paper into his breast pocket. "I got some thinking to do."

"Yup, you do," Thompson agreed. "And stay away from the wharf while you do it."

11
Beans and Sorrow

AUGUST 1942: Stalin presses Churchill and Roosevelt to open a second front to divert German assault on Soviet territory. Allied command convenes in Washington DC to strategize an invasion of North Africa.

WHEAT FIELDS SWAYED UNDER HOT, DRY WINDS. Roving teams of field crews hitchhiked on trucks, slipped out of train cars. Tractors started at dawn and ran till dark. The tractors powered the mowers and the binders, and the blonde fields knelt before the blades, stalks shuffled sideways and bound into bundles, left standing in the sun for the heads to dry. A few days later came the threshing crews. Everyone was baked, dusted, colored like the land. Maire had never imagined the vastness of harvest, the urgency of pulling everything in—alfalfa, wheat, honey, vegetables, sugar beets, hogs, and cattle.

"Rough men do the roughest work," Leo pointed out a threshing crew. "I'm looking around for a honey man. Someone I can have near the house."

She risked boldness, "What about Boyd? Doc says he's in Seattle."

Leo's brow furrowed as a field. "He never liked the bees. Always studious. He was more Jere's son than mine, her apprentice from an early age."

"Jesse then. He's the one you talk about most."

Leo blinked surprised. "He was the best worker, but he ran the year after his mother died. I did so much wrong with them."

"He's a man now, sir. And you're a wiser man." She touched his shoulder. "If he comes, you'll figure it out."

"Truth is, I'm not sure how to reach him. Don't know his draft status. Jere says he's on the reservation." Leo gestured out the driver's window, "I look at these men and wonder what drove them out of families, homes, places they used to belong."

The baby kicked and Maire positioned Leo's hand high on her belly. "Hello from your grandchild. Next summer, Hazel can babysit, and I'll be more help."

Most days Maire was outside by 5:00 a.m., walking rows of carrots, onions, and tomatoes, picking beans and zucchini, and opening the irrigation trough that seeped water to the garden's roots. Before heat came up, she baked bread and made both breakfast and supper, cold soups (page 192, JofC) seasoned with herbs, garlic, and lots of salt. They all needed salt. At 5:00 p.m. she called Doc to join them, cut chunks of Sunday's beef roast. Leo prayed. They ate outside, rocking on porch furniture, waiting for breeze.

While Leo walked Doc home, Maire sponged herself down, naked in the kitchen. She started top to bottom, pressing a cold washcloth into her hairline, wiping the cornices of her ears, lingering over her closed eyes, her lips, her neck. She rinsed. The hair in her armpits was crystallized with sweat. Her breasts large as cantaloupes with raspberry nipples. Her sun-browned hands moved over the white globe of her belly. The baby kicked again. "Don't you start now, wee bee, it's bedtime." She soaped her lowers, water dribbling down her thighs. Her fingers lingered over her secret place, but she was afraid release might start premature labor. Her passion with Franklin a long-ago dream.

By the time Preacher Boy gave his arrival bark, she was sitting on the footstool, dressed in Charlotte's nightgown, brushing her hair. Leo knocked his seed cap against his pant leg. "Washing's a good idea," he said, "revive myself to think on Sunday's sermon." He helped her up.

"You can think tomorrow," she urged. "Tuesday Club is canning in the church basement."

"You a member now?"

"I'm a curiosity." She smiled.

End of the day, Maire and Hazel pulled wagon loads of canned goods home to each of their cellars. It was a long block, and they treaded carefully not to jostle the jars. "We don't gotta do it all tonight," Hazel said after their third trip divvying up the bounty from shared gardens. "Always good to leave some stored in the church anyway, case of needy families."

"Are you friends with that girl Susan? The quiet one." They were in the cellar, chilled in their sweaty clothes, lining up a row of canned beets.

"We're *all* friends, Maire. I mean we all been together since first grade." Hazel took a breath, "Susan was sweet on Franklin, wanted to be the one he'd marry. Torgersons work ranchland, big spread, cattle, some alfalfa. Susan got two brothers in the Pacific." Hazel made a funny face like she shouldn't have told.

"I got to know such, Haz, so I don't mortify myself."

Two days later, Maire was sitting on a small stool in the garden rows, late afternoon light. Hazel cut across the road with her arms full of baby. "I'm behind the tomatoes." Maire called out. She had already filled a picking tray, and there was a peck in the cellar that would rot if she didn't can them. "I'm running out of jars and lids." Vine-ripened, sun-heated, she was eating one that had already split.

Hazel set Bonnie, a chubby six-month-old in a diaper and sunbonnet, down between them in the dirt and blurted out, "Ralph enlisted. In the Marines. He got a letter from Ronnie

Torgerson saying how the Japanese are claiming the whole ocean for the Rising Sun. Decided he had to be part of it." She handed the baby an Early Girl. "Told me someday Bonnie is going to ask, 'What did you do in the war, Daddy?' and he doesn't want to tell her he grew sugar beets."

Maire winced. "The radio calls farmers 'soldiers of the soil.'"

"In Ralph's mind, it still means he's home safe while his friends brave the real fight."

"Food is essential. Somebody got to stay here and do it."

"I made every argument and still lost the debate." Saltwater floated in Hazel's eyes.

"He could get stuck in a desk job like Franklin in Belfast. Or be a supply sergeant. That happens, growing sugar beets might sound the greater valor." Maire attempted a reassuring tone.

A green pickup drove by and Hazel waved. "Tim Sivertsen, Gloria's husband. He'll be here for the duration. Farmer, only son, married, three little boys. Not drafting him. Wouldn't of drafted Ralph either. Aren't Bonnie and me enough?"

Maire pulled the baby between her legs shading her with the apron. "There is something about this war makes men want to go see the world."

Hazel plucked beans into the lap of her housedress. "Caleb said it serves him right 'cause he did the same thing to his father in the First World War. And Ethel just sat there wringing her hands. I'm the only one who talked back to him, but his mind was made up." Hazel's voice brittle with worry.

"Next year, Doc and Ethel can take care of our babes while we do things men are doing now." Maire shrugged her shoulders. "Other'n that, Hazel, I don't know what to say except we will do it together."

They fell silent listening to the bees that came and went from the garden hives pollinating raspberries, winter squash, and endless beans. Bonnie was mashing the tomato in her tiny hands, seeds and juice running down her torso. "Good thing she's near naked," Maire said. "You can dunk her in the sink soon's you get home."

"Did I tell you how Ralph and I got engaged?" Hazel swiped at tears. "We were in fourth grade. The old Fort was the primary school. It was recess and I was hanging by my knees on the monkey bars, braids flapping, shouting, 'Hey everybody, the world is upside down!' And suddenly, skinny little Ralphie Pocket came alongside me swinging by his knees, too. When I turned to look, he kissed me. It was a child's kiss, but suddenly I knew he was the love of my life. Such a grown-up thought; it gave me the hiccups. He must have thought it too because right then and there he asked, 'When we grow up, will you marry me?' and I said, 'Yes.' And that was that. Every now and then he'd run by and whisper, 'Do you remember?' I always remembered. We didn't tell anyone until we were in high school, but by then people just called us *RalphnHazel* like we were one person." Hazel reached for the baby. "This is the first thing gonna take us apart. The Marines recruiter gave Ralph thirty days to finish harvest, then he'll be sixty days in boot camp and ship out at the new year." Hazel's voice sounded haggard. "He already wrote Ronnie he's coming."

Hazel put the beans in Maire's tray. The new mother helped the pregnant mother to standing. "We're friends, and our babies will be friends," Hazel declared. "And if it's a boy, maybe he'll kiss Bonnie on the monkey bars and promise to love her all his life. And maybe there won't be a war and they can live here in peace and we can be the grannies."

"Maybe." Maire smiled weakly.

Doc laid out cold supper for the three of them, setting homeliness into a space the letter in her pocket would soon shatter. Maire came up from the cellar and plopped in a chair. Doc hovered. "Let's get some food in you, girl."

"Just no vegetables! I've seen enough beets, beans, peppers, and pickles for one day!"

christina baldwin

"Put your feet up. I'll get Leo."

They ate. Made small talk. It was hot in the kitchen, but contained. It was cooler outside, but exposed. Where was the right place to tell a young woman her mother was dead? A small breeze riffled the kitchen curtains. *Just do it*, Doc scolded herself. She and Leo were the "uh-oh" team in the valley. Maire was the only one who wouldn't already suspect something if they entered a room together. Doc reached in her pocket, opened the letter. "Franklin wrote us. He is okay, Maire. He has bad news though, about your family. Please listen as best you can." They pushed their plates to the center of the table.

> *August 8, 1942*
> *Dear Auntie Doc,*
> *I'm writing to ask you to deliver some sad news to Maire so she can hear it in person with you there to help. It's about her mother, Ailish. She found me and told me some things about the night Maire escaped to America.*

Maire's eyes went big. She turned to Leo, "I was protecting my virtue, and my mother sent me away. I'm not bad, sir."

"I know that, Maire." He offered her his hands. "Let's listen together." Maire clutched Leo's gnarled knuckles.

> *I told her that we are married, expecting a baby, and Maire is far away from Philadelphia. She seemed greatly relieved but did not want to know where. She asked me to tell Maire not to write anymore, that she was okay, times were better. I didn't know what to do because Maire made me promise not to find her family. I didn't find them, but they found me. Then I was transferred to Belfast.*

Maire began to blurt random thoughts, looking first at Doc, then at Leo. "I dinna mean to put him in a hard spot, sir. I shoulda known the County were too small to avoid them. My Pa has such a braggin' mouth. And there's a bully, a'course. And did he tell you someone thieved his things?" Tears welled in her eyes. "But me mother, he got to see me mother. That's good news." Doc lowered her head and read on.

> *Mrs. MacDonnell brought me a letter to mail to Maire (enclosed). Then two days ago, my buddy Thompson brought me this clipping from the Ballymena press saying Mrs. Ailish MacDonnell had drowned.*

"No!" almost a shout. "She was afraid of the river. I'm the one washed our clothes on the rocks. But then she's had to do everything herself. Was it raining? Does it say?" Doc laid the news clipping on the table.

"Shall I read it?" He reached for his glasses. Doc watched Maire flinch as the facts unfolded. "Missing person… no investigation… drowning… accident or suicide… survived by her husband Patrick, her sons Gordon and George, and daughter Maire."

A fire ignited in Maire's eyes like oil burning on a slick of tears. "My father's a bastard, pardon Reverend, blaming her for acting strange. And no one to know the truth of it."

"There's more," Doc said, "Franklin wrote a message to you."

> *So, after you tend her sorrow, as I know you will, please read out what I have to say: My dearest Maire, I am so sorry for this tragedy. I know what it's like to lose a mother, though I do not know what it is like for you to lose <u>your</u> mother. I have tried to keep promises I made to you <u>and</u> to your mother. I met her only two times. She seemed a good woman, though burdened by the hardships she helped you escape. I wish we were together right now. I wish we could curl up like we did last winter and tell each other the whole story. We both got to trust that life is going to work out for us, now and in years coming. Love, Franklin*

A holy silence hovered over them. Maire took a breath, "He's a good man, our Franklin."

"And you loving him is good too," Leo's voice choked.

"My Irish life seemed so far away until he stepped into it." Maire caressed the unopened letter from her mother. "I need a bit 'fore I read this."

Doc leaned against the door frame. Franklin's old bedroom was Maire's now. She noticed a small photo of the young couple stuck in the dresser mirror. It was dated 11/15/41, exactly nine months earlier: before Pearl Harbor, before war, before marriage, before pregnancy, before his departure and her arrival, before whatever happened when Franklin got in a fight with a bully named Broin, before a mother reached out, before Maire took her place among the bee yards and garden harvests, before a woman named Ailish fell in the river, before now.

Maire settled heavily on the bed. "There's so much I want to know, now that it's all come apart." Tears were leaking down her face. "I never expected to see her again, but still, she was my mother. She did what she could with the life she had. She set me free. I sent her money. It was something."

"I suspect your freedom was her greatest joy." Doc opened the window to urge an evening breeze into the small square space.

"But I couldna protect her, Doc," Maire's voice broke. "And she couldna protect herself. What a woman like her does." Maire's breath sputtered in her chest. "All these years, letters sayin' she's all right. Her only advice is to find a good man. She never said who she was, how she came to marry my da. There was one Christmas, I had just started school and was so proud of myself, we had nothing. Da got out his squeezebox. We danced, my brothers and me. My mother's eyes were shining. My father was sober and charming. That day is my best memory. And now, her life is two inches of newsprint, and she would'na got that if she hadn't drowned."

The Beekeeper's Question

Doc sat on the footstool. "There's a river here, too. Folks fall in, some swim, some drown. You're not to blame."

Maire handed over the letter, "Please read this one too." Ailish's handwriting was small and cramped. Doc read slowly making it out as she went.

Dear daughter, Yur man is just what I dreamed for you. He says you are living among bees and away from harm. Broin talks that he's gonna make a accident for yur soldier boy and then go get yah, war or no war. I'm going to Belfast to warn him. All these years I been praying for you so I not letting B. get away with one more evil thing. I have my own surprise for him. I stake my life on it. I will write again when he is gone forever. I'm so happy you'll have a baby. I hope it's a girl good as you were. I always been proud of you. I shoulda tole yah more. Your ma, Ailish.

Maire was holding onto her belly, staring at the ceiling. "Is that what motherhood is, Doc? Risking your life for your child? Fighting a madman to the death?"

Doc patted Maire's foot. "People, animals, even the bees, have a fierce instinct to protect their young. You vowed to defend yourself against this man. And well, seems your mother may have done it for you, though with tragedy at the end." Doc paused a breath, "She found her courage. She intervened. She stopped him to keep you free."

"She died, though." Maire's voice sounded flat. "Do you think he's dead, too?"

"He surely deserves to be dead. But even if he's alive, he can't get here, dearie. There's a war, an ocean, fleets of German submarines. Then there's most of a continent between Philadelphia and here. We're going to trust your flight to Pigeon River is untraceable. Rest your heart. Grieve your mama. Love your man."

Maire shivered with tension, "Now I want Franklin outta Belfast, even if it means into the war."

Doc massaged Maire's swollen ankles until the girl's breath deepened. A drumming cadence took over Doc's heartbeat. She felt the war marching through her old bones. "Sing to the bees, Irish girl," she whispered. "That's what we got."

Part Two
Return of the Native Son

12
The Wandering Son

THIRD WEEK IN AUGUST 1942: *American bombers begin airstrikes from English bases. French Jews face mass deportation to Auschwitz. The German Army advances toward Stalingrad.*

JESSE COOPER LIKED TO FOLLOW A HARD DAY'S WORK with a hard ride, letting the gelding streak over open-range grasslands on the east side of the Reservation. Four hooves hitting dirt, divots kicked out behind them, the bellows of the horse's breath. Jesse had named him Windy. Bareback, he used his knees and ankles to keep astride, letting Windy set the pace. The earth echoed back *buttarump-buttarump-buttarump*, a cadence as old as these hills. He slowed them to a trot, then to a walk, and came to rest on the top of a rise. His fingers laced in Windy's tangled mane, Jesse felt himself seated in a thousand generations of peopled territory. From *Ponoka Sisitah* in the north to *Ootakoitatayii* in the south, east to the *Dakotahs,* and west leaning into Chief Mountain and the backbone of the world, Jesse inhaled the rolling vista of *Amskapi Piikuni*, Blackfeet homelands.

South, beyond this shrunken parcel of designated reservation, lay the territory recently known as Montana, where Jesse had been born and raised as a white boy, the preacher's son, in a town he had run from and people he hid from the past seven years.

A hurt and angry boy of seventeen—his mother dead a year, his father trying to work them through grief. His older brother Boyd escaped to college. Frankie was a torn-up mess of a kid. Jesse had kept himself together until the day truth poked him in the eye. They had lied. To him. Their son. Pacing the house before their father came home, Franklin's beseeching voice cracking with puberty, "Tell me, what's the matter, Jess?"

Cornered in the kitchen, Jesse had shouted, "Go away, Frankie, leave me alone!" His little brother twitched under the blow of words. He wanted to be sorry, but he was too mad. Jesse compared Franklin's wavy brown hair and blue eyes to his own near-black hair and brown eyes. "Impossible," that's what Mr. Dobson said.

Jesse had been staring out the classroom window when the biology teacher shifted from jabbering about pollinating pea vines to the genetics of eye color. He'd snapped to attention when Dobson joked, "So for extra credit, go look your parents in the eye, then look at the postman, see who your daddy really is." The class hee-hawed collective laughter. Dobson commuted home to Helena every Friday. He didn't know how unlikely it was that old maid, Gertie, had anything to do with the parentage of his fifth-period students. Jesse's mouth went dry.

He was the minister's second son, squeezed between the smart one and the sensitive one, kicker on the football team, his father's apprentice in the honey business. Tim Sivertsen buddy-punched him in the arm, "Dobson don't even know there's no *male* delivery out here. Get it, Jesse, m-a-l-e delivery." Jesse bolted for the crowded hallway, avoided looking into his friend's face. He threw his books in his locker, ran and walked and howled his way home, trying to make sense of himself. Had his mother been unfaithful? Did his father know? Was he an aberration of nature? Dobson had said it plain: Two blue-eyed parents, something about dominant and recessive jeans—no, "genes"—could not produce a brown-eyed child.

The Beekeeper's Question

He stood in the parlor, hyperventilating, in front of family photos. His parents' wedding; light eyes shining in the sockets of their faces. His parents with baby Boyd outfitted in baby rompers. Then himself in the rompers with Boyd in a sailor outfit. Next shot, Boyd in knickers, Jesse wearing the sailor outfit, Frankie in the rompers. Black and white, but still the telltale pale of their eyes and the darker dots of his. Charlotte and Leo's boys. Nobody ever said adoption, but if that was it, somebody knew. He scrutinized his parents' forthright stares into the black box of a camera. He needed out, now, before his father came home. Their Pa was a wreck, and Jesse's questions were too big to ask.

He took coins from the kitchen drawer, packed a rucksack with cold chicken and cheese, extra underwear, and walked away. East of town, Homer Torgerson, rancher from up the gap, offered him a ride, but Jesse wanted loneness, wanted country. He headed north, walking with the mountains on his left, seeing how far he could get before dark. Man-child howling in the wilderness of himself.

If Leo Cooper came looking, well, he didn't find him before the Blackfeet did. The man Jesse now called Uncle BB had pulled him out of darkness and brought him to backcountry reservation land where the Shines the Light family lived in the creases of the hills. He'd endured a week of nightly "visits" around the fire with Grandmother Josephine and a group of older men. She looked in his eyes, scrutinized his soul. "You got drops of Red blood in your veins," she said. "If you want to know, you can stay." Indianness was strange territory, but Jesse discovered lost traces of himself reflected in the brown eyes and skin and black hair of the extended family. How he had been claimed a Cooper remained a mystery. He made himself useful, drove a school bus, took odd jobs, leaned over BB's shoulder, learning to fix and tinker. Through their tolerance of his clumsy offenses and kind offers of kinship, he eventually felt almost at home.

Jesse held the two pieces of himself like drum beaters, one in each hand. In Cut Bank, he could be a white man; in Browning, he was a half-breed. Useful trait. Now, Gramma said, time to go back, get his story, bridge his worlds. He stared into the grasslands, working up courage, sucking in the aroma of horse and rider. Cowboy. Indian. Man.

"The honey house is a food processing plant," Leo leaned on a wet mop. "Always expect inspection." Though Leo suspected the Food & Drug Administration had other priorities these days, he was ready. And with every bit of metal being turned to military use, his equipment had to last the war, then he'd see what became of Cooper & Sons.

Maire prepared the backroom for the hired man that Leo sought with increasing urgency. A metal frame bed and a wooden box for stacking clothes. "No dresser," Leo explained, "these men don't have much, empty drawers emphasize the lack." But Maire tucked in clean sheets and fluffed a fresh pillow. She worked hard, but Leo noted to Jereldene, "She *is* more pregnant every day."

In desperate moments, he considered bringing in all the supers himself and training Maire to run the hot blade. Doc warned against putting the girl so long on her feet. Schoolmates of his sons were committed to their own family endeavors. If they hadn't been farmers, they'd have been gone, too. The absence of his boys bothered Leo like a dull toothache. He didn't talk about it. He didn't want the valley talking about it.

He knew Franklin was at a desk in Belfast waiting for the war to get real. He hoped wherever Jesse was that he was registered, finding his way. Boyd had been their big bet: That Doc could fashion her replacement in the valley, pass along the practice. He'd been at her elbow since he was ten, fascinated instead of repelled, bandaging his younger brothers, suturing Sunday's stew hen before it went in the pot. They'd gone to his graduation, marveling at Seattle, itchy and nervous in the bustling city, but so proud.

Rocking on porch chairs waiting for night breeze, Leo whispered into the dusk, "This war is a three-headed dragon, each black mouth round with teeth, consuming young men."

"That's surely the strain of it," Doc peered skyward, "We don't know what will become of them. Or us. Or our country." Caged between the Big and Little Dippers, Draco the Dragon writhed in the night sky.

Leo cleared his throat. "Philosophy, music, architecture, literature, democracy... I will not accept fascism as the final outcome of Western civilization." The porch boards creaked under their chairs.

"But it's terrifying! All those swastikas, and people who were like us a few years ago, burning books, throwing rocks, hating Jews." Doc rested her hand on Leo's arm. "How could this happen?"

"One charismatic demagogue." Leo stopped rocking. "Moral codes like The Golden Rule, the Ten Commandments, the Beatitudes, whisper in the human heart. Hitler has hypnotized the German people with promises of greatness in exchange for their souls. Now it takes the horrors of war to break the Nazi spell. Well, specifically, for the Germans to lose and for us to win without losing *our* souls."

Doc stared at the cosmic expanse of the Milky Way, "You're the local preacher and I'm an old country doctor, what can we do?"

"Help people live through the sacrifice required of us now. From the pulpit and the bedside, as best we can, we will comfort and cure."

"May I be that steadfast," Doc whispered.

"Me too," Leo sighed. "Honey needs harvesting. I pray help will come."

In an earlier time, Leo had painted the concentric rings of a target on the side of the honey warehouse and allowed his boys to practice aiming slingshots of spitballs. Once they outgrew the game, the paint remained faintly discernible. And on this August afternoon, as Leo came around the corner driving the flatbed into the yard, honey supers strapped down and Preacher Boy riding shotgun in the fender crease, a man was standing at the pitching point aiming pebbles at his warehouse. Leo hit the brakes. Honked. The dog barked.

Leo's heart knew before his mind caught up: Jesse. Father and son locked gazes through the dirty windshield and the swirl of dust rising out of the wheel wells. Leo stuck his head out and shouted, "It's okay, Preacher Boy." A message to both dog and man. The dog skidded to circling, and the last little stone, trajectory already launched, sailed out of Jesse's hand, missed the target, and hit a small pane in the ventilation windows high on the siding. A tink of breaking glass. "Hello Pa, sorry about your window." He turned fully toward his father and waited, arms folded over his ribs, hands tucked in his armpits, slingshot dangling.

Leo composed himself. What matter if the window broke? Here was his own boy who could handle supers and fix equipment. Someone he didn't have to train. Leo pushed back his seed cap, grit under the sweatband.

Jesse leaned into the rolled-down window, "I thought you might need a hand, what with the war… and well, time to come back."

"Son…" he said. The word sweet as a raspberry on his tongue. They shook hands. "You here for the honey?" Leo's voice cracked with dust. Jesse was fully a man now, Leo noticed, not the adolescent who ran from his grief-filled home.

"You have me." The two men nodded, identical dips of chin.

"Let me park." Jesse jumped onto the running board and Leo maneuvered the truck into shade by the honey house door. "I've been worried, you know. Where you been?"

The Beekeeper's Question

"Reservation, running cows."

"Registered?"

"Two-C: Invaluable to the homeland, letting Frank and Boyd do their parts."

Leo slid out of the truck. "Boyd?"

"There's a lot going on in the world, Pa. Boyd wrote General Delivery, Browning," he thumped the side of the truck like patting a horse. "He married a nice girl, nursey girl, Nisei girl, you know. Japanese. He's applying to do service in the camps. They need doctors and maybe liaisons, even spies. Minidoka. Someplace in Idaho."

Leo had received the wedding announcement. July 1941, before Pearl Harbor, before the war, before the declaration that all Japanese were suspected traitors, before relocation camps. "Jere and I been speculating for months," he scratched at his hairline.

Jesse paused, "He's in a delicate position, married to the enemy. White folks, yellow folks, nobody exactly happy 'cept, hopefully, the newlyweds."

"They're American citizens and God's people."

"His wife, Mariko, was born here, but her parents hardly speak English. As for being Godly people, we'll see how that goes."

"How do you know all this?" Leo swiped his brow with a damp bandana.

"I hitched to Seattle. You want to see someone, you miss your brother or your son, you go find them."

Leo's heart cracked. "It's complicated being a father, Jess. I hope you'll cut me some slack."

"Complicated being a son, too," Jesse's emotions cast shadows over his cheekbones. "I come to work, Pa. And I come to have some conversations you owe me and a couple I owe you. Am I hired?"

"You're hired." The honey-thief bear clawed at Leo's guts, but it was good to have his boy returned.

The next morning, Maire set eggs, bacon, slabs of bread in front of the men. "Thanks," Jesse grunted. "I started the boiler. Steam ready by 8:00."

Leo had gotten the steam engine the year before Charlotte died and trained Jesse to it that next summer. It was old industrial equipment out of a Great Falls warehouse now that everything in the city was turning electric. Leo was proud of his purchase, and Jesse was proud of his tinkering. A sweet August before a sorrowful September.

"I 'member wrestling that bugger into place, you and me, Franklin too scrawny to be much help. How it would run one day, not start the next, or not hold steam. Learning that engine was somethin', but we got it, didn't we, Pa?" Jesse swiped egg yolk with his toast.

Leo nodded mutely, his heart too full to speak. Jesse had hit his growth spurt and, in those golden weeks, he was the son at the center of Leo's world. Boyd was in Seattle taking summer school courses. Franklin had just finished sixth grade, still a soprano, working the garden with his mother. Something seemed not right with Charlotte, but every inquiry was met with reassurance. She was tired. It was change of life. Leo soldiered on, his household held in the throes of puberty, menopause, and his own unease.

That September, the honey in, the canning done, Doc knocked on his study door. "Charlotte's not well, Leo. I've made an appointment in Great Falls. I'll come with you and interpret the medical jargon."

Charlotte clutched Doc's hand while the man in the white coat poked and prodded and stuck the metal speculum up her most hidden place. He took a slice of her cervix and put it on a glass slide. Charlotte had grunted with pain and embarrassment her gaze locked onto Doc. Afterwards, shaking with tension, she let Doc snap her brassiere, button her housedress, tie her shoes.

The specialist recommended exploratory surgery and a hysterectomy. The specialist suggested inserting a radioactive tube up her vagina. The patient asked, "What are the odds of cure?" The patient asked, "If I accept treatment, how long? If I refuse treatment, how long?" The patient said, "Thank you for your honesty." The patient said, "I'm going home to love my family and set my life in order." The specialist said he was sorry. They drove back to Pigeon River, the three of them holding hands, Leo breaking his grasp only when shifting gears. Days before they spoke it.

Charlotte resumed putting up enough food for a year. She sent her husband to church and her boys to school and wrote letters to the son faraway. Leo knew she slept when the house was empty, rousing herself to make supper, fading before their eyes.

Charlotte had carried seven pregnancies. They had three living sons, one daughter that pneumonia took, three babes in tiny boxes alongside the cemetery fence. Now her womb had filled with something ropey and grasping and growing in secret.

February 1935, Charlotte Cooper died to frozen ground. Leo and Doc laid her out in a simple casket. Bill Sivertsen banked a smoldering charcoal fire to thaw the ground. Leo telegraphed Boyd, in his second year of premed at the University of Washington. Mother passed. Funeral Sat. Pls come.

Boyd had wired back, Catching train. Sad.

The western sky was roiling grey. Snow in the mountains. In a generosity Leo never forgot, Caleb Pocket drove up to Browning, brought Boyd down.

They sat on the sofa facing the casket, the Cooper men, scrubbed and picking at their collars, each wearing a tie, though Frankie's was hanging down over his belt. People came and went and said how sorry they were. Women of The Tuesday Club cooked, kept a pot of coffee going, answered the door. Everyone hushed around the ultimate stillness of she who lay in the wooden box in the center of the parlor.

christina baldwin

Leo watched helplessly as grief hollowed the last vestiges of childhood out of his younger sons and set a stubborn manhood into his college boy. The next week, Franklin went back to seventh grade, Jesse went back to junior year, Boyd went back to university. Leo perused the cellar shelves, began feeding Charlotte's love to her family.

Come next summer, Leo enrolled the boys in a grief cure of work: tilling the garden, planting vegetables, irrigating, weeding, milking the cow, churning butter. He lent them out to round up cattle or herd sheep, thin sugar beets or bring in hay, hoping other men and boys would pull them out of the daily absence that filled their house. He hoped they got silly, laughed in that snorting way boys do. Frankie cried himself to sleep in the room across the hall. Jesse stomped restlessly in the attic overhead. Boyd took a double class load. They toughed it out as seasons turned. Jesse ran the following spring, seventeen years old, six weeks from graduation.

It was nearly a month before Doc brought news, via her connection to a Blackfeet grandmother, that Jesse was tucked in the hills between Browning and Cut Bank at Josie Shines the Light's family allotment. How he'd ended up there, why they took him in, were mysteries that roamed Leo's mind in the wee hours. He prayed and waited and endured, a bruise to his shattered heart.

Jesse showed up a year later to get his things, "Moving out, Pa," he'd said stiffly. "I'm making my way. Don't worry." Two years later, they happened into one another at the farm supply store in Great Falls. Jesse muscled and strong. They shook hands. He smelled of sweat and horse, sage and tobacco, stories unknown. And now he was back. Leo could hardly eat breakfast.

August 20, 1942
Dear Franklin,
　　Your brother has returned to bring in the honey crop. Looks like a good season. I am grateful to Jess and

curious to hear how and where he's been. I pray some healing can occur in the father and son department, as I hope for you and me. He says Boyd is in Idaho doctoring the imprisoned Japanese. This war is certainly shaking up the world. Meanwhile—harvest full on. You know what that means. Jere says your wife is healthy and the pregnancy normal. Your wife says you are reading European history. Try to find a copy of William Shirer's Berlin Diary, *a horrifying account of the rise of the Nazis and the capitulation of the German populace. We're still the land of the free. Everyone sends love,* Leo

To liquify honey's natural consistency to a warm golden stream and soften the wax to moldable ingots, everything in the honey house was monitored at 95°F. The men wore coveralls that hung on pegs inside the door, outfits sticky with honey and encrusted with wax, kept separate from the taint of other chores. They off-loaded supers from the flatbed, running the dolly and stacking boxes. Bending, lifting, handing down. Jesse ran the hot knife, a hollow blade sixteen inches long, heated by steam tubed from the boiler. He decapped honeycomb, the shaved layers of wax falling into trays for later processing. With canvas gloves, Leo transferred each frame into a large metal barrel with wire spokes that supported the dripping forms. As a commercial operation, the extractor could hold twenty frames at a time, powered by steam, not cranked by hand. When loaded, the men sealed the top, turned up the engine, and let heat and centrifugal force fling the honey out of the beheaded comb and drain to the bottom of the extractor barrel. A metal screen filtered out remaining bits of wax, bee wings, pollen, and anything else the bees had hidden in the heart of the hive. Father and son kept busy clearing the filter and monitoring the critical temperature that would allow the honey to flow through a pipe and into metal cans that contained the honey for shipment and sale.

"It's amazing to watch you work, Jess. You were always good at it, even as a boy."

Jesse swiped a finger through the mix of wax and honey and stuck it in his mouth. Leo scowled. "Work is prayer, that's what Gramma Josie says. Work is giveback for the gift of life." Jesse looked his father straight in the eyes. "I come to extract the truth from you, Pa, 'bout that winter in Helena when I was born and who I am." He let the words linger. "I don't expect you to find your tongue all at once, but I'm not leaving without my story." He traded out a sixty-pounder, put a new gleaming tin under the spout and watched to make sure the golden river was flowing as intended. He hefted the filled tin onto the skid, turned his back on his father, and shoved a line of cannisters toward the warehouse.

13
Reckoning

FOURTH WEEK OF AUGUST 1942: *The Germans hold vast swatches of North Africa, but the British maintain control of the Suez Canal.*

THE SUN BORE DOWN WITH BLISTERING HEAT. "Hard on bees," Leo said, "and hard on beekeepers." The hives hummed with a hundred thousand wings as workers crawled over the supers making honey, filling combs, moving the air, dispelling heat. Airflow was life or death for the hive. Truth felt like life or death for Leo.

Jesse swung through the kitchen, grabbed bread and a hard-boiled egg. They were in the truck by 6:00 a.m., August dawn. He smelled of tobacco. Leo took a disdainful sniff. "Indians smoke," Jesse's voice edgy.

"Just don't smoke in the honey house."

"I know the rules, Pa."

Leo wanted to reach over and give his son's knee a friendly squeeze the way he used to grab the shift knob on the old truck and let his hand keep going. The boys would tussle over who got to sit in the middle where this game played out. Their legs grew up under his grasp, from chubby toddlers to lean boys and lanky young men. He longed to reach back to times when life seemed easier than it seemed today. He shifted into second, then third as they headed east of the river where they'd work the boundary of the diking district.

"Today the day?" Jesse asked.

"Today's the day," Leo nodded. Leo had slept deep for a few hours and then had laid awake from midnight to dawn. "Can't drive and do this, Jess. Let's get there, work in the cool, let this unfold."

"You're the boss…"

"No. I am your father. You are my son. This is our story."

By 1:00 p.m. they had loaded the flatbed with supers while rivulets of sweat and dust etched their arms. They gulped honey-sweetened lemonade and ate Cornish pasties, pocket pies stuffed with cubed carrots, potatoes, turnips, onions from the garden, canned beef from the cellar. There was no reason to put it off. "I'm ready," Leo said, "Are you ready?" "I've been ready for years, Pa."

"You've also been gone for years, son. We got to not blame one another just now. If you decide to be mad at me all your life, that'll be your business, but for the next half hour please listen. I will tell you anything you want to know."

"Deal." Jesse squatted on the ground, leaning against the truck tire, stuck a piece of straw in his mouth. He stared into the distance, giving Leo an occasional sideways glance. The dog lay under the truck bed panting a breathy cadence.

Leo settled on the running board, exhaled a silent prayer. "Okay. Summer of 1918, we finished the house, added the front porch, insulated the attic. There was a war on, like now, and beekeeping was an essential industry, making good money off beeswax. We were young, healthy, hard-working. The war didn't hit the valley so hard then because most settlers were too old for the draft and their sons were too young.

"That August, several local men went into Canada to work on the railroads and came home with stories of sick Chinese workers crammed into rail cars. They had to pull corpses off the trains, dig graves by the side of the rails. The men brought back sickness and four died. Doc wasn't sure what they'd been exposed to, but she wanted them buried quick. Two are in the churchyard, two in their own yards. One of the wives died. Three little kids got terribly ill. People were terrified. Articles in the Tribune were talking about this new influenza." Leo shuddered, even in the heat.

"Charlotte was pregnant again. Because I was ministering the sick, I doused myself in the trough and slept in the honey house. Your mother put food outside the door. Jere quarantined at her place, and every time she went out to treat another case, she started counting the days over. She called it a tipping point. There was a detention hospital in Great Falls for containing contagion." Jesse had chewed the grass stem into green spit.

"Your mother had already suffered two miscarriages. Boyd was our third try, a happy three-year-old. She was old to be birthing, mid-thirties. She was afraid, isolated. I thought a change of scene might do us good, so even though we couldn't socialize, I rented a little house in Helena. I lived with her when I could, drove the back road, took care of things, checked on Jere. We were lucky. A million people a week were dying, and with the war, it was horrible. The Indian tribes were sicker than the rest of us. Jere went up to offer medical help at the Holy Family Mission school and that's when she and Josephine Shines the Light got to be friends.

"Gramma calls her *Nississa*," Jesse nodded.

"Since Jere didn't drive, she hired a boy named Henry Beckner to get her around. After sickness left the valley, he drove her back and forth to Helena.

Jesse looked at him full on, "Are you getting to where I'm born?"

"The order of events is important, Jess. Young Henry tells Jere his mother has died, his father is overtaken with drink, and his sister, Lillian, is locked in the barn because she's pregnant and won't say who. Jere was outraged and, coming down from the reservation, she had Henry drive by his family's place near Valier. The girl was huddled in a stall with almost no food and her pregnancy quite advanced. Jere and Henry rescued the unfortunate girl and brought her to Helena. Lilly could help with Boyd, have the baby in peace, and then we'd see."

Jesse was twitching with tension. "So, Auntie Doc kidnaped this unwed girl who was *'great with child and living in the stable.'*"

"Exactly. And what happened next, to us and around us, had that biblical tone. November, at the eleventh hour on the eleventh day of the eleventh month, the Armistice was signed. Such relief. Charlotte and Lillian stayed in Helena. Jere and I continued back and forth. I preached on Christmas Eve then drove over the pass in a snowstorm, determined to share festivities with Boyd and your mother."

"Which one?"

"Hold on Jesse; you're coming. I arrived after midnight, and everything was falling apart. Lillian was in labor, everything looking normal and Jere attending her. But Charlotte was also in early labor even though she was only seven months along. Boyd was next door with neighbors. I drove Charlotte to the Lying-In hospital. It's Christmas morning, pouring snow, we slip-slide across the city and get her admitted. A few hours later, she delivered a tiny boy, cord wrapped round his neck, small as a puppy. And there we were, sitting in this hospital room with our dead baby. Charlotte was desperate to get away from the sounds of laboring mothers and newborns. She needed to be home with Boyd and Jereldene and to help Lillian. Because we were going directly back into doctor's care, they discharged her."

Leo shook with tension as the memories spooled out of him. "I bundled Charlotte, and we headed into a morning glistening after storm. That half hour was our time to grieve our little boy blue. We decided to put his tiny body in a pine box I kept for kindling and try to give Boyd some Christmas. But at the house, Doc was frantic. Lillian had given birth to a healthy boy, but now she was bleeding and bleeding. It's called postpartum hemorrhage when the uterus is a spigot that won't stop running. It wasn't Doc's fault."

Jesse sat curled into himself. "So, you and Ma walk into the house with your dead baby and…"

"And there is a healthy, beautiful little boy lying on his mother's breast. But Lilly is white as a sheet. Charlotte kneels next to the bed and takes Lillian's head and shoulders into her arms. And Lilly whispers, 'Thank you, Mrs., for helping me… Isn't he beautiful?' And you were, Jesse. A fuzz of dark hair and your eyes already looking intensely at the world." The wind licked them with a hot tongue, contrasting the scene of the story.

"I need you to see this scene fully," Leo said. "At one end of the bed, Jereldene is kneeling between Lillian's legs. She's got one hand deep up the birth canal and another hand on the belly and she's calling out, 'Stop bleeding, Lilly, stay with us. Leo, more towels.' I run out, come back. The girl is drifting away."

"You just traded us out!?" Jesse was hugging his knees to his chest. He brushed black hair out of his eyes and faced his father.

"Despite everything we were doing, this sixteen-year-old girl was bleeding to death. She could barely talk. She could hardly breathe. It is possible for the blood to just run out of a person. It's not that much, six pints, eight in a man. Doc was covered in blood, sheets and towels were soaked red. And at the head of the bed, Lilly put you into Charlotte's hands and pleaded, 'Love him.' The last thing Lilly heard was your mother's promise. 'Rest in peace, dear girl, he shall be ours.' She kissed your tiny face and your fingers wrapped around her finger and you became our son."

Jesse was rocking back and forth, making an indentation in the dried grass. "Were you ever going to tell me?"

"Please consider this moment fully. Your mother's heart was broken. We wanted a family. It was Christmas, there was all this high emotion about the end of the war, the baby in the manger, peace in the valley. Charlotte, Jereldene, and I were exhausted. No one had slept for two days. The world outside the window was blanketed with heavy snow. There was a little boy next door who wanted a baby brother. We stood there and humbly accepted the tiny miracle that was you."

"But were you ever going to tell me?"

"When you were little, it never seemed right to separate you out. We were all just one family. And when Ma got sick, she was afraid to tell you because it would be like losing two mothers at once. She left the task to Jere and me. But then we were all so heartsick. And…" Leo hoisted himself to standing, "I just fell apart as a father. I shouldn't have worked you boys so hard. I didn't know how to let us grieve. I'm sorry for that part, Jess. But I've never been sorry you are my son."

"What happened… to the girl?" Jesse's brown eyes bored into Leo's blue eyes.

"She's in the churchyard. Lillian Beckner."

"And the dead baby?"

"In the Little Lambs section. Baby Boy Cooper."

"Was his name Jesse, too?"

"No. Your name is your own. From the Hebrew *Yishai*, meaning 'gift'."

Jesse bent his forehead onto his kneecaps, a closed circuit of emotion. Even this couldn't stop a wracking howl from escaping deep inside him. Leo touched the back of his son's head, the silkiness of his black hair. Jesse shrugged him off. "And my father?"

"No one knows."

He looked up, "If he forced her… Lillian was only fifteen!"

"We don't know, Jesse. You make your own story about what runs in your blood."

Jesse struggled to his feet. "I gotta walk. Need to think."

"We're near ten miles out. It'll take a long time."

"I need a long time." Jesse whistled and Preacher Boy jumped at the chance to wander cross-country and swim ditches on the route they would take home. Leo poured the remainder of their water supply into one mason jar and Jesse took it, called back over his shoulder, "Don't worry, Pa, I'll be there to start the boiler come morning."

Leo watched Jesse's figure shrinking into the landscape, the dog a bouncing accompaniment. Eventually, he eased into the truck cab, laid his hands and forehead onto the steering wheel and held on. Soon as he stopped shaking, he'd go see Jere, catch her up on things.

Next morning, Leo entered the honey house before dawn. "Extracting can wait," he called, "Let's drive to Valier."

The '32 Chevy wrapped father and son in a bug-smeared bubble as they headed north on Highway 89. "When did you know?" Leo asked. The grain elevators of Fairfield came into view.

Jesse had his right forearm out the window, playing dip-n-dive with the wind. "Biology class, section on genetics. How two blue-eyed parents cannot produce a brown-eyed child. No one had ever hinted at adoption. I was scared Ma had had an affair. Scared you didn't know. Scared to break your heart more than it was already broken."

Leo pulled over on the shoulder, turned to look at his son, but Jesse did not look back. "I wish we'd talked instead of you running."

A flash of waterfowl, feathered white bellies glinting in sun, lifted off Freezeout Lake. "You were the parent trying to protect me. I was the boy trying to protect you. We both needed the truth."

Regret flooded Leo's heart with such force that he worried he might die right here, hands on the steering wheel, unable to finish the story unraveling between them. "I was lost too, Jess. Scared to add one more thing to our losses. It didn't seem the right time. I didn't know what was up for you." Leo's voice cracked. "You *are* my precious son, Jesse. I beg you, forgive me."

"Workin' on it, Pa." Leo pulled back on the road. A squawking V flew overhead. "Season changing early this year. We best get the honey in." Such a Cooper statement, Leo thought, relieved.

Outside Valier, inching west to east toward Lake Frances, the town limits, Leo squinted down one dirt lane, then another. The Beckner place rested in a swale between two humps of rolling countryside. Not the pretty landscape down by the lake. Not the interesting rock formations along Two Medicine River. Hard scrabble homestead. Windmill missing slats. Someone had painted "Beckner" in chipped whitewash on an old plank. Someone else had ripped it off the fence post and propped it half-hidden in tall grass. The Chevy kicked up a rolling dust ball behind their careful progress through prairie dog holes in the soft sand of the driveway. They could see the barn, grayed and sagging.

"Away in a manger..." Jesse snorted. "Probably conceived there too, no place else for privacy." Three dogs, barking, hackles raised. "Someone still lives here, Pa. We're gonna have to say hello."

A bearded man, stout as a barrel, appeared from behind the barn, shotgun draped cradle carry, probably loaded. "What you want?" The dogs wove in and out around his legs.

They got out of the car. Jesse wrapped his arms around his torso and gave Leo a son-to-father look. "I'm Leo Cooper, from Pigeon River. This is my son Jesse, and if you are Aaron Beckner, he's also a nephew of yours."

"Ain't got no nephew." He looked them over, a near-sighted man squinting in daylight.

"Mr. Beckner, twenty-four years ago your sister Lillian found herself in a delicate condition…"

"She brought shame on the family. My dad locked her up, gonna wait for that baby and maybe we could see-tell who the father was. But she disappeared." Leo and Jesse watched his expression as he realized his story was standing before him in the presence of his unexpected visitors. "You got no rights to this land!"

Leo continued, "We adopted Jesse fair and square. Your father had paperwork. And Jesse…"

"Father's dead. Mother's dead. Guessin' my sister is dead. My little brother's a hospital orderly in Billings. And that's all I know, 'cept this is my land!" The shotgun was cocked now, a quick sleight of hand. "Why you say you come?"

Jesse found his tongue. "Didn't come for the land, Uncle, no worry about that."

"What you come for then?" He looked like a bear wearing dirty overalls and a torn undershirt.

Jesse uncoiled his arms, floated them wide aside, and carefully down, palms exposed. He had a crazy smile on his face that twitched with nerves, "We just come to see the color of your eyes… Uncle." He stepped forward, stopped a second, stepped again. Beckner was taken aback. They were squinty eyes, set deep in a web of weathered wrinkles. Definitely blue. Jesse laughed, the old man lunged, tripped over one of the dogs, fell to all fours so the shotgun lay on the ground. "You get outta here you wormy half-breed! You and yer old man, 'fore I feed you to the dogs. Burned them papers, ever'thing but the deed."

Jesse backstepped, grabbed his father's arms and shoved him into the passenger side. "I'm driving." He turned the Chevy in a wheel of dust and careened back to the county road a lot faster than they had headed in. Maybe the dogs gave chase. Maybe a shot fired over their heads. They didn't hear because Jesse was singing at the top of his lungs, "Away in a manger, no crib for his head, the little lost Jesse lay down his sweet head. Come on, Reverend Cooper, sing with me!" And much to his amazement, Leo did, "The stars in the heavens look down where he lay, but little lost Jesse asleep in the hay!" And by the time they were back on two-lane blacktop, several variations, more and more irreverent, had escaped both their lips.

"Lord, forgive me," Leo called into the wind.

Jesse laughed. "Don't worry, Pa. Don't you think Jesus ever let loose? Out there in the desert with the Twelve Apostles, turning water into wine and making up naughty verses to the Psalms?"

After a while Jesse pulled over to the side of the road, the car facing into the front range of the Rockies that toothed the horizon. "You gotta let me have a smoke, Pa." He started to get out the door. Leo placed his hand onto the shoulder of his son. He started to cry and then, much to his surprise, Jesse started crying too. Side by side, the dam of grief burst and flooded cracks of broken-heartedness.

When, like all flash floods, the water subsided, Leo finally spoke, "Let's get out, eat lunch. You can smoke to your heart's content."

Jesse pissed into the ditch, blew snot out each nostril, wiped his nose with his shirttail. "Know why men don't cry? We're awful at it. And no way to wash up before we wrap our paws around Maire's ham sandwiches."

"I think we've been washed pretty clean, son."

A few bites later, Jesse added, "He called me a half-breed. Maybe Beckner knew more about who got Lillian pregnant than he let on."

"Maybe it was just the most awful thing he could think to say. He didn't know we wouldn't take offense."

"Pa, stop being so morally correct. You've always looked at me as a Cooper because you wanted it to be the only truth. But look at me—right here, right now. We're standing on Blackfeet country. The Valier Road practically touches reservation boundaries. Look at my eyes. Look at my cheekbones. Look at my nose. You're always talking about the beekeeper's question, how there's an essential inquiry that drives a person's life. Ever since that day I ran, I been asking, where do *I* belong? I was running from that question and running toward that question." He chewed a hunk of ham sandwich. "Ready to hear my story?" Leo nodded.

"I headed toward Robere, thought I'd hole up, it being a ghost town, think things through. I found this old cabin. It's dark. I'm cold. I push myself into the farthest corner and hunch down facing the door. I'm dozing, scared. Hear wolves. They sound close. I don't know if this is real or a dream, but it seems true that one wolf comes right to the doorway, its tail lifted against night sky. I shout at it, 'Hey, don't eat me! I'm just a boy.' And then the wolf speaks inside my mind, believe me, Pa, it says '*You are Walks Far Wolf. Go north.*' I tossed him a chicken bone. He took it and backed into the dark. Cold. I huddled under debris that the wind pushed in.

"When I woke again it was grey light and shadows. Something moved. There was snoring and snorting; three Indian men had come in for shelter late night. We screamed to see one another. They yelled to me, 'Who are you?' and I said for the first time, 'I am Walks Far Wolf.' And they asked, 'Are you going to fast on the mountain?' I didn't know what they meant but it seemed a good thing, so I said yes. They had dark eyes like mine. They saw through my pale skin. 'Oki, we'll take you to Grandmother.' They put me in the back of their old pickup, and that's how I met the Shines the Light family." Jesse gave his father a ham and mustard grin. "And today, we're goin' to follow those same trails so you can see how I came from the home you made for me to the home I was looking for." Jesse pinched tobacco into paper and rolled a cigarette. He exhaled cloudy circles, "Smoke signals. Let 'em know we're coming." He winked.

14
Two Medicine Women

THAT SAME AUGUST DAY: *Incendiary bombs dropped by a Japanese seaplane start a forest fire in Oregon.*

KNOWING LEO AND JESSE WERE ON THE ROAD, Doc fed the cat, watered the horse, and headed to Cooper's to bring Maire into the story. Morning light bleached the wheat stubble a bony white and she pulled a straw sunhat low over her eyes. Her tongue felt dry and fat in her mouth, filled with reluctance to break the silence that had encrusted their secret all these years.

In March 1919, the war over, the threat of flu lifting, the Cooper family returned to the valley with a beautiful second son who suckled at Charlotte's breast. Two years later, Frankie's arrival popped Jesse into the middle of the boys. He was theirs. Couldn't they just let him be? The three stopped talking about it, let life unfold. Gracie was born. The adults practiced forgetting; Jesse practiced not knowing. Then came Charlotte's bony hand in Doc's, her voice straining, "There are questions brooding in him, Jere. You'll know when."

Thrashing in grief, Leo pushed her back. Doc near wore a groove in the road, walking by to see lights on, dropping off cookies to make a trail of crumbs for Frankie and Jesse to follow up the road. They slouched on her sofa and shrugged in her hugs, walked home to Leo's table. She sent care packages to Boyd, wrote chatty letters, encouraging him to hold to his path, they'd be okay. It was hard work trying to tether these Cooper men. When Jesse ran, their world shook. She reknit a friendship with Leo that placed their common love for Charlotte safely between them. And now the truth was free at last.

She found Maire finishing breakfast dishes. Doc opened her arms and the girl stepped into her hug with the hard balloon of her pregnant belly pressing Doc's softer contours. "Everything is all right," Doc whispered. She handed over a bouquet of roadside blossoms.

"I dinna know how to help." Maire filled a Mason jar, set the flowers on the table.

"Come sit on the porch. It's a long story." Doc rocked nervously and spoke at last of that fateful Christmas Day. At the end of her telling, she reached for Maire's hand, "What happened to Lillian, that kind of hemorrhage, it's very rare."

"I'm not afraid," Maire responded. "T'other night I woke to see a shining wraith of myself sitting in the rocking chair. I were wrapped in Nana's shawl, holding a wee babe. So I know we'll make it through."

Doc leaned forward. "Oh Maire, how good that you are touched by light."

"Where are the men?" Maire placed Doc's hand on her belly and a tiny foot pressed against her palm.

"Leo is taking Jesse to the farm his mother came from. Then I expect Jesse will take Leo to the reservation."

"Is he an Indian, then?"

"We know who gave him birth, but not who fathered him. Lillian told me it wasn't rape. She never said more."

"But the Indians took him in."

"Maybe they see Native blood in him, or maybe they accept him because of what happened at the school."

"Wasn't it good to educate Indian children?"

"The children were kidnapped from their families, separated from their tribes, forbidden to speak their own languages or live their own ways. It was obliteration, not education. First year I was here, I set up a little infirmary to doctor them."

"Tell me," Maire nearly whispered, "I want to know."

Doc leaned into memory. "I had long blond hair, wore a black skirt, white blouse, and an apron with pockets that I stuffed with small medical supplies and pieces of hard candy. Often as I could, I pulled the children into the safety of my little house. They had chills and colds, tuberculosis, pneumonia, oozing sores. No immunity to white man germs. I let them play with my hair while I checked their lungs, listened to the thump of their broken hearts. Leo had been assigned by the Methodist Mission to be a teacher. Charlotte brought extra clothes. We tried to be a comfort.

"One night, Leo said, 'I cannot call myself a man of God and watch this treatment.' I said, 'I cannot fulfill my Hippocratic Oath.' And Charlotte challenged us, 'Let's do something then.' We took on a campaign to close the school and that's how we became friends."

Doc stared around the porch, "It's such a modern world now, Maire, hard to imagine that time with horses and Model T Fords. The U.S. government claimed the land was theirs to give away, people took it and that was that. I'm not saying it was right; I'm saying that's how it happened. People like Coopers and me, homesteading, trying to make our lives over. We were building up a town, raising church walls, starting farms and businesses. Indians were just in the way." Doc felt her body fill with sorrow. "All across the continent, Indians were murdered, driven from their lands, villages and crops destroyed. And lacking immunity to European diseases, whole tribes nearly wiped out. Out here, where tribal life depended on the buffalo, millions of animals were slaughtered and left to rot in the sun."

Maire started to shake. "You said you wanted to know…" The girl nodded mutely. "Leo was nearly thrown out of the church for dismantling the Mission. Folks refused to enter the same clinic room where Indians had been treated. Charlotte was having miscarriages from the stress. It was a rough beginning."

"But now everyone loves you." Maire searched Doc's face.

"Folks respect us. That's different." A hawk shouldered out of the wheat stubble into the sky. "To live your whole life in one place requires a delicate balance between forgetting and remembering, between forgiving and reckoning."

"And the woman Jesse calls Gramma Josie?"

"She came to get her daughters. Forbidden, of course." Doc's voice softened again. "It was October, my second autumn. I was down by the river when this Blackfeet woman stepped out from a stand of brush. She wore her hair in two black braids, and her dress was creamy buckskin with a yoke of thimbles and shells. Near jumped me out of my skin, but she smiled, so I introduced myself and she introduced herself. 'I have come for my daughters Áimmóniisi and Innaksistaki. Are they well?' I only knew the children by English names, but I told her they were well, hoping that was true. I told her we were working to close the school. I asked her to be patient.

"'This is not for patience,' she said. 'You and the Jesus man and his woman are good people. Look away.' She placed a small leather bag on a river boulder near where we stood and said, 'Thank you for protecting all my children.'" Doc reached under her shirt and pulled a tiny pouch on a fraying leather cord from between her breasts. "I've worn it ever since."

"And Mrs. Shines the Light's little girls?"

"That night they disappeared along with five other girls and four boys. There were occasional escape attempts among the children. As much as he hated to, Leo would get in the Model T and track them down. It was deep autumn weather, cold nights, fields harvested and gleaned. Leo found no one. We had to register them as missing persons, as they were wards of the state. I never spoke of meeting Mrs. Shines the Light."

Doc tucked the small pouch back in the moist crease of her bosom. "A month afterwards, the headmaster received a letter from the government saying that if the census of the students fell below sixty-five children, the school would be considered no longer financially viable and could be disbanded. With those eleven gone, there were sixty-four students remaining. The school closed. We scurried to return children to their families before anyone told us we couldn't. Those that lived through it still suffer. More homesteaders moved into the area, bringing more women and children. Few years later, the buildings got white-washed, new desks, new teachers—and presto—Pigeon River Elementary."

"And Jesse?"

"Jesse is who he is, a Cooper, raised as a white boy among white boys. No one here even knows he is adopted." Doc extended a hand and helped Maire to standing. "Most people want truth to be plain and justice to be simple, but neither truth nor justice are so well-behaved."

Sitting in the passenger seat, Leo played dip and dive with the wind. He prayed silent thanks for the wash his heart was in. He prayed for his dead wife and his living sons. He prayed to be wise in the place Jesse was aiming toward.

Jesse pointed at a small herd of Herefords. "Took the tribe three years to negotiate stock grazing rights. Indian Reorganization Act both giveth and taketh away. 'Course we're not permitted to eat' em," Jesse snorted in disgust. "Have to go to the store and pay for meat raised somewhere else or eat whatever wild hoof comes by."

It was high heat when they finally turned onto a long buckboard track. The end of the drive led to several weathered cabins alongside a gullied streambed. A lean-to barn and corral and several tipis were set to one side. The woman Jesse called Gramma waited in the shade of a windbreak cottonwood, dwarfed by two middle-aged men. Josephine Shines the Light was near eighty now, Leo thought, and still emanated an aura of authority. She flipped two silver braids behind her shoulders and strode toward the car. "Welcome Reverend," her English was spoken from the back of her throat, a second tongue. "I see you have given your son his story. Join me for tea when Wolf is done showing you around."

A horse was whinnying in the corral, and Jesse ran to it, grabbed a hunk of mane, and swung with ease onto the gelding's back. He bent forward and rubbed his face in the horse's neck. A man, not yet introduced, slipped a bridle and bit into the horse's mouth, tossed the reins to Jesse. Several dogs sniffed Leo's pants leg. "Pa, come along the fence. Can you still mount?" Leo stepped onto the second rung and Jesse hoisted him onto the gelding's rump. "His name's Windy." Pride in his voice.

Leo wrapped his arms around the strong torso of his son, felt the horse's muscles ripple with the urge to run. "Don't embarrass me, son. No trotting."

"This is Uncle BB." The man who opened the corral gate had cropped black-to-greying hair, jeans and cowboy boots, a smile with a broken front tooth. The horse lurched and danced, but Jesse held him to a walk. "This is the Shines the Light family allotment," Jesse gestured. "Folks live round here in various combinations of relations and generations. Gramma Josie lives in her lodge until BB makes her come in hardest part of winter." They clopped by several cabins, stick frame, tar paper on plywood, some with asphalt shingle siding. "Heart Butte settlement has a school. You can believe Gramma and the teacher have quite an understanding."

The horse sidestepped and Leo almost lost his seating. "Do you live here, Jess?"

A tension rippled through his son's muscles. "Gramma offered you tea. I'll drop you off. Tend to things. Then we head south, finish our beeziness."

"You're driving," Leo eased himself to ground and leaned against the horse's flank to get his legs under him. "Not too late, we got a good three hours on the road."

Jesse looked down. "No clocks out here, Pa. We'll leave when the visit is over." Leo watched his son, Walks Far Wolf, knee his horse into a gallop, raise dust, and clear the cattle fence, horse and rider running for sheer joy.

"Come in, Reverend," Josephine Shines the Light gestured toward the open flap of her lodge, "It has been many years…"

Doc had spoken of Grandmother's tipi and Leo knew he was crossing a portal of multiple dimensions. A single canvas panel was buttoned with willow branches and stretched over the circular bones of the lodge poles from the left side of the door, around to the right. Sunwise, he remembered. The entrance was a canvas flap hinged with a sturdy piece of chokecherry trunk and tied back to let in hot breeze. Old woolen rugs were laid over packed dirt to make a circle on the floor. Leo sat on an upturned round of cottonwood and took off his work boots. "I came from the corral," he said.

"These aren't new rugs, but thank you." Despite the heat, a small cookfire was lit in the center. She squatted, crumbling medicinal leaves into small metal mugs while Leo looked around. A mattress sat on a metal bed frame with a steamer trunk at the foot. An old chest of drawers, scarred from its long journey to this spot, made the headboard. Wooden boxes held cook gear and jars of dried berries and herbs. A large medicine bundle hung from the west wall along with other objects of Blackfeet antiquity—a bone breastplate, a bow and rawhide quiver that had seen many hunts, a buffalo hide from lineage inheritance, an eagle feather fan. It made Leo dizzy to look at them. He settled onto the stool, an older man in his stocking feet. Gramma

Josie poured hot water from a chipped graniteware pot. She handed him a mottled enamel mug. "Life is a long river," she said solemnly.

"And full of stones," he replied. Leo blew on the tea. "I think I owe my son's life to you."

"Your son owes his life to his own spirit and to *Iistapatapiop*, Creator. We who serve our people know each one must swim their own river. Jesse was drowning when he arrived, but he was reaching for the surface."

Regret twisted Leo's heart. "In that season of loss, I too was near drowning. I was not a good father when he needed me most."

Her eyes bore into him. "He needed you most on the day he was born. You took him as your own. You gave him a name, a family, a childhood."

Leo jolted at her words. How did she know his story? She sat across from him, inscrutable in their silence. "And here, Grandmother, it seems you have given him another name, another family, and his manhood."

"You were lying to him." She spoke plainly. "He could not become himself inside the lie. When my cousins brought him here, we made a fire and sat visiting with him every night for a week."

"He was barely speaking to me." Leo's heart cracked.

"He spoke to the fire." The old woman gestured toward her small flame. "My nephew BB took him to Badger-Two Medicine, our sacred lands, and held him in ceremony while we prayed and sent word to Doctor Jereldene that he was safe."

"She didn't tell me... not for a long time," Leo burned his tongue on the tea.

"It was not yours to know. You might have dashed up here and talked your son into going home before he had claimed himself."

"So, this is what you do, Grandmother, you take in wandering souls?"

She appraised him carefully. "What we do is hide our true nature from the white man. We are wards of the government. We are forbidden our ceremonies. We are devastated by the agency, the churches, the schools. We are deliberately addicted to alcohol, against which we have no defense. I speak openly because you have been an ally, and now your son has come to us."

"You think his father is Blackfeet?"

"His blood is a mystery. *You* are his father."

Leo sipped gratitude for her acknowledgment. "Will he come home with me and work the bees?" His hands trembled holding the cup.

"Jesse's path is greater than we can see for him." Josie shielded her face with the cup. "He will bridge between whiteness and Indianness in the world that comes. For now, the war grips people like a dark mouth round with teeth." Leo startled at her description. "But from this suffering much will shift in the world. It will be a new time for the Amskapi Piikuni." She smiled slightly, "I will live to see the beginning. He will live to see the middle." She poured more tea. "Meanwhile, a man needs daily work. He needs shelter in the places he comes from. He needs support from those who love him." Her gaze was piercing.

"I understand," Leo whispered, and hoped he did. "I love him," that he knew.

When Leo woke, he was stretched awkwardly in the Chevy's backseat. Car windows rolled down, night air washing over him, Jesse at the wheel. "What happened?" Leo asked, He could see stars.

"Gramma saw how tired you were and slipped some traditional medicine into your tea. BB and I helped you to the car. We're nearly home."

Leo sat up slowly. "I was dreaming. About the night she got her daughters out of the Indian school. The children were locked in. It's always been a mystery how she spirited them away." In the back of his mind, Leo saw Josephine Shines the Light glowing like the moon, laying her palm on the iron lock of the school dormitory. She was younger then, mid-life, the girls the last of her children. The door groaned in submission.

Opened.

Impossible.

He oriented himself among the familiar silhouettes of the buttes while Jesse drove south into the landscape of his life. White man.

15
Honey Harvest

AUTUMN EQUINOX 1942: *The battle of Guadalcanal rages in the Pacific. Rommel leaves North Africa for medical treatment in Germany.*

ALL LATE SUMMER AND INTO THE FALL, trains pulled onto the spur by the Pigeon River grain elevators in a procession of empty metal boxes waiting to be filled crop by crop. First was the wheat, rivers of grain pouring out of the elevator shafts into the empty container cars. Then flatbeds, stacked high with yellowing hay bales strapped down and covered with canvas. A bawling week when the ranchers drove their yearling steers into slatted cattle cars. Their harvest fed America, fed the military, fed the world.

Mid-September, two box cars marked "Sue Bee, America's Honey, Sioux City, Iowa" arrived. Jesse and Leo hoisted sixty-pound cans onto the truck and drove to the tracks where they used a forklift to transfer their harvest into the waiting cars. Back at Sue Bee, the load would be weighed, evaluated, and a check for a year's work printed out to Leo Cooper & Sons. The translucent alfalfa and clover honey would be mixed with the honey of buckwheat and fruit tree blossoms bringing the darker lots into the golden standard of Grade-A.

"Didn't Franklin say guys in his unit are from Iowa?" Leo nodded. "And here we are shipping honey there." Jesse slapped dust off his pants legs. "World is so big and so small at the same time, don't you think, Pa?" They came home dusty and worn. Jesse took off his shirt and bent his head, shoulders, and chest into the water of the trough, came up sputtering. He stretched in the late sun. Done. Harvest was done.

Early next morning, with no boiler to light or super frames to spin, Jesse ambled toward the church. The iron gate to the cemetery creaked on its hinges. He found the simple marker. *Lillian Beckner 1902-1918*. He squatted on his haunches alongside the bones of the girl who had given him birth.

"I'm sorry you didn't get to live," he crumbled tobacco into the grass. "You did leave me in good hands." He used his pocketknife to pick lichen from the engraved name and dates. "I hope the boy was good to you. Must've been a half-breed himself, my skin so white. But my brown eyes... at least it wasn't your brother..." Jesse lit a cigarette and stared hard at the ground, willing the grave to release its secrets. "Please tell me that I come from an act of love," his voice broke. Lilly had been sixteen, same age as Willow Shines the Light when she caught his heart.

When Jesse arrived at the Shines the Light allotment, riding in the back of BB's pick-up, the men had turned him over to Gramma Josie, who regarded him with such penetrating silence he felt his skin dissolve before her. Then the fire visits, how she and the men sat stirring the flames with a long stick, made him spill his life story into the flickering orange tongues. They put him to bed in an empty lodge beyond the cabins. He dreamt. They fed him. He shoveled manure and did odd jobs. At twilight, they lit another fire. Finally, Grandmother gave the slightest nod, and the men grunted. He could stay.

He missed his school, his friends, his brothers, his dead mother, his comforting auntie, his preachy father. He missed graduation. But whenever he thought about going home, anger stood like the wolf in the doorway. He'd been lied to. He wasn't his father's son. Who was he? That was the question that held him to Native ground. The man called BB Shoots Straight, and his wife Agnes gave him a bed, a second pair of jeans, and a canvas jacket that felt like a hug. BB took him under the hoods of reservation vehicles and taught him a trade.

Starting the next fall, he drove an antiquated school bus that picked up rural students and deposited them at the small school in Heart Butte. There was a girl, near his age, with chocolate-drop eyes and sheen of black hair. She watched him through the mirror, but whenever he watched her, she glanced away. Willow Shines the Light, Josie's granddaughter.

His third summer with the family they began to find moments of privacy picking berries, gathering kindling. She listened to his confusion between the red world and the white world, her ear bent to his heart. She confessed the challenges of carrying two minds, two languages, two ways of seeing everything, even her awe and fear of her grandmother. They were braiding sweetgrass.

That fall, the other young men began challenging him. "Gramma said you a breed, said to let you be. We said, there will be trouble. You *are* trouble, white boy." Their bodies twitched with pent-up energy. "You don't know how to live here. How to be one of us." A tangy smell like steel emanated from them. They worked alongside each other around the homestead, but they weren't like the valley boys, these were young braves. One sleight at a time, Jesse defended himself with fear-fueled sincerity.

The tallest and biggest among them, Horace, nicknamed Horse, put his foot in Jesse's way, "You play at being Indian." Horse pushed him in the chest and Jesse stumbled backward before catching his balance. "Anytime you get tired being one of us, you can disappear in Cut Bank or head back south," he taunted. "You can go back to being white. Go to college, get a good job, do whatever you want because that's what white men get, whatever they want." Jesse spun in place looking for the direction the next comment would come from, anticipating the fight building between them, words darting in, backing up. Hackles raised. Darrell, the one he called friend, snarled, "Now you want Willow. Will you want her when you go back? Will your family welcome her?"

Light flashed in Jesse's brain, "I'm not going back," he half yelled.

"You will go back." Horse appeared out of nowhere. "Why wouldn't you? That's where everything is."

Darrell stepped in, "You will break my cousin's heart if you leave her. And you will break my Gramma's heart if you take her."

A push from the side and then another, jostling him. "Bite first!" the angry wolf in him snarled. He punched out and hit Horse in the belly. Fists rained down on him. He took a set of knuckles to his nose, something crunched, he nearly passed out from the pain, blood running inside his throat.

A commanding shout swept over them—a force so strong everyone froze in the postures of the fight. Grandmother Josephine, five-feet-two-inches tall, strode into the middle of them, stood at Jesse's back. She did not help him, just stared the others down. "Fighting is not how this goes!" Darrell, Eli, Emmett, Stanley, Horace. One by one they averted their eyes and dropped their arms to their sides. Jesse struggled to standing. One eye was starting to swell, blood was streaming out both nostrils. Josie looked them over. "You boys clean up. I'll see you later. Jesse, come with me."

He sat on a cottonwood stump outside her lodge door. She emerged with a clean rag and bowl of water. "Head back." While he tilted his neck and pressed the cloth to his nostrils, she took her thumb and forefinger and before he could register her intent tweaked the deviated septum back into place. Jesse nearly fainted. "Your nose is broke. I think I got it. And... well, you look more a real Indian now."

"They started it, Gramma!" He swallowed blood.

"No, Christopher Columbus started it. And maybe you got mad 'cuz they're right," Josie daubed at his swelling eye. "They got no place else to go, no one else they can be, but you can pass for white and never look back. They know it, and you know it." She handed him another wet cloth. "I been watching. You want to be Blackfeet, one of the Amskapi Piikuni, then you best think what you got courage to say to them and what you got courage to admit to yourself." She snapped the lodge flap. "Don't move, I'm making a poultice." She reappeared and pushed a mash of yarrow up his nose, another jolt of pain. "Willow is young, but her spirit is old. When I saw you courting, I wanted to kick you off the place, save her from choosing you."

Jesse stammered, "I, I, I love her."

"See how you stutter, boy-man? The red world is full of hurt, and the white world is full of hate." She looked to the horizon, seeing what Jesse could not. "This road will test you hard, grandson. Every step is loyalty or betrayal." She pressed a glob of yarrow on a fresh cloth to his eye. "White people have ravaged our lives, our land, and our spirits. Many among us walk as ghosts. But in each generation, a few are taught to remember. We remind one another how to belong to *ksaahkoom*, the Earth, to respect our ancestors, and be loyal to our people. Willow inherits everything I know, as I inherited everything my grandfather knew. *Niitsitapiisini*, our old ways of knowing, are sinews stitching together who we are."

She whispered Piikuni words under her breath. "When you talked to the fire, I saw your longing to know yourself. I risked everything to invite that part of you home. I wagered that if you became part of the family, you would understand the need to protect the teachings, that you would be your father's son, an ally to the People." Grandmother stood with her hands on her hips, anchored to her ground. "I didn't see the love coming, but here it is. If you are not trustworthy, all my life work dies with me. Do you understand what I'm saying, Wolf?"

Jesse was shaking and didn't know if the shock stemmed from his nose, his heart, or his Gramma's words. He felt his *oosie* numb on the cottonwood stump. He felt his man parts twitch in his pants. He felt guilt and terror. He remembered the feel of Willow's silky black hair flowing through his spread fingers. He remembered the trust in her eyes when he had tilted her head into their first kiss. He remembered their bodies entwined; their stories entwined. He gulped air through his mouth, tasting the metallic trace of blood. "I promise you, Gramma, I will shield her, always."

A finger of wind brushed the back of Jesse's neck. He stirred from memory to present. One day, he would bring Willow here and introduce her to his two mothers. They would walk together onto the land of his father, over the bones of her ancestors. His life mission, whatever Gramma saw in him, would begin.

16
DOORS BETWEEN THE WORLDS

OCTOBER TO FIRST SNOW 1942: *General George S. Patton, sets sail from Virginia with troop ships heading to the Allied landing in North Africa. Military forces depart Northern Ireland, an armada heading for Morocco.*

THE PHONE RANG: THREE SHORTS. Doc reached for the earpiece with a habitual look of concern, followed by a smile. "When did your water break?" She glanced at her calendar; Leo and Charlotte's grandchild, right on time.

Doc was so pleased Maire wanted a homebirth that she decided to arrive by horse and buggy as she had when she delivered this baby's father. She rattled a can of oats along the corral fence. "C'mere, Bugle Boy, you old dodger." With the horse backed into his traces, Doc reveled in the jog of the wagon seat, the clop of hooves, the lift of Bugle's mane in the cool autumn breeze. It was the sum of her life that she drove down the road: Jereldene Jespersen, country doctor.

While Leo unhitched the wagon and put the horse in their empty barn, Doc walked Maire around the house, timing contractions. Hazel came over, Bonnie on her hip. "Don't worry, Maire, no baby's this big when it comes out... just feels like it!"

Leo hovered, paced, worked his sermon, hovered again. They had a light supper of soup and bread. The sun went down. The stars were out in a crisp sky. "Shall I pray?" He'd stuck his head in the doorway, once Maire was abed.

Doc didn't even look up. "You should always pray, Leo, that's your job. But don't pray worried, this baby's coming fine."

The door between the worlds opened. Maire went into transition. Doc spoke in a calm, firm voice. "You're doing it, dearie. Breathe short, short again, *whuh-whuh-whuh*, that's it. Don't push till I tell you. I can see the crown of the head…"

Doc's fingers were inside Maire's vagina. She felt the head fully in the birth canal and cupped one finger around the jaw and tiny chin. She called instructions through the panting, grunting, howl of birthing. "I've near got your baby's head in my hand…Take a big breath, get yourself some air." Doc felt the glide. "Now! Push for all you've got, Maire. PUSH!" Malleable shoulders. No cord around the neck. "Again—push!" A purple head was in her palms, eyes shut, cowl of vernix. Doc took her pinky finger and cleared the mouth, suctioned the nasal passages, turned the baby face down. The tiny body slipped fully into her waiting hands, squirmed, and gasped. Still connected to the cord, the newborn turned pink. Doc eased new life into the world. A trilling cry.

Doc laid the baby between Maire's thighs, cut and clamped the cord, wiped off the smear of birthing blood. Tiny blue tongue quivering in a scrunched-up face. She set the babe onto Maire's empty belly and watched the two of them touch for the first time. "It's a girl, Maire." It was 2:00 a.m., October 16, 1942.

Leo announced the birth at church, though Gertie had already told everyone. With sugar beets needing harvest, he drove truck to help Caleb. Then he and Bill Sivertsen mowed the churchyard and checked the gravestones. They pounded in stakes to mark potential sites that would be harder to find under snow, praying no graves would be needed. They tested the bell rope, checked the furnace.

The Beekeeper's Question

Ethel Pocket fussed in the kitchen. "Nothing spicy, no onions. It all comes through in the milk. You need iron and protein," she announced. "A nursing mother burns as many calories as a coal miner, you know." No, Maire didn't know. All those years reading and never a baby book. She had Hazel and Hazel had Ethel and they all had Doc.

Men's work. Women's work. Maire put a pillow on the chair at Charlotte's desk and began composing a letter to Franklin.

20 October 1942 #18
Dear Franklin,
You are father to a beautiful GIRL born early morning, October 16. We are both fine. I chose the name Flora, so she belongs to the bees and Charlotte, so she belongs to the Coopers. She has a fuzz of red hair, so she's a MacDonnell, too. Please go down to the harbor and say her name to the Irish sea. Flora is us, Franklin, and she will help us remember the love that made her. Your pa got film for the Kodak. Photos soon. We send our love.

Maire folded the letter, licked the envelope, addressed it with the strange APO. An address attached to the Army, to the man, not the place. She had no one else to write. She bowed her head and cried.

Hazel had cried too, curling Flora's tiny fingers around her pinky. "Two little girls, friends like us. Pigtails and scuffed knees, garden playhouses, doing schoolwork side by side." But then she whispered urgently, "Please tell me they won't be orphans together."

"I can only promise one thing, Haz, we are strong women, and we will raise strong girls." Her nipples hurt.

christina baldwin

November 7, 1942, #21 Flora is three weeks old!
Dear Franklin,
    I left Flora with your Pa so I could check for mail. I told him, "She's fed and wearing a clean nappy. I'll be back in 20 minutes." Then before he could worry (you know how he does), I walked to Gertie's. Coming back, I peeked in the kitchen window and saw your pa had propped Flora on the table surrounded by pillows and was making silly faces and baby talk. By the time I entered the kitchen, he was back being Rev. Cooper. Headline of the Tribune says: U.S. TROOPS HIT THE SANDS OF NO. AFRICA. There's a photograph of ships all pointed toward the Strait of Gibraltar. And I just heard on the radio that the U.S. Army landed in Morocco and Algeria. Where are you? Do you even know you're a daddy? I want you here making silly faces at our baby. I'm scared for you, but I'll be brave.
Love, Moy & Flora.

November descended with bone-chilling wind. Sleet that turned to snow at night. Paper-thin sheets of ice rimming any dip in the path to the outhouse. The bony fingers of the cottonwoods clacked in the corner of the yard, their fallen yellow leaves pressed into sodden piles against the fence. "They can wait for spring," Leo said, turning his back on the idea of raking. "We got enough going on." He made a cup of Postum and closed his study door. Saturday. Sermon writing.

    Maire was getting only three hours of sleep at a time, nursing twelve times a day, washing diapers and hanging them on the wooden drying rack installed beneath the stairwell. Heat wafted up the steps to her writing nook.

12 November 1942
Dear Jesse,
    I had a baby girl on the 16th of October. Flora Charlotte.

I'm still waiting to hear that Franklin has the news. Mail is slow, and if a ship gets sunk, there go the mail bags along with everything else. We think he's in North Africa, so there's the war now too.

Since becoming a mother, I have been thinking about your birth. Last April, when my employers found out I was pregnant, they offered to adopt my baby on the condition she would never know. Now that I see she has red hair, she would have carried a clue to their lie, just like you have brown eyes. Because I married a decent man with a family that took us in, I wasn't forced to sell her. I hope you come work again this coming season. I'll be stronger and eager to learn. Your sister-in-law, Maire

PS I will tend Lillian's grave. Quiet like, but so you know.

Then, one mid-November night Maire's nightmare returned. In the dream, Broin cornered her in the kitchen, his voice an evil hiss. "I come to kill the both of yah." She was not running. She would not cower. She was a mother. She made her stand with the baby pressed to her breast and a carving knife in her hand. Someone was shaking her. She couldn't aim true.

Leo's face was pale with sleep and concern, "Maire, wake up."

She grabbed for him, "Oh God, Leo, someone was trying to steal the baby." She sat up and burst into tears.

Leo patted her shoulder. "Hormones," he said. "Charlotte had strange dreams and moods afterward." Flora began to fuss. "I'll make us something soothing."

Maire changed Flora's nappy. Could mother's milk curdle? She rocked herself to calm, glad for the lamplight that pushed darkness from the corners. The shawl settled over her shoulders. Leo carried cups of steaming honey-sweetened milk. He read her poetry while she nursed. Maire tucked the baby in her crib. Leo tucked Maire in her bed. "You're a good man, sir." She slept again and did not dream.

The next day, sitting on the porch steps wearing Charlotte's winter coat, Maire decided to exorcise the demon. She had a pie plate and matches at her side and wrote furiously on a scrap of paper.

You are evil, Broin Mulvaney. Taking something by force does not make it yours. I will never be yours! Whatever happened with my mother, if you harmed her, if you killed her, you will go straight to hell. If you ever harm Franklin, I'll send you to hell myself. You <u>are</u> the war, and I hope it finds a way to kill you. You need be done with your miserable life. The rest of us need be done fearing you. You may not have one bit of me, not even my dreams. Begone!

She folded the letter into an envelope and spit into it three times. "Father, Son, and Holy Ghost." She licked the seal, held the paper over the plate, lit the envelope, and watched it burn. She carried the ashes to the outhouse and dumped them into the hole. She sat. She shit on the grey flakes. A growl rose from her: She-wolf under the full moon, dripping the last of the birthing blood. She felt the power of *Sheela-na-gig*, a squatting womanish creature carved on the stone lintels of Irish churches. This was no faerie, but a gorgon spreading the lips of her own vulva, birthing herself.

Leo came home with a letter in his pocket.

October 16, 1942

Dear Maire, I dreamed you called my name. Right now, it's 4:30 a.m., minus 7 hours—so 9:30 in the evening there. Maybe you are birthing the baby. The Army is getting ready for something so I'm back on base.

"It's written a month ago, on the night Flora was born."

I'm alone in the commissary with yesterday's cold coffee asking God that you both make it through okay.

The Beekeeper's Question

I don't get down on my knees like Pa, but I'm watching rain in the yard light and saying, "Please." That's a prayer. These months we've come closer to each other and soon the war is going to take us farther apart. I want you to have my baby for comfort and to keep you busy 'til I get home. I love you. Frank

Maire read it with tears in her eyes and then read it to Leo. A few days later another letter, carefully typed, King's face on the stamp, twenty days in a mail sack.

```
29 October 1942
Dear Mrs. Cooper,
     Do not be alarmed to receive this letter. I am a
librarian friend of your husband's. We arranged that
I would write you when he left. This is that letter.
The tens of thousands of American soldiers billeted
on Ulster soil are gone. A fleet of military vessels
shipped out of Belfast harbor yesterday morning:
destination unknown. I enjoyed meeting your
husband. He has a lively curiosity, and I wish you
many years to relish one another's company.
Most sincerely,
Malcolm Campbell, Belfast Public Library
```

Awake for the midnight feeding, wrapped in Nana's shawl, Maire sat in the rocking chair where Charlotte had nursed the baby who became her husband. Across the darkened room, she thought she saw the shining outline of herself lying pregnant in a tangle of hot summer sheets. "Look at us now," she whispered. She was holding her daughter, an American child.

17
Three Christmas Days 1942

One year after Pearl Harbor, the U.S. military is fully deployed into the war. Rommel retreats to Tripoli. December 22. The battle for "Longstop Hill" begins outside Tunis leading to a Christmas defeat for the Allies.

Pigeon River, Montana

ETHEL VOLUNTEERED TO COOK TURKEY. Maire volunteered to host. Leo spent two days clearing papers off the dining table. One letter had arrived, the envelope greasy and worn, the words a treasure.

> November 6, 1942 #27
> Dear Maire,
>   I'm on a transport ship headed into the fight at last. Radio silence, heading south. Seas rough. Everybody nervous, seasick. Lots of ships out here. Lots of us writing home. We got a mail delivery onboard, so I finally know I'm a new daddy! Flora Charlotte is a beautiful name. Did you get my letter that I was dreaming of you?
>   I'm glad we fell in love. I'm glad we got married. I'm glad I landed in Northern Ireland, so I know more about you and glad you're in Pigeon River, so you know more about me. I am a better man because of you, Moy. You told me to keep my head down, to keep thinking under fire. I have

your voice in my mind and your heart in my heart. Kiss our baby girl and try not to worry. This war is a job that's got to be done. I love you. Franklin

PS Please tell Pa I appreciate him even more. I'm glad Jesse came back.

She read it to Leo, gulping happy tears. She read it to Doc, who patted her hand the whole time. She read it to Flora who spit out milk. She propped it on the dresser top next to the tiny photograph taken on the steps of the Philadelphia Art Museum. On the piano, she played D-above-middle-C for courage.

December 24, 1942,
Happy Anniversary, dear husband
Oh Franklin, I finally got your letter written on the ship! Now you have landed, been in battle, and I don't know where you are this Christmas Eve. I am sitting at your mother's little desk. Snow is falling. We will always have so much to celebrate this day—our anniversary, then a candlelight service, then putting Flora to bed so Santa can come. Imagine us having busy and happy years.

I'm glad to be your wife. Happy to be the mother of your child. You said you wanted to liberate me from being a maid. Well, here I am. Your Pa and I are learning each other. He is a good man, like you said. Doc is bats over Flora. Your brother Jesse went back to the Indians after harvest. The bees are sleeping in their hives. Well, Leo says they are busy keeping the hive warm, making comb, and tending their queen. I wonder if they dream of flowers. I hope you dream of me. Your ever-loving wife, Maire.

The church windows cast yellow squares of light on the snow. The sanctuary was full of pine boughs and candles. Leo stood in his white robe (well ironed, and she knew the chore of that!) brightened with a green stole and red trim. They sang the usual carols. Leo read Luke 2, verses 1-20, "And lo in the time of Caesar Augustus..." He preached about miracles even in winter and war. He called the children forward to bestow each an orange, all the way from Florida, and placed a pastoral hand on their heads for Christmas blessing. "When you go home, say your prayers, hang your stockings, and go to sleep!" They giggled and promised nothing. Bill turned off the lights, everyone sang "Silent Night."

Gertie showed up the next morning knocking at the kitchen door. Her broad smile showed a missing tooth half back on her right jaw. "Letter came on the late truck and, well, seemed like special delivery."

Maire ripped open the envelope, scanned the news. "Thank you, Gertie, Franklin's fine. Come in, won't you stay for dinner?"

"I don't have anything to bring," she lamented.

"You brought good news and isn't that Christmas?"

My Darling,

I think it's the 17th of November and I just got three letters and a photo of you and Flora. My beauties!

Guess you know the U.S. Army is on African soil. We hit the beach and scrambled ashore under artillery fire from French Vichy troops. The Frogs switched sides after a few days. I did okay. Guys were worried we'd forget everything we learned in the sheep pastures. We're on the move now. Locals stand by the side of the road, old men, women, and children. They make a victory sign for whatever army is trudging by. Hate to say it, but chilling rain followed us from Ireland. Even palm trees are shivering. I'm kissing your picture. Love, Franklin

Leo returned from tending the church—hymnals straightened in the pew trays, pencils sharpened by offering envelopes, birdseed scattered in the cemetery. His arms were full of cut boughs. "Brighten up the parlor," he said. "Bring some yule in the house." Maire made him coffee and handed him the letter, watching his face while he read. "At least he made it through the first fight," he warmed chapped hands on the mug.

A swirl of ashes blew over the pristine whiteness of Maire's relief. She stared at her father-in-law. "It's Christmas morning, sir. Just last night you preached to keep believing in miracles. Couldna we have a breather from the worry of it?" She turned her back and chopped an onion, allowing tears. "I was happy, Leo. Now I'm scared again. The Pockets need cheering. I invited Gertie when she brought the post. She went to spiffy up." She blew a strand of hair out of her eyes and laid potatoes and onions into a baking pan.

Leo set down his cup. "I'm sorry, Maire, I didn't mean to ruin Christmas. I'm waiting for the plow, then driving to Vaughn Junction. I'll be back before dinner."

"On Christmas?"

"It's a surprise." He looked at her with soft eyes trying to shift her mood.

Medjez el Bab, North Africa

Rain. Mud. The sucking sound his boots made, every step trying to drag him down and every step knowing he could not stop. They were easy targets as the day greyed toward light. Rifles slung over their shoulders. Franklin stepped over a corpse. He wasn't used to that yet. Should he get used to it? What would happen to him then? What would happen if he didn't harden up? "Hey, Tommy, are we supposed to get his tags?" Blank eyes open. Why did the dead always look so surprised? Well, every guy had to believe it wasn't going to be him, that he'd always be the one stepping over what was left of a man.

"His unit'll get him." Thompson's voice was hoarse with exhaustion, "We just keep rolling wire." They were re-spooling the telephone line from Franklin's forward position back where they'd abandoned the Jeep stuck to its wheel wells.

Rain. Mud. They fought. Gained no ground. Franklin spent Christmas Eve hunched over the field telephone conveying messages and orders between officers and units. "I don't get it, Tommy. What's so fucking important about this hill? Was it worth…"

"Shut up, Bee Man," Thompson coughed raggedly. They all coughed. Cigarettes and damp chill, mildewed blankets. "We're infantry. We follow orders. Advance. Regroup. Push Jerries across this godforsaken terrain until we push 'em into the sea. Which hill is worth what, that's for command."

Franklin tried to catch his breath. "I had this notion," he panted, "that we were battle-ready, but man, these guys are tough." His stomach was growling, and his mind reeled from thought to thought.

At the Jeep, Thompson dropped the motor into first gear while Franklin and a couple other guys rocked and pushed. Mud spewed over everyone. Tommy began inching forward onto a roadbed cratered by artillery rounds. "Jerries have plowed through any European country they want. They're fighting the Soviets in dead winter. They been chasing Brits back and forth across North Africa for two years. We've been rehearsing with a Jeep and a sheep." He leaned into white-knuckle driving. "We got some catching up to do."

"They're madmen."

"Look at their *führer*," Thompson huffed, "Madman at the top. Madmen at the bottom."

Shines the Light Homesite, Blackfeet Nation

Jesse eased out of bed, reluctantly leaving the warmth of Willow's side. The cabin was divided into two rooms by a curtain—their bedroom and a living and kitchen space with a slumped sofa, small table, and a small woodstove with a cooktop.

The Beekeeper's Question

He layered on clothes and started the morning fire, adjusted the draft. He pulled on boots and stepped into the numbing tang of pre-dawn air. Dry cold froze his nostril hairs, that woke him up. Yesterday's snow blanketed the land. Christmas, his twenty-fourth birthday. He'd feed Windy, hunker into the stall, have a smoke and a thought.

Jesse was leaning against the horse's flank for warmth when a familiar face appeared over the stall rails. "I thought maybe the horses had taken up smoking." BB loved to amuse himself. "You waitin' for Santa?"

"He already left." Jesse smiled back, "What you doing, Uncle?"

"I hid a couple little things out here." BB shivered in a worn jacket, ran his tongue over his broken tooth. A youthful rodeo accident. That was the story BB liked to tell, always adding, "When I die, somebody close my mouth, so I don't scare Jesus." He cracked himself up over that. He was mid-forties, not anywhere near dying, less they froze to death in the barn.

"It's my birthday," Jesse blurted.

"I got oranges from the Methodist preacher in Browning. Got a couple extra, so Happy Birthday, one for you."

"Thanks, BB." Jesse took a drag. "Smoke?"

"Nope, only smokin' in ceremony these days." BB spread his arms along the stall railing and gave Jesse a long look. "I know something more of your story, Jess. Gramma said I could tell yah. Wanna hear?" Jesse nodded and settled in for listening. "I was sixteen, restless, sneaking over to Cut Bank. I'd hang around the rodeo with a few mixed-blood townies and a couple scruffy white boys. We all tryin' to figger how to make it into the circuit, be real cowboys. First big war was going on and if it didn't get over, we were all going in.

"Mixed-blood kid named LaVerne was part of that bunch. He looked like you. Coulda passed if he moved where no one knew his mother. Bragged that he had a girl who let him, you know… a white girl. We thought he was bluffing." BB shrugged. "No one out here thought Cut Bank was a good idea, you can imagine. I'd let Gramma talk sense to me, then be drawn back. One time, LaVerne said he wanted to see the Indian part of himself, so he drove me home in his father's Model-T. Well, Gramma looked him over that way she has, and pulled him into her lodge for a little visit. You know how that goes." BB winked and laughed. "He emerged an older and wiser boy. Told me the girl was pregnant. He was going to talk to her family, play up his white side, try to honor things. When I went into town couple weeks later, he was gone."

"You think LaVerne was my father?"

"Maybe. You see any other white Indians roaming around, invited into family? We got enough troubles without kidnapping lost boys, less they not lost, but found."

Jesse's mind was spinning. "Was LaVerne's mother Piikuni?"

"His Pa was white. His mother was mixed. Indian eyes, but light skin. Dressed like the wife of someone, church lady, store clerk."

Jesse winced. "Council said I can't enroll."

"We got a constitution now," BB said. "Write things down so we're more a nation. Blood quantum, you got to prove yourself. Maybe LaVerne was a quarter Indian. Maybe he fathered you. Maybe you got enough blood, maybe not. Even your preacher father got no proof. Just took you in 'cuz you so cute, I guess. Or you remind him of the baby Jesus." BB's laugh echoed in the barn.

"Didn't anybody look for LaVerne?"

"There was a war and a flu epidemic. LaVerne's father went to the police, and the police came to me and the other boys. Scared us good, but we didn't know anything. No body. No news. Police wun't of even made that effort except Mr. Gittels ran the hardware store. Best think he's dead, Jesse, drive you crazy if you don't." BB pushed himself back from the railing and slapped the wood, "That or he don't ever want to be found."

"Thanks, BB."

"Yah, well, Happy Birthday or Merry Christmas, however you play it. You and Willow come get your oranges." BB rummaged through the tack room and carried his presents into the house.

Jesse rubbed his face in Windy's winter-furred flank, felt the horse's muscles shudder under the touch. "Well, hell, at least I ain't LaVerne Gittels, Jr." He gave the horse a slap and a ration of oats and crunched back across the snow toward the cabin. The boy was still sleeping. Willow up and heating water for peppermint tea. He slipped off his jacket and came up behind her. "Merry Christmas, darling."

"Don't you wrap those cold hands around me," he could hear the smile in her voice.

He pressed his hands into his own armpits and shivered. "All this snow and BB still went to get oranges."

"BB likes a little risk." She turned and took his face in her hands. "Happy Birthday, my man." Her skin the color of brown sugar, hair a licorice black.

He tucked strands behind her ears. "He said he wanted to be a rodeo cowboy when he was young."

"Show me an Indian boy who doesn't want to be a cowboy." Her hair was not bobbed like many young women but long and usually braided. She let him brush it. She leaned into his chest. "You been hugging that horse before you came in and hugged me." She liked smell, Willow did. She knew the scent of sweet grass and wild herbs. She knew when to turn the fry bread, when the meat was cooked, when to take ears of corn from the coals. He was a lucky man, she liked how he smelled. She fingered aside his shirt, pressed her face to his chest inhaling and teasingly pulled the few hairs that sprouted from his sternum, his "white man hairs" she called them. He kissed the top of her head.

Dear Pa,

It's Christmas morning and I been up early trying to piece my life and myself together. This is the first year I have a true sense of my origins.

Their little boy tumbled sleepily into the room. Willow pulled him to her, wrapping them both in a blanket. Drummond Natoyii Isttookimaa Shines the Light Cooper, a child not yet as tall as his name. He sucked his thumb, fingering his mama's hair. "I'm thinking this is the year we cross the bridge together, Willow. Shall I invite them up—my dad, Auntie Doc, Frank's wife and the baby?"

"They don't know yet, do they." She inhaled the sweet smell of her son.

"I want them to meet you. Eat with us. Then I can ask how they're gonna support us if we come down to the valley."

"Winter is hard traveling. Then, when everything melts, no place looks good. Invite them for first greening when they can see the beauty."

Jesse went back to writing:

I think another year doing the honey together will show us the way forward. There's more to talk about that's easier in person. Maybe everyone can come visit this spring. Meanwhile, I hope Frank stays safe, and the U.S. starts winning. Maire wrote she had a baby girl. Congratulations and good luck getting sleep.
Jesse

He folded the paper for later mailing and joined his family on the sofa. "I think Santa has been here, Drummie."

"Dah fats man?"

"Yes. Let's get you dressed. Aunt Aggie made sugared fry bread and Uncle BB got you an orange."

Leo's Surprise: Pigeon River

Hazel and Ethel were back and forth across the road with news of the turkey's progress. Aroma of buttered bird clinging to their clothes made Maire's mouth water. "Leo promised he'd be back by 1:00." She kept the irritation from her voice. "Hand me Bonnie, you got enough going on." She reached for the chubby baby riding Hazel's hip, checked her au gratin potatoes.

Doc stomped into the entryway knocking snow off her shoes balancing a Pyrex dish of home-canned green beans baked with Campbell's mushroom soup poured over the top. "Specialty," she announced to Maire, "Wouldn't be a Cooper Christmas without my beans."

Gertie returned wearing gabardine slacks, a red and green sweater, and clip earrings. She carried a can of Planter's peanuts for the grownups, Zwieback for Bonnie, and a jar of Gerber's baby food for Flora. "Squash is my favorite," she said, "better than the peas, and don't even try the spinach." They hung around the kitchen. Hazel blustered in with bowls of stuffing, and then Ethel carried the turkey, steam rising off its crispy golden skin, in its final trek across the road. They set it all on the table, and, as if on cue, Leo drove the Chevy into the yard. A handsome young Marine jumped out of the passenger side.

In seconds he was at the door, full-sized, filling the frame, his smile as broad as his shoulders. Hazel let out a delighted scream and ran into Ralph's outstretched arms. "Merry Christmas, sweetheart, last-minute furlough before I ship out." Leo looked so satisfied that Maire forgave him for stirring her worry. Everyone cried for happy, and Bonnie smeared gummed-up Zwieback on Ralph's uniform.

After the feast, the grandfathers bounced the babies on their laps and listened to the radio. The women did dishes. Ralph and Hazel slipped back across the street. No one said anything, no one went home. Doc and Ethel and Gertie eased themselves down at the kitchen table and nibbled nuts while regaling Maire with stories of Christmases past.

The next morning, Ralph knocked at the door and let himself into the entryway. Maire looked up. "Is Leo supposed to drive you?"

"No, we're all going into Great Falls, walk along the river, have lunch at the Riverside Diner before I catch the bus back to California. Heading over at New Year's."

"You want a cup of something?"

He shook his head. "I just come to say I appreciate you being friends with Hazel. Now you got the two babies and Franklin in the war too, it helps her."

Maire wiped her hands. "It's good both ways, Ralph."

His Adam's apple toggled up and down in this throat. "I'm plannin' to get through this. But if I don't, well, you'll…"

Maire stared into his eyes, glimpsing in this one exchange everything Hazel loved about him, and his love for her. "Oh Ralph, you got to believe in coming through with your whole heart."

"Yes. I will. Of course. Thank the Rev for his help. Ask him, would he…"

"We're already praying for you, Ralph. Whole valley holding its sons, calling you safe back home victorious." He pumped her hand in his big farmer paw.

December 31, 1942 #27
Dear Franklin,
    Now I know what the word blizzard means! Snow drifted nearly over the door of the honey house. Your pa says it gets caught there. You know that.
    We had a lovely Christmas. Missed you. Missed Jesse. Got a card from Boyd. He's in Idaho at an internment camp. Did you know the government rounded up all the

The Beekeeper's Question

Japanese living on the West Coast and put them in places where they can't inform the enemy? It sounds like he's going to serve being a doctor there. Leo says they're mostly good people just like the rest of us.

Ralph came home. By the time he rode all the buses, he had only 24 hours here, but he sure made Hazel and his folks happy. He said Ronnie T. already got injured, patched up in Australia and sent back in. The Pacific fighting sounds even scarier than North Africa. I keep thinking that being signal corps keeps you a tiny bit safer than a regular foot soldier. If that's not true, don't tell me.

I'll be up at midnight. No champagne. Kisses only for Flora, hoping she'll go back to sleep. love, your Moy

18
Cold and Snow

JANUARY 14, 1943: *The Casablanca Conference begins. Churchill and Roosevelt strategize the invasion of Sicily and Italy and the principle of "unconditional surrender."*

THE FIRST WEEKS OF THE NEW YEAR were a blur of hardened weather. Not just snow, but a howling wind that bit hard on the land, sheets of ice brittle underfoot. Leo cancelled church, but kept the building somewhat warmed, unlocked, with blankets and a store of food. "Started sheltering during the Depression," he told Maire, "Some folks still in it."

Everyone hunkered down, ventured forth only for the most necessary tasks—keeping livestock alive, throwing hay off the backend of the pick-up truck, taking an axe to livestock drinking ponds. Up by their houses, people were milking a cow, tending barnyard animals, trying to keep the dogs from freezing their paw pads to the ground. The sun peered weakly over the landscape, its heat retreated to another galaxy.

Doc killed a chicken, stewed it with whatever onions and potatoes were softening in her root cellar amongst her doctor burdens. She huddled in front of the stove, rereading *The Journals of Lewis and Clark*, and leaving only to feed and water Bugle Boy locked in his stable.

The Beekeeper's Question

Middle of the month, Homer Torgerson missed a swipe with his axe and drove himself to Doc's with an old rag wrapped round blood-stiff pants. He limped into her parlor, sat by the coal stove and complained while she numbed, cleaned, and stitched his chilled flesh. "I'm fifty-seven years old, Doc," he said. "I shouldn't be ranching alone. Bought Tiller's old place. Fenced it in '39, me and the boys running Herefords. And where are they now? Out in the middle of the Pacific Ocean, one on a ship and one on some godforsaken island. Can't even say where. Ouch! I thought you numbed me!"

"Hold still then, Homer."

"Refused ag deferments. Got to go, they said, fight of a lifetime."

"You went into the Great War, I recall."

"Yeah, and there was nothin' great about it, other than we won. I was too old to be drafted, so enlisted with my younger brother. You remember Arnold? He didn't make it back." Doc adjusted the light of the gooseneck lamp as she stitched, her breath ricocheting back inside the cotton mask. "I tol' my boys war is mostly sitting in the mud, in some ditch with a pie plate on your head hoping nobody shoots it off." Homer glanced at his wound, then stared out the window into the cold, white day. "Me and the missus hold hands every night and just whisper over and over *come home safe, come home safe*. That's a prayer, don'cha think?" He cleared his throat.

Doc kept her head down. Homer was barrel-chested, beer-bellied, balding with a grizzled fringe and usually a couple days of stubble on his face. She wrapped gauze tight around his calf. "Good thing you sliced that nice and vertical. Runs with the line of the muscle. Should heal up quick, but stay off it rest of the week."

"Cattle be dead if I do. I should of seen it coming, the war I mean. Gone into pigs instead of turnin' heifers onto more land. I just didn't want to believe we'd get into the fight. Roosevelt kept promising to keep us out."

"You're a veteran. You know. Some battles got to be fought." She put away her suture tray, tossed used gauze and cotton balls into the stove. "Can Milly drive, maybe Susan throw hay and chop for a few days?"

"Would you send your wife and daughter into this weather?"

"I'd go out myself, but I've got twenty years on you." She paused to consider her words, "There's hobos. Belle knows where they are. And last fall, when Jesse Cooper was putting in the honey crop with the Rev, he said the Indians need paying work…" She let the idea float. "Men too old to draft, but still strong, or boys too young, but ready to put on muscle."

"Where Jesse at, Valier?"

"North of there. Between Browning and Cut Bank."

"On the Rez?"

"Last I heard." Doc was guarded, waiting.

"Why don't he stay here, help his own people?"

Doc pressed her point. "It's not just the valley that's stressed. The whole west is under orders to raise food production. It's an opportunity. Help the tribe to get into the modern economy."

Homer blurted, "What they need with modern economy? The lot of 'em livin' off our guv'ment money. Drunks and thieves."

Doc flinched. "Indians got a problem with drink, that's true, but we started them on that disaster." She adjusted his pantleg around the bandage, backed up, and stood with her hands on her hips. "White folks been drinking hootch for a couple thousand years, Indians, not even a century. You can elbow the bar at Belle's, rag about Roosevelt, and still make it home, wake sober, because white folks got a protein in our blood that metabolizes alcohol. Indians don't."

Homer snorted. "Don't know who I'd rather deal with—Injuns, Japs or Jerries—the devil you know or the devil you don't know."

"The ordinary man isn't the devil, Homer. Everybody just caught in the same slice of history." She took a breath. "Get home and change outta those torn up pants and bloody long johns 'fore I got to treat you for pneumonia." That was the "Doc" he expected, bossy for his own good, no philosophizing.

"What I owe yah?" She waved her hand in a gesture that meant "Oh, nothing." She knew he'd come by, drop off cuts of beef and a loaf of Milly's bread.

"I'll talk to Caleb, he ain't so busy. I heard the Army might ship in prisoners of war to ease the labor shortage, soon as they get some."

She gestured toward his leg. "You keep yourself alive. Think on what I said."

His truck started after a few wheezes and headed toward town. At Cooper's corner, he'd turn south on frozen gravel and follow the ditch line until it ran out, cut round toward the butte and the place he called home.

She put away her doctoring station, poured boiling water over a square yard of oilcloth that served as her portable surgical field and dipped her scissors and suturing needles in denatured alcohol. Dusk dropped suddenly over the winter landscape. Leo phoned, "Blizzard tonight," he sounded weary. "Come sleep here."

Doc shook her head in the empty room. "I should stay where folks know to find me." She stretched out on the old davenport, three cushions long, with upholstered arms that often cradled her neck and listened to the wind trying to blow her house down.

It was late when she startled awake. Leftover stew had congealed in a bowl set on the floor. Looked like the cat had licked it. The floor lamp cast a circle against the room's shadowed corners. Fire still going, though it needed stoking. Wind was rattling the old latch. Tapping, pause, tapping again. Not wind.

Doc opened the door to a figure wrapped in coats and an old blanket. "*Áisókinaki*... Are you Doctor Jere? Gramma Josie says you have medicine." Snow icicles froze in her hair, crystals matted her eyebrows and lashes. Her lips were cracked. Dried blood gave her a macabre appearance of lipstick.

Doc caught the staggering woman in her arms, pushed the door shut with her hip, walked the stranger to her sofa. Beyond shivering, advanced hypothermia. "Don't move," Doc said, though it was obvious the exhausted girl had expended all strength to reach the house. Doc filled up the firebox of the stove, fanned the coals until the new chunks popped and cracked to yellow flames. "Who are you? How did you get here?"

"I am Willow Shines the Light." Her voice wind-sucked, eyes a waning fire, "Jesse... truck broke. He walked... Help. Freezing. Couldn't wait."

"Dear God. Let's get these frozen rags off your feet. I'm tipping you back, lie down on the sofa." Doc carefully unwrapped layers of cut blanket knotted with leather strips. First layer frozen stiff. Second layer frozen. Third layer wet. Fourth layer, worn leather shoes, cold but still pliable. "Your feet are gonna hurt when they warm." There was a mewling cry. The woman was half-fainted.

"It's okay," she said. "You're safe." Again, that little cry. Something moved under the padding clothing covering the woman's belly. "Oh God, it's two of you."

Doc peeled back the blanket, two coats, wool stiff and now wet with melting. An inner blanket had been carefully trussed around the woman's torso. With surgical scissors Doc cut leather thongs, until she revealed a small child, bright with fever. A little boy two, maybe three years old, legs wrapped around his mother's waist like a bear cub on a tree. His head was resting at her throat so he could breathe. Doc lifted him gently, little arms and legs cramped into the position that had sheltered him through hours in the bitter cold. He cried out to be moved. "Oki, little one," she said, "I am your Gramma's friend." She caressed his fevered cheek. "We are going to warm up your mother and then cool you down." He wore only a flannel shirt, so the body warmth of his mother could reach him. His corduroy britches stank with pee. The cap with rabbit fur flaps looked familiar—Jesse must have raided the attic last fall. But oh God, where was Jesse now? She tried to piece together events from the woman's few words. Wind and white-out was death. How the woman had defied it, Doc had no idea. There was nothing she could do for Jesse in the midst of storm. She gagged down fearful ruminations and went into triage.

Doc wrapped the child in a towel and half-tucked him inside the bib of her overalls while she gathered bedding and draped it over chair backs near the stove to catch heat. She placed a pillow under the woman's head. Once a blanket warmed, she spread it over the woman's body. She wrapped her bluish hands in warm towels, counted her respirations. When Willow began to shake, two dark eyes searched Doc's face for reassurance. "This is good," Doc told her, "Your body is trying to make heat. Let it happen. I'm gonna check this boy of yours. You did a good job, Willow, he's not so cold as you."

"My son," the woman chattered through her cracked lips. Pink tinge to his fevered skin, eyes bright with inner heat and vacant. Doc laid him out on towels, unbuttoned the shirt, and pulled off his soiled trousers. She bathed his spasming body with lukewarm water, assessing symptoms. Bloody stool? Rosy bumps? Gurgling chest? A different fear rose in her: contagion.

She thought of Maire and baby Flora, of Leo and the town and valley folks hunkered in their farmsteads. She thought of Homer and others like him spread out over the homesteaders' plats that parceled the land into ownership and entitlement. *"Please, not typhoid,"* her thoughts rang loud in her mind, *"Josie... you wouldn't send me that..."* The face of her old friend shimmered in the corner shadows. Of course, she would send them if she thought Doc held a cure. Of course, Jesse would drive them because he knew the way. Love and family are like that. And well, typhoid isn't as fatal as it once was. She could quarantine with them, wait for the boy's fever to break, get antibiotics from Great Falls. She had read there was vaccine, though she guessed most of that supply was probably shipped to military field hospitals.

Willow propped herself on one elbow watching. Doc handed her a cup of lukewarm water and honey. "Sip this. Where did the truck break down?"

"Snow in my eyes. I walked toward the grain elevators. Crossed the highway."

The young woman's chances of wandering in the right direction and finding Doc's house, any house, in this storm were zero percent.

"My God, girl, how did you ever…?"

"I listened." Her shaking seemed a little less violent.

"Are you sick?" Doc wrapped newly warmed towels around the young woman's feet.

"Not so bad and better now, but my boy…" her eyes filled with a mother's tears. "Fever came after Christmas. Two have died."

Doc knelt awkwardly on the floor, one hand resting gently on the boy's exposed chest, gauging the balance between fever and chill. She didn't want him to cool too fast but needed to take the burn off him. "Is Jesse sick?"

"No, but he's lost." Willow's eyes went wild again.

"Look at me," Doc squeezed her ankles. "People catch this sickness from other people. The boy has bloody stool—his poo, his spit, his snot—all has sickness in it. If you have been sick and are better, you have protection, immunity. The people here do not."

"I am very sorry, Doctor Jereldene."

"No, Willow, you were right to come. There is medicine here." Doc stood by the stove, trading out towels, her mind spinning. She'd kept the Great Flu out of the valley; she could contain this fever in the four walls of her house and the strength of her own body. First, she needed to get her patients dry, warm, and clean. Maybe spoon a little chicken broth into the woman. "Do you still have breast milk?" she asked. Willow shook her head, no. She needed to get hydration into the boy. Anything that the boy soiled would have to be boiled. Doc peeled wet garments off the shivering girl and set them into a washtub for later. She offered Willow one of her own flannel shirts and a cardigan, pulled off her skirt and stockings, a rough wool weave held up by elastic bands that left a mark on the girl's thighs. She wrapped a warmed blanket firmly around her.

The small boy lay limp under her ministrations. Doc had no fresh clothes for him, and though he may have been toilet-trained, he had little control over anything just now. She made a diaper from a torn summer shirt, tied it to his waist, and threw his little pants into the washing bin, praying for a world where doing the wash would be possible again. She swaddled him in a flannel sheet and put him on the couch. "He needs fluids," she told the young mother. "He's too weak to swallow. I'm going to mix pure water and salt, the same as our blood—and put it in a bag that has a tube and needle." Willow's eyes grew large. "Then I'll put the needle in his arm—it won't hurt—but it will get the water into his body. He is dried out from sweating and fever. This is medicine your grandmother sent you for."

"Is he going to... going to live? Please say yes."

"I think so. You are safe. Your boy is safe. Jesse is in the hands of God." Doc made saline: 1 cup well water, ½-teaspoon salt, boiled for 15 minutes. She set it to cool to room temperature while she rigged the IV stand that she kept in the back closet, opened the sterile bag and needle and searched for a vein in the boy's thin arm. Once it was dripping, she tucked them under her quilt and sat by the stove on the remaining chair. She glanced at the clock. 4:00 a.m. Doc reached for her well-thumbed copy of *Physicians Medica*. She kept an eye on the drip and on the rise and fall of their chests. They were breathing. She was breathing. She prayed Jesse was breathing.

The clock ticked forward in the waning howl of the storm. She began to imagine Leo, an early riser, moving around under the light of the kitchen fixture. If Jesse stumbled home, he might expose the whole family. At 6:00 a.m., she traded out the blankets, cranked the phone and rang two longs for the preacher. He (and probably a few others) picked up the line. "Leo?" The tone was all he needed.

"I can get to you," he said.

"I need some things. And Jesse didn't happen to show up, did he?"

"Jesse?! No… what?" After all these years, she knew how he stood by the phone, one hand on the table steadying himself for news and need.

"I've got company. Bring the sheets we used when the baby came. Some diapers, pins, old towels. I hate to ask you to venture out in this…"

"Wind's down, I can find the road," he said.

She took a deep breath. "Anyone else on the line, listen. I'm going to hunker down with some out-of-town folks who need medical attention. I won't be available for a few days. Counting on everybody, take care of yourselves…"

"And pray for a Chinook," Leo added.

"Reverend," she addressed him formally in these moments, "If you can't make it, I can last out the storm. We don't have back-up in the valley these days, be careful." She and Leo could communicate in code, still she knew this conversation would raise curiosity. Well, Leo could handle that. Her job was rotating blankets, spooning broth into Willow, and offering a milk and honey-soaked rag to the boy to suck. She'd call into Great Falls for a prescription, the plow could bring it out.

When she heard the rumble of the honey truck, Doc dressed in her heaviest jacket, hat, scarf, and could hardly bend over enough to tie her boots. She pulled on leather mitts and stepped onto the porch.

"You can't come in," she intoned as he stepped into nearly two feet of snow, "but come up on the corner out of the wind."

"Oh my, Jere, what's going on?" He carried the bundle of requested goods.

"There's fever among the Shines the Light family. Jesse was driving a young woman and her little boy down for medicine, but his truck stalled. Jesse left them to find help, but the woman got too cold to wait. She walked for miles. Says Gramma Josie guided her. She was near frozen, and her boy is quite sick. Possibly typhoid," she admitted.

"Where's Jesse?" Leo's voice was hoarse with alarm.

She pointed north, "Somewhere out there." They had both seen death this way, the body a frozen curl around a fence post or splayed out in one last step.

"Dear God." He knew the odds, but he was also a father, "There's still a chance."

"Yes, Leo. There's always a chance." She was a doctor, but also an auntie. "The mother got here. The boy is still alive. Jesse will do what he can to survive."

"What else do you need?" his question muffled through the scarf around his face.

"I have a heck of an immune system from doctoring all these years. I got my usual supply of medications, but I'll have to get this boy to the hospital if his fever doesn't break. I'll order antibiotics sent out for him. Not happening until the plow. Keep an eye on the highway for me. Meanwhile, I got coal, food. Gertie has powdered milk, but don't come back until this storm lifts."

"I hate to leave you."

"You need be home for Maire and Flora. Willow said Jesse didn't have fever, but he might be contagious. If he shows up, put him in the honey house." She stomped her feet, "Talk God into letting them live, if you can. They've gone to quite the trouble to try and save themselves."

Leo hadn't turned off the engine, so just backed the truck into what was left of the tracks that got him there and headed down the road. When the phone rang a few minutes later, she began breathing normally again. He'd made it home.

Doc stared out her kitchen window toward the lost tracks of the woman, the stalled truck, the man who ran for help. She furrowed her brow and focused her thoughts like an arrow through the storm. *"Sister Josie,"* she whispered fervently, *"I have them safe. I can get medicine. I think the boy will be okay. Please watch over Jesse."* It was the only kind of letter she could send. No stamp, just trust in the ear of the storm.

19
CHINOOK

END OF JANUARY 1943: *Ending the siege of Stalingrad, Field Marshall Friedrich Paulus surrenders the starving remnant of the German 6th Army to Soviet command, and 91,000 German prisoners disappear into the Soviet gulag.*

AFTER LEO LEFT DOC'S AND DROVE BACK into the frozen, howling morning, he got only to the rise before shock overtook him. He held tight to the steering wheel through thickly padded gloves, gulping air and swallowing panic. He needed to get home and wrap his mind around what he was facing. He backed the truck snug to the honey house and tried to think. Well, stopping the shakes would be a good start.

While his outer layers dripped snow in the entryway, he paced the kitchen. "She wouldn't let me in the house. She's sorting what the fever is. Don't say anything to folks. She's going to quarantine with them. The broth was a good idea."

"Who are they?" Maire held out a mug of tea.

"Blackfeet mother, little child. Doc said Josie's granddaughter. Who they are to Jesse, I don't know, but he risked his life for them."

"And where is Jesse?"

Leo set down the mug and hugged his arms to his chest. "When his old pick-up broke down, he left them to find help. When they couldn't take the cold anymore, she walked too and made it to Doc's, God knows how."

"In this?!" Maire gestured out the window. "I've never seen weather like this, Leo." The whites of her eyes shone like snow behind the blue-grey storm of her irises.

"Yes. In this. Since last night." A whisper of surrender.

Maire slid onto a chair and dropped her forehead into the waiting cup of her hands. She couldn't look up, "So he's dead?"

Her question hit Leo like a punch. "He grew up in storms. He made snow forts and played caveman with his brothers. It's… it's possible he's applying those skills out there." He steadied himself with one hand on the back of her chair, and she reached round and grabbed hold.

"Shouldn't we pray then, Leo? It'd help me."

Leo bowed his head, "Dear Lord of many concerns, look down on us in this storm. Please watch over my son—your son—Jesse Cooper. Spare his life if you can."

"And the bees," Maire whispered.

"And the bees," Leo intoned, "bring the hives through the winter, and the flowers back in spring. Bring the beekeepers together again that we might steward your bountiful creation." He felt the interior inspiration began streaming through him. "Keep Jereldene strong and healthy. May the woman and child recover and not bring contagion. Watch over all who live in this valley, and all who have left it. Watch over the reservation and the Shines the Light family that all may be well. Into your hands…"

"Say amen," Maire interjected, "Flora's crying." She rose to tend the baby.

Leo slumped onto her chair, seat still warm, bowed his head to his hands. "In your mercy and understanding of Fatherhood, grant me another chance to be the father my sons need. Heal the grief-stricken regions of my heart. Help me serve my people. Uphold me. Guide me. That's the gist of it, Lord." Under the table, Preacher Boy laid his head on Leo's foot. "Amen."

Leo stared out the snow-whirled windows. He felt the storm whipping away all the distractions of daily life until there remained in him only a single focus. The hand of his love reached into the blizzard, searching, searching. He felt drawn toward faint heat, body warmth, a small flame. He pushed back from the table, grabbed his damp coat, hat, gloves, scarf. Maire's voice urgent behind him, "You not be going out?"

"Getting the truck ready," he was pulling on galoshes. "Soon as the storm breaks, I'll start the search." He felt on fire, possessed, determined to wrestle Jesse's death from the hands of fate.

"What shall I do?" Maire cradled the babe.

"Keep the fire up. Make soup and pasties." He pushed the door hard to latching and leaned into the storm as the shrouded truck took shape ahead of him.

As Willow's feet thawed, she retreated to an inner reserve, her body stilled. "You are truly a warrior," Doc said. The woman sipped broth and nibbled bits of soaked bread, cradled, and kissed her fevered child, singing softly in Indian talk. Wind chewed the corners of the cabin. Windows glazed thick with frosted steam from boiling water. The boy had stabilized with hydration and made it through the hardest hours. The three of them dozed in synchronicity, Doc jumping awake whenever her patients stirred. She called into Great Falls Hospital, ordered medicine. She counted hours, counted days. It had been Monday midnight when they arrived. Tuesday morning when Leo brought supplies. Tuesday night the boy let out a sharp cry, his body jerking as the fever broke. He lay weak in his mother's arms, but Wednesday morning his eyes held focus as he looked around. The storm began to soften. They needed medicine and more chicken broth. They needed clothing. They needed deep sleep. They needed Jesse. And Jesse needed a miracle.

The miracle came in hot breath. Chinook wind blowing down from the mountains. From nearly zero, in an hour it was balmy, and by noon the thermometer read fifty degrees. The snow, knee-deep in the yard, crystalized under the eye of the Sun, evaporating before Doc's eyes. Melting water ran desperate for a ditch. The Chinook exposed snow-bent grasses to the cattle's lips, thawed the water holes, gave everyone a chance to finish tasks the storm had stalled. Would give Leo a chance to organize the search for Jesse.

Willow sat on the porch in Doc's shirt and sweater and a pair of pants likely to fall off if she stood too fast. She held the boy, double-wrapped in one of Doc's flannel shirts and fed her son bits of bread soaked in broth. "Our people call this wind *si'kssopo*." The little boy tilted his face toward sunshine while his mother spoke a soft story in his ear. "Water is life. Snow is frozen water. Rain is wet water. See there, that shining," she pointed to rising steam, "That is spirit water. Nothing is lost, everything changes."

Two tears rolled down her cheeks. The boy, called Natoyii in Blackfeet, and Drum in English, poked his small finger at the trail of tiny droplets. "Water," he said solemnly.

She took his fingers into her hands and kissed the tips. "Listen, my son. In the beginning, before the world, everything was water. Napi, the Old Man, sent down four animals to find out what was beneath the water. First went the duck…"

"Quack, quack," said Natoyii.

"Yes. And then went the otter and the badger. They didn't come up with anything. So finally, Napi sent the muskrat who dived so deep he came back with mud on his paws."

"Dirty feets," he nodded seriously.

"Napi blew his breath of life into the little lump of mud." Willow cupped her hands around her son's small hands and blew on them. The boy smiled. "And from this mud, Napi made mountains and rivers. He made the grasslands where we live. He made all the trees and the food plants, the animals, and birds… and then he made us, the Amskapi Piikuni, from water and mud."

"Quack, quack." The boy rested his head on his mother's breasts. She sniffed his hair and held him close. He touched her tears again. "Na'á, where is my ninna?"

Doc opened every door and window to air out the cabin. She had prayed for this wind; it had come. She had asked for a day to do laundry, and the sun shined warm. Doc put on a surgery mask and gloves, gathered the fetid bedding and clothes. She poured boiling water into a galvanized washtub, added soap powder, and stirred it with a broom handle until it had cooled enough to plunge her hands into the scalded laundry. She knocked tiny icicles off the clothesline and hung little boy pants and shirt, socks, a woman's skirt and shirt, stockings, towels, and sheets to flap in the Chinook wind. Busy, busy, busy, but every breath echoed in her ears: Jesse, Jesse, Jesse. She aired blankets along the corral railing, cooking out contagion in the weakened beams of winter daylight. And finally, mid-afternoon, she sat on the front steps sipping watered-down coffee marveling at the metamorphosis around them. Then she saw the honey truck fishtailing on the mud-slick field roads.

Willow stood on aching feet and began luluing, a haunting treble cry like birdsong, used for celebration and welcome. Doc stood at the base of her steps willing herself to steadiness.

Leo had strapped hive boxes over the back axle for traction and made a pad of straw in the center, that he covered with canvas held at the corners with additional super frames. He eased the truck to a halt, stepped from the cab looking worn, but at peace. He gestured toward the flatbed with a tip of his head. The truck engine was shivering down like a horse at the end of a race. A body rolled in a blanket was laid flat atop the canvas. Doc thought she saw a twitch. She gasped. A hand emerged from the woolen cocoon and pulled down the edge that shrouded its face. He raised himself on one elbow. "Jesse!"

Leo was leaning against the cab door, tears streaming down his face. "Found him, Jereldene," he choked out, "In a cave he thought I didn't know about. He must've crawled more'n a mile."

Willow handed her boy to Doc as she ran past. Hitching up the pant legs of her borrowed clothes, she leapt nimbly onto the truck bed, cradling Jesse's head, covering his face with kisses. Comprehension hit Doc full in the heart. She carried the squirming boy toward his parents, "Ninna, papa!" and set him on the flatbed.

Jesse's eyes searched for hers. "My leg's broke, Doc. Can you fix me?" He managed a weak smile. "Pa, Auntie, this here's my wife, Willow, and this is our son, Drummond Natoyii isttookimaa Shines the Light Cooper." Jesse shifted and a line of pain sweat broke out on his brow. "Hurts, Doc. I rigged a splint."

"Ninna has owie?"

Willow took Natoyii's face in her hands. "Can you sit quietly? No wiggling?" He nodded solemnly. "We will move Ninna into the house and the doctor will make him better. You understand?"

Natoyii nodded again. "I has him." Little hands held Jesse's cheeks.

"Atta boy, Drummie," Jesse tried to smile.

Doc took Leo by the shoulders, each of them swaying in relief. He leaned into her grasp, pulled a bandana out of his pocket, and tied it bandit-style over his nose. Jesse was alive, safe, fixable. She squeezed Leo's shoulders. "I'll get kitchen table medicine ready to serve."

Alone in the cabin, Doc took a few breaths, dizzy with relief. She folded a freshened blanket to provide cushioning over the planked boards, then laid oilcloth over one end and prepped for cast-making: stockinette, cotton padding, plaster rolls, scissors. She fetched crutches from her supply closet and adjusted them for Jesse's height. She was the doctor. She knew what to do. She stepped onto the porch, ready for her patient. "Leo, I ordered a prescription for Drum. Once Jesse's off-loaded can you fetch it from Gertie?"

Jesse slid carefully to the edge of the truck bed. Doc handed him the crutches and braced him as he hobbled up the porch steps. Willow scooped her boy, brushed Leo's hand, "Thank you, father of my husband."

Jesse sat on the table edge and let the women take off his jacket and shirt and replace them with one of Doc's sweaters. Willow pressed her nose to his hair. "You made fire." He bit his lip hard as the women swung his legs and laid him out. Drummond Natoyii slid under the table and went still.

The splint was old newspapers dated 1935, wrapped in rotted string. "Where were you?" Doc asked, "These weren't blowing around some fencepost."

He grunted his story through pain, "I left the highway to drive the honey route, save time. Gas almost empty. Wind gettin' worse. Willow weak, Drummie, oh my God, he was near to dying, wasn't he?" Doc nodded. "But then the truck broke." His eyes were wild.

Doc cut his jeans above the knee, then cut off the legging of long underwear. The break poked under the skin, diaphysis fracture of the tibia. "I tied a red bandana on the antenna. If the truck drifted in maybe they'd be warmer, like a snow cave."

"Snow burying us," Willow whispered. "Natoyii was a hot ember barely breathing. I heard Grandmother's voice."

"The grid disappeared. I could see Crown Butte and aimed for it."

Willow petted Natoyii's head. "The ancestors were with us."

Doc focused on the break. "Jesse, I need to stretch your leg, get the bone realigned. It's going to hurt."

His eyes locked onto hers. "I shouldn't have risked us." His voice was cracking fear. "Instead of saving my woman and child, I was near killing them." Dry sobs began to wrack his body.

Doc pressed her hand on Jesse's sternum. "You're going into shock, Jess."

He was deep in story. "I was spinning in every direction. I was going to die. Willow and Drum were going to die. And now we were separated. No way forward, no way back." He grabbed her hand so hard Doc's arthritis screamed in her knuckles. "I decided to let the storm take me. Never have to face the shame." He gulped air.

"Hold on, son. Breathe into your belly. Willow, I need your help. Put your arms under his armpits, clasp your hands on his chest. Good." Doc moved to the foot of the table and wrapped a canvas strap around Jesse's ankle, below the break. Pain would send him over the line or jolt him back. Either way, Doc had to set the leg.

"Willow, hold him no matter how hard I pull, understand?" She didn't want to give either of them much time to think about her instructions, "Ready? One-two-three…" Willow braced. Doc pulled. Jesse screamed. Drum cried out. The lump in Jesse's shin smoothed under the skin. Doc felt up the length of the bone and Jesse screamed one more time when she fingered the break. Near as she could tell, the bone had found itself like two puzzle pieces snapped back into place. "We got it first try." She smiled into his eyes. "That was the worst of it, Jess."

Jesse kissed Willow's hand. "That's nowhere near the worst of it." Willow wiped his face with a damp washcloth. Doc slipped the stockinette gently as she could up his shin, padded the foot into a right angle, and prepared to plaster the leg from toes to above the knee. "I was singing my death song, begging forgiveness from all my relations. I shouted at the storm to take me," he took a deeper breath. "I fell. Hit something hard. Post or rock. Face in the snow, eating ice crystals. But then the wind started to talk. '*Get up!*' it whispered. '*Get up and be a man.*' It sounded like a snake made of snow. It said, '*You do not decide who lives, who dies.*' Pain awful. Cold helped. I dragged my leg.

The Beekeeper's Question

Crawled. I heard my horse whinnying. I heard my father praying to Jesus. I heard Willow singing the old songs. I don't know how I got to the butte, Auntie Jere, but there's a slit cave where Frankie and me, Tim and Ralph used to hide out and pretend we were stagecoach robbers." The cast was nearly finished. "We always kept a mason jar with matches and candle stubs and a pile of cottonwood twigs. I decided to wait out the storm. If Willow was dead, then I'd come back to the cave and join her, no matter what the wind said. If she lived, well then, me too." Willow kissed Jesse's forehead.

Doc had plaster of Paris smeared in her hair. "You got two families Jesse." The truth of it thumped in her chest. "You got two roads to walk." The challenges knotted her stomach. "You're gonna need two good legs." Twenty minutes later, Jesse was in bed, his hardening cast propped on a pillow. Willow was curled next to him, and Drum had wriggled into the space between. Doc stood in the doorway and wiped silent tears from her cheeks. Now she had time for relief.

Leo arrived with medicine, linens, clothes. "An attic is a marvelous thing," he smiled. "Remember how we scolded Charlotte for saving everything?" The smell of hot pasties rose from a folded towel. They ate, sitting on the porch steps, staring in parallel at the familiar contours of the vista. Leo spoke in a hush, "Some things, Jereldene, are so full of God they're beyond prayer, even for an old pray-er like me. How that happened. How they lived. Who has arrived."

20
Sermon in the Valley

FEBRUARY 1943: *Shoe rationing is announced. Guadalcanal is secured, the first American victory in the Pacific. Rommel launches a counterattack in western Tunisia. The Battle of the Kasserine Pass begins.*

OF COURSE, WINTER RETURNED. Chinook-softened ground froze in ruts that would make driving the back roads a spine-tingling experience until next thaw. And Doc's three-room settler's cabin was suddenly housing a restless man on crutches, a shy Native woman unaccustomed to cross-cultural housekeeping, and a two-and-a-half-year-old boy recovering his spunk and curiosity. After a week of sleeping on the sofa, Doc released her self-imposed quarantine and on a sunny afternoon, put on her coat and galoshes and hiked to Cooper's.

She found Leo in the attic prying loose the plywood vent cover with a crowbar. "Seems we might need more space around here," he grunted.

Doc leaned against the doorjamb. "Folks need you to talk to 'em, Leo."

A final prying and a whoosh of warm air rose through the grate from the coal stove positioned below. "Hard to write a sermon when I'm in shock myself." Leo sat with a thump on one bed. "When I plucked Jesse out of the cave, my heart was so blasted open it felt biblical, like God the Father was helping me save my son. I'm weeping in the truck cab, driving so carefully with him strapped down, the Chinook wind blowing resurrection over us... well, you saw."

"I thought you were bringing me his body." Doc sat on the other bed.

"Didn't mean to scare you. Then the woman is wailing, and she runs to him and then she's his wife, and there's a child whose half-Cooper and half-Blackfeet. Jesse hobbled into your house, and I haven't seen him since." Leo seemed near to tearing again. "Meanwhile, I'm up here wrestling a crowbar trying to make space in the attic, in the valley... and in my own heart." Leo sighed. "I just wanted him to come home, take on the bees. An Indian wife and child sure complicate things. I'm scared about it, Jere."

"Hard to trust human nature these days," Doc reached for Leo's gnarled hand. "When the world's uncertain, folks teeter back and forth between their good selves and their not-so-good selves. You're always pondering how the community can behave more like a beehive, so, call us to our best bee-havior." They pulled each other to standing.

Cars lurched over the ruts in the church parking lot as parishioners hurried against the cold, careful on the ice. Leo slid song numbers on the hymn board. "Don't suppose folks coming just because of Valentine's Day."

"'Suppose not." Doc bounced Flora on her shoulder. "Maire took the car to see if Jesse will come."

At 10:00 a.m., Homer Torgerson rang the steeple bell and limped into a middle pew alongside his wife, Mildred, and daughter, Susan. Everyone kept coats on as the church stayed chilly. Doc tucked Flora inside her jacket and hoped the warmth would lull the babe to rest. Gladys pounded out the first hymn and the service began. Leo had chosen specific texts.

Reading from the Old Testament: Book of Ruth 1: 15-20. And the people said, "Thanks be to God."

Reading from the Gospel: Luke 15: 11-32. And the people said, "Word of the Lord."

Standing in back, Doc cradled Flora's sleepy head on her shoulder. Besides Torgersons, she noted Gertie, Hazel, and the Pockets, three generations of Sivertsens, and several dozen outlying farm families she catalogued by ills and accidents from decades of doctoring.

Leo cleared his throat. "I address you this morning as both your pastor and as a father. And isn't that how God speaks to us? We pray 'Our Father who art in heaven…' Not Commander, not President or Prime Minister, but Father. The scripture readings this morning of Ruth and her mother-in-law, Naomi, and Jesus's parable of the prodigal son, are stories of families who redefine their understanding of welcome and belonging. This is my journey of the past year." People shifted in their seats. "Last spring, Franklin's bride needed a haven to have their child and live out the war. She came here trusting that I, and we, would welcome her. I was surprised, discomforted, but now see God's design in bringing Maire into our family.

"And she will not be the only newcomer to arrive from this war. Somewhere in the Pacific, Ralph Pocket, Albert and Ronnie Torgerson are telling their buddies how beautiful our valley is, making this place sound like heaven on earth to the war-torn and weary. Likely we will get to meet some of those boys and their families. But it's not the landscape that makes our valley heavenly. It's you and me and our willingness to welcome." Homer twitched.

"After Mrs. Cooper died, a family of males did not know how to grieve. I was hard on my boys when they needed me tender. Jesse ran away. He was welcomed into a Blackfeet family with long ties to this valley. He finished his schooling on the reservation. He made friends, worked cattle, fell in love, married, and has a son.

"I know intermarriage is hard for some to accept, but the Old Testament is full of intermarrying. The whole territory of the Bible is smaller by half than the state of Montana. The land was crowded with differing tribes, small nation states, territories held by one group and then another. They fought. And sometimes, they loved. In all this history, the Judaic code does not forbid or defame intermarriage. I am asking, in the name of God, that we do the same." A few grunts and grumbles floated over the crowd. "Ruth was a Moab woman married to an Israelite man. When he died, she returned to Bethlehem with her mother-in-law and vowed, 'whither thou goest I will go, and thy people will be my people.' This is Jesse's vow to his wife, Willow, and Willow's vow to Jesse. This is Franklin's vow to Maire and Maire's vow to Franklin."

Leo took a deep breath. "My sons challenge me to expand my heart, and I want to meet that challenge with open arms in this pulpit and in my own parlor. For Jesus said, 'I was hungry and you gave me food, thirsty and you gave me drink, I was a stranger and you welcomed me.' As a community of faith, I believe we can find room in our hearts to welcome the stranger. I am learning with you. In the Name of the Father, Son, and Holy Spirit, let us begin." That was it, then, Doc exhaled. His holy ask.

Flora was whiffling hot baby breaths against her neck while Doc kept watch on the crowd. A chill of air and a hand on her back, Doc turned to meet Maire's tear-stained face. "I was listening behind the drape. I'm sorry Jesse wasn't here…"

"It's a big request. Folks need thinking time." Gladys lit into the piano. Leo walked down the aisle. When he came alongside the two women, he turned and offered the benediction. "The Lord bless you and keep you; the Lord make His face to shine upon you and be gracious unto you; the Lord lift His countenance upon you and give you peace." The people stood and stretched. He tied back the blanket so folks could exit. "Well, Jere?"

"Exactly what we needed, Leo."

Ten pews forward, Doc overheard Homer complain, "Preacher shouldn't even speak the names of our sons alongside his sons." Torgersons slipped out without a pastoral handshake.

Their first family dinner was pot roast and potatoes. The little boy pushed one of Jesse's old toy trucks across the patterns of the parlor rug. With shyness and beginning, the young mothers did dishes; father and son bent their heads to the radio news. Leo drove the family home and came round the front of the house to find Doc wrapped in a blanket, rocking in the cold, grey light of late afternoon. "What's the matter, Jere?"

"I got no place to rest my thoughts… or my body." She turned her face into the shadows. "What you said this morning about God not condemning intermarriage. I think it can work in hearts that are reachable. At least for Jesse and Willow, but with a Japanese wife, Boyd can never come home." A racking sound traveled up her torso and she bent over the blanket. "I poured everything into him, hoping he'd take over. When we got the wedding announcement, I locked myself in the cabin and cried for two days. Pearl Harbor sealed their fate."

Leo settled himself on the other rocker. "I'm sorry, Jere. I know he was your dream."

"Gertie tacked a world map on the post office wall. She's poking pins in the locations of our enlisted. When I said Boyd was serving in the internment camps, she actually asked if he was spying for the U.S. or the Japs. What's going to happen to all this hate the day after victory?"

"There's a lot of mixed blood in the West, but I don't have a sermon strong enough to make Boyd's marriage acceptable after this war." Leo rocked nervously. "What's going to happen when we find out how bad it's really been?"

"We're not saints. Locking up Japanese citizens, burning crosses on the lawns of German families." She sighed deeply.

The Beekeeper's Question

"What we can do is hold steady, stay strong, do a little good every day." He pushed himself to standing. "Go get your toothbrush, Jere, come stay with us. The attic's toasty. The baby's a great distraction. We'll figure it out."

Sunday 14 February 1943
Dear Franklin,

I'm writing from bed, wee Flora asleep. I don't know where you are. I don't know how you are. I keep writing in hope you get my letters, or that someday you will get a whole stack of them, and maybe I'll get a stack from you.

Big news—Jesse returned a few weeks ago in the middle of a blizzard because he needed to get his Indian (!) wife (!!) and little boy (!!!) to Doc to cure fever. He also got a broken-down truck and a broken leg. They are staying at Doc's cabin. Doc is moving into the attic. Your Pa gave a powerful sermon saying God didn't care if the Hebrews intermarried. You are sure missing a lot being so far away.
Love, Moy

21
Sidi Bou Zid

MID-FEBRUARY 1943: The Allies advance into Tunisia
where German troops, defending supply ports,
are dug in and waiting for them.

THE SHADOWED LINE OF THE ATLAS MOUNTAINS rode like epaulets on the right shoulder of the 34th U.S. Infantry and Armored Division as they trudged across the edge of the great Sahara. Franklin hunched over his equipment in the jolting bucket of the Jeep: field switchboard, field handset units, spools of wire, radios. Anytime they reached a stable position, the spool runner would heft on his pack, start feeding wire. Sometimes they could splice into telephone lines the French had strung across the territory. Sometimes they had to plant their own poles, twenty-foot construction beams leaning out of the desert like the tower of Pisa. Dig in, hold the line, do the fight, dig it out. In forward battle, Franklin and everyone else resorted to radio, though transmissions were vulnerable. Germans listened to the Allies; the Allies listened back. Signal Corps' intercept units were college men who spoke educated French, Italian, German. They translated, out of harm's way. Franklin and Tommy were front-line infantry.

Christopher Cranston, business major from Iowa State, a "40-day Wonder" who had completed advanced training as a forward observer officer with the 82nd Armored Reconnaissance Battalion, had been assigned to their platoon. Code name: Cyclone, the school team. Corporal Thompson rolled his eyes. Cyclone was overly bossy, nervous, and four years younger. "Awfully early in the war to be raising puppies," he grumbled to Franklin, "but then, none of us been battle-tested yet, 'less you count our unfortunate sheep."

Franklin laughed but rubbed his ribs; still a catch in his breath from the boots of Broin Mulvaney. He sure hoped that bastard was dead. Training in sheep pastures and his Belfast desk job seemed another life.

"Making headway" in the Algerian backcountry meant swerving around potholes, artillery craters, and trudging soldiers. And if the lead vehicle, its driver blinded by mud-smeared windshield, veered too much to one side, the truck behind would follow it into the mire which meant winching and shoving, men slipping dangerously around spinning wheels. Sweat-wet at the skin, rain-wet at the surface, mud-covered troops marching another day. The real grind of warfare was between battles: endurance without adrenaline.

Now and then a town rose mirage-like out of the horizon, appearing and disappearing in the undulating hills until they eventually came upon it. Crumbling adobe buildings, people ragged with poverty under the heels of war. Refugee families with bundles on their backs or pulling handcarts or prodding camels, threaded through the convoy heading west while the Army headed east toward Tunisia.

"What's the buzz, Bee Man?" Tommy was honking at three goats and a tattered boy blocking the road. "Locals know something we don't?"

"Command's pretty hush, but I've seen the map. There's mountains running north-south, a town, Sidi bou Zid, a couple of highpoint hills, outcroppings, and a pass that cuts through.

Whoever controls the pass controls the supply stream coming from Bizerte and Tunis, ports currently in German control."

"Guessing that's our fight then." Thompson thumped the steering wheel.

> February 2, 1943
> Dear Maire,
> Army didn't outfit us for this much cold and rain. We camp a few days, move forward. Last platoon out shovels over the latrines. Bored. Tired. Muddy mess. Always tense. Germans like surprise attacks. I have the radio, field telephones, Thompson and the Jeep.
> I'm reading a book called <u>In Barbary</u> about the people here. Old men smoke hookahs (water pipes), children beg, women hide. They sell anything—black market stuff, tiny cups of thick coffee, real eggs, dates, almonds, their sisters. This is the backside of war. Keep writing, your letters put good pictures in my head before I sleep. Got your Christmas note. Ralph made it home, that's great.
> Love, Frank

He licked the envelope. The glue tasted of dissatisfaction. He had no words for the malaise that hung over him as weary as weather. Malaise was not good for a soldier. Malaise led to not caring. Not caring led to not getting through. He counted on Thompson's endless yackety-yack to keep him tethered, like laying wire for the field phone.

"High school football, I had one job, cut a path through the line for the boy with the ball. He scored, but I got him there. You got the equipment. I'm your offensive guard. This is scrimmage, Bee Man, but you and me are heading to the big game. Gonna be a helluva season, then playoffs and we take the trophy home!" Thompson gunned the engine, "See our ladies. Make more babies." He let out a whoop.

Franklin laughed, "You, Corporal Thompson, are wasted in Iowa. After the war, come to Montana, trade pigs and corn for cattle and wheat. My brother Jesse's a cowboy, he'll show you the ropes."

Thompson was quiet longer than Franklin expected. "I just might," he shouted into the rain. "Give Bev something to think over, 'sides worryin'. Never thought to leave the farm, but then I never thought I'd be cruising alongside the Sahara. Before this is done, we'll be driving the Appian Way."

"Rome? How you figure?" Franklin was startled.

Thompson gestured into open space. "Brits gonna hold Egypt, guard the Suez Canal. Americans gonna use Tunisia to take Sicily, use Sicily to take Italy, use Italy to kick the ass off the Third Reich." He grinned, proud of his military strategy.

February 7, 1943
Dear Maire,

When I said I wanted to be part of history, nobody mentioned that in the middle of it you got no idea what's really happening. Scholars will write about this war. And when I am an old man, I will read how other old men made sense of it. Right now, I'm hiding behind a bush with field equipment or sleeping under my rain poncho in the same clothes I've worn for weeks. There are skirmishes, moments of terror, that churn up mud and blood—but not mine. I'm keeping my head down. Your broody man, Franklin

PS: Almond orchards blossoming. Go figure.

The U.S. Army's hike across North Africa, from Christmas to Valentine's Day, repositioning troops to take on the Reich's Afrika Korps, was referred to by Command as "military inaction." But for the foot soldiers, every day was hard labor in a harsh land. Cold, coughing, hungry, thirsty, bad food, tinny water. Bigger battles ahead. Soon.

Dear Moy,

Cold. Raining. I don't know what to write. When sun comes out, Arab men show up and guys trade a pack of Camel cigarettes to ride a real camel. LIFE photographer takes photos. Relax America, war is Boy Scout camp.

The Army resorted to mule trains to supply advancing troops. "Great idea," Thompson scoffed. "Livestock gotta be grazed and watered and they shit on the trail." Thirty thousand men tried to keep boots on, socks dry, weapons cleaned, while the desert turned to grime and slime. Battalions scattered, picked off by German mortar fire, harassed by Stukas. Command in disarray behind the scenes, ordered troops one way and another, spread men and artillery thin across miles of desert scrub. Ambushed on open terrain, terrified and untried men, sometimes a third of them without even a rifle, scooped shallow foxholes with their helmets. Swore or prayed or both.

~~Dear Moy, I don't know what to write. Scared boys tape the New Testament over their hearts, praying Jesus will stop a bullet. The Germans are vicious and trained.~~

Franklin tossed a trail of crumpled paragraphs in one ditch after another. It stopped raining. Wind started blowing. Dust blinded them to how close they were to all hell breaking loose.

~~Dear Moy, I don't know what to write. I don't want you to see what I see or know what I know.~~

Sunday, February 14th, 1943: At 4 a.m., under the cover of a howling windstorm, elements of the 10th Panzer and 21st Panzer Divisions under Generals von Arnim and Ziegler, attack Allied forces near Sidi Bou Zid and Bir el Hafey. At 6:30 they obliterate Company G of the 1ˢᵗ Armored Regiment. At 7:30 a squadron battalion of U.S. Sherman tanks is destroyed. One after another, units fall in the first major clash between American and German armies.

Sixty-ton Panzers lumbered like elephants down the only roadway. The impenetrable German tanks, armed with 88mm cannons, slammed armor-piercing rounds into the Shermans whose smaller cannons couldn't stop the onslaught. Inside their metal boxes, cooked-off ammunition ignited infernos. The ground shook. The men shook. The deafening battle fueled terror.

Machine-gun fire exploded from invisible positions, mowing down men as they scrambled for cover in a terrain that did not provide it. Tommy and Franklin were hunched in the Jeep behind an overturned transport vehicle with Lieutenant Cyclone. Peering through field glasses with his map shaking in his hand, the untried officer worked to make sense of the hellish scene. "Radio Command. Tell them we're getting creamed," he yelled at Franklin over the deafening ratatat of artillery fire. Franklin thumbed the press-to-talk lever on the SCR 536 field radio. He looked to the lieutenant for coordinates. The radio sputtered with static. Franklin pressed his ear hard against the headset, communications in chaos.

"This is Sierra Charlie Cyclone two niner foxtrot. We are taking heavy fire! Stand by for target coordinates. Over." Shouting left grit on Franklin's teeth. Winter silt, blowing toward the Mediterranean.

Using compass and map, the lieutenant marked their position with his grease pencil and estimated the source of the machine gun fire. He grabbed the radio from Franklin's hand. "This is Sierra Charlie Cyclone two niner foxtrot." A pause. "Affirmative! Now, give me one round and stand by to adjust for fire," he barked the eight-digit target coordinates. They waited. Nothing. "Do you read me?" The lieutenant was shouting.

Paused for reply. A tinny tone drilled through the headset. Cyclone handed the set back to Franklin. His face was ashen. "They're not in position. No cover. We're fucked." He scanned the chaos enveloping them. "This isn't battle, it's a rout." A shell rocked ground near their position.

Thompson shouted into the roar, "There's men behind that burned-out tank. They need leadership, sir."

The lieutenant took a long breath, seemed to gather himself, turned to Franklin, "Cooper, come with me. Corporal, get the Jeep outta here. It gets hit, we're a fireball."

A range of expressions crossed Thompson's face. "I'm his driver, sir."

"I need the radio by me. I need you to run recon, assess and report to someone in command."

"Yessir." Another round of artillery landed nearby. Franklin grabbed his rifle, pack, and radio and hit the ground. He felt like a snail that had just lost its shell.

"Live to fight another day, buddy." Thompson turned the Jeep and began swerving through the end of the world.

Lt. Cyclone and his radio man crouch-shuffled over to the bedraggled cluster of sand-blown soldiers. "What's our mission, sir?"

"Get to cover. Survive to nightfall." To Franklin, he added, "Monitor talk, get us a plan."

The German battle plan, personally approved by Hitler, was to counterthrust through the passes, penetrate to the northwest, disrupt the Allied rear. Facing the Germans were fragmented and untested units of the 1st Armored Division, stretched thin along a 60-mile front. Quickly marooned, radio frequencies unsynchronized, American forces descended into chaos.

A hundred-yard dash, zigzagging to avoid fire, Cyclone led his straggly group to a bit of high ground, boulders and

The Beekeeper's Question

brush. They hunkered down, rifles at hand and lived the day. Others did not. Twenty-yard line, men screamed for help, then whimpered, prayed, fell silent. German patrols moved among the burning tanks and smoldering debris, executing anyone left alive. Pistol shots, one to the head, over and over. Cyclone sat with his back to a boulder and commanded. "Do not move, do not shoot… they figure we're here, we all die." The Germans kicked over bodies, stripping guns, ammunition, shoes. Rag-tag locals fingered through pockets, mining trinkets for the black market.

Franklin was shaking with rage. He remembered Tommy yelling at him to toughen up. This was toughening: His finger on the rifle trigger, aimed, but holding fire, the guttural shouts, their disrespect and pillage. Around him, men muttered strings of expletives, twitchy with tension. Wanting revenge, wanting not to be the next body picked over by enemy hands. "Please, God, get me through this," Franklin prayed. Every hour he turned on the radio, reported in. Down the line, one order, "Maintain the mission." What the hell? Franklin imagined high-ranking officers holed up in some Tunisian farmhouse miles behind lines, clean shaven—hell, just clean!—fresh uniforms, trying not to spill hot coffee on their maps while they squinted over a game plan that did not jibe with the carnage and chaos playing out before him.

Cyclone kept scanning west. "Jerries took the day, but we'll get back in the fight, you'll see." Bold words, but his voice was strained and hoarse. Franklin swallowed bile and a dozen questions. The air wafted acrid bands of burning fuel, rubber, molten metal, dead men. It hurt to breathe.

"Cover of darkness, we get to those rocks, hook up with other units. Ration your food and water. Sleep. We move out at 0200." The lieutenant hunched down, pleaded hoarsely into Franklin's ear, "Cooper, for crissakes, get me some orders."

What do you do on what may be the last night of your life? Not sleep, Franklin discovered. A slop bucket of extraneous memories kicked over in his mind. He replayed the scene at the kitchen table when he told his father he'd enlisted and wondered now if the look on Leo's face, which Franklin had interpreted as disappointment, was maybe fear, even love, for a son he did not want to imagine in harm's way. Well, he was in harm's way now.

At 2320 hours, Lt. Col. James D. Alger arrived at a Tunisian farmhouse miles behind the line where Combat Command, with no account of German strength, was preparing a counterattack to rescue their infantry. At 0330, two reconnaissance lieutenants, driven by Cpl. Tommy Thompson, made a firsthand battle report: field situation desperate.

Monday, February 15, 0200, the lieutenant roused his men. One kick, boot to boot; he didn't want to get shot. Litany of mumbled swearing. They packed gear, pissed from a full squat. Some apocryphal private, the story went, had stood up to pee and been cut in half by machine gun fire. Franklin hefted his gear with the radio, front sling. The lieutenant gave the signal, Franklin staggered from shadow to shadow, keeping out of moonlight, not casting a silhouette. Spotty gunfire.

The day dawned dry and sunny. Lieutenant Cyclone braced his elbows on a boulder, assessing the scene through field glasses. The two hills, Djebel Ksaira on the horizon and Djebel Lessouda to their left, overlooked the lone ribbon of Highway 13. Midday, a column of tanks, tank destroyers, and infantry in trucks and half-tracks, lumbered in from the north. "U.S. battalions." Cyclone squinted through his binoculars. "Scott assault guns. Mounted artillery. Tank destroyer platoon. Shermans. Great formation, right outta the book." A truck-mounted radio blared "Stars and Stripes Forever."

Franklin sat hunched with the radio. "Orders, sir. All outlying infantry to fall in with the troop force, sir." He had barely relayed the message when twenty Stukas swept out of the eastern sky and strafed the advancing battalion. The textbook formation began to break apart. "Goddamn it!" The men ducked deeper into their sparse cover.

"They're okay. Heading toward Sidi bou Zid," the lieutenant nodded. Tanks rolled over freshly plowed fields. Advancing artillery units took out German machine gun emplacements. A half-dozen explosions popped smoke into the clear air. "Finally, we're on offense." He lowered his glasses, turned to his men. "Get ready to join the band," he was humming along with the sound truck.

"Scrimmage," Franklin whispered to himself. Where was Tommy? And well, German ground forces? That question soon answered.

At 1500 a flare soared over Sidi bou Zid. Upon signal, enemy artillery turned full force on the advancing American guns. An ammunition carrier took a hit, detonated, flames leaping, black smoke, shells exploding skyward in crazy spirals. The counterattack was falling apart, along with any sense that isolated units had a rallying point. Lieutenant Cyclone was speechless. Below them, tanks blew, men scrambled, fell to fire. No wind, twenty-seven columns of heavy black smoke—burning tanks. The U.S. Army, ambushed.

"Get down, sir!" Franklin jerked his officer's pant leg.

"We can't stay here. They'll pick us off." The lieutenant spun in place. "Follow me, men!" He jumped over a hump of stone and aimed himself toward the Stars and Stripes Forever. Three men followed; three hesitated. Franklin clutched his radio. Equipment? Rifle? Seconds that saved his life. Young Christopher Cranston, destined for third generation management of Dubuque's finest hardware store, codename Cyclone, took a machine gun round that splattered Franklin Cooper, the beekeeper's son, with the bloodied bits of his CO. *Piff, piff, piff.* Bullets skidded into sand. A man screamed in pain, another grunted last breath. Franklin heard Maire's commandment howling in his bones, "Dinna raise your head, broody man!" He bowed his helmet toward incoming fire. Laid low.

The battle raged until nightfall. Franklin wiped bloody smear off Cyclone's field glasses and watched the mayhem. He and other stragglers winced again and again at shells screaming overhead, and the deep pop of the Shermans exploding into fireballs. Tank crews often fried inside, but every now and then flaming uniformed flesh leapt out of the turret or scrambled out the bottom hatch, dropped and rolled, trying to suffocate the torch he had become. Stukas screamed across the sky, dive-bombed their artillery, the convoy, the crossroads. He shouted skyward, "Where the fuck are the Warhawks!" His finger on the rifle trigger was numb and cramped. He was out of range, low on ammo, saving his shots. His radio was dead. He and Tommy had no idea if the other was still alive. He gulped back something that might have been sobs; he couldn't spare the water. It had never occurred to Franklin that America could lose—a battle, territory, the war. It occurred to him now. All he wanted was to go home. He would walk it if he had to. He would swim for the far shore of peace. Come nightfall, he would crawl toward what he hoped was an American line.

Without food or water, he had one night to make it. Tongue swollen in his mouth, parched was a sensation that ran all the way to his gut. He hadn't peed or shit for a day, his body saving everything for this last effort at staying alive. He crawled through a wadi, an open scrub grass trench, prayed the scuffling of other men was friendly, prayed they were out of range and heading in the right direction.

Dawn rose fierce on the eastern horizon. Running for brush and cover. Thousands of them. Bugs on the desert's skin. "History in the making." A faint image of Maire floated in his mind. He thought he smelled honey.

The Beekeeper's Question

~~February 17, 1943~~
~~Dear Moy,~~
~~I'm alive.~~
~~War is hell.~~
~~I can't find Tommy.~~

    Late. Dark. Maire felt herself lifting into her dream body where she roamed the war in her sleep. The bellows of his breath sucked air out of her world, then his exhale put it back. He was alive. Like photos in *Life* magazine, she hovered over terrain that presented itself in half-tone shades, grey men on grey battlefields, bleeding black blood from black holes in their young bodies. Behind the mangled men sprawled the mechanical carnage of overturned Jeeps, derailed convoys, grey tanks aflame on grey sand. She saw him. Reached for him. Her eyes blinked; her body twitched. She came awake gasping in the night tones of the farmhouse, in the womb of Montana midnight. She whispered his name into the room he had left her. Wrapped in her shawl, the sound of Nana's voice seemed to whisper from the woven threads. "You've got the fey, me girl, dinna be afraid. The wyrd will teach you." She was afraid but equally determined to practice fearlessness.

    Years earlier, dusting the Annenberg's library, she had discovered a cache of hidden pamphlets. Desperate in her longing to have a child, the Missus once confessed to visiting the author, Edgar Cayce, for a medical consultation. Cayce wrote of telepathy, clairvoyance, psychic trance, all new concepts in her mind. Nights after reading, she dreamed of flying over scenes of her life or dancing in caves spattered with firelight. One night her mother's face had floated before her, "Careful, daughter. Dinna lose yur path to Jesus or some'un will light the witch's fire!" Maire had startled awake, jumped out of bed, knelt on the hard floor, and recited the Lord's Prayer until dawn. She slipped Cayce's booklets back into hiding, but the mind is sticky, and knowledge set into it is hard to forget. She was older now. She had her own fierceness. She had protection in the faith of her father-in-law. What could be the harm if she hovered in the astral realms, praying Franklin's safety in a tongue called forth by dreams?

> February 17, 1943 (Flora is 4 months old.)
> Dearest Franklin,
> Reports of the war are frightening, and those LIFE photos.... I fear for you. First for your physical safety, but also for your soul. Battle requires young men to commit acts that go against all Christian character. You were raised to hold a deep moral code and I pray you can protect who you really are. You left here to discover your beekeeper's question, to let the world and the war reveal what inquiry will shape your life. Remember that mission, my darling man. We are waiting for you. I love you, Moy

She licked the envelope, took her prayerful breath, felt the echo of his breath. She settled into a duality of ordinary days coupled with extra-ordinary nights. She ached for the brief fire of their lovemaking, and while she fingered her own pleasure, it was not the same. She missed his bookish correspondence from Belfast. She missed his tender condolence over her mother. She memorized his letter written from the ship before it all got real. Since Christmas, only two letters. She whispered to the baby who slept on her breast, "I am watching over him, Flory, and that is all we can do." The moon shone in the window. Owls hooted early mating calls from the cottonwoods. A mouse let out a tiny squeak as it became a meaty offering from the darkly feathered male to his mate. Maire shivered in half-light, floating in the space between. She twirled the baby's one curl around her finger.

22
Freezing and Thawing

MID-MARCH 1943: *Devastating convoy losses continue in the North Atlantic. German forces liquidate the Jewish ghetto in Kraków, Poland. General George Patton leads his tanks into Gafsa, Tunisia.*

JESSE CROSSED DOC'S PARLOR FLOOR in three swings of the crutches, the bedroom in two swings, the kitchen in one. He was afraid of knocking things over, stepping on Doc's cat, tripping over his son. Six weeks of stumbling; halfway to freedom. His father had brought over a pair of wool pants that Maire had sliced open along the inseam. Willow scrubbed the kitchen and set Natoyii to play at his father's feet. A set of worn wooden blocks had materialized from the Cooper attic. He remembered them well. Sounds of a farm truck rumbled into his awareness.

Tim and Bill Sivertsen drove into the yard towing Jesse's pickup. Seeing it in daylight, he felt ashamed of the old vehicle, but when he opened the cabin door, Tim smiled and tossed him keys. He still had a haystack of blond hair and an amused grin. "Good to see you, Jess. Thought we'd get your truck off the road before melt." Jesse noted the manhood in his friend's face, creases of weather and work.

"Think it's repairable?"

"Can't tell." Tim had taken off his leather cap, flaps lined with flannel and was slapping loose dirt from the bill. "We can get under the hood once weather warms up and your leg heals."

Drum squirreled his head between his father's knees. "Who dat, Ninna?"

Tim tousled the boy's hair, and took a good look at the almond-eyed, honey-toned features of a mixed-blood child. "Your pa told us, you know, in church."

"Yah, I heard." Jesse tried to compose himself. "You were sweet on Gloria Davis," he said, "You marry her?"

"Sure did. Four-year-old twin boys, a little brother. Gloria's due again in May." He flashed his smile, "Trying to figure what's causing 'em." Old joke.

Jesse opened the door wider. "Come in. Meet my family." The men crossed the threshold with a huff of cold air and closed the door behind themselves. "This is my wife, Willow." Jesse regarded her through white eyes, her copper skin, the bridge of her nose, black braids tied back with a kerchief, the deferential shyness of a carefully raised Piikuni woman. "Willow, this is my friend, Tim Sivertsen and his father, Bill."

She reached out her hand to touch theirs in the respectful way. "Glad to meet you." She was dressed in her skirt, a plaid shirt and sweater. Jesse thought she looked beautiful, original, self-possessed. Tim took her hand, one strong shake. White man's greeting.

Drum had wrapped himself around his father's good leg. "This is our son, Drummond Natoyii isttookimaa." He watched Tim's eyes go round, and laughed, "Don't worry, buddy, just call him Drum."

Willow spoke softly, "The doctor is away. May I offer you tea?"

"Oh, no, ma'am. We best get home; just glad you all made it safe in the storm." Tim smiled at Drum. "Need any little boy clothes?"

Jesse swallowed embarrassment. "That would be great. We weren't planning to stay, except now I can't drive, and got nothing that will drive."

Bill suddenly found his voice. "You got plans for spring, Jess? We got 250 acres going into sugar beets and not near enough manpower. If your leg's still bum, you can run tractor. Your dad don't need you till the hives are full." He cleared his throat. "Labor Department declares farmers are short-handed all over the west. Then raises production quotas. Then tells us good luck." He was a craggy man with grey hairs sprouting from his ears. "Homer's running Herefords on a thousand acres above the ditch with both his boys in the Pacific. Guv'ment buying everything we can plant, grow, and harvest."

Jesse defended his other life. "Tribe has men fighting and ranching, too. Reservation mostly grassland, horses, and cattle."

Bill scratched his head. "Ralph left after harvest. Caleb don't know how he's gonna manage. Women will be in the field this spring, and every child old enough to handle a horse or a hoe." Tim was squirming. "I keep saying no food, no fight. Farmers shouldn't be called from the crop field to the battlefield." Bill glanced around the small house, "This place could be a starter for you Jess. Doc shouldn't be out here by herself anyway."

Tim pulled his father's jacket collar, "Jeez, Dad, don't go laying out Jesse's whole life. Nor Doc's." He turned to Willow, "Thank you for your hospitality, Missus. Jesse, call me when you're ready to look at the truck."

"Remember what I said," Bill was still pitching his offer from the porch steps. "Pay you good. Get yourself a newer truck."

Jesse shut the cabin door. Willow wrapped her arms around his chest and wrinkled her nose in the folds of his shirt, "Ah, you were nervous, too."

When the door between the worlds is open, a thing not intended can weasel through the crack of space and time. Maire had been drifting home after her nightly search for Franklin when something grabbed her astral flight and clawed her down. A ship. An engine room. She heard the shish of water as the grey metal hull sliced through grey waves. Below deck, grey men working in grey light, steam pipes and gauges, smell of diesel. His intent had summoned her, but he could not see her. She floated over the boiler as she floated over the desert. She. Did. Not. Want. To. Be. Here.

Broin Mulvaney muttered into the machinery noise. "Comin' for yah, gurl. Army pulled out 'fore I could get your soldier boy. Nobody to warn yah, what with yer muther floatin' in the river, unfortunate accident that." He scratched himself. "Got the address for the fancy lady you was hiding behind…" A sound gargled in the back of his throat. "Maire MacDonnell, thinking yerself too good for the likes of me. Wait 'n see. One day you be proud ta be my wife." He spit. She froze, suspended. She had to breathe, now, before a gasp of desperation might stir the air over his greasy head. She turned to face a hiss of steam and let go a spent breath. Then through her nose, silent as the owl's naris she inhaled. Full lungs lifted her out and back into the ethers where she swung her arms wildly, paddling through sky tunnels.

Her eyes blinked open to darkness, adjusting. Her room. Her baby's sigh. The small photograph of herself and Franklin glowing in caught moonlight from the dresser mirror. These four walls. Safety. Hers. Far. Away. America. Big. The Missus could not direct him. Maire scrunched deeper into sheets and blankets warming her bones.

This was not the Westerlies of Nana's faery realm, nor Cayce's soulful astral travel, but something the war called and behind that, the evil that had called the war—a black hole, round with teeth, that chewed the hearts of men. She sat up, panting. "Believe me, Franklin Cooper, I am your wife and no other man's." She wrapped the ordinary reality of Pigeon River around her trembling shoulders. In the back of her throat, she practiced D-above-middle-C to signal the bees hiding in their hives, waiting out the days until spring. Fearlessness her only protection. She'd work on that.

A few days later, Leo knocked on the cabin door. "Getting bored? We can repair supers."

"Sure." Jesse twirled slowly on the cast, putting weight on the walking platform the Great Falls doctor had added to the original. "Want to come, Willow? Drum can play with the baby."

She kissed and sniffed him. "Natoyii and I will walk."

"Road's muddy," Leo stuck his head in the door.

"Earth softens," Willow replied. "We leave footprints, so she knows our names."

Jesse eased himself, cast, and crutches awkwardly into the Chevy's back seat. Leo started the engine, "Is she always like that?"

"Yes," Jesse smiled into the rearview mirror. "Willow is Gramma's lineage carrier. She speaks spiritual, like you speak philosophy, scripture, literature into any conversation."

The car fishtailed on thawed mud. "Am I really like that?"

"Yes." Jesse leaned on the seatback.

"And do people have to work to understand me?"

"Yes. Sometimes. I do." He watched his father's brow furrow. "It's who you are, Pa. Anyone can make small talk, people need you for the big talk." Jesse was enjoying the moment. "In or out of the pulpit, you're the purveyor of Pigeon River moral standards."

"Well, is it working?" Leo glanced in the mirror.

"Hope so. For our sakes. We'll see."

Winter work meant repairing supers, bringing them back into true, slipping the frames in their slots, readying hives for the industriousness of summer bees. Father and son kept both hands busy, eyes focused on the glue line. "Does Willow inherit Grandmother Josie's role?"

"She will be *iiokamiiks*. One who carries the Beaver bundle. It's a big responsibility." He lowered his head over the super. "When you are an Indian, the survival or loss of essential wisdom often rests on just one person. Where is the grandfather who knows how to make a drum or say the prayer before hunting? Where is the grandmother with words to speak of the world that made you? If one person dies, or falls into drink, or slips off the road like we did in the storm or, like most within our tribe, are forced into schools, separated from sacred teachings and way of life, generation after generation, whole sections of the map of our existence can disappear forever."

Leo handed him a hive tool to scrap old wax. "And your role, my son?"

"I am Willow's safekeeper in the world that comes. I am her husband, her provider, the father of our children." Jesse's voice trembled to speak it aloud. "When you are an Indian, you hide in plain sight. You do menial work, without becoming a menial person. You find purpose in a world that doesn't see purpose for you, that doesn't think it would even miss you, that in fact thinks you are already dead. I'm twenty-four years old, unregistered with the tribe, mostly blood white by all looks and guesses. Willow and I are charged by Gramma Josie to stand between the worlds."

"Yes, Mrs. Shines the Light told me, last summer. Do you understand what they carry?" Leo inquired.

"I arrived too late, too white, too educated in non-Indian ways… but I have faith in what I do not fully understand." He glanced up, "I don't know what story to tell, Pa. Even that I'm adopted. I don't want folks to stop seeing me as your son."

"You are forever my son…"

"Being a Cooper is part of my protection for Willow." Jesse looked deep in his father's eyes.

Leo laid his hand over the knuckles of his son's hand. "Being a reverend is part of my protection for you both."

"Thanks, Pa. You know what Willow carries is secret."

Leo nodded. "Does Maire understand?"

"Yes. Willow says they will be *aakim*, like Auntie Doc and Gramma Josie."

The Beekeeper's Question

Leo laid his gnarled hands on the spread of repaired hive boxes, "Maybe beekeeping is how you can live in both worlds and support your family. On the road to Valier last fall you said you had the beekeeper's question."

"I said my question is, where do I belong? Bees are the uncomplicated part."

Two weeks later, there was a knock on the cabin door after dark and a familiar voice called out, "Hey White Man, you got my cousin in there?"

Willow leapt up, "Darrell!" She wrapped her cousin in a hug that squeezed another laugh out of him.

"*Oki Niksookowaiks*, I come to bring you home, Gramma says it's time." Darrell limped into the room, his one leg four inches shorter than the other, wearing his clomping shoes, the left sole built up. Ticket out of the war whether he wanted it or not. "You gonna walk like me now, Jesse? Heard you broke your leg."

No, he would not walk like Darrell because of Doc's skill, and because he'd been driven to Great Falls to the bone man for x-rays. "We got the same broke-up nose, that'll have to do." Darrell was BB's nephew, that's how Jesse figured it. Raised under Gramma's strict rules and BB's skills, Darrell could fix anything. Jesse was glad to welcome him.

"Stew is still warm." Willow handed him a plate and a water glass.

Darrell nodded acceptance and sat on the floor to play with Natoyii while he ate. "War-time sure is different. Hitching down I got two offers for work," he shook his head. "Maybe they thought I was Mexican." He laughed.

Jesse nodded. "Even with my broke leg, farmers want whatever I can do."

Darrell gestured with a toy truck in his hand, "Yah, but lots of our people still half-starving, making do."

Jesse swallowed with a gulping sound. "I been kinda thinking we could bring a crew down here for a couple weeks this spring. Plant sugar beets. Come back in June and thin 'em, come back in October and harvest 'em."

"For money?" Jesse nodded. "For fair money?"

"I'll see it's fair," Jesse said. "We need a deeper well, bigger windmill and cistern. Make sure we don't get fever again."

Willow turned from the stove, "Natoyii was burning hot. We all near died driving for help, Darrell. Men gone to the war or factory work, there's women and children who need shelter, help, and education. We need sweet water." She handed Darrell a second helping. "Eat up, stay strong."

He popped a mouthful and smiled. "*Iniiyi'taki,* Willow, good stew." He looked at Jesse. "You sayin' we make money off the whites, bring it back to help the people. But young women don't come down. One white man marrying into us is enough." He smiled, teeth rimmed with gravy, "You're a half-breed learnin' respect, but we're not lettin' our beautiful women marry farm-boys."

"Farm boys mostly gone, that's the problem. So, you in?"

Darrell chewed a few bites in silence. "And for this, they'll pay us how much?"

"Tim and his dad are offering $2.50 a day. And if all goes well and we come back late fall to pull beets and load trucks, they'll pay $3.00 a day."

"I could maybe bring the Boy Scouts down." Darrell had influence over a pack of younger teens. "See how folks take to us. I can talk the boys into the adventure. You can talk the mamas into letting them come." Darrell's chuckle wasn't really a laugh. "No offense, Jess, but white folks got money, power, and police on their side. I wouldn't do it without you. Anything happens, you ready to stand up against the folks you come from and side with the folks who took you in?"

"I don't think we'll have trouble if it's just young boys." Jesse made his voice sound confident though his stomach clenched.

23

Old Men and Young Men

APRIL 1943: *German troops hold the Mareth Line, but American tanks defeat the Germans at El Guettar and the British break into southern Tunisia.*

DARRELL AND TIM GOT THE TRUCK RUNNING and Darrell drove the family home. Doc's parting advice rang in Jesse's mind, "Don't you stress that bone or you'll mess up your leg for life." She knew him well.

Jesse gave Drum horsey rides until his calf ached. He stepped up and down entryway steps of his cabin. He curried the winter fuzz off Windy and rode him out to the road and back. The cast protruded at an awkward angle, but reminded the horse of who he was and who they were together. Hard to rein it all in—himself, the horse, his longing for the next stage of his life to kick in. Jesse eyed the teenagers: Which boys were already handling horses? Who was strong enough for field work? Who was patient enough to thin seedlings? He was edgy and unsettled. Days were lengthening. Temperatures warming. A green haze began to shoot up in the grasslands between the stubble of last year's haying.

End of the month, Jesse turned over a shovelful of dirt registering the warmth in his hand, assessing the moisture level, the smell of soil coming back to life. Everything would come on at once and the coordination made him tense. He tacked the order of sugar beet farming on the wall of their cabin next to a calendar where he marked off the days.

> Furrowing: using the push tractors for the deep plow.
> Leveling: using the horses and the tinged drag.
> Harrowing: using the horses and the chain drag.
> Seeding: using the seed cart followed by the roller.
> Sprouting: 9-11 days, then two weeks for seedlings to grow.
> Thinning: hand work with short-handled hoe.

Tim emphasized the dance of temperature, weather, and the life cycle of the crop—from seeding to harvest, 170 days. "Early in, late out," he'd said. "The beets need heat to mature, and then cold to bring out the sugars but not get frozen into the ground." Going south also meant getting his cast off, the itch under the plaster as fierce as his frustration. One afternoon, engrossed in mental planning, Jesse bumped into his grandmother.

"*Oki, iisohko*," she hailed him, "Were you going to look up, grandson, or just plow me under?"

"I'm sorry Gramma, I wasn't looking where I was going." He braked mid-stride, one foot in his cowboy boot and the other in his heavy plaster cast.

Josie gave him the eye. "No, you were *only* looking at where you are going, but not looking at where you are!" She stood in the sovereignty of an elder's space. "You are standing on Piikuni land. If you got plans for Shines the Light people, you talk with the community elders." His throat went dry.

That night at supper, Willow asked, "What do you want?"

"I want to help my people," he said. His knife and fork clinked on the plate.

"Which people—Piikuni people? White people?" She puffed a strand of hair out of her eyes.

"Both."

"*Why* do you want this?" She stroked the back of his hand.

Jesse felt confused. "Shouldn't a man strive to be of service? To enrich both communities?" He was cutting a hotdog into Drummond-sized bites while the boy bounced on a chair.

"That is not my question," she shook ketchup onto Natoyii's plate. "Why do *you* want this, my husband. You—*ipisttotsimakoyii*, Walks Far Wolf. You—Jesse Cooper. The elders will ask what you seek and why."

He took her hand, lifted it to his cheek. Her fingers uncurled like fern fronds and caressed his face. He kissed her fingertips and searched her eyes, grabbed a jacket, and headed into the dusk. "I'll be back," he said softly.

"I'll be here." she whispered. "Sit down, Natoyii." She tucked a napkin into the boy's collar. "Use your fork and dip the pieces in your ketchup."

Jesse limped west. The night wrapped itself around him. His leg ached. The outline of the cabins and the conical shape of Gramma's lodge poked the horizon. Each lodgepole leaned as though to fall, but together formed an interlaced circle of strength that, like Josie herself, could stand a blast of wind from any direction. And isn't that all Jesse wanted—to be laced together, to lean in, to hold his own part, to feel the weight of weathered skin covering his own bones? He sat on a small rise. He allowed himself to howl. At the bottom of the howl was a cry. At the bottom of the cry was the wind.

Two days later, Darrell drove Jesse to Browning and the visiting nurse cut through his cast and scrubbed layers of dead skin off his leg. Jesse put on a sock and boot and walked free. Two days after that, trucks full of families, men on horseback, streamed into the yard. "Moccasin telegraph," Darrell smiled, "Folks heard we got a big idea. Come to see how we do."

"That's good, right?" Darrell shrugged. At the entrance to a ceremonial lodge, a braid of sweetgrass smoldered. The two washed themselves with the smoke and entered.

The elders, a line of five men, were seated cross-legged on the dirt floor, closest to the small center fire. Two wore traditional bonnets, signifying military service in the war before this war. All were dressed in jeans and flannel shirts, here and there a necklace of bone and beads. A bundle was hanging on a tripod behind the honorary carrier. "*Máakópiit.*" Jesse and Darrell were motioned to sit down.

The birdsong voices of women buzzed in his left ear; the mumbling bear voices of men buzzed in his right ear. Folks settled. Pipes were smoked. Prayers were spoken. They sang *kaamotani*, a protection song. Two aunties brought in stewed elk and frybread. The men ate. Jesse followed Darrell's demeanor: the nod of the head, the averted gaze, an attitude of respect. On a regular afternoon, these men were mid-life and older uncles who worked the odd jobs of daily life, but here in ceremony, they bore ancient authority. Jesse remembered the day his nose got broke and Darrell's taunt of "fake Indian." He bit the inside of his cheek and waited to be addressed.

Gramma Josie met his eyes. He heard her admonition in his mind, "Look at where you are, so you will know where you are going." He waited his turn. Afternoon light moved over the canvas skin of the lodge.

Uncle Stanley, an elder and veteran, leaned slightly forward. "We hear that you wish to take our boys, to leave the lands that remain to us and return to the lands that were stolen from us to help those who stole them." His tone held ironic amusement, but his eyes were serious. "Why is this a good idea?"

Darrell gave Jesse a quick nod—*you first, your plan.* Jesse straightened his spine and leaned into the voice of the wind that blew through him, calmer now. "The government tells the farmers that an army marches on its stomach. Food must be raised, processed, packaged, and shipped to keep the soldiers fed. The farmers are charged to grow more food, but because of the war there are fewer young men to work the land."

The Beekeeper's Question

An old man Jesse knew from Birch Creek, shook his head. "Piikuni warriors have always fought with empty bellies and only our courage to eat."

"I do not question the courage of Piikuni men, Uncle. My question is, will the tribe cross Two Medicine River to help the war effort?"

"The white man's war effort." With a chunk of frybread, Uncle Stanley wiped the last of the elk gravy from his plate, "If America wins or loses this war, will it be better or worse for us?"

Jesse took a huge breath. "If America loses, it will be much worse for all Real People." The men sat silently with this message.

A grandfather grunted. "The white man has been killing us for hundreds of years. Even now. How could things be worse?"

The gaze of the elders tingled against his pale skin. "Hitler has a plan to create a pure white race. The Japanese are determined to be the master race controlling all of Asia." He bit hard on his cheek. "America must stay in the fight until we win. And when the war is over, Blackfeet soldiers will have training they could not get in Browning, opportunities for work, and the brotherhood of war."

Uncle Stanley held his standup warbonnet in hands veined with age. "Indian warriors may shed blood for the white man's troubles, but we are veterans of a thousand wars and broken promises. Do not say we will be honored once this fight is done." He commanded silence to receive his words.

In that space, a flash of comprehension blew through Jesse's heart: Grief was the battle these elders fought with empty bellies and only their courage to eat. Every day these men worked to protect their people from the ravages and neglect of modern America. White America. They endured the kidnapping of their children. They prayed the forbidden traditions of Amskapi Piikuni spiritual life would restore their Indian souls. Jesse sat motionless, biting his cheek, swallowing the enormity of what had gone wrong on the land of his birth, in the bloodlines that mingled in his veins. The council waited. He composed himself and spoke to the fire. "History sits with us, Uncles, that is true. Injustice is a pile of twisted rope that seems impossible to untangle. Yet I offer my life to this unraveling. I hold out my hands. I surrender my bones. This is all I know to do."

Grunts of acknowledgment traveled around the circle. A slight smile creased Uncle Stanley's face, "So, *ipisttotsimakoyii*, to stop Hitler you come to ask our boys to plant vegetables?" A string of Piikuni sentences followed and the old men laughed.

Darrell whispered in Jesse's ear, "They wonder if the Army grinds vegetables into gunpowder."

"Sugar beets are a cash crop. The farmers will pay well for help in the fields. This can benefit both peoples." Wind still blew through his ribs.

"Ah, benefit…" the uncles nodded, "If we help the farmers, will they help us?"

"No," Jesse admitted. "They will not." Wind hollowed him.

"Will they pay our boys the same as white boys?" another uncle asked.

"I have known these farmers all my life. They are honorable men. I will negotiate fair pay and good treatment. That is my role as a son of the valley and a husband of Shines the Light."

Another elder leaned forward, "Will they return to us *Niitawahsin*, the lands they stand on?"

Jesse sighed. "That time is over, Uncles. Just as the People are no longer free, the Land is no longer free."

Uncle Stanley nodded. "We see that you are willing to speak true. Tell us why we should help them."

Darrell leaned forward, brushed Jesse's arm. "My uncles and grandfathers, you have told me the stories of our great days, how we ranged over these lands raiding horses and riding home with the wind in our ears. Money is now the horse. This sugar beet work is a raiding party. We bring home the money, and we decide how this benefits us."

The uncles turned to one another's counsel. Jesse and Darrell waited. Uncle Stanley regarded the two young men. "The world is changing. It is ours to protect the old ways. It is yours to decide the new ways. It is ours together to never forget *Niitsitapiisini*. Do as your hearts show you. Darrell Good Feather, you may ask the boys and their parents who will raid for horses in the modern way. You will show them how to stand among the white farmers in their Piikuni bones. You will keep them safe. Do you agree?"

Darrell nodded, "*Áa*. I am ready."

"Jesse Walks Far Wolf Cooper, you will see the boys are paid fairly. You will interpret the customs of the whites and command respect for those we send. You will protect the boys from violence or liquor. Do you agree?"

Jesse nodded, "*Áa*. I am willing."

Uncle Stanley looked Jesse in the eye. "You are here because you are the son of Leo Cooper. You are here because you carry our blood. You are here under the protection of our Grandmother. You are here because you are the husband and shield for our Granddaughter. We are the community elders. When something needs to be decided, it is decided through talking with us. Do you understand?"

Jesse bowed his head, "*Áa*," he said. "I understand, Uncles."

The men nodded. The people stirred. The council was over.

Waiting for him, Willow rose from the cabin steps and the two began walking into the grasslands where they could talk and be alone. "We go south," she said. It was not a question. "Natoyii will be happy. He likes his baby cousin."

"Where *is* our boy?" Jesse slipped his fingers through hers, caressing her bones in his hand.

"Auntie Aggie is making frybread with the children."

They tucked into the slope of a small rise in the early evening light. Jesse spread his jacket for her to sit. "And you, my woman?"

christina baldwin

"I will cook and stay at your side." She stroked the greening stems that held them. "And you, my man?"

"I am responsible for fair pay and respect."

"That is what the council says. What did the wind say?"

He stared at the colors gathering in the West. "I am a man broken in half. I keep asking how to belong with my father and white people and with you and Piikuni people when I am neither."

Willow traced the lines of his palm with her fingernail. "None of us is whole, Jesse, but we are on the road to wholeness."

"You are whole." He tucked a loose wisp of her hair.

"No one asked me if I wanted to be Grandmother's *minipoka*, her chosen one. Claiming me preserved the teachings. Claiming me caused pain." Willow searched his face. "I was a baby. There is a hole in my heart where my mother should sit."

"The People revere you."

"The People revere the teachings. It is mine to carry our spirits' survival. Everything has been torn from us—our language, our history, our land, our families. Gramma's ordinary homesite is where Amskapi Piikuni remember how we belong to ourselves."

"That's my search," Jesse sat up, "How do I belong to myself?"

Willow bowed her head. "In our ways, you go on the mountain. You sit up all night. You ride the wind. You pray for your people. When you come back, wise ones look into your heart. They see you. They welcome you. You do not have to be whole. You just need be on the journey. What the elders trusted in you today is the direction they see you traveling."

Jesse breathed her words into his chest. He kissed her fingers folded around his. "Maybe it will be good for you to get away, let responsibility rest. You can work the garden with Maire, get to know each other, be friends."

She looked puzzled. "In my early years, I longed to be like other girls, to laugh over nothing, fuss with my hair, tease boys. I have kinship, but not what you call friendship. You say that

Maire and I should be friends. I do not know what you want for us."

"Maire is far from her land and her people. Is that not a common bond?"

"Binding two wounds together makes more blood, not healing. Healing requires bonding with the drive for wholeness. You want your heart to be whole, on the grasslands and in the valley. I want that for you also. And for myself, I want peace in my heart to fulfill my duty. I want to feed tradition to the hungry minds of my people. I will plant sweetgrass in the garden of your father's home. We shall see what grows."

Silence floated between them until Jesse asked, "What do you want just for yourself?"

Willow's face spread into a mischievous grin. "I want you. With all your questions, your awkwardness, your good heart, your passionate nature. You are my rebellion. Stinky white boy, stuttering in our language, clumsy in our ways of knowing. I had to wrestle the ancestors for permission to claim you. My treasure. My love." She pushed him back onto the grass. He let her.

24
The Fort and the Farmers

MAY 1943: *The British capture Tunis. The Americans take Birzete. On May 13, German and Italian troops surrender North Africa. The Allies have 267,000 prisoners of war on their hands. Churchill is in Washington DC planning the invasion of Sicily.*

DUST BALLS OF SORROW SWIRLED AROUND THE ANKLES of the young farm wives as they swept debris from abandoned corners, eager and nervous to welcome Jesse and his crew. Built by the U.S. Army in 1867, the Fort housed cavalry that provided military escort for gold shipments coming out of Helena. In 1869, a fur trader named Malcolm Clarke, who had beat his Blackfeet wife near to death and raped her sister when she tried to intervene, was killed in a fight with the sister's husband, Owl Child. In retribution, in January of 1870, Major Eugene Baker led fifty mounted soldiers out of Fort Shaw toward the Marias River with carte blanche orders to "strike 'em hard." Baker stumbled on the encampment of a peaceful band of Blackfeet whose chief, Heavy Runner, carried script identifying them as "friendly."

As he stepped out to show the paper, the soldiers shot him.

Then they murdered over two hundred women, children, and old men.

Then they burned the encampment.

And then they slaughtered the buffalo.

And then the People starved.

And then the People surrendered.

After the railroads came, and the Blackfeet and other tribes were pushed onto designated reservations, the Army turned the Fort over to the Bureau of Land Management, which later turned it over to the Bureau of Indian Affairs. Between 1892-1910, the Fort housed a vocational training school for Indian children. A few decades later, after significant whitewashing, the buildings served as the primary school for the children of valley homesteaders. Tim and Gloria, Hazel and Ralph, sat in the same desks, ate lunch in the same kitchen, but without the trauma of kidnapping, imprisonment, and the forced obliteration of their language and culture.

Technically, the Fort belonged to the Department of the Interior, but as far as anyone local was concerned, if the diking district granted permission, the Fort could be commandeered as needed. It was their valley. "Pete said bringing in a sugar beet crew, no problem," Tim spoke around a mouthful of ham sandwich, "I wasn't specific about Indians, but I didn't lie." He flashed a charming smile and Gloria leaned into him, resting her back.

On a day the wind blew warm, Uncle BB brought a letter from Tim back from town. Jesse sat on the cabin steps and read it aloud:

> *Hey Buddy, hope you have been successful in finding a crew. The soil is ready. The women have cleaned out the barracks. There's pots and pans in the kitchen, and electricity is connected since the Diking District operates out of the officer quarters. Next week's weather looks good. Come on down. Tim*

They could spare three trucks, had enough gas to get them to the valley. Darrell announced that ten boys, ages fourteen to seventeen, were ready to go. They had all been sufficiently prayed over and the schoolmaster had provided a week of lessons. On the morning of their departure, Darrell wheeled a horse trailer onto his hitch. "Raiding party, remember?" He flashed Jesse a grin that was definitely not community elder approved. "We can ride between fields, give folks something to talk about at the store."

"How do you know what folks talk about?" Jesse urged Windy into the trailer and slipped the halter lead into the tie ring. "I been around Cutbank. Fixed cars for country folks. That's why I understand the white side of you so well." He slapped a dusty cowboy hat against his horse's rump.

Gramma Josie strode into the yard, the elders beside her, and the families of the boys clustered around. They sang *kaamotani*. Jesse at the wheel with Willow and Drum alongside, three boys stuck on hay bales on the back. Darrell at the next wheel, pulling the horse trailer, three boys crammed along the bench seat with him. Uncle BB and Aunt Agnes occupied the third truck with four boys. They headed onto the broad expanse of *Niitawahsin*, now known as Cascade County, state of Montana, U.S.A.

Three hours later, sun warming the day, they crossed the bridge over Pigeon River, and the Fort came into view. Sitting alongside him, Willow spoke softly, "Don't drive in yet, I need to say prayers." Jesse halted by a clump of cottonwood trees. "Wait here." She reached over and caressed his cheek and Natoyii's. BB got out of the third truck unwrapping a hand drum. Everyone turned off their engines. The boys stood and leaned elbows on the roof of the cabs. They looked around the central yard where an old guard tower stood forlorn, the stockade long gone. On their left, a row of small houses, on their right, two low buildings where stucco had been layered over the original construction of clay bricks. Across the yard, a cookhouse and classrooms. Along the river, a stable and corral.

Jesse watched Willow stand by the trunk of the oldest tree, the shiny green clusters trembling in light breeze. The women were dressed in skirts, long blouses. BB began drumming a two-two-beat. Aunt Aggie called between the worlds.

Willow knelt to the soil of the Fort, picked up a spoonful of dirt, spat on it four times, and mixed a paste in her palm. She marked her face with the mud, brown rivers of tears down her cheeks. Her face to the sky, arms outstretched, feet planted on the soil, her prayers petitioned the ancestors in their own tongue.

Jesse squeezed his squirming boy tightly in the circle of his arms. "Be still, Drummie, your mama is in her power. Watch and learn like the big boys."

"Dwum, *naá*, dwum, mama."

A door opened in the old infirmary. Doc and Maire stood in the doorframe. He had wanted his worlds to come together, Jesse thought; well, here it was. He felt safer with Doc as witness, comforted that his first Medicine Woman, she who had delivered him, half-raised him, and traveled the road to the reservation many times, was welcoming his work-party to the valley. He put his hand on the chest of his son, palm spread over Drum's heart.

The next morning Tim and Bill showed up with two other sugar beet farmers. "We got three farms; you got three trucks. We each take a team of boys and one man to drive and train the boys to the equipment." Jesse thought Tim's voice carried a nervous pitch.

Bill stepped in with introductions. "This here's Harry Rickard and Calvin Gladd. They got outfits on the benchland. Your pa has yards out their way. They run beets and clover."

The two men shook Jesse's hand. "You the twin's father? I remember them." The farmers appraised each other through acquaintance and history. "Calvin, good to meet you." Mr. Gladd's Adam's apple was sliding up and down his throat.

Jesse gestured his team leaders into the cluster of greeting. "This is Darrell Good Feather and his uncle BB Shoots Straight.

Taught me everything I know about horses and engines. We run cattle and hay." Commonalities was Jesse's ploy—speak the lingo of the land. Everyone shook hands. Jesse was pretty sure it was the first time any of the farmers had touched the skin of an Indian. "Darrell and BB are in charge of the boys, and I'm in charge of making sure everybody understands what the work is so there's no disappointments." The farmers nodded. "And $2.50 a day to start." The men nodded again. They would work out the kinks as they went.

With a driver, a passel of boys, and a farmer to point the way, the trucks headed into the landscape. Jesse sent BB with Sivertsens; Darrell went with Harry. Jesse drove around the back of the butte with Calvin to the end of the honey route. Pressed against the cab to keep out of the wind rode the "3Rs"—Robert, Russell, and Ricky-John.

Jesse stood on the truck bed at the edge of Calvin's fields assessing the work. The land undulated in patchwork fields around the feet of the buttes. Treeless, except along a slice of creek, arid except where the river's meander toward the great Missouri had been siphoned into miles of irrigation ditch. Home.

Harrowing meant pulling a heavy blanket of chain and tines over the roughly plowed fields, breaking the big clods of soil into a smoothed surface for planting. "Take us two days, most likely," Calvin broke a long silence. "I got a team and a push tractor. Boys handle horses?" Jesse nodded. "Good. I don't think any of 'em got enough muscle to manage the tractor. You and me take turns running that. Then we disc harrow, get ready for seed. Planting by week's end. Radio says rain come Sunday. Good for germination. You folks go home, come back down in a month, we'll thin."

The 3Rs were subdued as the farmer put his horses in harness and taught the boys how to lay out the harrows, tines down, the weight of the chain requiring two of them to move it into place and fasten it onto the metal bar the horses pulled. Ricky-John nuzzled the big-boned Percherons, laced his fingers into the stiff bristle of their manes, cut short to keep hair out of the harness. He whispered sweet to them, blew his breath gently up their velvety nostrils. He and Russell stepped behind, took the reins, and began walking the first row. Calvin walked beside. "The horses know the routine. Don't fuss too much or you'll confuse them. They walk the straight and narrow, you boys best learn from them." He meant it as true advice.

Robert, the smallest, looked forlorn. "Come on, Robbie," Jesse put an arm across the boy's shoulder, "Mr. Gladd thinks you're too small to walk tractor, but I need some weight on the seat, hold the harrows to the ground, and Darrell says you're strong for your size."

The cadence of man, horse, machine was slow and deliberate. The sun warm, but not yet hot, Calvin signaled the noon stop. "Water them horses," he called to Ricky-John. "There's a ditch yonder." He pointed east. The three boys unhitched the team and headed in the direction of the farmer's gesture.

"Guess they'll find it," he said, turning to Jesse. "Either that or fall in." He dug a hand deep into the gap under his overalls, scratched someplace Jesse didn't want to think about. "Sivertsen was right, they're earnest boys. Never would of thought of it myself. Never would of gone up there to ask, either. Good to have you make arrangements, find the right kind of folks." He gave Jesse a long look. "Said you one of the beekeeper's boys?"

"Yup," a longer response crouched in Jesse's mind.

"I got a boy in the Navy and two girls in Portland making ships."

"I don't remember any Gladds in school."

"Wife kept a house in town. Kids went to Great Falls schools. She died after the last one graduated and I moved out here. Needed the horizon to put life back in perspective. The sight of them mountains."

"Blackfeet call them Backbone of the Earth."

"Yeah, I can see that. Don't mind me asking… How'd you get to know Indians?"

"My mother died when I was sixteen. Family sort of fell apart. I ran away. A Blackfeet family found me. Took me in."

"Heard the younger woman is your wife."

"Yes, and the little boy is our son."

"Well, takes all kinds."

"Yes, it does." Jesse was not exactly sure what he was agreeing to, but the comment seemed benign. "Looks like the boys found water." They watched Russell and Ricky-John each holding onto a halter, Robbie astride, the horses still slobbery-nosed from sucking out of the ditch. "We got plenty food…" Jesse said.

"Got grub, thanks. Set on the truck, rest a bit. Things are going good."

Jesse retrieved the wicker basket of water jars and field lunches that Aggie and Willow had prepared. He had glanced into the truck's rearview mirror as they pulled out of the Fort and watched the two women turn back toward the dormitory. The physical world and the spiritual world commingled in that abandoned room: those who slept in the present, and those who slept in the past. He had wakened in the night enveloped in the sense of not being alone, not just the whiffling breaths of those asleep around him, but the souls of children who didn't know where else to go.

What Willow and Aggie would do with their morning made him shiver. Man's work was harnessing horses, breaking clods of Montana soil, getting dusty, and running a sweat. Man's work was practical and productive. Jesse loved it. Willow's power was real work too, but Jesse liked to come in afterwards with his dirty hands and sweaty brow. He liked to stand at the basin of water she offered and wash their worlds together and play with their little boy. He liked to make love in the middle of the night, plowing her field, planting his seed, bringing her back to the raw pleasures of an ordinary life.

At the end of the third day, BB pulled him aside. "There's a man sittin' on the back of his pick-up truck with binoculars and a hunting rifle watching us. Mr. Bill said to switch, Tim wants you in the fields."

Jesse's stomach lurched. "Beat up blue Ford?" BB nodded. "Older guy, stocky?" BB nodded again. "Homer Torgerson. Ranches next to Sivertsens. Not a man in a good mood. One of his sons is missing in the Pacific war, and he's mad I didn't marry his daughter."

Darrell walked by, "She good lookin'? His daughter? For a white girl."

"You did hear Uncle BB mention the part about a rifle? That, and to quote Mr. Torgerson, he 'don't trust Injuns.'"

BB huffed, "Well, I don't trust a white man watching me through his hunting glasses. I told the boys, ignore him and work harder." This was the moment the elders had trusted Jesse to be "their white man."

Next morning, Jesse joined Tim in easy tandem. They kept their eye out for Homer, but he did not return. Jesse relaxed until they saw a car speeding across the field roads.

Tim shouted, "Moving at that speed, I'm guessing Gloria's not bringing us cookies." They jogged to meet her.

"Trouble at the Fort," Gloria rolled down the window, her pregnant belly pressed awkwardly against the steering wheel. "Maire called from the store, says white men are threatening to throw them out. Says they're dressed like cavalry or something."

"Stay here, tell Dad."

Gloria eased out of the driver's seat. "Your hunting rifle's in the trunk. I couldn't find the ammunition, but it'll make a show."

Jesse shook his head, "You don't put a gun in your hands that's not loaded because everyone else thinks it *is* loaded. And you don't load it unless you're willing to take the situation all the way." He looked at Tim, they agreed.

"Homer's prejudiced, but not crazy. Besides, he's our neighbor." Tim took his wife by her shoulders, held her in strong hands. "Everything's gonna be fine. Just don't drop that baby out here." His father had turned the corner of the field with the push tractor and was walking their way at a steady pace behind the harrows.

As they approached the Fort, they saw Homer's pickup doing wheelies around the parade ground, in and out among the buildings. "Wasting gasoline!" Jesse's first thought. Another truck and car, each with a reckless driver and a whooping and hollering passenger. One waved a bed sheet, one raised a rifle, an intimidating ruckus. Tim drove his Chevy straight into the middle of the grounds, honking his horn, making a hub in the whirling wheels. The two friends stepped out in unison—Jesse on one side, Tim on the other.

Maire, flat out Irish, was defending the tipi Willow had erected, swatting a broom at any vehicle that came close. Willow, holding Flora, and Aggie, holding Natoyii, stood in the doorway of the cookhouse. Jesse made a dash toward the women and children. Tim leapt alongside Maire. A driver Jesse didn't recognize aimed straight at him but had to swerve to avoid collision with the building itself. "You okay!?" Willow and Aggie nodded mutely. Drum reached for him, and he swept the little boy into his right arm, put his other arm around Willow. They made the expected tableau, but he knew if the two women unleashed their powers…well, they weren't going to play that card today.

Tim shouted. Another vehicle was racing toward the Fort. It was Doc. It was Belle. It was Bugle Boy at a full canter, pulling the medicine wagon that had served the valley for thirty years. As the horse galloped into the courtyard, the circling vehicles slowed, uncertain what to do. The car gunned toward the gap by the old guard tower and headed into countryside. The other truck was blocked by Tim's car. The third exit was now occupied by the two women and the horse and buggy. Jesse nearly whooped. "This situation is gonna be fine," he smiled at Willow, "Nobody messes with Doc and Belle."

Doc steadied the old gelding and drove the buggy onto the field. She stood in the wagon and flipped her stock whip over the scene. A loud snap. "Everybody out. Feet on the ground!" Truck engines complained in neutral. She cracked the whip again. Engines went off. A driver door creaked open. Homer exited his blue pickup along with an old cowboy Jesse didn't recognize. A rusted red truck dumped two other grizzled men onto the parade grounds, one wearing a beat-up black hat, with a cavalry brim and a "flag" he'd been waving now wadded up in his hand. Tim looked at Jesse and shrugged. Except for Homer, they didn't know them.

Belle jumped down from the buggy seat, circling the strangers. "Well, well, well—recruits from Vaughn Junction. Drinking buddies of Mr. Torgerson's, I recall. You got nothing better to do for the war effort than drive around terrorizing women and children?"

"Don't like Injuns," one of them mumbled.

"Really. Do you know what is happening here?" Doc's voice carried across the empty yard from her perch on the wagon, whip still twitching in her hand. The men studied their feet. "Ten young Indian boys are taking a week off school, doing lessons in the evenings, working to help our farmers put in the cash crop that'll keep families going for another year. And their prize mechanics came along to fix equipment we got to keep running for the duration." Doc eased herself to ground, boots scuffing dust where she walked. "One of our own young fathers bridging two communities. Women cooking, taking care of babies, making sure schoolwork is done." She was strutting and Jesse was grinning. When Doc got mad, she was mad. Only happened every few years, far as he knew, but it was impressive.

"And what are YOU doing this week, gentlemen?" She pointed the butt of the whip at the Junction men, "You got so much time on your hands, folks could use more field hands."

Maire took hold of Bugle's halter; the horse was still breathing hard. Doc walked up to Homer, stood in his face, her hands on her hips and her face stern. Whatever she said, it talked him down. He turned, face flushed, strode to his truck, and gunned out of the parade yard. The three "cavalry" guys slid into the other truck and eased off the field.

"Jesse, you and Leo are calling a meeting," Doc announced, "Friday night before you head north. Homer agreed to come." She and Belle looked satisfied. Maire put down the broom.

25
Town Meeting

MAY 20, 1943: *The Warsaw Ghetto uprising ends with 14,000 Jews killed, and 40,000 Jews deported to extermination camps. Winston Churchill addresses Congress.*

JESSE SLICKED BACK WETTED HAIR as he watched people slide into rows of pews. There must have been over fifty folks. He smiled weakly at Darrell. "Doc reported the incident to the county sheriff, and he decided to show up." Darrell stood still so no one saw his limp. "Polish. Everyone calls him Buzz, real name is Vladimir. Knows Pa and Doc. They've been at the scene of things before." Darrell's eyes got wider. "Don't worry, we've done nothing wrong."

"You are such a white man." Circles of sweat dampened Darrell's clean shirt.

"I'm going to shake hands, talk farming." He resisted giving Darrell a slap on the back. Here in the valley, he was Reverend Cooper's son, a do-gooder trying to get employment for his wife's family. And who knows why he had married that Blackfeet girl when half a dozen local daughters had tried to be his comfort after his mother died.

Jesse had urged the boys to stay at the Fort, but they'd held their own council. "People got to see us," they said, "or they'll make up stories of who we are. Besides, the meeting is about us." So, in the end, everyone came. The Shines the Light family sat up front, filling the first two pews on the right side. Leo had positioned them there for protection by proximity. In the pews just behind them, were several rows of "young friendlies" as Aunt Aggie called them. Maire and baby Flora, Tim and Gloria, with their boys bouncing around, Hazel and little Bonnie, Ethel and Caleb Pocket.

In the front rows of the left side sat the farmers: Bill and Esther Sivertsen, Harry Rickard, and Calvin Gladd. The men pulled at their shirt collars like it was Sunday morning. Behind them sat Gertie, Belle, and Doc—the three old maids. Then the ladies of the Tuesday Club—middle-aged and older women who looked pretty determined to keep things civil. Jesse choked to see his mother's friends together in the same pews where they had grieved their sister Charlotte. Then, pushed into the very middle of it all, sat the Torgerson family, and a pew where the old cowboys from Vaughn sprawled, along with other farmers who shook hands with Jesse because he held out his right arm until they did. Back of them, widespread valley folk who didn't want to miss the excitement, should there be some, which seemed likely.

The altar had been lifted aside and replaced with a long table and three chairs. Leo, Sheriff Buzz in the middle, and an empty chair for Jesse. Over the heads of the crowd, his pa gave him a look that meant, "Let's get going." Jesse took his place.

"This here meeting shall come to order," the sheriff shouted in a tone of authority. Everyone quieted, faced forward. The sheriff's tan shirt stretched taut over the barrel of his chest. He had one bushy eyebrow running straight across his forehead, and it raised and lowered itself as he made his points. "Some of you come here on Sundays, this ain't Sunday but it's the biggest room in town. I'm here to make sure things stay orderly. Rev is here… is here to… Rev, you say it." The sheriff turned to Leo with his eyebrow raised in a questioning wiggle.

The Beekeeper's Question

"I'm here to moderate," Leo spoke up. "We have differing opinions, and we are going to listen to one another and take turns talking. You have up to three minutes to speak your piece."

"Heck, Rev, you get ten minutes on Sundays," a call from the crowd.

Leo let himself smile. "Yes, but as the sheriff noted, this isn't Sunday." He looked over the room and cleared his throat, "As you know, the government has set goals for American farmers and ranchers to increase food production to feed the country, the military, and the Allies. At the same time, we are hugely short of manpower. Last year's quotas took a toll in the valley and this year we are asked to produce 20% more. And Washington says we got to solve these labor issues ourselves." Leo nodded to Jesse.

Jesse pulled a clipping from his pocket. "This piece in the *Great Falls Tribune*, estimates a shortage of 10,000 laborers in western states." Someone let out a whistle.

Another catcall, "You got 10,000 Injuns you planning to bring down then, Jesse?" One of the Tuesday Club women turned and glared at a man behind her.

"Let him finish," Buzz sounded firm.

"In Nebraska," Jesse continued, "They estimate thousands of high schoolers, even city boys, will need to help farmers. We only got about 500 people in the whole valley, and that includes babies and old folks." Jesse gulped a breath. "These boys are a gesture of goodwill." He motioned to the front row where the boys sat, hardly moving. "They are…"

"They're getting paid!" Homer's voice boomed over the crowd. "That's employment, not goodwill. They better be working."

Bill Sivertsen stood up and turned to face his neighbor. "Running cattle isn't the same as crops, Homer. In the past five days, with these boys working, Tim and me, with Rickard and Gladd, we got our fields harrowed and planted. We grabbed the good weather. They earned their money, and I need 'em back to thin."

"They should be volunteering for the patriotism of it. Everybody's making sacrifices," Homer retorted.

Bill stood his ground. "I'm a patriot and I'm gonna get paid. So are you when the calves go. Farmers got to admit this war came in the nick of time for us. Commodity prices bounced back. Demand went up." A murmur of agreement filled the back rows. "The world needs what we're doing here in Pigeon River, and we're determined to do it."

Homer folded his arms over his belly. "You gonna make me hire Injuns? You settin' a president?"

"Precedent," said Leo.

Bill kept going, "So what if I hire these boys." He gestured to the row of clean-shirted, black-haired, copper-skinned youth who sat across the aisle, "What's in your craw, Homer? Nobody's bothering you. Nobody's trespassing."

"Injuns are Injuns," Homer stammered. "You want them working in the field alongside our kids? Alongside white girls fresh out of home economics class?"

Bill stared at his neighbor. "I don't see the harm…"

"You watch what gets thieved." Homer sounded sure of himself, like a man predicting rain by morning.

The meeting stalled. Folks held their breath, shuffled their feet. The sheriff coughed and Leo cleared his throat. Jesse prayed for guidance. But it was Doc who leapt to her feet, stood in the aisle, and whirled to face the man three rows behind her. "Homer Torgerson, who taught you to think so mean? Anybody in this room should be accused of thieving, it's us." No horsewhip, but her authority was crackling.

Homer hefted himself to standing and shouted back, "That's old history, Doc. We got this land fair and square from the U.S. government."

"It may be history, but it wasn't fair and square." Her voice reverberated with tension. "Come to mowing, to baling, come next winter when that slice down your leg is throbbing, you are gonna need *more* friends, Homer, and more help, not less." Homer looked like a carp thrown out of the river, the bellows of his big body gasping, mouth opening and closing. "Are these cowboys from Vaughn putting themselves out for you?" She gestured at the row of men seated mid-church, "They working for $2.50 a day?!"

Homer shouted to the rafters. "I'll go to Great Falls and get a truckload of Chinks before I let Injuns on my land." Mildred yanked her husband's sleeve.

Doc's hand clenched the pew finial. "You solve your labor shortage however you want, Homer. The farmers are solving their shortage how they want. These Blackfeet boys are here to help because your boys are not."

Homer nearly lunged, "Don't you speak of my sons in the same sentence with Injun boys, Doctor Jesperson!"

Jesse wished he had a gavel. He wished he had an idea how to break the deadlock between Doc and Homer. He glanced at Willow and felt her trust pouring over him. The rest of his Blackfeet family sat utterly still, not drawing attention to the fact they were overhearing what white folks say about Indians when they think Indians don't hear.

Though she was huffing hard, something shifted in Doc. The woman who lived under her weathered skin, a younger woman with long hair before her chopped bob, a woman in a blouse and skirt before her overalls, rose to the surface. Her stance softened and she spoke to the room at large. "In 1910, I got off the train, an old maid doctor driven out of Ohio by men who would not let a woman practice medicine. I came west because here is where I was needed. Some valley people started out prejudiced because of my sex, but when you were bleeding or fevered or in labor, *I* was all you had." She stared at Homer, "I sewed you up last winter, and I'll sew you up again because I am your doctor. My life work is to be here when you need me." She scanned the crowd. "Now the whole world is having an emergency. The world needs more food, and the government says you *must* produce it, because *you* are all this country has." Her voice cracked. "Millions of people are sacrificing to win this war, and they need to be fed. We are soldiers of the soil. Raising food is our part. These Indian boys were invited into the valley by folks who need help. They give us a chance to do together what we cannot do separately."

Harry Rickard stood up, cap in hand. "You know, Doctor, I never even shook hands with an Indian until last Monday." She looked at him with encouragement. "Me and this fellow Darrell been working together all week with a crew of four. He fixed my tractor. I 'preciate him and 'preciate the help. The boys work hard and I'm glad to pay 'em." He gulped and sat down.

Tim stood up. "Jesse and I were high school buddies." Heads swiveled. "I missed him when he left, and I'm glad he's back. He's welcome home. And he's welcome to bring home his family and his friends." Tim took a deep breath, "This war is a hell of a fight. Making sure we got a crop in 1943 is how we care for our Service boys, Indian boys, and each other."

Gloria, so pregnant she could hardly balance in the narrow aisle, pulled herself to standing. "I was born here. I expect to live here my whole life. I want to stand in a Montana big enough for everyone."

Maire jumped to her feet, Flora asleep in her arms. "I'm Jesse's sister-in-law, I stand as a Cooper, working the bees and praying the father of my baby comes home safe."

Hazel stood up, squeezing Bonnie so tight the toddler fussed. "I stand for doing whatever we need to get food on the table and off to the troops. Torgerson, Rickard, and Pocket, we got men in the Pacific. Franklin Cooper's in Africa. Two more classmates are in England flying missions over Germany. Geez, let's just do our part!"

All around Doc, the ladies of the Tuesday Club stood up. Belle stood up. The three little Sivertsen boys jumped up on the pews. Their grandpa Bill and grandma Esther stood up and pulled the shyer farmers up with them. The room held a collective breath.

There was a rustle from the right front rows. Poking one another into action, flipping hair back with a toss of their necks like young horses, all ten boys stood up and turned their brown faces to look at the white faces of the valley people. Ricky-John, Russell, and Robbie stood with hands on each other's shoulders. Then BB and Aggie stood up. Darrell stood up. Willow and Natoyii stood up. Jesse stood and came round to the front of the table. The people of his childhood, the people of his manhood were standing together. Everybody began pivoting in place, looking at each other. Gazes swept over the crowd as folks craned their necks, nodded acknowledgment. And then, before anything else could happen, there was a stir in the middle pew. And holding one another's hands, Mildred and Susan Torgerson stood up.

"I'll be goldarned!" Homer swore into the hush. He pushed his way out of the row stomped down the side aisle. The outliers slouched in their seats.

Mildred called after him, "Don't we have enough war goin' on, Homer? What's wrong if we make a little peace in the valley?"

Homer spun around from the narthex, "What's wrong with it, Milly? My grandpa came west after the Civil War, staked our land before statehood. Dug his own well, plowed through buffalo bones. Cavalry at the Fort because Blackfeet were raiding horses, taking a man's livelihood out from under him, threatening white women." Homer's eyes were like searchlights scanning a night sky. "There's not a man or woman in this room responsible for what happened back then. You people think you're so righteous standing alongside these Injuns, as though you can make things right by them, but you can't. It's done. White folks won. Everyone got to live with the circumstances we got."

The sheriff pushed back his chair. The reverend harrumphed. Doc was nearly lurching out of Belle's grasp. They had had their moment; it was his turn now and Jesse prayed to tap the source Gramma Josie believed was in him. He stepped to the center of the chancel, standing opposite Homer, and called out to the angry rancher. "I am not your enemy, Homer. Coopers and Torgersons been neighbors my whole life. Albert and Ronnie my buddies since grade school. I've worked alongside you getting the hay in." Jesse locked his gaze on Homer and did not blink. "You want to live in the circumstances we got? Well, this is my other village, my other family. We're in the middle of a world war. I'm asking can we make some good happen in both communities?"

"Well, ain't that a noble thought." Homer glared up the aisle. "You Coopers always decidin' how folks should live our religion, how we should read the Bible, and then you determined to drag the rest of us along with your highfalutin ideas." Jesse heard his father gasp. Homer huffed for breath. "You're right, we're neighbors. You need help, I'll give it to yah. We gotta live side by side. I gotta live with my wife. But I got my own ideas, my own plans. Anybody interested in an alternate to Injun labor, you let me know." The church door thudded closed behind him.

Sheriff Buzz pushed his chair back and raised his hand. His eyebrow was jumping like a caterpillar on hot asphalt. "Calm down," he commanded the room. "Everybody take a breath." There was a collective intake of air followed by a slight whoosh of exhale as folks followed the sheriff's order. Buzz spoke into the stunned silence, "Ladies and gentlemen, you got things to think about and I got public safety to protect. I'm assigning a deputy to the Fort tonight, make sure nobody does anything you later regret." His belt buckle clanked against the table. "For now, this meeting has gone far as it can." He shook hands with Jesse, with Leo, and stood down.

The night exhaled a perfume of lilacs and apple blossoms as Jesse and BB walked back through town. "Mr. Torgerson is right about some things." Jesse turned a surprised face to his uncle. "We live in circumstances that can't be undone. Indians can't have America back. We can't live as we did. And so much civilizin' been done to us we can hardly remember ourselves."

"Then what's the good of Gramma's teachings and what she asks Willow to carry?" Jesse thought his heart was going to break.

"The teachings hold our spirits and bodies together. The teachings prove we're still here." BB looked down the block of modest homes, lights on in windows, glimpses of folks putting themselves to bed. "And truth is, white people need us to be here." He scuffed his boot on the moonlit gravel, "There are things we remember for you."

When Jesse eased into the dormitory, the boys were laid out on bedrolls whispering. Russell called out, "Jesse, Darrell, I just want to know, did we win?"

Darrell let out a whoop, "We're going home tomorrow with the money we earned. That's our horse raid."

"It wasn't only money," Jesse added, "People got to meet you, you got to meet people, and tomorrow this valley will be a friendlier place. That's winning."

"But that one old guy and the woman who shouted at him..."

"The woman, Doctor Jesperson, is Gramma's friend. She stood up to Mr. Torgerson, so he knows people are watching out for you. Even his own wife and daughter stood up."

"So," Russell's hushed voice traveled across the bedrolls, "We won, right?"

BB spoke into the shadows, "You stood tall in who you are. Be proud, but don't be fooled. Indians do not win."

Part Three
The War Comes Home

26
Homefront in Summer Days

SUMMER 1943: *German command withdraws their U-boat fleet, putting the Atlantic in Allied control. July 10, the Allies invade Sicily. July 12, the battle of Prokhorovka, the largest tank battle in history, rages on the Eastern Front.*

MAIRE DEVOTED HER MIDNIGHT HOURS TO WORRY. Each breath sought the echo of Franklin's breath. Tangled in insomnia, her fingers twitched on the tenuous cord that tethered them. But since the night she had been sucked into the engine room, seen the face of Broin's maniacal pursuit, she was terrified to travel the night clouds. She woke tired and prayed into dawnlight, her hands folded over the sheet. "Thank you, God, for bringing me safe to Pigeon River. I know you are besieged with prayers for protection, but please keep mine on the list. Thank you for victory in North Africa. Watch over me broody man. Cover me trail that the evil one never finds me. Bless the bees and the Indians and all folks doing our best. Thank you for me baby and me life. Amen."

Doc came down from the attic. She held Maire's face in calloused hands and noted dark circles under her eyes. "You got to take care of yourself, too, mama."

"It's the war, Doc. We all doing more'n what we ought."

Willow walked up the road. The little family was back at the cabin while Jesse set supers with his pa. The two young mothers stood side-by-side cutting bread. "You have bad medicine on you." Willow spoke so softly Maire barely registered the sentence. "He is a black mouth round with teeth." Maire stared at her sister-in-law. "You need to call on your protection."

The knife shook in Maire's hand. "What do I do?"

Willow lifted a piece of bread to her face and inhaled the yeasty aroma. "Long ago, before church religion, white people carried tribal teaching. You did first to yourselves what you did later to us. You been forced to forget your old ways. But your grandmother had the long memory, like Gramma Josie has ours."

"My grandmother is dead."

"Her spirit is not dead. You can find protection in the Medicine ways of your tribe."

"Like *Tsi-ksi-ká-ta-pi-wa-tsin*," Maire struggled to pronounce the Piikuni word.

"The sources are the same. *Ksaahkoom*, the Earth and Great Creator. A people belong to their original Way of Knowing. Listen with your Irish ear." Drum wanted toast. The baby woke. The day shifted into ordinary.

"I will try." Maire hummed to the waking-up bees.

Leo's thoughts rattled around the truck cab. Ever since Homer had challenged his pastoral intentions, familiar faces seemed unreadable, heads bowed in private opinion. Making their way through the lectionary, Sunday by Sunday, year after year, he preached of the prophets and teachings of Jesus. That's how it went; that was his job. When they stood for the Indians, wasn't that gesture proof his beekeeper's question had spread like honey over the bread of valley lives?

Leo watched plumes of dust rise over the greening haze of sugar beet fields as various vehicles made their way toward the work of thinning. United Methodist Women, young wives, local teens would co-mingle with the Blackfeet boys. Working for common good. People behaving more like bees. Leo headed toward Torgerson's ranch.

Mildred stood on the porch wiping her hands on her apron.

"Morning, Milly. I was out this way. Thought I'd chat with Homer, see if we can find a truce."

"He's not much in a peaceful mood these days." A squarish woman in a faded flowered dress, she squinted into the brightness gathered at Leo's shoulders. "Took a bit to find our own truce after that showdown. Not sorry I stood up to him, but it's complicated, the mind of a man. My own mind too, for that matter." She pushed at her hair. "Susan and I not doing field work, so you know."

"I'll pass on word." Leo hoped he sounded understanding. "Jesse and his crew arrived last night. The church women are organizing lunches."

"Try not to rile him up again." Mildred hunched her shoulders. "Last I saw he was headed towards the field parcels to check on stock, watch his alfalfa grow, says he's going to cut soon. You got bees over that way."

Leo met the woman's gaze. "I'll be mindful. I know you're carrying heartache."

"It's anticipation of heartbreak that's wearying. If Albert's ship don't sink, he's likely okay. Ronnie, well MIA don't tell you much. Homer says it means they haven't got a corpse or a dog tag. I say it means he's outta the fight but not outta the war. Japs probably got him, and that's not good." She turned back inside, "Good luck."

Highland yard #14: Leo could see Homer's pick-up from a quarter mile away but couldn't make sense of the scene. Man. Cattle. Field. Hives. But not in their right positions. Cows had broken through fencing and were up to their knees in clover. Homer slapped at them, trying to drive them back through the fence gap onto the drier range grass, but the animals weren't eager to move from the lush feast. Leo leaned out the cab window, "Help you, Homer?"

The rancher was red in the face, sweating frustration. "They're gonna bloat," he shouted with a note of desperation. Preacher Boy barked. "That dog got any herding sense?" Leo opened the door and prayed instinct would click in. Preacher Boy crouched in clover, darted at the cattle, barked, backed up, circled round, darted again. "For a dog used to workin' bees, he's doing pretty good." Leo grabbed a canvas tarp to flap at the stolid creatures. Soon he too was red-faced, sweating, and frustrated. At least he and Homer were working too hard to disagree. The rumble of a pick-up made background noise.

When the truck pulled into the bee yard, a familiar voice hailed them. "Morning, gentlemen... looks like you could use a cowboy." The two older men stopped in their tracks. Two cows frisked past them.

Homer had his hands on his thighs, half-bent to catch his breath. "You actually got a horse in that trailer, Jess?"

Jesse was standing with one foot still in the cab. "It's an Indian pony, Homer, but I'm a valley man, and I'm offering." Homer twitched a kind of nod. Jesse backed Windy out of the box, pulled a saddle out of the truck bed, and in minutes was mounted. Homer positioned himself by the broken barbed wire section, Leo stood alongside the hives. Jesse and horse maneuvered the cattle while Preacher Boy's barky darting kept them from wandering too far into clover. Twenty minutes later a dozen head of cattle were pushed back into the grassland.

"Where you learn to ride like that?" Homer sounded impressed.

"Reservation is running beef too, and a hard-fought battle with the U.S. government to allow it, but meat is meat. We're part of the war effort now." Jesse dismounted and handed Leo the reins while the horse helped himself to trampled clover stems. Homer tossed him a pair of leather gloves. Jess grabbed the string of barbed wire pulled hard while the two of them laced it back together best they could. "I can stay and watch 'em while you get the tubing and squeezebox."

"Thought you were here to pull helpless little beet seedlings outta the ground."

"Tim can boss the field crews." He appraised Homer's mood. "And my friend Darrell taught me everything I know about handling stock."

"The limping guy?" Jesse nodded. "Those boys here?" Jesse nodded again. "Working alongside white girls?"

"Working alongside most of the junior class, young wives and ladies of the Tuesday Club making sandwiches. Everything's chaperoned. Likely done in four, five days. Then everybody's going home. It's not a land grab."

Homer's face flushed red. "I got plans come fall. Don't you expect to come down takin' more of our money."

Jesse breathed as steady as the horse. "Today, you need a cowboy. I'm a cowboy." He stuck out his hand.

Homer stared at Jesse's palm. "Pay you same as the Injuns."

Jesse extended his hand a couple inches farther. "Not like that, Homer. This is neighbor to neighbor, doing what needs to be done."

Homer shook on the deal. "I'll get the stall and hose." He turned and spit, swung his truck into the road.

Leo was holding Windy's halter. "I don't understand what just happened, Jess, but the Lord works in mysterious ways."

"I'm doing what Gramma calls bridging the worlds," Jesse pressed his face into Windy's mane. "What are you doing out here?"

"It's been bothering me, what Homer said in church."

"For Homer, actions speak louder than words, unless they're his words." Jesse stroked the horse's neck, "You flapping that canvas probably did more good than anything you could say. Got a hammer? I can better stretch this fence." Leo began digging through his toolbox. "Alfalfa this green—good for bees but not for bovines—makes gas in their stomachs. They swell up. Lungs get pressed until they're suffocating, heart gives out. Bloat is a painful death." Jesse began torquing the wire.

"Makes a swarm of bees look pretty tame." They were standing in the buzz of a summer day.

"Best to catch 'em before they're down. Put 'em in the squeeze stall, tie up their heads and make 'em swallow a length of garden hose. All that gas comes belching out. Homer's got to keep the bunch separated, watch 'em." Jesse pulled the barb wire taut.

"He sure could use his sons," Leo sighed.

"Guess the son of his neighbor will have to do, even if I'm one of those uppity Coopers." Jesse grinned. "Leave me the dog. Can you swing by Sivertsen's, tell Tim?"

"You be okay?"

"Torgersons always had their own ways, Pa. What he said in the meeting I've heard before. Today, I'm gonna be his ranch hand." Jesse swung into the saddle, adjusted his seat.

"Al and Ronnie, why do you think they enlisted?" Leo felt small on the ground.

Jesse leaned on the saddle horn. "Pa, for the rest of our lives people are going to be asking what we did in the war. We're gonna live around men telling stories of the Big Fight. There's gonna be mamas, widows, and orphans with their Gold Star sacrifices." He stretched in the stirrups, ready to ride, "And then there's gonna be the guys who didn't go. Tim talking sugar beets. Darrell with his short leg. I promised Gramma Josie that protecting Willow would be my first concern, always. Even the U.S. Army not gonna get me to break that vow. I'm guessing Al and Ronnie thought enlisting's just what a Torgerson does. Makes a better story, assuming they live through it." The horse stomped sideways, nervous among the bees.

The Beekeeper's Question

Dirt under her fingernails, Maire eased to ground and leaned against a fencepost, admiring her garden. Flora pulled at her shirt, and she felt the tiny tributaries of her breasts release their milky creek. After sucking, the baby's lips went slack with sleep. The sun was warm, the breeze just perfect. Bees were buzzing from the hives kept close for pollinating gardens and orchards. Maire dozed in the safety of sunlight.

Nana walked toward her through a field of lavender light. "There you are, me gurl," she called. "The faeries and I been looking for you." Her grandmother's wispy white hair shone like a halo.

"I dinna believe in faeries, Nana." In the dream, she saw herself as the saddened girl she had become after Broin yanked her from the hedgerow and taught her the world was even meaner than she already suspected. "Broin hurt me. I called them to help. They dint come." Tears flooded her dreaming eyes.

Nana handed Maire a handkerchief with a shamrock embroidered into the corner. "It's hard to understand how life pieces fit together. 'Specially the hurting bits, but would yah have come to 'merica, if not on the run?"

"I got away, but..." tears spilled down Maire's dream cheeks, *"The faeries let Broin break me."*

"You're not broken, mo chroi.*" Nana pushed back Maire's curls and kissed her at the hairline. "Love is a healing balm. Quit mooning in the dark and learn fey in the daylight."*

"It's not that world anymore, Nana. There's a war. My man's gone silent. Ma drowned. Evil is loose."

"There's always war somewhere, darlin'. As for evil..." Nana spit sideways three times, *"Father, Son, and Holy Ghost. Mother, Daughter, Faerie Queen, it's always lurking about. You jes' keep it outta yur heart." Nana seemed infused with light.* Maire blinked. *"As fer yer Ma, we always promised we'd have a cuppa tea in heaven, and we do." She offered Maire the sweetest smile. "When the Old Ones went to the West, the faeries stayed*

with the humans to keep magic in the world. Do you well to make friends again."

"There aren't faeries in Montana, Nana." Maire now felt herself turning full grown.

"They bee all around you." The old woman looked flustered. "Oh my, I'm fluttering. Yur me special gurl, Maire. Keep your heart open. All things under heaven have reason, even hurt, even dark." Her voice grew faint, "You got the olde blood, listen to the wee."

"Wait Nana!" Maire's call bridged the dream and the garden. She woke. Her back was sore where she'd pressed against the fencepost. A tiny droplet of milk drooled down Flora's chin. She wiped the baby's face, astonished to be holding a handkerchief embroidered with a shamrock.

Bees floated over the garden. Inside their *hmmm* seemed the tiniest song, *"Wee are the ladies who dance from flower to flower. Wee are the ladies who know the honey power."* A small cluster flew out of the strawberry bed and arrived six inches in front of her face, fuzzy yellow shoulders, striped bodies, their wings a blur as they hovered and darted.

Maire clutched the baby and extended her other hand. Three bees began walking in tickling steps across her calloused palm. She raised her hand to her ear. *"Wee are the ladies who dance from flower to flower. Wee are the ladies who know the honey power."*

Maire flicked her wrist and sent the insects buzzing overhead. Amidst her surprise, something shivered awake in her. "If a handkerchief can come through the veil, then both worlds must exist. And if bees can sing, maybe the Irish Way of Knowing is not lost." As if in answer, one hovering bee flew directly at the center of Maire's brow, six tiny legs touched her skin. *"Hmmm,"* resounded in her mind. Her heart filled with honey. Her blood ran golden. Every part of her felt cleansed. "So, I am not broken then?" She held onto Flora while the day held onto her. *Hmmm.*

The Beekeeper's Question

Time drifted in sunshine. She began to hum D-above-middle-C. After a while she came back to herself, rose and did laundry, but she was not the same.

Doc stood on her porch counting lightning strikes and clutching her forearms under a roiling thunderhead that filled half the horizon. It had been a month since the beets were thinned, the broad-leafed plants could withstand a bit of wind shredding, but green wheat was vulnerable. Hail would ruin the crop. "Don't do that!" she yelled at the storm, "We got enough going on."

Fourth of July had been somber: production quotas, rationing, shortages of nearly everything. At least the lack of firecrackers meant all the valley fingers were still attached. The radio carried a nightly stream of serious news interspersed with Big Band music as though to offer worried listeners a chance to get up and dance between battle reports and the weather forecast. Fierce fighting in the Pacific. Everyone knew that Ralph was in it, that Ronnie was missing, that Al was supply sergeant on a munitions ship. Coopers assumed Franklin had landed in Sicily. Doc counted twenty valley boys in service, six on deferments, and a dozen young women at the coast working shipyards.

As news of fighting shifted and the whereabouts of the military men became clear, Gertie moved thumbtacks around a map of the world tacked behind the register. Along one side she listed their names. With no one else in earshot she whispered to Doc, "If we lose one, I can't just cross out his name."

"Maybe outline the name respectfully in black," Doc suggested.

"Maybe we'll be lucky."

"We won't be that lucky."

Doc scanned the storm, waiting for trouble. Within minutes, the rain hit so intensely it blurred her view. Waterfalls gushed off the porch roof. The yard funneled with runoff. She heard

Bugle Boy's whinny of alarm and called into the gusty roar, "Get in the stable, you darn fool!" She decided to follow her own advice, patted the wall of the sturdy cabin, giving thanks to the men who had built it.

They had withstood the test of time together: the neighbors, the doctor, the house, the horse, the land. They were in a test now when the world would swing toward the Allies or the Axis, toward democracy or tyranny. That's what Roosevelt said. And squatting on landscape her President could scarce imagine, Jereldene Jesperson cringed under flashes of spiked light and roaring thunder that confirmed his warnings and stirred the worst of her fears. The cat curled her claws into the weave of Doc's summer sweater as a howling night tore around the house.

Next morning, Doc woke sprawled on the couch, still in her clothes, and peeked into a sky of faded denim blue. She put on boots to go feed Bugle Boy. The corner of the shed was charred. A black vein of patterns forked down one wall and burned onto the shoulder of the old horse. The gelding's body had crumpled with his legs under him, head dropped in wet straw, eyes blank. She eased down, stroking the familiar contours of his withers, shoulders, the cowlick of hair in the middle of his forehead. She lifted his heavy head onto her lap, kissed his soft lips, and wept.

Bugle Boy had been an Army horse, headed for trenches in The Great War, but he bolted at loud noises—guns or thunder. Homer's father bought him at auction. Turned out he wasn't much good at plowing either, so in the spring of 1915, Torgerson had shown up in Doc's yard with the horse and a buggy. The gelding became her partner in the delivery of medicine, careening into farmyards, even as the Model-T and a parade of vehicular descendants took over delivering everything else. He was old, but she grieved that he'd died in terror. She'd ask Bill to bring down his front loader, dredge a hole and roll the ole boy into it.

The Beekeeper's Question

Three days later, Homer arrived with a bouquet of zinnias. "Bugle Boy is the end of an era," he held out the flowers. "Time you corral up with the other unmarried ladies. You, Gertie, Belle, institutions in this town, but none of you fillies. I'll give you fair price, cash. Mitchell house behind the store is sitting empty, you could put a clinic in front, live in back."

"We've had this conversation before, Homer." Doc hid her face in the blossoms. "I'll put these on his grave. Please thank Milly."

"You've been lucky out here, a woman alone. But today's world got Hitler and Hirohito, Nazis, and kamikazes. It's not the good old days." He gave her a stern look. "You said at the church we got to move forward." He tipped his seed cap. At the truck door, he turned, "Whatever Sivertsen offers you, I'll raise him."

Doc put the flowers in a mason jar, wiped pollen off her nose, and set the bouquet into the mound of loosened dirt that used to be her horse, the man of her life. "Not for sale," she muttered.

July 23, 1943
Dear Jesse,

Would you and Willow like my place? You both need a homestead here. Drum can play with Sivertsen's crew, a corral for your horse. (She stopped writing and blew her nose.) Fix it up however you like. The stable got hit by lightning Monday night. The bolt charred one wall and killed Bugle Boy, but it can be repaired for Windy. Garden is probably redeemable. I'm thinking of moving to town. Folks need a modern doctor, a real office, metal table and trays, sign out front, clinic hours. Have to keep up the practice now that Boyd's not coming back.

I don't want money, just to keep it in the family. Love, Auntie Jere

Entering town, she walked to the Mitchell house. She peered through dirty windows, trying to imagine herself at home in the clapboard building, hearing people, trucks and trains. She overheard Gertie's voice from half a block away and watched her come out of her own living quarters at the back of the store. Doc turned, waving the letter.

Gertie wiped her hands on the postmaster smock she wore in that part of her domain. "You just made the pickup. And I got a letter you can take by Coopers. Come here, Jere. I'm so sorry about Bugle Boy." Doc let Gertie give her a sideways hug. "Don't suppose I got anything on the shelf that can soothe your grief. Want some canned Spam? Made for the Army, of course. Calvin Gladd came by. Fresh shaved, clean shirt on a Wednesday, lingering over Campbell soup cans." Doc clutched her letter; Gertie carried on, "Turns out Mr. Gladd is a widower. He's making a supply run to the Falls this Saturday, wondered if I'd like to come along, maybe see a movie." Gertie snorted. "Imagine that man courting on me. Should I go? Susan Torgerson could run the store a few hours. Do her good to come into town, talk to folks. What you think?" She reached for Doc's letter.

Doc backed up. Coming to town made her feel like she was surrendering something, like she was going to be old now. She swatted tears, which Gertie misinterpreted. "Ahh, Jere, at least Bugle went out with a flourish what with you and Belle driving buggy into the middle of Homer's raid on the Fort, war horse at last. Mark my words, he'll be a legend." Gertie seized Doc's letter, popped it into an official canvas sack stamped "U.S. Postal Service" and zipped it closed. Then she pulled a cream-colored envelope out of Cooper's slot. "Came yesterday." Gertie held the envelope to her nose, "Perfume."

Name of sender, Annenberg: return address, Philadelphia. Doc's mouth went dry. "Talk to Susan. Say yes to Mr. Gladd." She backed out of the store, crossed the highway, and slipped through the cemetery gate where she slid to sitting pressed against the sunned heat of Charlotte's headstone.

"What should I do now, old friend?" How Mrs. Annenberg had found out about Pigeon River was assuredly not good news. Doc fussed half-consciously at the corner of the seal. Fancy stationery, not much glue. A flattened twig pried a gap.

July 15, 1943
Dear Mary,

    I am sure you are surprised to hear from me. One day in your courtship, I overheard Franklin say the name "Pigeon River," and it stuck in my mind. I never spoke it to another soul as you seemed so intent on your privacy, but I must break silence and hope a general delivery letter will reach you.

    I think of you often, hoping you had safe delivery of your baby. I am finally pregnant myself and begin to comprehend the fierce stirrings of mother love. It is this that compels me to warn you that a derelict and violent man showed up here last week. He forced his way into the kitchen and threatened Regina with a knife until she confessed all she knew, which was the date you left and that you were headed to your husband's family. The man went into a rage, throwing pots and dishes until Regina was able to shoo him out with a broom and call the police. Other than a general physical description, there was nothing we could tell the authorities. Roger hired a security guard to stand duty on our stoop and there has been no further interaction.

    I presume you were once acquainted with this man and may understand he is pursuing you. Regina would beg your pardon if she knew I was writing. It's a big country. I pray you stay safe. If you wish, let me know how you are.
Sincerely,
Eleanor Annenberg

The letter shook in Doc's hand. Montana was thirty times larger than Northern Ireland. That would take a man from Cullybackey a lot of figuring. Broin couldn't know about Pigeon River. Could he? Maire and her baby were still safe. Weren't they? She didn't have to tell anyone yet. Did she? She folded the letter. She had glue at home.

Maire watched the activity of the garden hives. The busy insects a blurry cluster landing at the lip of the hive box, greeted by guard bees, allowed to enter with their cargo of pollen. Outgoing clusters lifted into air and beelined for destinations untraceable. "Bee calm," something inside her whispered. "Bee a flower. Open." Maire breathed stillness.

The bees seemed to move in slower motion, their wings stirring sun motes, tiny legs dangling. "Wee are the hmmm," a whispery voice greeted her. "Wee are the Unity." They aimed for raspberry canes thick with blossoms and greening berries.

"Why are you talking to me?"

"You have honey mind."

A thought twitched to the surface of her thoughts. "How am I hearing you?"

"The ear in your heart tunes to the hmmm."

Maire looked down at her full breasts, dirtied shirt. "How is it possible you speak English?"

"Wee don't speak English. Wee speak hmmm. You hear in English. And when you speak, wee hear in hmmm." Several bees drifted in formation around her. The whisper continued. "There is within all things, an Under Tongue, a language of Unity. This is how the bee speaks to the flower and the flower speaks to the bee. This is the Song of Creation."

Maire felt something in the vicinity of her heart begin to vibrate. "How could I not know this?!" She looked at the garden. She looked down the dusty road. She looked to the hills. Everything seemed to be vibrating.

The Beekeeper's Question

"You have not been taught," the voice responded, "You are learning."

Learning would change her, this much Maire understood. "The faeries gave you listening. Now we pollinate your understanding."

"And my man?" she asked, "Is he listening?"

"War is loud. Fear is deafening. But wee hold him."

21
Summer Sorrow

JULY 24, 1943: *American and British aerial bombing of Hamburg, Germany, creates one of the largest firestorms of the war, destroys the city, kills 37,000 civilians, and wounds 180,000.*

TWO RINGS. MAIRE WIPED HER HANDS ON THE APRON and picked up the phone, along with anyone else who was interested. "Hello, Coopers." Well, everyone knew that.

"It's Gertie. Is the Reverend around?" Her voice sounded strained.

"He's out back." She had just retrieved Flora from Hazel's care. "We've been checking bee yards."

"Would you send him up. I have a message." She hung up.

Whatever Gertie wasn't saying slammed Maire's heart so hard she staggered. She ran to the honey house with Flora riding her hip. "I'm coming with you," she announced. "If it's serious, we're together. If it's not serious, we'll get Flora a teething biscuit." They tried to look casual, walking the long block to the church and crossing the highway.

Gertie handed Leo a telegram and blew her nose in her apron. Leo read quickly and looked into Maire's eyes. "It's Ralph."

Maire swayed with nervous relief, then wanted to howl, but she knew it was Hazel's right to cry first... and his parents'... while Bonnie watched in puzzlement.

Leo patted Gertie's shoulder. "Signal Doc. Give us an hour."

Hazel's smile froze when she saw them. "No, no, no." She backed up, letting the screen door bang in their faces. "I thought you were my friend," she shouted to Maire. Then desperately, "Rev, Rev, is it the worst?!"

Leo looked her straight in the eyes through the mesh that separated them and firmly but kindly spoke the words that would cut her life in half: Ralph/no Ralph. "Listen to me, Hazel. What is, already is. What remains is the necessity of bearing it." He opened the door, "We need to come inside." Ethel Pocket stood in the doorway between kitchen and parlor biting her knuckles. Maire helped Hazel into a chair. Bonnie came running on her stout toddler legs and Maire slid down to pull the toddler onto the half of her lap not already occupied by Flora. Leo kept a grip on Hazel's shoulder. He looked Ethel in the eyes. "Official telegram. Your dear Ralph has been killed in action."

Ethel backed into the dining room and wrapped her arms around Ralph's empty chair, the one with his shirt draped over the backrest and a seed cap resting on the seat. "He had the deferment," her voice cracked raggedly, "Now look what's come of my sweet boy." She collapsed onto the chair beside Ralph's and hugged the wooden frame against her sagging breasts as through to hold him. Maire sat at Hazel's feet, one arm solidly around Hazel's knees, as if to tether her to the ground. Her friend was shaking uncontrollably, teeth chattering in the late afternoon heat.

The screen door banged. Doc strode in, the parson's steady partner. She raised Hazel's face to look into hers. "You're in shock, Haz." The girl's eyes were dilated and far away. "You can't go with him, dearie. It doesn't work that way." Doc pinched Hazel's cheeks. "Stay here. Bonnie needs you. Look at me, darling." Maire hugged Hazel's shins and watched. "I'm going to give you some honey to balance your blood. Open your mouth."

Doc pulled a small jar of granulated honey from her bag. It was dark and grainy. Wildflowers, South 13, Maire thought. Doc spooned a glop onto Hazel's tongue. "Let that dissolve." Doc cradled Hazel's face with calloused hands, kissed her forehead. "I'm so sorry. He's a fine man, your Ralph. We will miss him forever." Hazel was still shaking. "Let's make you a cup of tea," Doc's presence filled the room, "Maire, get the kettle on. I'll see to Ethel."

The heat of the day was pouring off Maire, but if Doc wanted tea, tea they would have. She handed Bonnie up to her mother's lap and, with Flora still in one arm, fetched the kettle.

"There's cold in the fridge." It was the first thing Hazel had said since, "Is it the worst?"

The ordinariness tore at Maire's heart. "Cold for us then, but hot for you, Doc wants you regulated."

"If I'm regulated, will this be a bad dream?" Her eyes searched Maire's face.

"No, Haz. It's going to stay real. And I'm going to stay your friend. We're going to raise these girls to be brave, strong women like their mamas… And that's all I know." Hazel nuzzled Bonnie's head, hair the color of straw, straight as a stick and full of cowlicks, Pocket hair. Waiting for the kettle to whistle, Maire stroked on Hazel's hair. "Here if you need me, girl." Leo left to find Caleb. Doc was sitting alongside Ethel, who sat leaking tears, one arm still clutching the empty chair.

Kettle whistled. Tea made. No one cared. The only thing they wanted was to roll the sun backwards, to savor a few more moments before the yellow telegram destroyed their ordinary happiness. Her wedding ring clinked against the cup as Hazel sipped chamomile tea. The new time, the widowed, orphaned, sorrowful time ticked mercilessly forward.

"Shall I set some food?" Maire whispered, "People will come by soon's they hear." In her mind, she already saw the traipse of older women and the schoolgirls turned young wives and mothers; she saw the farm men clustered on the porch, slapping jeans and caps, stomping the day's dirt out of cleated boot soles. Ralph and Hazel's friends, Caleb and Ethel's friends, everyone mingling together as they had all their lives. Hazel clutched her toddler and the telegram—what remained.

August sweated by. Alfalfa was harvested into bales, wheat swayed in mesmerizing waves, hives filled with honey, sugar beets grew. Summer looked normal, but the community was unsettled. Like a hive with disturbance deep in the box, the buzz discordant. The losses of war sat amongst them, a bear they could not shoo out of the valley. "We need one of your Good Shepherd sermons," Gertie implored Leo at the store.

He offered her a worn smile. "Been waiting on Pockets to say they're ready."

Gertie nodded, "Sunday, then."

The church simmered with heat, windows open, doors ajar. On the altar, a collection of photographs. Ralph as a baby. Ralph as a schoolboy. Ralph with his slicked-back hair at high school graduation. The bride and groom at this very altar, and one final pose of the little family taken last Christmas, Ralph in uniform, Bonnie on his knee, and Hazel with her hair done in a Victory roll forcing a smile.

Maire set a vase of gladiolas at the altar's base and studied the plain wooden cross that hung suspended from the front of the church, cottonwood timbers the men had jointed and shined. "This fight better be worth it, God," she whispered, "It sure causing pain." She slid into a pew alongside Jesse, who smelled of honey and beeswax. He handed over Flora. Drum crawled onto his lap. Willow held his other hand. Family.

Susan Torgerson sat up front in a line of Hazel's girlhood chums and, just as the service started, there was a slight ruffle as Homer and Mildred slid into the back pew. It was the first time Torgersons had entered the church since "that night with the Indians," as everyone now referred to the community meeting. Their faces looked set with determination to stay at the back, to not be the next family seated in the front row of grief.

christina baldwin

Gladys brought the final chords of "Nearer my God to Thee" to a vibrato ending. Leo took a drink of water. "We are gathered this morning to honor the sacrifice of our valley son, Ralph Elfrid Pocket, and to uphold the sorrow of his family. Ralph's valor and courage took him far from Pigeon River. His body is buried on a shore we will never see and cannot even imagine." A sob escaped from Hazel and half a dozen hands fluttered to rest on her shoulders. "To find comfort in this moment, requires trust, as the hymn proclaims, that beyond the scope of our understanding, Ralph's soul rests nearer to God." The words of the beekeeper wafted over the garden of his congregation. He recounted Ralph's too-short life. He prayed for the family. He prayed for all the boys gone to war. He prayed for the hardworking soldiers of the field. Sunlight streamed stained glass patterns on their bowed heads. When all was said and done, Ralph Pocket was still dead, but at least they would bear it together. Gertie drew a black box around his name and pulled his thumbtack from the map.

Maire laid Flora on a blanket in the grass beside her at the edge of the garden and stroked her wee back. She had grown confident that the bees would not sting the one she had named in their honor and relaxed as their hypnotic scent and sound floated in the air around her. The high-pitched *hmmm* of their lullaby coalesced into words through the Under Tongue. Maybe they would understand her sorrow. "We have suffered a great loss," she whispered. "One who was beloved has died."

"*What is died?*" the *hmmm* asked.

"It's when you stop. Fall out of the sky. Do not return to hive."

"*Hmmm. Wee maidens die all the time. Die is not important: Hive is important Hive is Unity.*"

"Don't you want to live?" Maire felt her heart jump.

"*Maidens fly so Hive survives.*"

The Beekeeper's Question

"But what about you?"

"There is only Hive," the wee responded. *"Wee are Hive. Bee-ing is Hive. Hive is our song, our queen, our pips, our honey, our story, our gift."* Maire held out her hand and several small, fuzzy beings landed on her palm. She raised her hand until they were eye to eye. She cocked her head one way: the bees cocked their heads the other way. *"What is suffer?"* the *hmmm* asked.

Maire thought a long time. "Suffer is when the bear has come and wrecked the comb. When the Queen is dead."

"Ah, suffer is Hive not in balance." Their opaque black eyes seemed to search hers. *"Balance is order,"* the *hmmm* said.

"That's what Leo said. He studies your balance."

"Balance is peace. Peace is unity. Unity is Hive. Wee are Hive that flies, makes honey, makes wax, tends pips. Queen is Hive that makes generations and holds center. Drones are Hive that bears seed. We are Hive. Hive is one."

Maire sighed. "Human beings want individuality. Everybody is different, like flowers in a garden."

"Ohhhh, difference is how flower tastes, smells, what it offers to Hive."

"Yes. And one flower has been cut from our garden. This makes us sad." A tear slid down her cheek.

"There is only garden. Flower blooms to call the wee. Wee come to gather pollen. Flower seeds and withers. Why suffer when flower gives way so that more flowers may come?" The bees lifted off her skin.

"We did not want this flower to give way," she whispered after them. "He was young. We hoped he had more life. We suffer in his honor." The bees flitted among the bean blossoms. Carefree. Maire resigned herself to loving, to suffering, to being human.

28
Hot Nights

SEPTEMBER 1, 1943: *Sicily conquered. Soviets struggle at great casualty cost against German forces. Allied command debates how to advance into the Reich.*

AUGUST ENDED IN HEAT. The sun rose, the sun set; honey needed extracting, house needed cleaning, meals needed preparing, baby needed tending, vegetables needed canning, dog needed combing, Doc needed help settling into town. Jesse needed to refurbish Doc's cabin. Tim and Darrell needed to excavate the side yard to lay a septic tank. Hazel needed a friend. Leo needed to keep an eye on the souls of the valley folks. Wheat needed harvesting. Alfalfa needed baling. Everyone needed more sleep. Everyone needed more time. Everyone needed more help. Everyone worked as hard as they could. Every evening, elbows propped on farmhouse tables, people listened to radio news. Allied troops fought over tiny dots on the map in Gertie's store. Pockets couldn't abide to look. Homer drank sympathy beers at Belle's.

Maire paced the edge of the garden yard hurling stones against the wall of the old barn. No letter from Franklin. British and American bombers were wrecking Axis supply lines, bombing munitions factories and petroleum plants and killing thousands of civilian Germans. The bees were a tornado around her. Her arm whipped back through the haze of tiny companions, then forward as she pitched the pebble. No letter from Franklin. The leap from North Africa to Sicily had been declared victory in five weeks. She collapsed into a heap of weeping. The bees swirled over her, some landing on her back. D-above-middle-C a dirge of *hmmm*. No letter from Franklin. Mussolini fell from power. The war seemed spring-loaded. No letter from Franklin. She no longer trusted the APO or herself to reach him.

> 26 August 1943,
> Dear Franklin,
> Where are you? How are you? Why don't you write? I'm holding our life together, and I don't know if you even care. I'm exhausted, Frank. It's not bloody battles, but it's hard. Everybody sacrificing. Ralph got killed. Leo says you are alive because the Army hasn't said different. I say you are alive because I feel your breath in the world. But how are we going to find each other again? Please don't let the war eat your soul. The news says we are winning though the road will be long. There is life ahead for you. Where are you? How are you? Why don't you write? One word is all I need. Have mercy, please. Moy

Night blows hot breath across the sheets. The hairs in her ears vibrate at the frequency of Hive. Hive in distress. The *hmmm* is screaming. Maire bolts up, listens. Now that she has tuned to it, the death buzz is all she can hear. *"The bear has come. Unity burning."* She is not dreaming. She pulls on jeans and a work shirt.

Maire carries Flora across the hall to her grandfather's room and lays the sleeping baby alongside the sleeping man. One of them waking will wake the other. His face is worn with work and wind, one side slack against the pillow. She wants to ease his mouth back into symmetry. She wants to tell him everything

christina baldwin

will be all right. She needs to move fast, to follow the wisdom he has poured into her these honey seasons. She scrawls a note, "Gone to check on bees. Flora's morning bottle in the fridge." She sets the message under his cup.

Maire slips into farm boots. The truck keys are under the seat. Bee bonnet, hive tools, and smoker boxed in among extra supers. She summons the dog from his curled-up shadow at the mouth of the barn. "Preacher Boy, come to truck." He stretches, rolls his tongue along his jaw. She needs him with her, not standing in the driveway barking. Slowly, easing the clutch and the low grind of gears, she stops at the highway. A thin black signal rises from the bench road. The sound is her heart breaking. Her fear rising. The bees *hmmm* at a pitch she has never heard before.

Preacher Boy, riding with his head out the window, eating the wind through his mouth, howled as Maire careened down the dirt road toward the smoky plume. CR14—Creek Road, fourteen hives, furthest out, isolated under the shadow of the buttes. She spun the truck to a halt and sat a few seconds in shock. Something—someone—had set the hives on fire, smoldering painted wood, other boxes shooting flames. They had harvested the yard weeks ago. It wasn't the honey loss; it was the malevolence. Tiny Amazons, any bees still alive, divebombed woman and dog. She pulled on bonnet and gloves. Preacher Boy yipped and spun, cleared the perimeter, and ran toward the irrigation ditch. Dried grass crackled and sparked, blackened fingers reaching toward the wheat field beyond.

Shovel. She needed a firebreak between the yard and the field. She stomped spots of small flame. Thousands of little carcasses crunched under her feet. "I'm so sorry, ladies. I'm so sorry." Five feet ahead of the fire's edge she positioned the shovel against the prairie grass and came down hard with her boot. Again, again. She couldn't even break the root mass. She shoveled ashes onto the fiery edge to tamp down flames, then stomped with her boots. Little potholes of flame seemed everywhere. She started to cry but did not stop.

Bucket. She stumbled toward the deep cut of the irrigation ditch, water running blacker than night, brought up what she could carry, and staggered back to the yard. She doused a flaming hive, turned again. She wished Jesse had not gone north. She wished she had wakened Pa. She wished she had called Tim. She wished she was stronger. She bent over the bucket. She bent over the shovel. Again. Again. She feared she'd drop dead like the bees had done.

Headlights pierced the darkness. Homer Torgerson and a man she didn't know stepped out of his pick-up in a roil of dust. "You, little lady, need help," he said.

She leaned, swaying, on her shovel. "I woke up, smelled smoke, and drove out without alerting anyone."

"Same as us, coming out of Belle's. Thought we better come see." He seemed a bit unsteady on his feet. She couldn't read his face in the dark.

"Most the bees are dead or gone, but if you could trench a firebreak between the grass and the wheat, I'd much appreciate it, Mr. Torgerson." She handed over her shovel.

"Name's Homer, Irish. We do for each other. We save crops." Homer reached another shovel out of his truck bed. "This is Zemke's wheat. His clover, too." The two men started to dig, blades breaking through the thatch, turning over sod to stop the crawling flames. They grunted with effort and belched beer.

Maire carried water buckets from the ditch. The air stank of sodden ash. Stars crawled overhead. Finally, the fire calmed. "Thank you, Homer." His name felt strange in her mouth. "I can watch it now." She stood her ground, dismissing the men. Exhausted as she was, she needed solitude to survey the scene.

Homer looked her over, "Say this for you, Irish, you're tough. Middle of the night. Woman alone. Could have been someone rougher than us find you. Where's that Injun-lover brother-in-law of yours?"

Maire stomped down a fiery response that ignited inside her. "He's back north a few days, working two harvests."

Homer grunted. "How you think this fire got started?"

Maire had to think fast. "There was a line of cloud earlier this evening, dry storm over Fairfield."

"Yah, I saw. But no lightning."

She grabbed back her shovel, rose to her fullest height. "Where you were, you're not in a position to know about lightning."

"You say so." Homer smiled; a line of crooked teeth that looked grey in the shadowed light. "But more'n likely, somebody round here either don't like honey… or don't like Injun lovers." He gave his buddy a little punch on the bicep. "C'mon Virge, get us some sleep 'fore sunup." He looked over the yard, steaming and charred. "You know what a lightning strike looks like, Irish girl? Leaves a burn hole, sometimes a snaky pattern spreading from the center. You can check out your theory come morning." He slapped his seed hat, "Anyway, since we helped, we're not suspects, right?"

She forced herself to remain standing until they were far away, then opened the cab door and collapsed along the seat bench. Light woke her. She sat up and rubbed her eyes, slid out of the truck, and faced the wrecked yard. "Oh, dear God." She peed, squatting against a tire, jumped on the flatbed to get perspective. No hole in the ground. No exploded hive box. No snaky filigree webbing the yard. She walked the perimeter. The men had done a decent job and she stomped the blackened grass edge making sure everything was out cold. Some hive boxes had burnt to the ground, others tilted like tiny bombed buildings. Melted wax and honey, ash and mud, clumped on her boots. Here and there an unmistakable wisp of gasoline lingered on charred frames. With Homer off the suspect list, there was only

The Beekeeper's Question

one person who would send her such a fearsome signal. She slid down the side of a half-charred hive, crumpled onto all fours. Dry heaved. Broin had come. Indelible in her mind was the slash of his mouth, the spit of his words, "I ruined you, Maire MacDonnell. You belong to me."

Hot tears of surrender streaked her ashy cheeks. "Come on then," she groaned, "I'm spent and empty. Me muther is dead. My lovely man is broken by war." Maire had only one condition: She would kill herself before she went with him. Death was sweeter than any life under the rough hand of his rage. She clutched the hive tool and fell into an exhausted swoon.

Ashes to ashes… Maire's body made only a small lump on the landscape under the opening eye of summer sun. Dust to dust… The morning breeze began covering her with the ghosts of bees. Then… buzzing. Persistent. *Hmmm.* "*Rise up mistress. Wee bring you our Queen.*" Maire groaned in stiffness, rubbed her eyes. The morning air was spotted with tiny flying bodies.

She raised her arms. "You came for me?" Her voice a dry cracking sound. The swarm dove on her upraised arms as though she were the branches of a tree. Several pounds of insects cloaked her shirt sleeves in a living, thrumming ball. Outliers clung to strands of her hair, crawled over the pockets that covered her breasts. Scout bees floated before her eyes. The swarm trembled. She staggered to her feet, eased herself carefully to the flatbed and knelt next to an empty super. She lifted the lid revealing hanging frames and began scooping bees into the box. She handled them bare-handed. The burning colony was like the war; many die but some survive to start again. She poured handfuls of bees into the slats. She mourned for Ralph; thought of Hazel.

"*Hmmm, hmmm,*" the swarm parted, and there on her left elbow the queen was revealed. Her majesty stepped onto Maire's right index finger and Maire lowered her onto the frame. The queen slipped into the dark that was her life and the ladies followed the One into the safety of All. She shook the last bees from her hair, brushed them gently off her shirt. "Go home," she wept, "take your place anew." She would take her own advice. If it was Broin, she needed to warn them. If it was Broin, she needed to hide Flora. If it was Broin, she would fight for her life. She found an intact bottom board, faced it east to catch morning sun and set the vibrating box on a new foundation. Life started over in the ruined city of CR-14.

Standing on the truck bed overlooking the devastated yard, she shouted into the empty vista, "I am Maire MacDonnell Cooper, keeper of the bees! Whoever did this, you may not destroy the hives! Whatever you want, you may not destroy me! However you come, you may not hurt this place, these people, my child."

She was hungry. Thirsty. Where was the dog?

29
The Button

SEPTEMBER 2, 1943: *Italy signs a secret armistice and drops out of the war. Mussolini is deposed after a 21-year regime.*

LEO STARTLED TO WAKEFULNESS, surprised to find his granddaughter tucked against his back. He jostled the babe in one arm, made his way to the kitchen, read the note. Doc was now just two blocks away. Leo cranked the phone. Thirty minutes later, they were both seated at the kitchen table, two matched sets of age-spotted hands curled around china cups; Flora in her highchair with the remnants of Pablum smeared across her chin. "She took the truck. She shouldn't have."

In unison, they looked at the kitchen clock. It was 7:45. "Let's give her another hour." Doc wiped Flora's chin. "Don't want to posse out too soon."

"Or too late," Leo blew on hot tea.

At 8:15, the honey truck rumbled into the yard. When Maire entered the kitchen, Leo's face crumbled into a deep frown. "We were about to call a search party. Do you understand how big a deal that would be, pulling everyone off harvest?"

"I left you a note," Maire defended herself.

"Alone! In the middle of the night!"

"I had a nightmare. It turned out to be real." She stood before them covered in ash, mud, and honey. "Someone torched

CR-14, sir. It's burnt to the ground. I've been stomping out grass fires and dousing hives." She swayed on her feet, "Might I sit?" Leo nodded, recalibrating from anger to concern.

"Mamamamama," Flora reached out her arms.

"I'm too dirty, *mo chroi*." She slumped in the chair closest to the door.

It took a few more seconds for Leo to comprehend the specter of his daughter-in-law and the news she reported. "A yard burned?" He paused. "Was there lightning?"

"Does lightning smell like gasoline?"

"Who would waste gasoline?"

"Who would kill bees?" Maire searched his face. "It was awful, Leo, thousands and thousands of charred little bodies. Grass flaring and hives aflame. All I had was a shovel and a bucket. Afraid I'd melt my boots." Doc handed her a glass of water. "Mr. Torgerson and his hired man arrived half-drunk from Belle's, worked to save the wheat field. I tried to convince him about the lightning. I didn't want him in our business."

"And what exactly is our business, Missus?"

Maire emptied the glass and looked him in the eye. "My childhood village had a horrible bully. When I was sixteen, my father got sotted and promised me to marry him. My mother gave me money to run away." She swallowed hard. "When Franklin was in County Antrim awaitin' the war, they accidentally crossed paths, got in a fight. He may have stolen letters I wrote. He may have pushed me mother in the river. He may have come to America to get me." She was hiccupping with tension. "It's the only thing I can think."

"Why have you never told me?" Leo's voice was softer now.

"I dint want you to think me tainted." She tucked her hands into her armpits to hide her shaking.

"Did you see anyone?" Maire shook her head. Leo finished his tea with a long swig. "Struggling in the dark it's easy to imagine the worst. I'll go look. We'll figure it out." Leo was putting things in the truck when Doc appeared with a sandwich and a jar of water. "Did you know this, Jere?"

"Franklin wrote her about the fight. She told me, woman to woman. I promised to keep her secret." Doc pulled the letter from Eleanor Annenberg out of her pocket. "This arrived a couple weeks ago. Sort of came open in my hands. I've been carrying it around, not sure when to show Maire."

He read quickly. "Call Buzz."

"And say what? That there's possibly an Irish boogeyman loose in Montana." Doc folded the letter.

"A man like that leaves a trail of trouble." Leo slapped the side of his truck. "You seen the dog?"

Maire closed the kitchen curtains and dropped her clothes down to bra and underpants. "I'll put these stinkers outside," Doc said. Maire washed her hair, sniffed it, washed it again. She sponged and soaped and rinsed her face, her arms, her breasts, her privates. Brown scum floated on the water. Doc handed her a towel and turned her around in the sure grip of calloused hands. "You'll not face him alone, Maire."

Maire's voice was hoarse with smoke, "I near died out there, Doc. I fell and couldn't rise. I saw life going on without me like I was on the other side of the veil. But I was not defiled. After a while that knowledge gave me strength. Some bees survived. In morning warmth, a swarm flew to me for help. They called me back. I saw life with me in it. I saw bits of coming years, Flora a growing girl…" Maire's eyes flooded with tears. "And Franklin," she whispered, "Just a glimpse, from the side, but I'm sure t'was him. Broin was nowhere and Franklin was alive, Doc, alive in our future."

"Well, that's a sweet promise. We can live from this day to that day, knowing everything will come out right." Doc took the towel tip and wiped Maire's eyes. "I'll take Flora; you rest until Leo comes back."

Leo stared into the tiny blitz of the bee yard. The charred hives, wood crisp in summer dry, had burnt to black cinders, while the tightly packed supers of brood and honey tipped wildly, or lay scattered sideways on the ground. Cooled pools of weirdly shaped beeswax, yellow soaked with ash and bearing the mark of boots, lay softening in the morning sun while disoriented survivors buzzed overhead. Leo rough-estimated 500,000 bees had died in the conflagration and the only sound was a soft thrum of hidden industry coming from one intact brood box, hastily placed. The scene wrenched his heart.

Was this the work of a madman? A lure to cull Maire away from the safety of town? Had Homer's arrival prevented something worse? Leo's heart ratcheted weirdly in his chest. The silhouette of a man would be visible out here quite a way in daylight. He saw only far-off farm equipment. He whistled for the dog. A slight breeze swirled the nearly weightless ash at his feet, and a smell hidden within the essence of smoke, gasoline, and under that something rotten. Leo grabbed a hive tool and set about excavating what he could from the remains of several hives. There. Evidence. Sunken brood comb caps, larvae turned into stinking mucus by the bacterium *Paenibacillus larvae*. Leo's heart sank. American foulbrood was a highly contagious disease spreadable between hives and colonies. His entire honey operation was in peril.

He was a careful man, well-read in prevention, well-practiced in cleanliness; a man who held himself accountable for the purity of his product. American foulbrood was an act of sabotage, introduced when nurse bees fed the larval bees infected honey. Once sealed in the brood comb, the bacterium invaded the larva and devoured it from the inside. A generation of workers dissolving into stinky goo could take down a hive in weeks. Millions of spores became embedded in the comb, the supers, the walls of the hive, a scourge transferable via bee movements and beekeeper tools, capable of lying dormant for decades. One deadly spore, probably carried in on the body of a rogue bee who made it past the entrance guards, had introduced disaster. The only known treatment was to burn infected hives to the ground. Bury everything. Sterilize all equipment. War had entered his perfect miniature world.

Either the firestorm of the colony was coincidence beyond credibility in Leo's mind, or it had been deliberately torched by someone who knew beekeeping. Someone educated enough to detect the health or disease of a hive. Someone strong-willed enough to ignite destruction for the larger good. Someone who managed to lug enough gasoline cross country to set the blaze. Someone who did not want to be seen in daylight.

Leo tried to take a breath; his chest cramped. "May the sacrifice of this yard save the whole." He spun slowly, searching the farm roads, the far vistas. His heart locked like gears suddenly unmeshed and grinding. The pressure spread; he couldn't breathe. He steadied himself on the crumbling edge of a hive, bent over and gasped to force breath into his lungs. His left arm throbbed. His jaw was clenched, he could barely whisper, "Help me, Lord." Hands on his knees, he crouched dizzily over the destruction. The world spun around him. Something glinted in the dust. His whole chest hurt. The sound of his heartbeat throbbed in his ears, irregular, racing. He had to reach the truck. Glovebox. His jam jar of heart tonic: cayenne, vinegar, honey, aspirin. What might save him. All he had. Gasping. Stumbling.

Button.

Maire dozed fitfully, dreaming of screaming bees. Doc came in, changed the baby, handed her over for feeding. The two women picked at cold food. No sign of the honey truck. They paced the porch. "Let's go get him," Maire said, "It's midafternoon. It's hot. He shouldn't be alone. Isn't that the scolding I got?"

They knocked on Pocket's screen door. The family was seated around the kitchen table with glasses of iced tea. "Nothing's wrong," Maire quickly assured them, "or we hope nothing's wrong. Leo hasn't come back when expected. Can you take Flora?" Hazel reached for the child.

Caleb pushed his chair back. "Heard one of your yards burned last night. My truck'll do better than the Chevy." He wiped his whiskery chin. "That where he was headed?"

Maire wrung her hands. "Oh, he'll be so embarrassed."

Caleb harrumphed. "If he's okay, he'll get over it. If he's not okay, he'll be grateful." They swung by the Mitchell house and Doc grabbed a blanket, her doctor bag, water jars. They headed toward CR-14, Caleb driving, Doc squeezed into the middle, Maire with her head out the window, looking for the honey truck silhouetted in the sun. "Sure is disorienting with the hives gone," Caleb noted.

"Lightning strike..." Maire said.

"Don't recall..."

"After midnight." She was clutching Doc's hand.

"Huh," all he said.

They found Leo leaning dazed against a front tire, out of direct sun, his legs splayed out in the ashy dirt. Doc knelt in front of him. "Leo, it's Jereldene, Maire, and Caleb. We've come for you. You hear me?" His eyes didn't focus.

"Heart," he whispered. His breath smelled of vinegar. In his lap, an empty mason jar.

Doc pulled out a stethoscope, listened, took his pulse. "You've had a heart attack, Leo. And you're lucky you're alive. Now we're going to keep you that way." The worried eyes of the friend peered through the competence of the doctor. "Headache?" Leo shook his head, no. "Sharp pain?" No. "Funny vision?" No. "Move your left foot for me and then the right." Leo waggled his legs. "Sometimes your heart beating like this can set off a stroke. I'm going to rub aspirin powder on your gums and under your tongue, thin your blood quick. We need to get you to Deaconess. Run an EKG, get you stabilized." She took out a paper of medicine, broke it open and gently swabbed Leo's mouth with gauze, then rubbed the aspirin around his teeth and under his tongue. He made a grimace, "It's the best I got for field medicine."

Maire got a canvas tarp from the honey truck and made what padding she could in the back of Pocket's pickup, she covered it with the blanket. Caleb took one side, Doc the other, and Maire gently pulled his arms. Leo rose. They walked him the few yards to Caleb's truck and helped him onto the bed. Doc eased herself up alongside him. "Drive easy between here and asphalt. Stop at the store. Gertie can call an ambulance to meet us in Vaughn." Caleb closed the tailgate. "Maire, drive the truck home."

Maire leaned over the side and Leo gestured her toward him. "Bees sick," he wheezed. "Page 363." Her mind was blank. His gaze bored into her.

"Oh, *The ABZ*." He nodded.

"Bu-b-b..." he tried to speak again. "But-t-t..."

She kissed his ashy hand and let him go. "Don't worry, Leo. I can take care of things. Go get well." As Caleb threaded his precious cargo back to the highway, she stood alone on the landscape. Leo had been digging around in the ashes, examining the charred remains of the hives. "What were you looking for?" Boot prints were everywhere—hers, his, Homer's. It was hard to tell what had happened, except that a bunch of folks had tracked the ground and put out a fire—and someone had lit one, whose original tracks were long obliterated.

Maire knelt and touched the spot where they'd found Leo propped against the tire. She looked to the heavens, "Please, God, we still need him. Well, *I* still need him. I'd appreciate You let him live. Amen." Book, she had understood his meaning, but then "bu-b-b..." Had he meant Broin? Did he even know the name? What had happened here? She was shaking, her hands clawing dirt. Something glinted in the ashy dust. "Bu-b-b..." Button. Brass. Embossed with an eagle.

Once upon a time, she had stood with Franklin at the train station on a cold winter's day, nervously fingering his uniform jacket. The button was an impossibility. The button was in her hand. She clenched her fist and opened her palm; it was still there. She bit it gently; it was real. The day spun dizzily. This was the thing that had exploded Leo's heart. She heaved herself up, bracing on the honey truck, breathing raggedly. When she was calm enough to drive, she steered the honey truck into the western sun before turning south and east toward home. Blind in the glare, something moved.

It was dark. The baby was sleeping. She had wrapped the button in the Irish hanky and laid it on the table in front of her. She drank deep from a glass of water, cooled in the fridge. She composed herself.

September 2, 1943

Dear Jesse,

When you get this, please come straight away. Your pa had a heart attack. He's in hospital in Great Falls. Doc is with him. Last night CR-14 was torched. We don't know by whom. And Leo suspects foulbrood. I read about it just now. It sounds scary. Remains of the yard need to be buried. I've sterilized all the equipment. Boiled my clothes. Bleached my boots. I'm waiting to hear from Doc how things are in town. I'll tell you more when you get here. I called the minister in Browning to please get word to you, so this letter is a backup. It's 1943, you need a mailbox. We need a bathroom. Sorry to ask. I know you are busy haying. Thank you. Maire

The house seemed hugely vacant. She dashed to the outhouse, looking over her shoulder. She whistled for the missing

The Beekeeper's Question

dog. She didn't know whether to open the doors in welcome or lock herself in. Bu-b-b. She wanted Jesse's strength. She wanted Willow's knowing things beyond ken. She found the skeleton key on the lintel and locked the back entryway, propped a dining chair against the porch door, closed a few windows. Anyone entering would make enough racket to wake her. She took a knife from the kitchen drawer and laid it on the nightstand, slipped under the sheets, curled into a ball, cried herself to sleep. Flora whimpered.

30
Coopers Return

SEPTEMBER 5, 1943: *Allied forces invade mainland Italy. The German Army occupies Rome and northern Italy to fight back.*

"HONEY HOUSE ISN'T MEANT TO BE A ONE-PERSON JOB!" Jesse shouted over the hiss of the boiler and the whir of the extractor. It was late afternoon and Maire leaned on the blading table, half a super of honeycomb glistening under the heated knife. She stared at him, tears welling. "Did you get my letter?"

"No. Preacher in Browning sent someone out. Said you called. Said Pa's in the hospital." Jesse took the heavy blade from her trembling hand. "I can finish this, call it a day." He checked the boiler gauge, untangled the line of the steam knife, straightened supers in the extractor, tested the temperature of the trough, kicked a pallet under the next tin. "You did good," he said. A man born to the job, confident and strong.

Maire trailed him through the routine, telling the story bit by bit. "This honey's clean," she assured him, "And I sterilized everything according to the book."

Doc returned that evening. "Told Gertie, so at least the story will start off accurately." The adults were seated around the table with Drum chasing Flora crawling on the kitchen floor. Doc attributed Leo's heart attack to the discovery of foulbrood.

"On top of everything else, it was just too much." Her eyes were sad. "There's always permanent damage to the muscle. Medicine can't change that, but much of his heart still looks good."

Maire felt her prayer rising, "But he's still the Rev, still Leo, still Pa?"

"Yes, but he will have to discover a new version of himself."

"And dat ole man still Grumpa." Drum's voice floated up from under the table.

"Yes, Natoyii," Willow reached down and petted her son.

"And da bear?"

"What bear, son?" Jesse asked.

"Da bear in da cave." He grabbed Flora's foot, making her squeal.

"There's no bear, Drum. You're pretending that part." Jesse gave Willow a look.

"No. I not. Hims a honey bear."

The phone rang. Jesse answered. "Great, I'll come in a bit." He turned back to them with a plan. "Tim will bury the yard, that'll be the first thing Pa asks. Tomorrow I'll start checking other colonies around the creek for any sign of disease and see if Tim can start on the septic field and bathroom, give Pa something to supervise while Maire and I finish harvest."

Doc and Willow at the sink, Jesse preparing to bicycle to Sivertsen's, Maire joined the children under the table. "What about the bear?" she asked Drum quietly.

"He wivves in a cave. Hims paw fell off."

"How do you know, Drum?" She stroked his sheen of hair.

"Dweaming." He sounded very matter of fact.

"I believe you," she whispered, and lifted Flora into her lap.

"I bewieve me, too," his smile so like his father's.

Next morning, cool shouldered over the valley under a blanket of high cloud. Maire and Jesse visited bee yards, pried open hives, looked for sign of the dreaded disease. "Foulbrood doesn't affect adult bees: they just spread it. On the comb, convex caps cave in, turn dark and shriveled. The smell of rotten larvae gives the infection its name." He carefully pried up the lid of the next hive. "Smoker." Maire puffed the calming waft over the workers. The tone of the buzz changed. Jesse sighed with relief, "We were lucky. C-14 is our most isolated yard, but heightened inspection will be our everlasting routine."

"Where did it come from?" They were leaning against the truck door eating tomato and mayo sandwiches swished with warm tea from Leo's Stanley thermos.

"Drifter bees, wild swarms, contaminated hobby hive. Foulbrood is bacterial sabotage. Fitting to the times, don't you think?" Jesse regarded her closely, "The fire saved us, but it was a desperate act, valley so dry. Any suspicions?"

A jumble of nightmares and secrets raced toward her tongue. "At first I thought it was an Irishman…" Jesse looked totally puzzled. "An evil bully I'm feared is chasing me. But then…I found this." She reached deep into her pocket and offered him the button on the pillow of her palm.

Jesse ran his thumb over the raised image of the eagle. "Military?"

"It was in the ashes. Your father found it. It's… it's impossible, but—" She searched Jesse's eyes, looking for belief.

"You're not thinking, Frank?" She nodded shyly. "You're right, it's impossible," he handed back the button as though it was hot.

"Something happened out here, Jesse," she met his doubting gaze, "Someone risked torching a yard. And the only one we might have blamed stumbled out of Belle's bar and helped."

"Homer knows fire is danger."

"It's not Homer." Maire's thoughts tumbled forward. "Think about it—I'm alone in the night scairt near to death that my nightmare man has found me. Come morning, Leo surveys the damage, finds foulbrood. Finds the button. Gets a heart attack.

The Beekeeper's Question

No local arsonist would have known the yard needed torching." Maire's voice broke as she remembered the bees crisp on the ground and the swarm that had saved her. "January '42, Franklin shipping out, we're at the train station." She blushed. "Details get burned in your mind. I remember this button, Jess." She couldn't read his reaction. "He hasn't written in months, not since spring, early spring. I been preparing myself for a telegram, but this..."

"Meaning what?!" Jesse's voice flared, "That the Army mysteriously sent him home for not writing his wife?!"

"You tell me how a brass Army button arrived in our bee yard?!" Maire went Irish, "Maybe he's wounded. Maybe he's got that battle fatigue."

"Stop it, Maire!" Jesse whirled in place. "This is fantasy."

"Where's that cave, Jesse?" She put her hand on his arm. Squeezed hard. "The one you crawled to in the storm."

"Froggy's? Our boyhood hideaway?" Jesse shook her off. "No, Maire. We're in the middle of a goddamn world war. Men do not just show up!"

"But their buttons do?"

"There are millions of Army buttons. And jackets. And loose threads. The war is massive bureaucracy, procedures and paperwork."

"The war is also men missing in action, bodies on a battlefield picked over for souvenirs. Men evacuated who can't talk or can't remember who they are 'cuz they're shell-shocked or I don't know." A tiny fist of incarcerated hysteria hit against her ribs. Jesse refused to look at her. "Tell me, Jesse! The cave..."

Jesse pointed west, "At the base of the first butte," then, "A half-mile beyond CR-14." He stared into the vista, silent for a very long time. "Jeez, Maire, what if it *is* him? Burning the bees, not exactly a friendly hello."

"Unless he knew exactly what he was doing."

"All this because of a button!"

christina baldwin

"All this because war is not orderly, it's also chaos. If it's him, he needs help, Jess. If it's not him, whoever it is needs help."

"Or whoever it is, is that crazy sonofabitch, that might or might not be chasing you?! But okay. Willow can watch the kids. After supper, you and I can take the Chevy, go see what's out there."

"Who," she said quietly. "And the dog."

Maire fed Flora, diapered her, gave into a bedtime nursing. She rummaged the back of the closet and gathered a change of clothes: jeans, underwear, clean shirt, socks. He had boots, there'd not been any bare footprints at the bee yard. He had an Army issue jacket, missing a button, that he'd worn even on a hot night. She wrapped the clothes in a blanket, tied it all with a belt. His belt.

Willow packed a basket of dry meat, thick cut bread, hunk of cheese. "It is not the evil one," she whispered.

Maire's heart jumped in her chest. "What else can you see?"

"What happens now will bring you your Medicine." She handed over the basket of food and smiled shyly. "And you and I will become what Jesse calls friends." It was their secret, the three of them. They worked around each other, nervous, quiet. Jesse eased the Chevy out the backyard, driving west into gathering dark, Maire clutching the arm rest. They passed the burned yard, now a fresh grave of humped dirt, and followed tractor tracks toward the shadowed hulk of the butte.

In Froggy's cave, Franklin and the rattlesnakes had reached a truce. The snakes hunted in heat; he hunted in cool. He stepped around their sleeping coils on his way to nightly marauding—vegetables from gardens, apples off trees, scraps in the hobo box Belle kept behind the saloon. He knew where the church key was hidden and after the Ladies Club spent days canning in the cool basement, he filled every pocket with jars of tomatoes, beans, pickles. He took candles from the altar supplies, a box of matches, a spoon and fork. He stole a gas can from the back of a pickup, glad for the swish of fuel. "Insurance," he'd thought. He really didn't want to douse the snakes, he'd seen enough bodies writhing in flames.

It was ten years since he and Jesse and their high school chums had discovered the shallow cavern hollowed into the side of the butte. They checked for skeletons and ghosts, hooting echoes against the back walls. Nothing hooted back. They cached boyish treasures: mason jars with matches and fire-starters, dried beef and wrinkled apples, a quart of booze tailings from the saloon where Jesse washed glasses and filled a jar with anything left at the bottom of the bottle. Froggy's they'd called it to signal each other. Franklin had found the mildewed remnants of a blanket scrunched in one corner and evidence of a recent campfire, but nobody bothered him. Nobody knew where he was.

Honey yard CR-14 was closest to his hideaway, at the edge of the route. Maybe swipe himself some honeycomb. Through the field binoculars, liberated from what was left of Lieutenant Cyclone, he watched his father, his brother, and his wife, moving through the life he'd left behind. It had been a couple of weeks since they'd harvested, time enough for the bees to build more comb and sweetly fill it, and the hive lids would be loose enough to pry open one-handed.

The night of the burning. Preacher Boy had tracked him to the cave and hadn't left. "You with me, now?" he asked, his voice croaking from disuse. "Things rough out here and I get first bite." The dog licked his face and curled at his feet. "Got nothing for supper but each other's company." He sunk his hand deep into the dog's ruff as they sat side by side and watched the dusk come up. And then he noticed the Chevy. "Shit."

As Jesse and Maire approached the base of the butte, Preacher Boy skittered down the rubble of rock that surrounded the cave mouth. He was barking excitedly to alert whoever was hiding that someone was coming, and whoever was coming that someone was hiding. Jesse eased the car to a halt to make sure the dog didn't tangle a wheel. "Well, probably a good thing we're not surprising someone trained in combat," Jesse sounded as nervous as she felt. They stepped out each side of the car.

"Stay where you are!" a gruff voice shouted from the shadows.

They stopped. Jesse looked at Maire. Maire looked at Jesse. The man's voice was flat, American accent. "That you, Franklin? It's Jesse, your brother. And Maire, your wife." She rolled her eyes. "Well, what am I supposed to say?" he whispered. "We don't know it's him."

The dog twirled on the rocks. "Well, Preacher Boy knows it's him," Maire whispered back. She called out, "We brought you dinner and clean clothes. I come to ask you home." She took a step forward. She was shaking with nerves, queasy and unsure.

"I told you. Don't come up here!" Well, he could see them even if they couldn't see him. The cave man continued, "Leave me be, you hear me? I'm not fit company for man nor beast."

"That's not what your dog thinks." Anger flared in her, and she wanted to yell at him that he was a husband and a father, a son and a brother. His father had just had a heart attack. They needed him to get on down here. Instead, she breathed herself calm, looked around the silhouetted boulders. "I'm going to leave you things." She spoke loudly, intending him to hear. "You can keep the dog for company. I brought kibble, but you best come get your dinner before he does." She turned and aimed back toward the car, shouting a bit overloud, "Come on, Jesse, the man wants to be left alone, let's leave him alone."

Jesse's mouth was opening and closing, and he was kind of step dancing with his fists clenched, trying to think what to say or do. He looked at her astonished. "Just leave?! Him not coming with us?"

"Get in the car," she whispered urgently, "we can drive a ways and talk."

"Okay, like she said," he pointed to her and called out to the voice, aiming his words at the opening of the cave hidden maybe fifty feet up the side of the butte. "We'll leave you tonight, but don't go torching any more yards."

There was a hollow laugh. "Did you a favor, you want the truth," the voice said.

Jesse called back. "Pa figured it out. We been checking the other yards. Seems we caught it in time."

"You're welcome," the voice said. A pause, then, "Thank you for the food and clothes."

In the switch from defiance to politeness, Maire heard the voice her heart remembered. A man well-raised. Charlotte's boy. Leo's son. She cupped her hand over her mouth to stifle whatever sound was rising in her and slipped into the car. Away from the butte, Jesse stopped, hands on wheel. "It's a good thing I was with you, or I wouldn't have believed it. I mean, it *is* Frank, right?"

She studied Jesse's face, dim in the night shadows. "I need you to say you're sure so I can be sure."

Jesse bit his lip. "I've hardly seen him since his voice changed, but he sounded like a Cooper man to me. So, what do we do now?"

A wind of relief blew tumbleweeds down the fence of her spine. "We help him remember himself. Bring up food and water. Give him space and support and talk him in before freezing." Maire slumped into the backrest of the car seat. She was trembling. "I am so tired. I haven't slept for worrying. Flora is teething and fussy. Leo's coming home a convalescent. We need a toilet and a bathtub. It's still full-on harvest and then the beets and the Indian boys…"

"You can't list everything like that, Maire. Drive yourself crazy. You just gotta do a day's worth and not think too much ahead." Jesse started up the engine, and they drove in silence. Maire stopped by the outhouse, kicked her boots off in the entryway, and staggered to bed, face unwashed, teeth unbrushed, clothes on, asleep. She didn't even hear the attic stairs creak as Jesse headed up to join Willow and Drum. Three of them knew now, and a little boy who dreamed of a honey bear.

Franklin woke screaming. The cave barely lit with dawn; Preacher Boy was licking his face and whining. "You be careful," he told the dog, "I don't want to kill you." Franklin's mind was filled with days far away and under fire, but the day he dreamed was the day it was his turn. Artillery, grenades, blood, infection, transport. The ether cap coming down over his face, waking in the stump ward. At night he screamed in concert with the other dreamers. By day, he stared at a wall in the evac hospital. Exhausted beyond exhaustion. The pills made him addled and angry. A stack of letters rested in his lap, no energy to read the homely news, no idea how to answer messages from a life he barely remembered, from a wife he barely knew. June rain over English countryside beyond the glass of hospital windows.

One day a doctor and an officer had presented him paperwork marked CDD—combat disability discharge. They shook his remaining hand and said he'd been valuable to the war effort. The doctor filed orders for rehab and more pills. The officer gave him a clean uniform and a Purple Heart to wear alongside his North Africa campaign ribbon. They put him on a ship going the wrong way across the Atlantic.

A week later he'd been processed through Fort Dix and taken on the stump bus to a military medical complex on the Jersey shore. His military service come full circle. The Army issued him an artificial arm and a week of physical therapy, training him in the use of the heavy appendage—leather sleeve, metal hook. He signed himself out and headed into the bustling civilian territory of America.

The Beekeeper's Question

Heading blindly westward with a wad of severance pay, Franklin rode trains, buses, hitched rides. Folks around him making small talk or tongue-tied. He was a newsreel, a headline, a photo in LIFE. Every now and then, a saluting look from an older vet. He got off the train in Havre and decided just to hoist his duffel and walk while he figured what to do. He slept at hobo fires where nightmares were a midnight chorus . He tucked into haystacks or barns. He knew how to find county roads, to rest from heat and roam in cool. One August night, as though he'd been aiming there all along, Franklin staggered into Froggy's and laid his body down.

Flora's whimper roused Maire from exhausted slumber. She bent over the crib soothing the child as she stepped out of her clothes and slipped a worn nightgown over her head. The brush of soft fabric made her arch with waiting desire. "Your da is here." Maire lay them together on the bed, the baby splayed across her torso. Flora nuzzled haphazardly on a nipple. "He needs a bit more time," she whispered. "Don't you worry *mo chroi*, I'll find the way." Flora's head lolled heavily to one side.

Franklin was back. Was nearly here. Was surely retrievable from the cave that held him and the dark that emanated from him. She had heard his voice. "Go away," he'd said. "I need help," he'd left unsaid. She retraced the grid of tractor tracks in her mind, memorizing the route from house to cave. No more night flying. She could drive. She could bicycle. She would crawl if she had to. She gathered herself for the work of rebinding them.

31
Pollen Portals

MID-SEPTEMBER 1943: *The Allies push north from Salerno. The Italian fleet surrenders in Malta. Hitler rescues Mussolini from captivity and sets him up as head of a puppet state.*

PREACHER BOY ROAMED BETWEEN HOUSE AND CAVE taking up his duties as Franklin's dog. Maire left food for them both, a cracked bowl, a plate, a jar of honey, a tiny sock of Flora's. Doc was close in town now and showed up to tend the baby and watch over Leo while Maire and Jesse finished the honey harvest, while Maire and Hazel finished the canning, while Bill and Tim finished the bathroom, while Willow and Jesse refurbished the cabin.

Maire stood over the kitchen sink so tired she could barely do dishes. She was strung tight between the demands of the day and the enormity of her nightly pilgrimages. Doc wrapped strong arms around her shoulders, "Remember your vision of Franklin here in our future," she whispered, "Your love and courage is his guide."

She leaned into Doc's embrace. "He's always in the cave. I sit outside and talk in the dark. He dinna talk back, but I hear him breathing. He's shaggy. He stinks. He doesn't tie his shoes."

"You do know he's been wounded. Army wouldn't send him home unless he can't soldier anymore."

Maire nodded solemnly. "Drummie said his paw fell off." Last night, she had brought him pencils and paper. "I caught his silhouette once." She wrote him a note:

Dear Franklin,
Thank you for saving the crop. It was brave necessity.

A tiny challenge. His turn. Which arm?

Leo woke mornings in his own bed, grateful to be alive. With his hands resting on his sternum, he assessed the beating of his heart. They'd kept him in the hospital a week—unnecessarily long, he thought—but he'd overheard Jereldene tell the city doctors "It's the only way he'll rest." He chaffed not to be out harvesting and was equally terrified he might drop in the field again.

"You're a lucky man, Leo," Doc informed him. "With heart attack, survival is a one-time grace." She spoke in her doctor voice but clenched his hand as a friend. He had pills the doctors thought better than the *Farmer's Almanac* recipe he'd been sipping earlier in the summer whenever an unusual twinge got his attention. He had mixed the concoction in the cellar, hiding a few pints to keep Doc from asking or Maire from worrying: eight ounces of apple cider vinegar in which he soaked eight cloves of garlic, juice of raw onion, quarter cup chopped parsley, quarter cup chopped basil, couple powdered aspirin, sweetened with honey so he could stand to drink the stuff, filtering liquid through gritted teeth. He credited the elixir with saving his life in the bee yard and, well, here he was, heart steady, far as his untrained pulse-taking could discern. He intended to make another batch, for luck.

Jesse had picked him up at Deaconess Hospital. The young folks must have been working day and night for the septic field had been dug, tank installed, ground moved back into place. Jesse's friend, the man who limped, came down from the Reservation and laid plumbing pipe. In a few days, apologizing for the noise, Bill and Caleb had fashioned a bathroom expanded from the old linen closet, carpentered walls, found a tub and sink at the building surplus store (porcelain not even chipped), and installed a toilet and faucets. Leo had been too tired to be embarrassed, thanked everyone, nibbled at light suppers, fell into long sleeps.

Confused and orienting himself in the morning light, he recited the days of the week until he realized it was Wednesday, September 15th. Half a month gone. Supply minister had come out from Great Falls. This would be the first Rally Sunday he'd missed in over thirty years. Jesse was managing both the septic business and shipping the honey harvest. Darrell, that Indian fellow, was sleeping in the honey house and working with Jess. Maire was rendering wax, and Willow was filling cellar shelves with jars of vegetables. Seemed everybody was getting on just fine without him.

"It's a different time in your life now, Leo," Doc warned. "And if you ignore whatever you were ignoring before you got laid down out there, you won't have a second chance, and none of us is ready for that." She searched his eyes making sure he understood. He did.

Gentle tap at the door. Maire came in with the baby on her hip and a cup of tea in her other hand. Flora stretched toward him. "Gaga." A pearl of drool hung off her lower lip.

Leo hitched himself to sitting. Maire set the baby on his lap. He made his grandpa face. "Well, one thing is normal," he searched Maire's eyes. Without a word, she held out the military button. A curtain of grief descended. "I've been wondering when you'd consider me strong enough to speak of this." He felt his sharp intake of breath, but his heartbeat didn't skip like it had when the button first caught his eye. He rolled it in his

The Beekeeper's Question

palm. "Sometimes the dead leave the living a token, like they're signaling from the other side." Maire stared at him. "Gracie had a doll that lost its shoes. We looked for months and, eventually, I painted little Mary Jane's on the doll's feet. After the funeral, Charlotte found one tiny doll shoe twisted in the bedclothes. We wept with wonder and grief. And after Charlotte, I swear I still heard the piano some nights." He handed back the button. "Has the telegram come?"

Light shined in Maire's eyes. "Franklin's not dead, Pa. He's hiding in that cave where you found Jesse." Leo slapped his hand to his chest. Everything kept beating. "Jesse and I drove out there. He was standing in shadow and wouldn't let us see him. Told us to leave him be. I go out every couple of nights and bring him food and little supplies. Preacher Boy pretty much staying by him." Her eyes searched his face. "He's wounded and got battle fatigue." Her eyes teared, "I'm feeling my way, trying to respect him, and still break through to him."

"He cared enough to burn the bees and save the crop. That's something."

Maire nodded. "We start there, for sure, help him remember himself."

"How can I help, Maire?"

"Follow Doc's orders. Build your strength. When Franklin comes in, he will need you." She took the baby and handed him the tea. "Whatever he's going through, he needs privacy and protection. Jesse and Willow, you, Doc, me, we're the only ones who know." She left for the kitchen and the start of the day.

Leo eased out of bed and onto his knees. This prayer required the full posture. "Thank you, God, that my son is alive. Help Maire find the key to his heart. Help him return to himself and to us. Thank you that it's not that Irish devil. Forgive our relief in the face of the Pockets' sorrow. Guide us day by day. In Jesus' name, Amen."

christina baldwin

He looked around. When had his room become an old man's space? Pills on the nightstand, chair with a needlepoint seat to ease his bones down, pull on his pants, a footstool for bracing one foot then the other to tie his shoes. Leo hefted himself to standing and pulled on his lightweight union suit, feeling his skin come back on, feeling weakness and willfulness begin a dance in the new time in his life. He would get dressed. He would walk to the kitchen with his shoulders back. He would trust himself to resurrection.

Late that night, Maire came back from a food drop at the cave, checked on the baby, checked on the old man, grabbed her shawl, and threaded her way through the garden to the backyard hives. She eased down amongst the ghostly white boxes shining in moonlight, pressed her forehead to the weathered wood, and whispered into the wall of the hive. "Dear wee ladies, please help the beekeeper's son and me become the bee and the blossom to one another again." Only a quarter inch of wood separated the industry of the night-duty bees from the skin of the beekeeper. She stopped. Listened. The *hmmm* took her into a swoon. She surrendered where it led.

Sometime later, Maire groaned awake, stretched, and put herself to bed for the remaining hours of night. The *hmmm* had given her a dream. Four bees had hovered before her, bodies folded with stingers hung low. *"We make our offering to the pollen portals. Place us to crown, to heart, to neck, to center-eye. The way in will open."*

"What do you think it means?" she asked Willow the next morning.

"The bees are stepping in to guide you. They bring you the lineage that is tuned to your heart." Willow was buttering bread for Natoyii's morning snack. "When Hazel can take the baby, we will find a private place so you can take the stings, and I will stay by you."

The Beekeeper's Question

"Stings?!"

"Bee venom is powerful medicine. You prayed. They answered."

"It has to be warm enough for them to fly and it's near to Equinox." It took a few days to coordinate space, time, and weather. The next Monday morning, Leo took to his study, Hazel took Flora across the street, Jesse took Drum on the honey route, and Willow took Maire to the back of the barn. Together they laid out straw and blankets and opened a window that faced the garden bee yard. Maire propped herself against a stall's sideboard. "Now what?" "Call the bees, tell them you're ready." Willow settled herself on an old milking stool and flipped back shiny black braids, adjusted her skirt, nodded encouragement.

Maire buzzed quietly, her teeth and jaws vibrating. After a few minutes the buzz spread, and her body relaxed. Four bees came through the open window. "Place them as the dream instructed," Willow whispered. Maire opened her hand. One bee landed. She took it gently by the thorax and held it to the crown of her head. A sharp sting through her hair on the very top of her scalp. She set the dead bee in her lap, opened her palm again. Another landed. Maire shifted her blouse aside and placed the bee on her sternum. Another sting, hard on bone. The third sting she placed in her jugular notch. She felt the venom diffusing. She began to tremble. "Trust the bees," Willow sat firm across from her. "I'll stay right here." Willow's eyes anchored her. "Let yourself be taken. This is the Way of Medicine." Maire took the fourth sting on the center of her brow. She entered the Unity.

Alone in the house, facing a stack of envelopes he had no desire to open, Leo shuddered at his desk. His legs twitched with the desire to stand, to stride, to drive boldly into the countryside and gather up his soldier son, no matter his condition. His arms longed to lift supers, to clean the honey house, to heft tins alongside his beekeeper son, sending their golden elixir to soothe the ravages of wartime shortage. He opened his Bible to a random page: Gospel of Mark 4:9, the parable of the sower and the seed, what grows and what cannot, what falls on fertile soil. Leo prayed, "My heart is broken open, God. I pray to germinate for the good of family and community. Let the seed of my soul come to full harvest. Turn my actions into bread and my words into honey." He glanced down at the page again and there in red ink Jesus said, "He who has ears, let him hear."

He heard buzzing. The sound of bees filled his study. No, not his study, his head. Leo cupped his hands over his ears and closed his eyes. The sound carried him into a vision. He watched a cluster of bees crawling on his heart. The diligent workers filigreed the chambers with comb that dripped honey into his veins infusing him with well-being. He smelled flowers. He was held in place, commanded to witness. In all his years of asking, "Why don't human beings live as bees live?" he had never been invited into the hive—not like this. He entered the Unity.

And there, inside the hive mind, he saw Maire, clothed in gold and striped in black, multi-legged, two reaching arms, a queen among queens. Her face alight, she danced in ecstasy above the mass of the maiden workers. In all the ways he gave them nurture, Leo had never been transported to the bees' inner sanctum. But here, this bookish housemaid who had married his son because he smelled of honey had entered the trance of the hive. This was not a scene of dark industry, but a temple infused with light that emanated from every cell, every bee, every glistening drop of honey. The drones gathered around her, urging her flight, but she held herself back, preparing for Franklin, calling his soul home.

The buzzing subsided. Leo awakened with his forehead on his Bible. Words of Isaiah swirled around him, *"Fear not, for I have redeemed you; I have called you by name, you are mine. When you pass through the waters, I will be with you; and through the rivers, they shall not overwhelm you; when you walk through fire, you shall not be burned, and the flame shall not consume you.*" He opened his palms in silent praise.

Outside in the barn, Maire wakened in the straw. Willow massaged her feet. "You smell like honey and beeswax," she smiled, "It is a golden pathway."

Out on the benchland, Jesse settled a hive lid in place and talked to his son, "All summer the bees make honey. And when we take honey, we also leave honey. They are heading into naptime, and we are giving thanks."

On the truck bed with his face turned to the sun Drummond Natoyii isttookimaa spun slowly in place, "Listen, Nínna, dah bees am singing to dah bear."

On a rock at the entrance of the cave, Franklin sat hunched with the sun on his back, learning to lace his boots one-handed. He did not hear singing, but the pollen portals were open.

32
OFFERINGS

OCTOBER 1943: *October 1, citizens revolt and free Naples from German occupation. October 5, Allies cross the Volturno Line penetrating German-occupied Italy.*

THE TWO YOUNG WOMEN STOOD SIDE BY SIDE sorting dishes and linens to divide between Cooper's and Doc's kitchen. That's how it went: Things moved around, got shared, mended, repaired, had history in several families. "The bees have said yes to you," Willow said, counting forks of various patterns. "They are your ancestors now."

Maire pulled plates off a top shelf. "But their teaching is all mixed in with baby care and housekeeping, honey business, Leo's recovery, chatting with Hazel. I don't know how to be in both worlds."

"It's not two worlds, Maire, it's just one." Willow held out an odd-shaped spoon for identification. "To live with medicine means to see what is truly around us. Unity doesn't come and go; we open and close our noticing. That's what Gramma says."

"But the bees," Maire added, "are always in the Unity. They gather pollen, make honey, extrude wax. They take an element into their own bodies and turn it into something else. Every day they are magicians." Just then, Flora let out a howl from under the table. When Maire turned quickly her vision went strange, her daughter turned a bluish-white, Flora's red hair a shade of grey, her mouth a ring of yellow and a center of red. This was bee-sight, and her daughter had momentarily become a flower. Maire gasped and blinked. All she could manage to say to Willow was, "Gravy ladle, that odd spoon."

Willow set it aside. "Creator didn't choose human beings because we are so advanced but because we need teaching."

A pattern developed in the following weeks: gifts of food and water, a clean shirt, even a pillow. Franklin had found a note, *I'm not going to come in after you.* Her handwriting familiar from the unopened envelopes he wouldn't read crumpled in the bottom of his duffel underneath the heavy Army-issue hook he wouldn't wear. *But I'm not going to leave you either.* Franklin held his breath, wanting and not wanting the reach she extended.

After she deposited paper and pencil, he wrote her back. *Don't get your hopes up about me, Maire. You don't know what I have become.* An Army shrink had told him, "Battle fatigue makes you a man of two minds." The doctor spoke in the clipped accent of the proper schoolboy he'd been. Now, his clinic was two chairs in a windowless room in a British military hospital. It was the day before Franklin shipped Stateside. "Your battle mind is trapped in a repeating newsreel of your war experiences." The doctor looked weary with explaining, "But your benign mind remembers yourself before the war. Use benign mind to design a man capable of carrying on."

The next night Maire replied. *You don't know what I have become either, Frank. We got to talk our way home.* A food delivery was placed in a wooden box tucked near the entrance. He stared at it, imagining her so close. The thought made his stomach churn with hunger and something else.

"It's a tough fight, old chap," the shrink had cautioned, "Deciding which mind will run your life." Franklin needed the cave, the dark, the bare necessities, the stink and stumble of himself walking for miles in the companionship of the dog. "Battle mind will not surrender, but to make truce with your life you must let benign mind become your commanding officer." The doctor shook his remaining hand. "Don't give up." Both his minds took that as marching orders.

Don't give up, Maire wrote, *You can't live in Froggy's the rest of your life.*

Well, he thought to himself, that depends on who wins. He found dark comfort in the hellish consistency of his inner newsreel. He knew how it would end. If he couldn't stand it anymore, well he had his bayonet and a box of dynamite he'd found in an old mineshaft. He didn't really want to die; he didn't know how to live with what he and the war done.

Pasties showed up, his mother's recipe wrapped in newspaper. He bit into a mouthful of memories, gave a crust to the dog. "You never knew her," he told Preacher Boy, "but this is what my mother tasted like. When I was a boy. When the Coopers were happy." The dog chewed once and swallowed. Franklin glanced at grease-stained headlines: War in Italy.

Maire kept coming, kept cooking, kept talking. Had to admire that. Middle of the night, he would wake to the lilt of her voice, tendrils of words that reached through enveloping darkness. He found things on his forays: a hawk feather, an antler, a snakeskin, and left them out for her. He scribbled: *I got no stories a woman should hear.* She brought him a book of collected poems, a baby picture stuck on the page "Invictus." Benign mind read it aloud; battle mind scoffed.

One night, she said, "Let's talk back to the beginning, Franklin." He sat up, the voice continued. "Say again things we said in Philadelphia. Add things we didn't know to say." Franklin grunted, his battle mind a dark cloud. "Remember ourselves afore anything bad happened, start fresh."

He wrote: I hardly remember that Philly boy. His hand poised over the paper: But I want to remember him. Was it true? His life depended on it. Some nights, valley life, Irish life and Army life ran together through his dreams; he considered that progress. Sometimes shouts of his boyhood buddies echoed in the cave, their honking laughter, voices changing. That had been a rough time, middle of the Depression, his mother dying. Benign mind knew about survival, too. He wrote: I'm listening.

Well, at that moment he was drifting, until Maire said, "I'm glad you didn't go to the Pacific. All those islands, Japanese dug in, ships getting sunk, Ronnie Torgerson missing, and then there's Ralph…" Her voice broke, he snapped to attention. "I dinna know him much, but Hazel and I are friends, and our baby girls."

"Ralph?" The name escaped his lips.

"Killed on the Solomon Islands. July. I wrote you. When you dinna write back, I thought sure I be next."

"I'm Signal Corps. I knew guys. Told 'em I sent a telegram," Frank's voice was crusty.

Her teary breathing trapped him at the back of the cave. "We got the chance Ralph and Hazel will never have," her voice quavered, "Please take it with me, Franklin. Call me Moy. Meet your baby. We can figure it out."

"Go home. Go to bed." It sounded gruffer than he meant.

"Dinna you be mad to me, Franklin! You be mad at the war; heck, I'm mad at the war. We're doing ever'thing we can around here." Her voice went steely. "All these miles wanderin' about, you best think on something happy. Tell me something good." Her advice sounded like that shrink. He watched her stomp down the scree and pedal off in darkness. God, he was going to miss Ralphie.

He couldn't admit to her the pile of unopened mail in his duffel. He couldn't explain his terror that news from home would have destroyed his ability to withstand the war. He'd

christina baldwin

seen men throw down a letter and stand up to take a bullet. It wasn't all sweetness, letters from previous lives. The winter's march across the top of Africa eroded his connection to any other world. Month by month, he let the story slip, cached the letters, turned his life over to the frantic ruminations of battle mind.

Late night, mid-month, frosty half-moon, he was cutting cross field when he saw her riding the old bicycle, jouncing carefully along the tractor paths that cut around the crop plots. His heart leapt, and he loped diagonally through the stubble to head her off, get there first. Preacher Boy was jumping at his dangling jacket sleeve making a game of it. It was not a game. He scooted into the back of the cave just ahead of her. Panting. Hiding. Not wanting her to see him. He heard her talking sweet to the dog, settling onto a smooth rock, going to be a story night. "Case you decide to come home," she began, "We got indoor plumbing now. Toilet, bathtub, hot and cold running water, all the modern conveniences. It's Jesse's new business, along with Tim and Darrell."

"Who's Darrell?" Franklin grunted.

"Jesse's Blackfeet friend. Deferred 'cause of having one leg shorter than the other."

"Jesse got an Indian buddy?"

"Jesse got an Indian wife."

Franklin's mind went into a spin. "He married an Indian?!"

"Jesse *is* an Indian, well partly. I mean, he's adopted. I wrote you. His mother was a white girl Doc took in."

"My brother?!? How come I never knew?"

"No one knew 'cept your Ma, Pa, and Doc. When he ran away the Blackfeet took him in…" Her voice trailed into whispery darkness. "Dinna you get my letters?"

Franklin slumped against the cave wall. His father's stories of the residential school swirled together with boyhood games and cap pistols, hunting arrowheads at the buffalo jump, baling crew by Fairfield with a giant Indian kid they called Horse, and the vacant eyes of dark-skinned men down by the tracks. "You asked me if there were real Indians out here, guess you got your answer."

"Indians aren't stories in a book or Saturday matinees, these are real people. Willow and Jesse are good for each other. And their little boy, Drummond Natoyii isttookimaa, his name means holy drum in two languages, is like a big brother to Flora." She paused, proud of her pronunciation.

"I don't know," Franklin was half in shock, "My brother adopted, Indians in the family, that little boy around my daughter…"

Maire's voice quick and flaring, "You dinna decide who's in your family afore you know them. And you dinna choose your daughter's friends when you won't even come meet her!"

Frank's mind flipped to battle mode. "Having family, making friends is a luxury, Moy. I'd get to know a guy, trade stories and photos, and next minute he's dead."

"It's a different war, here," Maire retorted. "Fighting shortages. Fighting prejudice. You got a foreigner wife, Jesse got an Indian wife, Boyd married a Japanese nurse. You best be ready to stand up for all of us, not just for some." He sat frozen in the challenge she laid before him. She called out before getting back on the bike, "I want to love you, Franklin Cooper. And there's things we got to have sorted from the start."

Next morning, he opened a jar of peaches and forked a slice slippery with nectar and popped it in his mouth. The sweetness was so full of boyhood summers that tears sprang to his eyes. He laid out her letters, slicing them open with the tip of his bayonet, arranging them by date, a clumsy process, one-handed. As he read her heartfelt correspondence, benign mind began to reweave a sense of valley life. Then. Now. Tomorrow. Peach juice ran down his chin. He wiped it with a baby sock.

Late October. Wheat sold. Alfalfa cut. Honey shipped. Steers sent to slaughter. Franklin watched over the harvest routines, his body camouflaged in khaki. When farm equipment started up one more time, he knew—sugar beets. Maire said Jesse was bringing back the Indian boys. He sent Preacher Boy home and veered toward the Fort to see for himself.

Franklin squatted in the scrub brush on a rise overlooking the dilapidated square that had framed his school days. Except for the Diking District house, most buildings had been boarded up and left to weather. Not today. Today was commotion. He pried Cyclone's field glasses out of his jacket pocket and watched Jesse and his crew unloading gear. There was a limping younger man, an older guy with a banged-up cowboy hat, several women, and a dozen teen boys, black-haired and shades of brown skin. He flattened himself on the cold ground and scrutinized his brother for the first time with knowledge they shared no common blood, only common childhood. Among white folks, Jesse looked white, heck everybody was white. But in the company of the Indians, Franklin could see the true black of his hair, the way he moved with a different sense of space. He was lean and muscled, a working man.

A sound engrained in battle mind intruded on the scene, the distinctive rumble of deuce-and-a-half transport trucks. Franklin swung the glasses around to see an Army convoy turning off the highway with an old blue pickup leading the way like a drum major. Two Willys MB Jeeps, officer and driver, peach-fuzz privates on the back bench, rifles glinting in the morning sun, four canvas hooped Jimmys and some cargo carriers. Franklin knew that interior. Wooden benches for the lucky, squatters on the floor, men and gear spraddle-legged, bouncing over terrain. Last vehicle a gunner Jeep with a mounted 30-caliber machine gun scanning his hometown. Fear tightened his stomach and heightened his senses.

The Indians scattered as the Army drove into the old Fort compound. Homer Torgerson stepped out of his truck. Bits of

Maire's story and her letters from last spring came back to him: confrontation at the church, prejudice, threats. An officer stood at the roll bar shouting, "Trespassing... government property... orders." Franklin was half hearing words, half reading lips through the glasses. Riflemen positioned themselves at the canvas flaps.

Torgerson strode up to Jesse, poking, shoving. Jesse shoved back. Homer pushed him aside. Jesse grabbed at Homer's jacket. Every muscle in Frank's arm twitched. The limping guy made a lopsided tackle. Homer went down and the three of them rolled in dirt. The older Indian corralled the women and boys into a doorway. Franklin held his position. Something metal flashed. The young officer raised his pistol and fired. A warning shot sailed off into the Big Sky.

Franklin could hear bits of command, "... labor shortage... sugar beets... ranch hands... POWs." Homer dusted off his overalls, postured with arms across his chest and nodded at whatever the officer said.

"Be good, Jesse," Franklin whispered as his brother staggered to his feet. "Live to fight another day." Tommy's same instructions echoed in his mind. Metal bolts clinked. Tailgates dropped. Dozens of German soldiers jumped out of the troop carriers and stood blinking in the Montana daylight of his hometown, his valley, his refuge, his return. Rage belched up his gullet. Battle mind howled. He pitched sideways, unable to balance with only one elbow spread on the dirt.

Franklin's nightmare thrashed in daylight. He shook his head side to side, trying to hold focus on the scene in the Fort below. Adrenaline pumped through the broken boundary of time and place. Now. Below him, shouts of confusion in English, in German. Then. Thump-thump-thump of artillery fire. The war ricocheted in his skull. He struggled onto the tripod of his limbs. Phantom pain tore up his disappeared arm. He couldn't tell if he was screaming his mouth so full of dirt. And what if Homer charged up the hill and found him writhing in the underbrush? Tourniquet, for god's sakes, Homer, I'm bleeding to death. Do for me what you pray someone does for your boys! What if a Jerry bastard jerked him to standing, the whole mess of himself exposed? Name. Rank. Serial number. Then. Now. There. Here. Hands—well one hand—on his head. What if the prisoners grabbed rifles from the slack hands of the guards and opened fire. Franklin knew how fast this scene could turn ruthless. His brother needed his help, but he lay shaking on the ground, sweating, crying, useless, crippled, vomiting peach slices onto dead grass.

"It's not a fucking football game, Tommy!" Tanks exploded in fireballs. Men were blown out of shallow foxholes. Why was all the artillery firing from the Pass? Didn't they have guns? Boys who used to hunt pheasant and corn-fed deer were shooting off rounds at rocks and boulders that shot back, rapid fire. After days of useless chaos, covered with the smear of battle—dirty, bloody—American troops had fled backward in panic, scattered into fifty miles of desert and brush, cut off from resupply. Sidi bou Zid and Kasserine Pass was the fight that changed him. He learned to hate. Hate war. Hate passing orders that killed young men. Hate Germans. That was February. He still had two arms. Found Tommy. Repaired his radio. They headed toward Hill 609, their destiny with death and dismemberment.

If the sun hadn't shone this October day, Franklin might have died of hypothermia lying on a ledge overlooking his hometown, his body turning into a shriveled hairy carcass. But the damn sun did shine. Pale light baked through the Army jacket, kept him warm enough to survive the long swoon as his mind reeled through war to the moment he could not forgive. When he came to, the scene below had changed. His brother was gone. The Indians were gone. Military grunts and orders

The Beekeeper's Question

were turning the Fort into a fortress again. Homer Torgerson strutted around the parade grounds like Patton.

Franklin Cooper, U.S. Army Signal Corps, rose on shaky legs. There. Here. Then. Now. Yes. No. Live. Die. He surrendered to shame and shadow, turned toward Froggy's planning his death.

33
Truths and Visitations

OCTOBER 21, 1943: *Early winter storms bog American troops in the Italian mountains. The Japanese American 100th Battalion begins its distinguished career fighting up the Italian peninsula.*

FOR SEVERAL DAYS AND NIGHTS after the scene at the Fort, Franklin refined his plans for departure. He wrote Maire a letter saying he was sorry and set her free to marry again. He wrote his father requesting burial next to his mother. His words rang hollow in his shelled-out mind. Battle mind and benign mind fought for his soul.

It was a moonless night when she returned, easing the bicycle over rough terrain, the small headlamp flickering in the unevenness of her pedaling. She brought food. "I come to say the full story about Broin." She pushed a covered dish into the shadow of the cave and eased onto a flat rock. "I ken he's in America, Franklin, looking for me."

Franklin kept the veil of shadow between them. So many greater horrors overlaid his long-ago pub brawl. He smelled venison stew. A bully wields power because no corresponding violence matches him. He wondered how Broin Mulvaney, the terror of Cullybackey, would have fared in the real fight. His stomach rumbled. He'd have to wait out the story.

The Beekeeper's Question

Maire took a deep breath, sucked in night air. She was shaking with tension and chill. To tell the story she had to enter the nightmare, let the worst happen to her again. She unfurled the shawl she'd carried in the bicycle basket. Comfort, and something more, the one possession that had been with her all along. There. Then. *I was ten years old, my birthday, summer coming on, the longest day. My mother said I could do whatever I pleased. I wanted to have tea with the faeries.*

"All right for now," Ma said, *"but after today you be too old for fancy."*

"They're not fancies, Ma, they're real!"

"You such pals with faeries, well you ask 'em to send us growin' weather for the potatoes and a cow to give milk. And by the by, some sheep who need a shepherd. The fey folk got to be useful, me gal, or you bid them goodbye." She handed me a biscuit and a crock of weak tea, like she gave my Da when he went to work.

"Nana believes in faeries," I said.

"Nana is an old woman prone to foolishness." Maybe Ma blamed faeries for her dead babies. She showed me one, once, when I came home from school—tiny pink body, size of my finger. She said it was my sister, but I think it was a mouse. I took the tea and set off to my secret spot.

Maire closed her eyes remembering shades of green, patterned hedgerows, how the land tilted toward the sea, moist wind. *I laid out biscuit crumbs and dribbles of tea, like Nana showed me. I sat still, waitin' for the wee. Weren't faeries who came, but my brothers, George and Gordon, and their buddy Broin. Broin already a bully. He skipped school, never went to church, did what he pleased. No one stopped him. Because they friended him, they were the only boys who han't got a black eye or bloody nose. They had slingshots, looking for birds, perfecting their aim. I scrunched down small at the base of a bush, but Gordy, who was twelve, called me out. "Whatcha doing there, Maire?"*

I was prayin' the faeries to make me invisible, but I couldna say that. "Ma said I could take me tea outside. Leave me be." Maire shook her head side to side, trying to keep hold of herself on the rock, stay grounded in the October chill, the ear of the cave, the point of her mission. Adrenaline pumped through the broken boundary between sleeping and waking. Then. Now. There. Here. "Come out where we can see you." Broin was fifteen and already manly with a smear of hair on his lip that made him look dirty all the time. He was jumpy like he was deciding to be mean. When you're little, you know that feeling.

Maire tugged the shawl around her. *Broin grabbed me foot.* "A girl got to learn to do what we say when we say it!" *My brothers din't move at first, but he goaded them.* "I'll show you how to be a man." *There was nothing fer me to hang onto. The tea got spilled. The faeries din't come.*

Broin pulled me onto the grass like you pull a sheep down for shearing. He sneered at George, "You don't gotta do anything, just hold her while I show you what's done." Gordy looked like he was near scairt as me, "She's... she's my sister," he stuttered. George poked him in the arm. "Grow up, baby face... we won't let him really hurt her." *But they did, Franklin. They let him. Really. Hurt. Me.*

Words bunched in the back of her throat. She didn't want to say it. *My own brothers pinned me to ground. Broin reached up my dress and got inside my knickers. He stuck his finger in my pee place. He poked his sharp dirty fingernail into a secret hole I didn't even know I had. He jabbed his finger inside me. It hurt terrible, like an eel slithered up in me. And then he said,* "You're my bride now, Maire MacDonnell. Your bras are my witness. I ruined you for myself." *He was kneeling between my legs. George and Gordy sat frozen beside me. He pulled out his finger and licked it, made an ugly face.* "Still sour, but it sweetens when you turn sixteen. I'll have you then. You belong to me."

Georgie and Gordy lifted me up and brushed me off 'fore running after Broin. The spilt tea had got my dress wet. I was too shamed to go home. How could I say what been done me? That night, Gordy and me were by the outhouse. He tried to hold my hand, but I pulled away. "I din't know what he was ginna do," he said. "It got over and I helped you up."

"You heard Broin," I turned on him, "I'm ruined." I was crying. "You helped me too late, Gordy. Now I'm dirty inside." The faeries deserted me. Nana took sick and died. I had no one."

"Oh Moy," his voice croaked into the dark that held them. Benign mind scrambled to the surface, gulping air. The lump of coal that had served all these months as Franklin's heart took a beat.

"We just went on, my brothers and me, that's all we could do. We grew up and never talked more of it. The night I ran with the passage money, Da was too drunk to follow and if the boys gave chase, they made a show of not catching. They owed me to get away." Sobs choked Maire's voice. "I never told anybody. But you are my husband, Franklin and I need to know: Was there anything about me that made you question… made you think I was impure?"

Franklin gulped so loud it echoed on the cave wall. Words rose in him from the time before his own ruination. "You were exactly who you said you were—a proper girl—a woman who waited for what you knew was right." The voice of her letters, finally read and organized into a chronology of absence, streamed through his mind. Her steadfastness during his desert silence had brought him to tears. Ink that had made it through the war blurred in his hands. The blackened coal reddened in his chest. He felt warmth. "Broin raped you, but he didn't ruin you. He couldn't."

He knew what she did not, that men can do unforgivable things that darken their souls forever. Things he hoped Maire couldn't even imagine—a woman's body in the desert raped so many times her vagina was hanging out. He and his buddies buried her in the sand cursing the Germans. Their outrage a defense against their own feared cruelty. Admission crawled up his throat. "It's possible for a man to get so broken he can't be fixed."

The coal that was his heart beat stronger. "He had no right to hurt you or to force his claim on you." In the chilly darkness of the cave, the fight that had been buried under so much other fighting surfaced in Franklin's mind. A man fights to bluster, to bloody, or to kill. Broin swung to kill. He remembered now.

And then she said, "He's coming." Her words hung in the air. "I prayed the war would stop him, but he *is* the war. Nothing has stopped him." She reached toward him, fingers extending through the darkness, voice still broken by tears. "When the bee yard burned, I feared it was him. Turned out t'was you. Then your Pa got sick. Jesse and I had to finish harvest. You needed to walk. We needed to talk. It was Flory's first birthday. Everything so busy, but nights get haunted." She took a long breath. "For years, I been fighting how he's a monster in my mind. Doc said be fearless, and I try, but seems like fear and courage get stronger together. It's like I got two minds—one that lives in daylight and one that cowers in darkness. Do you know what I mean?"

Yes. Franklin knew. Battle mind hoarded his box of dynamite, outdated and unstable, like the caveman himself. The past few days, since spying the POWs living in his grade school, he had imagined hugging the bundle to his chest, lighting enough sticks that at least one would blow. He knew what she did not, how death, for all its random horror, solved everything. That's what he saw in the vacated faces of battle corpses: secret relief.

But what if the man who would die chose to live? Not just breathing, but stepping into the whole mess of life, because he had a woman who knew how to love, and if he let her, if he met her, they could be something together. He heard the voice of his younger self, spouting dreams into the attic bedroom, tapping 'i love u' in Morse code on Maire's back. He remembered now. "I am your rightful husband, Moy. He will have to face me first." Something uncoiled in his spine that felt like courage. "In that Irish ken of yours, do we got time?"

"He's close," she whispered. "Please come in."

"If he's close, I'll meet him here." Franklin's stomach tightened with hunger and tension. "In the Army, I knew this scrawny kid who couldn't sleep until he made himself a foxhole. Howie the Hole Man we called him. One night, during especially hard shelling, Howie dug himself so deep he couldn't get out." Franklin cleared his throat, "That's where I been, Moy, dug in. One mind wanting out; one mind digging down." He was inching forward as he talked. He could see her shivering in that big grey scarf she treasured. "I didn't want to bring the war home."

She shifted on the rock, her hand balanced on cold dirt. "You're not bringing the war home, Broin is." Her fingers crossed their demarcation line into the cave. "I need you, Franklin. We can fight together."

The lump of coal softened into flesh; his bruised heart pulsed with his life's blood. He cared for her. He cared what happened to her. And if he cared what happened to her, he'd have to care what happened to himself. He stared at her fingertips. Benign mind moved his hand across inches of darkness. Battle mind tried to pull it back. His hand, the survivor, kept clawing forward, insisting his mind let his body go. He was three inches from caring. He was two inches from wanting. He was one inch from touching. Skin, fingertip to fingertip, connected.

She gasped. "I'll send Preacher Boy out to keep you warm. You can't stay here much longer."

"Pa got sick?"

"He's better. Don't worry over everything at once."

"I'm scared for you now."

"He's not here yet." She slipped her fingers down the shaft of his fingers. He gasped. "That soldier, Howie, how did he get out of the hole?"

"Tommy and I grabbed him and hoisted him up."

"Remember that part," she whispered, "Jesse and me, we're right here."

Franklin stood at the mouth of the cave slurping cold stew, watching his Irish girl cycle bravely through the uneven dark.

34
TROUBLE

OCTOBER 23 & 26, 1943: *Five hundred RAF bombers target Kassel, Germany, setting off a seven-day firestorm.*

DOC TIED HER PANTS CUFFS WITH STRING and wobbled out of town on Maire's bicycle, her medical kit jiggling in the basket. The day was swinging between sun and shadow like Doc's emotions, vacillating between optimism and worry. Things were coming to a head. Maire was quietly preparing room in the house and the mind of the family for Franklin's coming in. Once she confessed that she hadn't fully seen him, Doc determined to head out herself. So here she was, huffing up the slightest hill, coasting down the slightest dip, the butte seeming to advance or retreat as she aimed her way. At the base of the cave, boot prints, paw prints, bike and car tracks, a lingering odor of latrine. She set the kickstand. "Franklin! It's Auntie Doc. We need to talk." Preacher Boy ambled toward her from the mouth of the cave, tongue out, tail wagging.

His familiar voice shouted back, "You can talk, but I don't come out."

"I'm your auntie. I'm your doctor. You come out or I come in." No movement. "You know I've seen the worst. You can't scare me."

"I been a mess so long, Doc, can't just switch it off."

"That's why I've come—to help you bridge from cave to house." She was heaving breaths of anxious anticipation. The dog circled her legs. Sounds of scuffling, a ragged cough. A shaggy form emerged into daylight: tangled hair and beard that hadn't been cut or washed, rumpled jacket, wool pants slung low in the crotch, boots flapping with curled tongues. His left sleeve hung empty. "Oh Franklin…" Doc bit the inside of her cheek. "Come here, my boy, let me check you over."

He slid down the grade. "I'm not getting naked it's cold."

"I just want to see that stump, other inspections can wait." He sat on a boulder and looked away while she unbuttoned his coat and shirt, assessing his condition under the disarray.

"Do you know how long it takes to button those?" his voice cracked. "Tunisia, last spring. Artillery fire." Doc bared his shoulder. "Lost my buddy, my arm, then my mind." She opened her kit, got out gauze and alcohol, swabbed old scabs from the suture lines. Normal color under the dirt. He stank, but not of infection. "I've been trying to walk myself back together, but now those Jerries are living at the Fort."

She rebuttoned his shirt, slid the jacket sleeve back on. "Those men are prisoners. If you can let your war be over, you are free." She lifted his chin, stroked his matted beard. No nits. She kissed his grimy forehead. "You've been so brave out here, dearie." The boy beneath the man began heaving tears with no water. Doc pulled him to her soft bosom. She felt his arm slip round her waist. "You can make a good life for yourself, Franklin. Maire loves you. Your baby is the dearest thing. Everyone is waiting to welcome you." She rocked his torso and held on.

He choked out words, "I will come in, Auntie, but first I got to finish Maire's war. You know about him?" Doc nodded, her chin hitting the top of his head. "Figure to use myself as decoy. Lure that bastard here, keep him away from the house."

"A letter arrived last August from Mrs. Annenberg. I, uh, opened the envelope, never sure when to show Maire. And then everything else happened—the hives, Leo's heart attack."

"Pa had a heart attack?" Franklin pulled back, looked at her.

"I thought you knew. He's okay. Weakened. We try to keep him from worry." Doc tucked the crumpled stationery into Franklin's pocket. "It verifies he's on Maire's trail, and that they told him nothing, though she knew where to send the letter."

"He burgled my Quonset hut, stole stuff, rifled through letters." The boy submerged again beneath the man. The man had work to do. "Send Jesse here, I'm gonna need help."

Two days after Doc's visit, Franklin and Preacher Boy sat on a rock at the mouth of the cave sharing stale bread and watching Jesse's rusted-out pickup make its way across the field roads.

The truck rolled to a halt and Jesse strode to the bottom of the scree. "Hi Franklin, Doc said we got to talk!" Preacher Boy dashed down, and Jesse reached distractedly into dog fur. Franklin stood and watched a wave of shock cross his brother's face. "Holy smokes, Frankie. I wouldn't have known you." Jesse wiped sudden tears from his eyes. That was love, wasn't it? Crying at the sight of your brother. "Maire, see you like this?"

"Hell no. I hide in the cave. And it's night."

"That's probably good. You look a wreck, but you're still you," his brother looked him over, "I mean... Aren't you?"

The box of dynamite rolled a quarter-turn in his mind. Nothing exploded. "Yes," Franklin croaked. "Yes, I'm still myself." He stood, reeling in the truth of it. "I hear you got in trouble bringing the whole Indian thing back into the valley."

"It's in my blood."

"But red blood or not you're still my brother." Franklin felt his own cheeks suddenly wet, "I mean... Aren't you?"

"Yes, I am your brother." There was a catch in Jesse's voice, "Been worrying 'bout you. Maire said to give you time, let the two of you find a way. You finding your way?"

Franklin snorted back snot, "Yah… I am. But got to find a way through one more trouble 'fore I come in." He watched Jesse shifting his weight one foot to the other, jittery and chilled. "There's a violent sonofabitch hunting Maire."

Jesse nodded. "She told me bits. And this morning at Gertie's, Homer was saying he met some Irish guy in a bar in Great Falls, drifter type, looking for a family name of Cooper. You know how Homer likes to be the one who knows everything, 'specially after a few beers. Said he's going back into town, maybe hire him to oversee his POWs."

"Shit." Franklin went twitchy. "That bastard finger-raped Maire when she was just a girl. Terrorized her until she escaped to America. Then she worked all those years in the big house waiting for someone good." Anger and sorrow swirled in him. "So now, I got to be that someone. Prove it to her… and to myself." Franklin felt strings of memory working to bind the man he was to the man he wanted to be. "I need you to get him before Homer does. Broin Mulvaney, from Cullybackey. Bring him here to Froggy's, keep him away from Maire."

"And then?" The Cooper boys appraised each other, man to man.

Franklin started pacing. "I already fought him once, front of a pub in Maire's hometown. Mulvaney's body is a weapon. He will take you down, break your neck, stomp your heart. Would'a killed me 'cept my Army buddy put a knife to his neck."

Jesse winced. "You been living in a rougher world than the rest of us, Frank. Shouldn't we call Sheriff Buzz?"

"Unless his face is in the post office, the sheriff can't intervene until Mulvaney does something illegal. Police get involved *after* someone gets killed, hurt, kidnapped, or raped. Who do you want that to be, Jess?" Franklin stared at his brother. "Mulvaney breaks into the house, if Pa stepped in front, Broin would kill him in minutes. That leaves Maire and Willow with a mop handle. You want our kids in the middle of that?" It was the first moment Franklin felt himself a father with someone little to defend.

"Would he take money? Ticket to California?"

"You've never met anyone like this, Jess. Getting Maire is Mulvaney's endgame."

"The law *is* on our side, isn't it?"

"First someone's got to stop him, turn him in." Franklin stepped around the boulders that guarded the cave. "I am all that stands in his way. Find him, Jess. Tell him I want to make a deal. Get him in your truck. Drive straight here."

Jesse pushed his hands deep into jean pockets and hunched his shoulders. "So, I get him here and…?"

"We lure him into the cave. I knock him down with our old baseball bat. You tie him up good. We leave him overnight. Let him consider the error of his ways. When he's ready to talk, we get Buzz."

"Yah, well after we've kidnapped and hogtied him, how are we still the good guys?"

"Man like Mulvaney leaves a trail. He's already been to prison. Who knows what he's been up to making his way here. Once he's in custody, Buzz can trace his path from one sheriff's department to the next."

Franklin saw the Adam's apple working in his brother's throat. "I've got rope in the truck. Got a deer rifle at the cabin. You hear that Doc gave us her place?"

Franklin felt his chest tighten. "No guns. A gun makes this a battlefield. We're not gonna kill him. Just restrain him before he introduces a level of fear this valley doesn't ever want to think about. Homer got no idea what he's dealing with."

"All the more reason to get the sheriff."

"All the more reason to intercept him. Turn him over to the law. Let Buzz make some official calls. Keep everyone safe."

"Okay, I think." Jesse gulped. "I'm making a supply run to the Falls. I can leave straight away."

Now Franklin gulped, "Today's the day then. Big guy, red hair, crooked nose, fists like bricks. Be careful. Just say you can bring him to me, Maire's husband."

"What are you going to do?"

"Get ready for our little ambush."

"What you got out here besides the baseball bat?" Jesse ran his hand through his hair, that common Cooper gesture.

"Sixteen-inch steel bayonet blade. And, like you said, underneath all this filth… myself."

"What do you think Mulvaney's got?" Jess sounded nervous.

"Rage. Revenge. Probably a hunting knife he stole from my Army buddy. Two arms."

Jesse winced. "We got three arms, Frank. I'll do my best." Before he got in the truck, he called back, "Don't clean up. The sight of you is terrifying, and the smell up close is your secret weapon." Jesse drove off, the engine making that jittery sound, heading toward the highway.

Franklin watched the pickup get smaller and smaller in the bigness of the land. "Stay smart," he whispered. He was an infantryman. He knew what Jesse did not—what it takes to stop an enemy gone mad.

35
The War Comes to Froggy's

EVENING, OCTOBER 26, 1943: *The Japanese Burma/Siam rail link through dense tropical jungle is completed. Of the 61,000 Allied POWs used as slave labor, over 12,000 die.*

FRANKLIN HAD NO WATCH, but it was long past dinner (of which there was none) and moonless dark. It would be a cold night, not winter, but cold enough for a man tied and bound. Well, he'd throw a dog blanket over Mulvaney and stand guard, send Jesse for the sheriff. He had talked over their strategy with Preacher Boy, and the dog was in for the plan. The baseball bat was propped where he could grab it. Jesse's rope was coiled just inside the entrance. The bayonet was stuck in his belt, hidden under the woolen Army jacket that had become his outer skin against the autumn chill. His stump ached as though remembering its last moments as an arm with a hand.

The distinctive sound of Jesse's truck, headlights bouncing on the rutted farm trails, coming fast. Franklin waited, heart pounding, prepared to follow Jesse's lead. Preacher Boy growled low in his throat, straining at the short rope Franklin had wrapped around his neck. He took a long breath, and Tommy's battle cry rang in his mind, "Scrimmage, Bee Man!" They'd finally take down Mulvaney together, if only in spirit.

Around the kitchen table, the family laid plans for the coming months. Franklin would come in. Jesse, Willow, and Drum would head north. Leo would get stronger. The farmers would winter down. Out on his ranch, Homer used POWs to stack hay and mend fence. He bragged how lucky the valley was to have cheap labor and armed guards both at hand. He was training a couple prisoners who spoke some English to take over winter tasks. "Gonna give my leg a rest. Send 'Adolf' out in the storms." Folks bundled in layers. Kids planned Halloween costumes. The edges of the days were downright cold. Midday sunshine offered weakened warmth or rain soddened the bare fields. Frosty mornings. Everyone waiting for the season to thoroughly turn to first snows and hard freeze.

Since the day of the pollen portal when she had danced in the trance of the hive, the *hmmm* had taken residence in Maire's body as though bees made honey in the skep of her ribs. Pressing her nose into a chunk of beeswax she entreated the Unity, "Fly high. Watch for the demon. Let me know." Jesse hadn't come back from town and the *hmmm* vibrated with increasing intensity. She and Willow set his plate, then ate without him, the two women maintaining a veneer of calm in front of the young and old. They gathered around the radio for evening news. Leo retired to read himself to sleep. Maire put Flora to bed. She stepped outside to get a sense of the night, assessing the temperature Franklin would have to manage in the cave. She stood in the yard, wrapped in her shawl. The vibration of guard bees messaging alarm hit against her chest. Her pulse ratcheted up. Something was happening. Now.

Willow joined her, wrapped in a blanket. "I put Drum to bed in the attic. We need to stay together." She sniffed the night air. "Jesse goes to Franklin. There is trouble."

Maire spun in agitation. "What do we do?"

Willow pulled at the edge of the shawl. "We sit. Prayer is

power. This is our part." The young mothers sat on the porch steps. Maire folded shaking hands in her lap, closed her eyes. The hmmm was deafening though only she could hear it. She spoke to Willow, "In a hive, there are bees who stand at the entrance to defend against intruders. They do this trembling thing, moving up and down on their legs, like a final warning. If the intruder—a stranger bee or wasp, even a mouse—does not retreat, they attack." Something glinted in the shadows at the edge of her sight.

"There is a knife," Willow said, "In the hand of the hunter." She chanted in her ancient tongue. "I am talking to the knife. It was stolen from a good hand and does not want to harm. I am singing to Jesse. He is *ipisttotsimakoyii*, Walks Far Wolf. He needs to be cunning, to fight with the pack."

Maire willed herself to focus. She whirled the guard bees into a cyclone of protection and sent the men a swarm of determined fighters.

"There is another knife," Willow spoke softly, "In the hands of your man. It will be bloodied one last time." They leaned into one another, shoulder to shoulder, steadying each other, calling on the lineages that thrummed through their bloodlines. Then everything went dark. They grabbed hands. White skin, brown skin. *Aakim.*

The truck stopped with a squeal of brakes, headlights making two ponds of soft light. The passenger door flung open. A burly man stepped out and violently jerked Jesse across the seat, dragging him headfirst out the door. The headlock wrestling hold could break Jesse's neck if he didn't get his feet under himself. Not good. Jesse pulled one leg out and found his way to half-standing in the grip of his captor, upright but head twisted in Broin's rough grasp. Hostage. Also, not good. In the cast of light and shadow, Jesse's face looked blood darkened. Very not good.

"Hey brother," Jesse's voice raspy inside the chokehold, "this man claims Maire is his rightful wife; something about when they were young."

Broin looked even bigger and rougher than Franklin remembered. "You know how many Coopers live in Montana?" a laughing sneer, "Some of 'em pretty damn sorry to share your name, boyo." Broin stepped belligerently in front of the truck yanking Jesse around in a terrifying manner. He peered into the dark trying to locate his foe. "Fat old rancher thinks you're in Italy fighting Nazis, him cryin' in his drink over his own boyos. Was plannin' to hide at his house, figger how to liberate my woman." His silhouette played along the ground in exaggerated shadows. "But this is ev'n better. Since you here, I kin finish yah, take the grievin' widow and get the hell gone."

"She's not your woman, Mulvaney." Franklin needed to buy time, assess how badly Jesse was already hurt, and if his brother could free himself for the fight that was surely coming.

"Oooh you so brave for a deserter. Show yourself and let's get 'er done."

Franklin shouted from the mouth of the cave. "I'm a cripple. Didn't Jess tell you? War tore me up. You want to fight me, come get me. I'll give it my best." He tried to sound defeated, hesitant; he was bait. He shifted enough so Broin could catch movement, but not see him. He was dressed in his saggy pants, a flannel shirt, two sweaters, and the jacket. He felt awkward and overstuffed, but anticipated the advantage of padding if it came to fists and boots before they got him tied.

"Cripped?! Now that's sweet. Crybaby, too, living out here in your own dirt, leaving your woman unprotected." Broin blurted a guttural laugh. "You wasn't much a puncher back in Cullybackey. Would a finished it then, 'cept for your buddy. Liberated his knife, I did, on my little trip through your duffel bags. Got it right here. Gonna slit your brother's throat with it, less you got enough courage to come down." Mulvaney jerked

Jesse hard enough that Franklin saw him stumble. "A little revenge for that humiliatin' moment in front of me gang." Broin coughed and a cloud hung for a second in the cold air. "I've been chasing what's mine halfway 'cross the world. Stopped in Philadelphia, got meself pointed in the right direction, worked my way west. Montana, what a godforsaken piece of turf."

Jesse hung slack in the vise of Broin's hold. Franklin prayed it was a ploy. He played the unseen voice booming from the cave, hoping the chamber would amplify his commands and the dog's growl. He let Broin carry on, buying time for Jesse to figure out how to rally, counting on Broin to get more jittery. Praying, oh God, that Broin didn't kill his brother right before his eyes. Maybe they should have called the sheriff; designed a plan that included reinforcements, squad cars, deputies with drawn guns. Well, wasn't that what the government had inducted *him* to do? If Mulvaney's name was Mueller or Morimoto they'd be heroes for whatever was going to happen here. Two against one, though Franklin wasn't sure if it was him and Preacher Boy or him and Jesse. He sucked air through his teeth. "Yah got a big mouth on a little brain, Broin. If you had stuck me in Cullybackey you'd be in prison missing the best years of your life, such as they are."

"Fuck you, Cooper." Pointed eerie shadows, lit by truck lights jerked across the darkened grass and stiffened mud tracks. "I got money. Set us up. Maire and me. Back where we belong." Broin's speech got faster and faster. "Get my girl, get some sheep, get some respect. You not takin' that again, neither is she. We get home, she'll forget you. We get home, I go to the pub with a story to tell and a round for the reg'lars. Her da beat his wife good for giving Maire that cash. 'Spose you know the old lady fell in the river." His laugh gargled like muddy water. "Now, this war. Everything's gone wrong. What you hidin' anyway?" Broin pulled at Jesse's neck, knocking him off balance again and again. The Irish ran hot with rage, his body near to steaming in the lights of the truck; he wore just a shirt. That might help.

Franklin held steady. Let the enemy walk into range. He wanted the night to witness. "You raped a ten-year-old girl!"

"I decided her!" Broin shouted back. Maybe he'd drop Jesse and charge the cave. "I hear you proved her a breeder. She'll make me strong Irish lads. Someone else can raise your punk, but I'm taking my girl."

Franklin blurted a laugh. "You do not separate a mother and her child like taking puppies from a bitch. Maire is not yours—not mine either—she belongs to herself."

Broin made a half-crazed and wild sound. Preacher Boy lunged against the rope almost pulling Franklin over. "You the one dinna get it, Yank, I am not leaving without her, and I dinna care what I leave behind. Cripped or not, come down or I'll slice your brother ear to ear." A blade glittered in the headlamps. Buck knife, five-inch steel, Thompson's prize possession.

Franklin let out a growling bellow and watched Broin searching for him in the shadows. He released the dog who shot down the rocky slope and lunged himself in full canine fury toward the stranger. In those seconds of distraction, Franklin screamed to his brother, "Jesse, go for his nuts!" Headlights and night-shadow. Preacher Boy dug his teeth into Broin's raised arm. Jesse twisted in a spurt of strength. Bent in front of Broin's torso, Jesse grabbed his tormentor's crotch, a vise grip and twist, yanking Broin's dick and balls. A scream of pain. Jesse tore himself loose and the dog tore flesh. Franklin flung himself off the ledge, watching his balance on the loose stones, and raced toward the writhing of men and dog. Broin still had one arm free and was slashing wildly, trying to knife Jesse before Franklin got to him. Bayonet drawn, Franklin watched for the hole in the fight. That's what he'd learned in the heat of combat—there was always a sweet spot where the bullet or the blade could do its rightful job. One chance, or you could kill your buddy. One chance, or your enemy could kill you.

The Beekeeper's Question

Buzzing. Angry. High-pitched bees. Impossible in the cold and dark. Inside the maniacal *hmmm* that surrounded him, Franklin slipped into an altered realm of perception. He knew he was moving fast, but every action registered in slow motion. He saw Broin grabbing at Jesse. Saw Jesse twisting Broin's prick and balls. He saw the knife raised to deal a slicing blow. He saw the dog's teeth clamped onto Broin's forearm, saliva flinging in the headlights, restraining Broin's wild stabbing. Franklin pushed himself into the writhing combat. The growl coming out of him matched the dog's tenor and ferocity. He saw Broin recoil at the smell and sight of him. He screamed at Jesse, "Get outta the way!" Jesse twisted his whole body around, pulling out of the headlock, flinging himself to the side, buckling Broin to his knees as he jerked on his genitals, nails digging through the crotch of the pants. Broin a screaming animal now. Jesse pulled back from him, kicking hard, farm boots landing on Broin's torso, ribs, groin. Everything raw and chaotic.

Broin tossed the knife from his right hand into his left to free it from the painful wrestle with the dog. And in that instant, he slashed down, gashing deep into the meat of Jesse's thigh. Jesse howled. Broin tore the blade out of Jesse's leg and raised his arm to do it again. Franklin knew what they did not—somewhere in that flesh the femoral artery pumped its lifeblood along the leg of a man. He'd seen men bleed to death, red geysers shooting out of their thighs. Not tonight, at least not Jesse, because there it was— the hole in the fight. The dog had captured Broin's right arm. Broin's left arm was in the air, raised high. Broin hauled himself to sitting, thrashing his head side to side like a shaggy bear. He aimed for another slash. If he got to his feet they'd be bested. But for a second, Broin's whole left chest was exposed. Franklin shook with memory, how he'd lost himself to battle mind, mangling the body of a German plowboy. Plunging his bayonet in and out, screaming hatred and terror, he'd carved the corpse to shreds. That rage cost him, body and soul. Tonight, he commanded battle mind—one plunge. Franklin turned his blade sideways and, using the weight of his body in full trajectory, drove the bayonet deep between Broin's ribs. He felt the point pierce skin, slice the pectoral shield, cut through the intercostal muscle, and push deep into the chest cavity aiming for the ticking bomb of Mulvaney's heart. Even if he missed, the sixteen-inch blade would damage Broin's lungs enough to kill him. The night vibrated with the sound of angry bees.

Time came back to itself. Franklin lay sprawled across Broin's torso, his hand cramped around the bayonet handle. With a small surge of desperation, Broin tried to poke Thompson's knife through Franklin's jacket. The point bounced away. "You're dying, Irish." Franklin watched realization rise into the black pupils of Broin's eyes. "You're going to hell, and Maire is free."

Broin began gurgling pink slime. Franklin pushed his dirty, hairy face closer to his enemy's. "You called this down, Mulvaney," he growled. "You could have walked away. Saved us trouble." Broin's eyes went glassy. Franklin hefted himself up. He was the great bear now. Preacher Boy mouthed the dead weight of Broin's arm, growling fiercely. "That's enough, boy," Franklin panted, "We got him. Good dog."

Survivor shakes. Death in his face. How had it come to this, again? He shouted at the implacable sky, "I had to save my brother!" God did not reply. Jesse lay crumpled alongside Broin's body. Bleeding. Franklin crawled to his brother.

"I'm sorry, Frank, I was no help." He sounded shocky and fat lipped.

"Yes, you were. You ripped his dick. You took him down, gave us a chance." Franklin reached inside his jacket and pulled out a flashlight. "I got to see how bad you're poked."

"He broke my nose. Can hardly breathe." Franklin shined the light in his brother's face. "My eye's swelled shut."

"It's your leg I'm worried about, where he stabbed you." Franklin aimed the beam on blood darkening jeans. The wound was seeping heavily, but not pulsing.

"He stabbed me?" Jesse hoisted himself up onto his elbows. "I can't feel a thing."

"Well, that's not so good." Franklin reached in another pocket. "I thought we might need to gag him, so I tore up a shirt." He jammed the flashlight in his useless armpit to aim the beam and ripped the denim back. Raw muscle opened like steak. "Hang in there, Jess. You got to press the wound together best you can. Hold the skin closed." Jesse started to shake. "Don't faint!" Franklin grabbed a strip of shirt cotton, used his teeth to hold one end in place and wrapped the length tight around Jesse's leg. The flashlight rolled onto the ground, but he felt the bandage take on pressure, "Ease your fingers out when you feel it tighten."

"I'm all bloody." Jesse wobbled.

"I need your hands, Jess. We got to slow the bleeding until we get you to Doc's. Tie it off, tight as you can. You got it? This is important." Jesse was shaking so hard he could barely control his fingers, but he managed a knot.

"It's the same leg I broke last winter." He sounded sad.

"Welcome to World War Two, brother."

Jesse searched his face. "That was horrible, Frank. How'd you live through stuff like this?"

"You just do it. Like we just did." The dog pushed his muzzle under Franklin's armpit. "Then you get the shakes. Like we got now." Tremors shook them both. "All this terror starts sweating to the surface, and you have to go live in a cave for three months, so you don't accidentally kill your wife in your sleep." Both men fell silent, until remembering the third man in their fight, they looked at Broin.

"I thought we were just gonna tie him up?" The corpse lay in the glow of the headlights, eyes half-open, chin covered in bloody foam, skin dead white. The bayonet plunged to its handguard protruded from the left ribcage. "Are we murderers now, Frankie?" Jesse stuttered.

"We're soldiers now, Jess. With soldiers' courage, soldiers' wounds, and soldiers' guilt."

An engine noise penetrated their shock. "Honey truck," they said in unison. "Can you stand? Help me drag him to the cave. Maire doesn't need to see this." They each staggered to their feet, swaying to find stability.

"We gonna lift him?" Jesse asked.

"Deadman's drag. Grab one foot, I'll grab the other." It was nearly impossible. Franklin's one hand wrapped around an ankle, Jesse stumbling to pull with his one strong leg. It was maybe twenty-five feet from the fight scene to the cave mouth, but Broin outweighed them by a good forty pounds, and he wasn't helping any. The sound of the oncoming truck summoned a reserve of strength as they dragged the body up the scree.

"His head's banging rocks." Jesse was facing backwards, trying to put most of the chore on his uninjured leg.

"A corpse is meat, Jess. The man, mean bastard that he was, departed with his last gasp. Get him into Froggy's, and I'll give him proper burial." Broin's torso bumped heavily over the loose stones. His arms flopped up alongside his ears. Twice a wheezing whine escaped his lungs, making them jumpy. Franklin's nerves were still zinging with taunts and danger. "We've dressed out a buck, a body does weird stuff, but he's dead. I know he's dead."

Jesse mumbled. "He's not meat, though. We killed a man. In our own backyard. At Froggy's!" Jesse was groaning but moving. "This was our hideaway, Frankie. Where we hung out with Ralph and Tim." The brothers pulled the dead weight into the cave mouth. "Last winter it was me that hid here in a storm. Froggy's saved my life." Jesse had a two-handed advantage, but his leg kept crumpling under him. "Who'd have thought it'd come to this?"

"It was self-defense." They dragged the body inside. The honey truck braked to a halt. Preacher Boy danced around the vehicle. "Good enough." They dropped those dead legs and grabbed onto each other. Franklin held Jesse in his one right arm, supporting Jesse's stabbed-up left leg. Jesse put his arm around Franklin's shoulders. The brothers stepped out where Maire could see them and hobbled down the slope. Before they reached the bottom, Franklin whispered urgently, "The killing rests on me, Jess. Broin is the last man of my war."

"Not alone, though," Jesse whispered back, "You're my brother." He swayed, near to fainting. "Now do I call Buzz?"

Franklin halted, "No. I'm going to blow the cave. Broin got no people. Nobody seen him. Nobody miss him—least of all, us." Jesse was losing focus in the throes of shock.

The two women were shaking in the chilling night, the porch skimmed with frost. They roused from their twin entrancements and Willow spoke first. "It's over. There's blood, but our men live."

"I'll go get them. Can you go prepare Doc?" Maire pulled on boots and jacket. Hunched over the wheel, she steered the clumsy bulk of the truck toward the cave. Jesse's truck was parked askew on the gravel, the dog was racing around the perimeter, and the silhouetted figures of the Cooper brothers limped down the familiar slope. They met halfway, stopping only a hive's width apart, standing in rutted tire tracks, lit by headlights, searching each other's shadowed faces. Maire ran her hand over the surface of his jacket. Her fingers were slick with an unmistakable stickiness. "Oh my God, Franklin, you're covered with blood."

"Not mine. I'm okay." A low buzz resonated under his words. "Homer found Broin in town, told Jesse he was going to bring him out here." She felt herself recoil. "We decided to get him first. Tie him up, call the sheriff, get evidence on him."

"Yah, tie him up," Jesse mumbled.

"Broin got crazy. We fought. He's dead." Preacher Boy lifted his leg on blood-soaked soil. Jesse hung off Franklin's side, half-conscious. "Jesse got stabbed." They half carried him to the honey truck cab, opened the door, propped him inside. Blood had seeped through the makeshift bandage soaking his pantleg.

She closed the truck door. "I want to see for myself."

Franklin held her with the strength of his gaze. "Maire, be sure. If you look, you can never unlook."

"If I don't look, he'll always be my nightmare."

Franklin handed her the flashlight, "We have to be quick, Jesse needs Doc, fast."

Maire crossed the threshold she had always respected, night after night, waiting for him to emerge and shined the light up and down the corpse. "He was always bigger than anybody. Beating littler kids, making people give him his way. He din't care the cost to anyone else." She swallowed back nausea. "Did you talk? I mean, did he say anything about my mother?"

"He said she fell in the river." Maire flinched.

"That your dagger?" Franklin nodded. "Through the heart?" Franklin nodded again. "Seems fitting." She searched his eyes. "Are you hurt?"

"I got him first."

"My God, Franklin... he's really gone." Maire spun dizzily between relief and emergency. Wanting him dead, praying he's dead, seeing him dead, a logjam of thoughts and feelings in the back of her mind. "Now what?"

"He's just an unreliable drifter who drifted on. I can blow the cave. Bury him under a ton of rock."

Tears welled in her eyes. "I'll come back and help."

"I need to finish this. Me and Preacher Boy. I can drive the pick-up. You take my duffel," Franklin gestured to the mouth of the cave. "Careful, it's got all your letters... and an arm the Army issued. Go save Jesse. Watch for me after."

The Beekeeper's Question

She grabbed for his hand, it wasn't there, so she held the end of his empty sleeve and kissed the dirty, bloody, woolen cuff. "I'll be waiting, Franklin." She closed the cab door, popped the clutch into drive and headed into the blood-curdled dark.

36
Burial Rites and Rebirth

MIDNIGHT, OCTOBER 26, 1943: *The Soviet Army liberates the Ukrainian city of Dnipro from German occupation. Part of Hitler's "Annihilation Zone," and Soviet "Scorched Earth Policy," the war cost Ukraine 6.8 million civilian and military lives.*

ADRENALIN COURSED THROUGH FRANKLIN'S VEINS with a sensation like his heart was pumping crude oil. He wanted a cigarette. He wanted a drink. Well, he really wanted a pint in a pub in Belfast with Thompson, the two of them smoking Luckies. He wanted to tell him, "I got the sonofabitch, Tommy. What he did to Maire. And probably Ailish. And I got your knife back." He turned off the headlights, saving enough battery to drive home, but plunging himself into darkness.

    Franklin had spent the afternoon tidying evidence of his three-month occupancy. When Buzz arrived to take their hostage, he wanted his hideaway to look like a sane man had made a sane choice to live here. Now the cave was a crypt. He needed to drag Broin deep enough into the cavern that he could light a dynamite stick and throw it at the box—praying it would finally explode while he ran like hell for Jesse's truck. Dead men required a blanket drag. He sat with his back to the cave wall and used his legs to roll Broin's body over on its side, slid the blanket lengthwise along his spine rolled him back and then repeated his actions from the other side. He was sweating in padded layers of clothes, and he hadn't budged the corpse an inch.

The Beekeeper's Question

Preacher Boy watched, cocking his head one way then another. "You gonna help, or not?" Franklin balled a corner of the blanket in his right hand and pulled hard against the deadweight. The drag slipped a couple inches on the cave floor. He changed corners, pulled again. Preacher Boy mouthed a wad of cloth, braced his four legs, and tugged. He was only a forty-pound mutt, but he tried. "War is something you do with your buddies," he told the dog. "Fourteen of us in the squad walked into that battle and only five came out—me and the men who carried me. God, I hope they're still alive." They grunted on. Inch by inch. "Not always grateful they saved me." He raised his stump in the dark. "I got shrapnel in my ribs, scars on my back. Even after I clean up, I won't be pretty." The dog listened for words of interest: come, sit, food, good boy. Man and dog, panting with effort. "Far enough, good boy."

Franklin shined the dimming flashlight on the dead man's face, dropped to his knees and pulled the bayonet. Bile rose in him. "You evil sonofabitch. You could have had a life, a wife, though not my wife! You could be sitting on some rainy hillside counting sheep. Plenty of ways you might have lived and died. But here you are, all dead and no one to mourn you." The bayonet came free in his hand, along with a torrent of grief. "I was done killing. I was waking from my nightmares." Franklin slid to sitting in the space between the cave wall and the corpse. "Then you show up all crazy and violent, make us risk everything—Maire and me, Jesse and me." Spasms of tension washed through him. How close he and Jesse had come; how high the stakes had been. He put his head between his knees, breath heaving. "I killed, but I didn't lose it, not like then." The dog nosed into his armpit.

A voice began resonating inside his mind. "Bear Heart," it called him. Franklin looked up. An old Indian woman, silver braids lit like moonlight, buckskin dress, stood at the mouth of the cave. She glided toward him. "What the hell..." Franklin tried to believe his eyes.

The Old Woman mind-talked him. "A warrior fights his own dark mirror. Your anger at this man is your anger at yourself. Your fear of him is your fear of yourself." Preacher Boy whined, buried his head between his paws. "You have killed to save your way of life. You have killed to protect your people and land. You have walked the valley of the shadow. This is what a warrior carries." Franklin began to shake. "If you honor his death as sacrifice, you will you be free." Two large, black, severed wings dangled from her outstretched wrists. "This is Eagle Medicine." She took the wings firmly in her hands and held them aloft. "*Pita* flies where there is need."

He felt the air stir around him. Real. He heard the whistle of the great bird echo in the cave. Real.

"Stand and be doctored," she commanded. He rose and stood still. The cave went totally dark. Four times the wings swooped over him from head to toe. He smelled cleansing and strength, maybe sweetgrass, maybe pine. The wings scrubbing now.

"Thank you, whoever you are." His voice was creaky and raw. He took a breath that seemed to fill his whole body with night and stars. Spirit of eagle flew through the terrain he held deep inside. Eagle behind his eyes. Eagle whistling in his throat. Eagle circling his heart and careening down the canyon of his battered torso. Eagle flying through the hollow darkness of his pain. Eagle landed in his belly, perched on the bone of his pelvis. In one talon it tore at the small, rank body of his nightmare, devouring terror that he might be free. He wept as men do not admit they weep.

When he shuddered to stillness and opened his eyes, the Old Woman was gone. He touched the contours of his manbody and sank to his knees. The dog let out a whimper. "No shit, Preacher Boy." He pressed his face into the comforting doggy rankness.

Franklin Cooper had become himself.

The Beekeeper's Question

Proper burial, that he could do. He laid the body out. He laid the war down. He set the bayonet at Broin's feet. He would never kill again. He maneuvered Jesse's pickup so it faced away from the butte, put Thompson's knife in the glovebox. He shut Preacher Boy in the cab, engine idling.

Flashlight barely glowing on the uneven cave floor. He dragged the box of dynamite to Broin's head, keeping several sticks out. Took the box of matches from a Mason jar, backed up, pacing himself and careful. He needed to aim toward the box, a straight-line throw, and give himself time to run. If one stick went, the shock waves in the cave would set off the box. That was his plan, a theory gleaned from late-night grumbling among enlisted farm men experienced at blowing stumps and boulders out of Iowa fields. "Why don't the Army let us dynamite the Jerries out of their machine-gun holes instead of risking our sorry asses?" Everyone had agreed it was a reasonable question.

Franklin held the dynamite stick pressed between stump and ribcage. He lit the fuse. The chemical sparkler blinded him a precious second. Now! He threw the lit stick at the box, turned, and ran into the night. Twenty seconds. He hoped he was far enough away. He hoped it would explode. He scrambled into the truck and drove a couple hundred yards. Stopped. Waiting. Counting. Night air cool in his lungs.

BOOM. A stick went up. Dust steamed into the night.

KABOOM. The box went up. Froggy's collapsed. Broin Mulvaney was blasted and buried. Franklin put the truck in second gear and steered one-handed, heading home.

The lamp on the kitchen table shone through the window. He parked next to the honey truck and stepped into the shadow of the small barn. Preacher Boy sprinted for the mudroom door and barked. Maire came out carrying an old-fashioned oil lamp. "Jesse'll be fine," she called softly. "He's with Doc. It's cold. Come in."

"I... I want out of these stinking clothes. And I need some help." There he'd said it. His new life starting... and hers. "Try not to look. I don't want this to be a lasting impression."

Maire hung the lantern on a nail. She unbuttoned the bloody jacket. She pulled the sweater over his head and unbuttoned the worn shirts. The closer he got to naked, the stronger he smelled. "I'm sorry, so sorry," he whispered.

"You, alive, all that matters."

He dared to touch that one independent curl. "Is everybody asleep?" she nodded. "Just you and me?" He let her loosen the rope of his belt and his pants fell to the dark ground. She handed him a towel. They made their tiny pilgrimage from the door in the shadows to the door in the light.

Past the kitchen, she opened a door into an added-on room. "Welcome to Jesse's gift." The bathroom was lit by two tapered candlesticks set on the sink's edge. Hot water was steaming in a claw foot tub. He lowered himself. Blissful immersion. He closed his eyes.

"Rest, *mo chuisle*," she whispered to him. "Let me, let me... please." She started at the top, washing his hair, her fingers strong on his scalp, massaging the tightened skin, loosening the mats. She tilted his head back and with an old teacup ran water over and over his head until his hair squeaked clean. She washed his beard, his ears, his neck. "You look like a shaggy professor," she said. She bent him forward and scrubbed his back with a long-handled brush. His blood rushed to the surface, begging purification. He remembered his mother's calloused hands when he was a small boy hunched in the tin tub that had served for baths on Saturdays and laundry on Mondays. Candlelight played on his eyelids. He floated between his mother's scrubbing and his wife's caress. Loved as a boy; loved as a man. She took his strong right arm and soaped the crusted dirt, set his hand on the tub rim and cut his nails. "You'll be holding our baby, soon," she whispered.

"Can you stand?" He obliged. She lathered and rinsed his buttocks, his legs, and then he felt the curve of her hand cradling his balls. He didn't know if what she beckoned in him had survived the war. He held his breath and prayed to be a man.

In the act of ritual bathing, Maire enters the Unity. The fey and the real swirl in the *Hmmm* as she disrobes him. The *Hmmm* imbues her hands with honeyed magic as she washes him. She takes his privates into her hands. His balls with their hidden sac of child-seeds. His member, remembering, stretches under her fingers. He opens his eyes, pupils black in the candlelight. Their gazes lock onto the other's eyes. He moans. She rises, dries him, leads him. She is a priestess at the tomb of Clontygora, Queen of the Bees. His boyhood room is now his marriage chamber. She lowers him onto clean sheets and fluffed pillows. She unbuttons her dress. She mounts him. Her breasts drop like softened fruits into his hand. His eyes are wild with longing. Hers the same. She whispers. "Let me... let me, please." She is dripping honey. She eases him into the crevice between her thighs and slowly begins to slide the branch of him up and down. She rocks her pelvis, elbows by his shoulders, her hands holding his head. She does not blink but watches him arching below her. She travels a sublime territory of desire. She is the ancestor of herself, running across the golden fields of the faerie realm toward the well of souls. His fingers are rolling one nipple into a pinpoint of fire that courses through her body to her hidden bud. She bursts into flame. He does not blink but is running toward her now across a great expanse of barren ground. He is dodging minefields and mortar shells. Faster than bullets, he outruns his war. His breath is hoarse. He grasps her whole body and wraps his strong arm and the broken-off limb around her back. He is howling. He is coming. He is coming back. He is coming to her. They are heaving. One rise. One undulation. There is the honey in her womb. There is the milk in his loin. Riding, riding, riding.

They are bursting. Green flames envelope them. They explode together.

    Tears of release.
    Laughter of amazement.
    Drifting back from urgency.
    They rest, he is still inside her.
    She will wake first, resting in the tuck of his half-arm.
    She will feel the ghost of his hand lying on her belly.
    When he wakes, there will be his baby and an old man.
    There will be making breakfast and tending chores.
    It will be Montana and taking one step at a time.
    It will be valleys and mountains of decisions.
    There will be that secret death.
    Now, they sleep.
    Sweet dreams.
    Hmmm.

37
Morning in the Valley of the Shadow

OCTOBER 27, 1943, MORNING: *U.S. 1ˢᵗ Infantry Division departs for England to begin training for a cross-channel attack into Northern France.*

JESSE REMEMBERED LYING ON THE TABLE while Doc stopped the bleeding and did the stitching. The light of the gooseneck lamp hurt his eyes. "Is my leg still there?" he'd asked.

Maire leaned over him. "Doc's got you, Jess. Leg's just numbed." She looked fright-faced with a deep line pulled together at her brow that ran right up into her curls. She had blood on her sweater. She kept saying thank you. Oh yah, the fight. Someone dead. A man who hurt her. The man in a bar. When he'd said, "I'm Jesse Cooper," the man had pulled a knife. He'd driven the guy into the trap they'd laid. Was it always going to be murder? His own or Frank's or that man's? His brother had a bigger knife. The Irishman got killed. Oh yah, the cave. He and Franklin *had* a plan. It didn't work. He could see it all now. He was on the ceiling looking down at Doc stitching his leg. What a bloody gash. And his face looked like steak, red and dark blue. Doc's voice sounded urgent, though far away, "He lost a lot of blood. He's drifting on us." She shouted at him, "Stay here, Jesse. You got family. We need you."

Willow was holding his hand and praying in Indian. He tried to say, "I love you." Thump. He fell back inside his skin.

Willow stitched his spirit to his bones. She touched his face, his chest, he felt safe. But wasn't he supposed to keep her safe? Wasn't that the promise he made Gramma Josie?

Jesse opened his eyes in a strange room. Willow lay stretched alongside him. "Where are we?" His lips were cracked. He breathed through his mouth; his rebroken nose was stuffed with cotton.

"In the backroom at Auntie Doc's." It hurt to turn his neck. Those burly arms, bristly red hairs like a cinnamon bear, the chokehold.

He had found the Irishman in a diner down by the river, eating greasy potatoes and a piece of meat that looked like it'd been dead awhile. Maybe horse. Out here they just took a deer. It wasn't murder, killing for meat. What happened at Froggy's, that was murder, even in self-defense. He began to spool the story. "Franklin said to keep the Irishman away from Maire. I went to town. Had anybody seen him? Someone said he had a big mouth and a bad temper. Someone said to watch my back." Willow sat up, listening. "I had the honey money. Thought I could bribe him. We go out by the truck; I make him the offer. He sticks his knife against my throat, says 'Take me to Maire MacDonnell or I'll kill yah.' I drove… only to the cave, not the house. Things went bad." Jesse winced, his leg a heavy weight.

Willow fingered his hair. "I could smell storm coming. Maire was jumpy. The children were fussy. I wanted to go to the little house. Calm Natoyii. Maire going to talk her man in before snow. We fed Grandfather and the children. Then everything began happening. We did Medicine." Willow shivered as she talked. "Maire said 'He has come.' I told her, 'There is blood on the ground. That is all I see.' I prayed life for you and your brother. Prayed evil to be removed. I saw Gramma carrying the eagle's wings." Her gaze explored Jesse's battered face.

Jesse shivered about the wings. Before he married Willow, he had stood for the ceremony of cleansing. He kissed Willow's hand. "When I was twelve years old, a mad dog showed up around town. Pa and I took our hunting rifles. Pa said, 'We fire together, share responsibility.' We dropped the dog. Pa said, 'Once he was a puppy. Once he was a good boy. It's not his fault he got the rabies.'" Jesse gulped air for breath and story. "Mulvaney got the rabies. Frank and I fought him together. The knife was Frank's though. Franklin took that burden to save us all."

Willow inhaled his smell. "You are a good man, Jesse Cooper. We will walk far together." He drifted back asleep while she softly sang a song for healing.

Leo had dressed in pajamas and laid himself to bed in a posture he called "flat out praying": sheet folded over the quilt edge and hands clasped over his breastbone. He recited the Twenty-third Psalm, the Lord's Prayer, the Prayer of St. Francis, Numbers 6:24. After that, he prayed his own heart's worth of words, entreating God that his sons and these exotic women they had chosen and the beautiful children they had made, would come safely through whatever was going on. He rubbed his thumbs, one over the other, comforting himself.

He heard the kitchen door slam. The honey truck started up. Had to be Maire. His heart called after her, "*The Lord is thy keeper: The Lord is thy shade upon thy right hand. The Lord shall preserve thee from all evil.*" He prayed it was so.

He feigned sleep. Willow placed the children around him. The heat and breath of their sleeping bodies entered his dreams. He was not the young shepherd of the Judean hills, but the weathered old reverend who knew the crags and crevices of life's terrain. "*Yea though I walk through the Valley of the Shadow of Death, I will fear no evil, for Thou art with me; Thy rod and Thy staff they comfort me...*" Drum's small hand wriggled into his palm. Flora curled against his belly. "*Thou preparest a table before me in the presence of mine enemies; Thou anointest my head with oil; my cup runneth over.*" They slumbered. And goodness and mercy held them until morning.

Flora's whimper pulled him from a dream of bees. Maire came down the hall. "G'morning Leo," she whispered, "Franklin's here. Jesse and Willow are up at Doc's. Everything is okay. I need to introduce this baby to her papa."

Franklin lay sprawled in his own bed, tucked in clean sheets. He'd been dreaming of those last moments in the cave when the eagle wings had swept through him, and the Old Woman summoned him back to himself. Then, to come home, to make love after all that had happened. He stretched one leg into the spaciousness she had made for him. Maire, his good choice. Her honey scent lingered on the pillow.

A baby cried. He'd forgotten how sound moves inside a house, as though the walls, the floors, and the people all wake up together. Footsteps down the hall, a murmuring exchange, the crying stopped. A bell-like voice inquired, "Is him sleeping?"

Maire's head peeked round the door. They smiled shyly in the morning light. Riding on her hip a small replica of Irishness who sucked her fingers. Tears sparkled along her lashes. Mother and daughter stepped over the threshold and Maire plopped the little girl on the bed. "Flory, this your Papa." He stared at this living being, his daughter. "Papa, meet Flora Charlotte Cooper."

Waves of emotion rolled through him. He steadied the child on the lumpy terrain of his blanketed body. "She looks so like you." The feel of her skin a softness that buzzed in his fingertips.

"It's the hair. But look at her eyes and you'll see yourself."

The baby crawled up his torso and stuck slobbery fingers in his beard. "Am I passing inspection?" The reality kept hitting him. This was his seed come to fruit, his wife, his daughter. He'd come back. A second child slipped into the room. He had skin the color of goldenrod honey, eyes two acorns of curiosity. Jesse's demeanor cut through with a shy and charming smile.

"Are you still a bear?" the boy was slight of build, agile, watchful. He coiled his little body around the footboard.

"Why do you call me a bear?"

"Because you's fuzzy. And you's paw got in a trap. You bited it off to get free. You a brave bear." The boy nodded, sure of his story.

"Ah, I see. But I am your uncle."

"Uncle Bear?"

"Uncle Franklin."

This caused a pause. "Do you like honey?" The little boy tilted his head, "I can make you toast."

Minutes later, Franklin sat at the familiar table in his familiar place looking out the window at the familiar sight of the yard and honey house and down the familiar block-long road. "Looks like snow," he said.

"You got out just in time." Maire had popped Flora in her highchair, handed her a Zwieback that the baby began gumming. She mixed mush from a box marked Pablum, handed Drum two pieces of toast. "Show Uncle Franklin how nicely you butter the bread." A crock appeared out of somewhere, "Then let him put on the honey." She set down the bowl of mush and a tiny spoon. "I need to get dressed. If Flora fusses, feed her cereal." She wiped her hands on a dishtowel and was gone.

Franklin sat stunned in the blur of domesticity. His stump was shaking inside the sleeve of his robe. Flora gave him a disgusting crumby grin. Drum had buttered two pieces of toast, taken the spoon out of the honeypot and dribbled a trail of honey over to his side of the table, including a little bit on the bread. "Here's you breffast," he said, sliding a plate back through the mess. Preacher Boy was thumping his tail hard against the linoleum. A measured step was coming down the hall.

Leo appraised himself in the bathroom mirror. Hair thinner and grayer, a two-day stubble, clothes that hung off shoulders, bony from lost muscle mass. Himself as he was. He straightened up, buttoned up, and stepped around the corner to greet his soldier boy.

In the kitchen, Maire spooned mush into Flora's mouth, grabbed a dishrag to wipe Drum's sticky fingers, and poured two cups of coffee rations. "I's making dah bread into a bear," Drum held out nibbled toast for inspection.

"Don't play with your food, Drummie. Let's go see *náa* and *ninna* at Doc's house." On her way out the room, Maire stroked Franklin's bearded cheek and kissed the top of Leo's head. "Eggs in the icebox. Corn Flakes in the cupboard. Take care of each other."

Father and son nodded in unison as the room emptied. "I'm so sorry, my boy." Leo gestured toward the empty sleeve.

Franklin shrugged. "Seems we're both somewhat worse for wear."

Maire took the children out the parlor door. They watched Drum stomping ice-rimmed puddles as they came round the house and back into view. It began to sleet. "Is she always so efficient?"

Leo smiled. "She's a fine gal, your Maire. Shook up things in a good way. Hope you find me improved." He studied his son, this soldier with weathered eyes. "You and I were not so good for each other when you left. If I'd been a better father, a lot of things might be different."

"If I hadn't left... well, there'd be no Maire, no Flora." A line of tears rimmed Franklin's eyes. "Last week, when the German POWs arrived, I determined to kill myself. Then Maire told me a story that determined me to live. Every day I got to find enough good in life to carry on." Franklin swiped tears on the woolen shoulder of his robe.

"There's a heap of good right there," Leo gestured at the receding figures. "Thanks for burning that bee yard."

"Jesse said the other yards are okay."

"It was a shock. Maire out there, middle of the night, risk of grassfire, wondering who would do such a thing. But then I found the foulbrood and your jacket button, then Maire found you, and it all began to make sense."

"Didn't mean to give you a heart attack."

"My ticker was signaling SOS. Should'a paid better attention. I made a tonic from Farmer's Almanac and just kept going. Good that we made it, you and me." Leo swirled honey into his coffee.

"You warned me, Pa. About war..." Leo felt Franklin's gaze search deep inside him. "Ralph should have stayed home. What was he thinking?"

"Do his part, I reckon." Leo blew on his steaming cup. "Tragic, though."

"Yah, and if Ronnie is still alive... Japs don't follow the Geneva Convention." Tears were starting to leak unbidden down Franklin's face. "You think I'm a mess, Ronnie gonna be a mess."

Leo patted his son's empty sleeve. "I don't think you're a mess, son, I think war broke your heart."

"The first part was good—Maire, Northern Ireland, Belfast library, my mind full of ideas. I hitched a transport to London, England. I'm standing where white people come from, trying to understand what we bring to the history of the world. So much culture in rubble, and our flyboys doing worse to German cities." Franklin tumbled on, "Then Maire here, having our baby, writing about bees and scenery and people I've known all my life. I couldn't write what war is really like. After a while, I couldn't even read her letters. Homefront and battlefront, too big a gap."

In the back of his mind, Leo began praying Psalms 19:14 in a continuous loop: *May the words of my mouth and the meditations of my heart be acceptable...* "You can tell me," he whispered.

Franklin huffed deep breaths. "Army lived outside all winter, marching east toward Tunisia. Corporal Thompson and me followed the field officer with my field telephone and radio pack. Mid-February, Kasserine Pass was a bloody disaster, whatever the press said. We got tested, flunked. But by spring, Brits and Yanks, we're finally pushing the Jerries into retreat. Two weeks of mountain fighting." Franklin shook uncontrollably. "Those Nazis are rabid dogs, gonna take down everything while they die. My radio's blown, and I'm on the line, just another gun. There are dead bodies everywhere, the smell is horrible. We tossed corpses into old earthquake rifts and bulldozed them over. Neither side taking prisoners. Soldier next to me takes artillery round. Blew him in half. The shrapnel shredded my arm, just bone splinters, fingers hanging off a few tendons, half dozen holes in my torso. Command says we're winning, just one more hill, but I'm bleeding to death."

Franklin was drowning in the river of recall; Leo prayed his listening was a life ring. "Fellows pull me out of the shell-hole, yelling for a medic. Thompson comes careening up in his Jeep that's been turned into a stretcher ambulance, big red cross painted on the hood. Anyone could see that. International law. Medics allowed to transport wounded off the field. I'm half in/out of consciousness. Artillery shell—maybe it was an accident, maybe they aimed for him—direct hit on the Jeep." Franklin was out and out sobbing now. "He grew potatoes in Iowa, Pa. Three little kids. Loved his wife. Helped me be a husband. Had my back. Kept me sane. But in the end, we couldn't protect each other. Last thing he saw was me bleeding. Next thing I saw was him blown to bits. A medic put a tourniquet on my arm, a shot of morphine, packed the shrapnel holes. I came 'round in an evac tent, screaming. They knocked me out again, transferred to a hospital ship. Woke up in England in the amputee ward."

Coffee sloshed in tiny turbulence in Leo's cup. "Go on, son."

The Beekeeper's Question

Franklin dropped his voice, "Tommy got killed coming for me, and that still wakes me screaming. Weeks later, on the cripple ship heading back to the U.S., I met this lieutenant, both legs blown off at the knees in Sicily. He said somedays there were so many dead soldiers they used bodies to sandbag the bridges." Franklin gulped for air. "Holed up in Froggy's, I dreamed of corpses blocking the bridge over Pigeon River or folks digging sugar beets in fields full of landmines or artillery blowing the church some Sunday morning, leaving the Catholics and agnostics to bury the faithful." He wiped tears from his beard with his empty sleeve. "I listened to that lieutenant and thought maybe I traded my arm so I wouldn't be a sandbag on the road to Palermo."

Leo felt a wrenching inside himself like a bridge giving way, footers of faith and civility swirling into the torrent. Storm in the mountains. Dams bursting. His line of Psalm was a canoe rocketing him downriver seeking an eddy of wisdom. "My son, my son."

Franklin pushed back from the table, began pacing the small room. "A psych doctor said guys like me got to lock up the war and move on. Figuring that out required a lot of valley miles. All the while, Maire is bringing up food and telling stories, believing in me. But every time I touch my own peace, the war blows back in my face. Homer fightin' Jesse. POWs billeted in my old school. A violent bully stalking Maire."

Leo's head snapped up. "He's here?!"

"He *was* here." The past tense hung suspended between them. "We wanted to tie him up, a little present for the sheriff. But he got Jesse by the throat. He had a knife. I had a bigger knife." Leo braced himself. "I killed him, Pa. Last night. Before I came in. Jess and I pulled his body into Froggy's. I blew the cave with old mining dynamite." Franklin hunched into his shoulders, "Self-defense, but still, hand-to-hand combat and violent death." Sleet hit against the window. "Family secret. Jess and me, Maire, Jess's wife, Doc, and now you in the know." Franklin stopped. Waited.

The Psalm kept ricocheting in Leo's mind: *May the words of my mouth and the meditations of my heart…* He prayed for words to rise from some wellspring of his soul. "Thing about evil, my son, it doesn't dissipate by itself. It demands reckoning. Evil unchecked can devour a man… even a nation. Like a black hole round with teeth, evil can consume men's moral nature until it falls to men of decent moral nature to fight back." Leo shuddered at his description.

Franklin stood backlit by the small window. "It's tricky business though, Pa, not to become evil while fighting it. My buddies and I entered the war with moral natures, but we had to become soldiers who could maim and kill and walk over the dead and keep going. We hoped love of our buddies and hatred of the other guys would keep us from being devoured. At least we felt something." Franklin turned, spoke out the window, unable to face his father. "I lost myself out there, Pa. To kill in battle is horrible enough but, one time before I lost my arm, I was face to face with this German. It was him or me. I shot him, but he kept coming. Shot again. He lunged. I lunged. Bayonets drawn. Like last night, we fought hand-to-hand. There's no barrier, no pretending you're not killing another human being to save yourself. That day, rage completely overtook me. I stabbed him until he finally went down. Then I straddled him and stabbed again and again, cutting him to ribbons. Artillery is deafening. Chunks of machinery and human flesh fly around you. You wonder if you're already dead… how to tell? I'm on top of this corpse. My arm is doing this terrible thing. I'm swearing, 'Goddamn fucking war!' I'm screaming, 'I am not this kind of man!' But I'm pulling his guts out with my bare hands." When Franklin turned again, heavy tears were soaking his beard.

"A few battles down the road, I paid for that rage with my own arm. Since then, I been hiding in Froggy's trying to reconstruct my moral nature." Franklin paced the length of the small kitchen and back. "I finally convinced myself war is such an extreme situation that normal rules cannot apply. I found a way to separate war and homefront. There. Then. Battle mind. Now. Here. Benign mind. And then I had to break those barriers down and kill one more man."

Leo tried to read every nuance in the face of his battle-weary son. "All I know, Franklin, is you and Jesse ended up in a life-or-death fight with Maire's boogeyman because those who should have stopped him did not. People cowered before his violence. They did not make him reckon with his actions. They accommodated and excused and stayed out of his way until his wrecked-up life became a journey to the knife in your hand."

Franklin nodded. "Broin Mulvaney was a sonofabitch. Who knows all he did—and would never stop doing—in the way of hurt. The problem is, Mulvaney's death occurred on a patch of dirt outside my hometown where normal rules are supposed to apply, instead of on a battlefield where death and destruction are sanctioned. How do I live with that?"

Behind the tired eyes of the soldier, Leo saw the seeking eyes of his boy. *Be acceptable in thy sight. Oh Lord...* He reached for words. "As a man of faith, I am instructed by the commandment 'Thou shall not murder.' As a citizen, I am obliged to respect the law. As a father, I am humbled by the courage of my sons." Leo's voice cracked. "I don't know how you will reckon with that death and the others before it, but I will come to this table and be in this conversation with you as long as I live." He stared over Franklin's shoulder into the gray day. "You are alive. Jesse is alive. A terrible threat is lifted from Maire. The valley is ignorant of impending disaster, yet safe because of you. For now, this is justice."

Father and son rested a few heartbeats in silence. "I fought fair when he did not," Franklin sighed. "I kept control. I saved my brother, and he saved me. I dynamited my demons. I came home, slept with my wife, met my baby. We had this talk. For now, this is grace."

"You have become your own man, Franklin. You have walked through the valley of the shadow." Leo swallowed the last sip of cold coffee. "That's what you sought. What will you do with this hard-earned self-knowledge?"

A tiny light flickered in Franklin's eyes. "That sounds like one of your beekeeper's questions, Pa."

Leo nodded. "Amen, then." The Psalm lifted off his shoulders. *My Strength and my Redeemer...*

Franklin reached for the frying pan that hung on a hook over the stovetop. "I'm starved. How you want your eggs?"

"Over easy."

"Well, wouldn't that be nice." Franklin turned with a hint of smile.

38
WE'LL FIGURE IT OUT

OCTOBER 27, 1943, AFTERNOON & EVENING: *New Zealand troops make an amphibious landing on the Treasury Islands. The Italian campaign pushes up the boot of Italy.*

A SECRET IS A THOUGHT WITH A FENCE, that's what Doc always said. And then she'd quote Robert Frost, "Good fences make good neighbors." Life in the valley required choosing what to remember, what to forget, what to say, and what not. Some secrets were docile and crawled into her root cellar to compost at the edge of thought. And some secrets were headstrong and demanded she bolt the lid of rumination. Doc didn't know what kind of secret Broin's death would become, but she and the young wives were determined to contain it while Jesse healed and Franklin adjusted. It was their turn now, and in the aftermath of the fight, the women devised a plan.

Midday, Doc hunched into her jacket, collar up, and strolled toward the Cooper house with feigned composure. Franklin turned from the sink as she came through the vestibule. She hugged him and took the cup of cold coffee he offered. "This evening, soon as shades are drawn, Maire's going to drive Jesse and his family back north, away from curiosity and questions. Plan is, you ride along, Maire drops you in Great Falls, and you hitch back out like you're just arriving." Doc pulled the kitchen curtains closed. She fussed at his shirt buttons. "Rest up. Stay out of sight. We'll figure it out as we go. Where's Leo?"

"Said he was going to the honey house. We had an intense morning." An unreadable depth owled in the back of his eyes. "War stories. Maybe not the best for his heart."

Doc stroked his bearded cheek. "Having you back is best for his heart."

Leo needed to walk his perimeters, fill his lungs with cold air, make room in himself to bear the heartbreak of Franklin's stories. He slipped into his woolen jacket, dug for gloves left in the pocket last March, pulled on an old fedora, and tied his boots. The weight of winter clothes reassuring; he was still a man who could face into the storm.

He thought to reposition the honey truck parked askew in Maire's midnight hurry, but the sight of Jesse's congealed blood on the floorboard made his heart clench. He kicked Franklin's filthy clothes behind the barn door. Tik-tik-tik, sleet hitting his hat brim. He went round the building to the garden hives and laid his gloved hand on the top of a box. The vibration of deep hive life tingled into his palm. They were in there, keeping warm, eating honey, tending the fire that was their queen.

Listening, Maire told him. That's when she could hear the bees, not just buzzing, but a message. Well, he could use a message. Leo had spent decades admiring his bees. Sunday by Sunday, he had faithfully carried his inquiry into his sermons: *How can humanity become more like bees?* Mixing scripture and beekeeping, he translated the wisdom of the hives into the lives of the people. It had seemed a worthy endeavor until this morning. His beekeeper's question had been shattered by Franklin's anguish and blown off arm, by the pool of Jesse's blood in the Cooper & Sons honey truck, and by knowing what violence had happened at their boyhood hideaway. Leo's heart filled with dreadful realizations: Men were bears, not bees. Men were meat eaters, not honey suckers. Men were fighters, not pacifists. The Old Testament was a bloody chronicle of God's Chosen People dominating a small piece of land. And in the New Testament, when the Good Shepherd finally came to offer love and redemption, they crucified him. Tik-tik-tik, sleet hitting the hive lid. And then, in the name of Prince of Peace, look what horrors unfurled! "Onward Christian soldiers" was a hymn Leo would never sing again.

Leo slid to sitting on a cottonwood stump. Nothing got better. His life work hadn't changed a thing. He had asked the wrong question. Tik-tik-tik, the rain worked on his thoughts. A different question rose in him that shook him to the core. *What if...? What if God had chosen the wrong species?* Leo stuttered his doubt into the cold ear of the day. *What if humanity is not the right choice to grant dominion over the earth?* The sleet spit in his face. Mankind is brilliant but brutal, inventive but destructive, compassionate but murderous. Bees are perfect. Bees provide. Their life work pollinates creation. Leo pressed the heels of his palms against his eye sockets until he saw flashes of light. Tik-tik-tik. Sleet and doubt squirmed down his jacket collar. His breath wheezed through his nose and the beat of his heart drummed in his ears. *If it was possible for God to make such grievous error, what hope was there for Leo Cooper? If the question that had framed his whole life was the wrong question, how then could he help his sons?* The theologian, the beekeeper, the widower, the father, the friend, all the aspects of self that comprised Leo Cooper, sat frozen in place before the silent altar of the hives. He folded over like an old animal who took no shelter. Tik-tik-tik. Sleet and chill weathered him down.

A tiny sound tickled the hairs in his ears. Leo turned his head slowly one way and another, tuning his perception. *Hmmm.* Barely discernible. *Hmmm.* Maybe this is what Maire heard. *Hmmm.* Maybe this is the sound she had danced with when he envisioned her in the temple of combs. The *Hmmm* shaped into words. "*Leo Cooper, wee come to speak true to your heart. You are one of the Dræn, a wizard, a priest, commonly called drone. Dræn are the fathers of bees. Dræn carry the seeds that keep Unity strong. Dræn sing the Song of Beeing.*" Leo shook his head, scattering raindrops off the hat brim. "*Before the pips are born, the maidens sing them the song of function; Dræn sing them the history of beekind. Dræn teach them the spiritual purpose of beeing. Because of the Dræn, bees are born with knowing.*" A tiny hexagonal light began to shine behind Leo's closed eyes. "*Because of you and others in the Order of the Dræn, humans are shown the path to remembering. As the beekeeper, you tend the Unity. As the preacher, you sing purpose to the people.*"

"But they're not listening." Ineffable sadness washed over him. "I have failed to bring order to the valley. I have failed to bring justice to the land. The world is a horrifying mess."

"*Hmmm,*" said the *Hmmm*. "*To know why you are born is honey in the heart. Your words awaken longing to know true nature. Though for many nonbees, this journey completes only in the Great Flowering you call death. You have watched remembering flow into the heart, even in the final moments. Trust the people to listen, Brother Dræn. Bee assured. The Unity you call God has made no mistake in choosing you.*" Swooning in the trance of the hive, Leo bowed before the Queen and stood in the Council of Dræn.

When Doc came around the corner of the barn and saw her crumpled-over friend, fear knotted in her throat. "Leo?" she called tentatively. He stirred. "Oh, thank God." The eyes he turned to her were dilated and huge. A crease ran down his forehead from under his hat to his brows, a seam of light. "Are you okay?"

A small humming sound seemed to vibrate off him. "I was dreaming."

"Out here? In the cold and rain?"

His head was cocked in an odd way. "It was terrible to witness Franklin's suffering. I needed air. And help. Something."

"You were in shock."

"There's blood in the truck." His speech sounded dazed and deep.

"Jesse will heal. Franklin has no infection. Your sons have strong bodies and souls." Doc stepped beside him and reached out her hand. "You're hypothermic."

His eyes filled with tears. "Jere… I saw the Great Flowering."

"And hallucinating."

"Death is all light-filled and honeycombed. But she said it wasn't yet time."

"Who said what?"

"The Queen of the Bees. She gave me time. She said my life is not in vain."

Doc shifted modes. "Of course, your life is not in vain, Leo. Come inside. I'll make tea. We'll sit by the stove, figure things out like we always do."

Leo looked at her. "I was somewhere else."

"Yes, but we need you to come back, be here."

"That's what she said: Bee here." Leo wrapped his square palm around hers and to her surprise lifted her hand to his lips and kissed her knuckles. She hefted him up and they crossed the yard toward the threshold of the farmhouse under the tik-tik-tik of icy rain.

The young couples left after the radio news hour when valley folks were tucked into houses that glowed here and there out of the black patchwork of plowed fields, spent harvest. The rime of the day's sleet edged the roadside. Maire drove to Doc's new house and eased Jesse into the backseat. Then she drove to Doc's homestead and picked up Willow and their sleeping boy. The family tucked in the back seat.

Finally, she drove to the honey yard where Franklin waited in the barn shadows looking as "Army" as he could muster. Maire had washed and ironed his uniform pants, sewn buttons on his blood-stained Army jacket. Franklin held his year-old daughter awkwardly but proudly in his arm and stepped toward the car. Something gleamed off the cuff of his left sleeve, a folded hook, pincers of metal. "I need it to drive. Pa helped me." He waited until Maire realized he couldn't open the car door. She took the baby and let Franklin into the driver's seat, slipped around to the passenger side. The clandestine carload eased into the night.

Franklin met Willow's eyes in the mirror. "Hello my sister-in-law," he said.

"Hello my brother," she dipped her head into the shadows, adjusting the weight of the boy, positioning Jesse's leg.

Maire slid her hand onto Franklin's thigh, Flora stretched across her lap. "You get tired," she said, "I'm right here."

"Counting on that." They rode in silence, listening to the little family's deepening breaths. "I'm driving the same car I learned on. I've got a wife and baby by my side. Twenty-four hours ago, Jess and I were fighting for our lives." Franklin's voice was shaky. "I'm scared I might screw this up."

"I'm scared that I won't know how to help."

"What if the nightmares never go away?"

"I'll wake you and hold you, however long it takes."

"I can't be a beekeeper," he said.

"That's okay, I am." He glanced at her.

"I need education and a desk job."

"I saved your pay and our share of the crop money." Maire stroked his thigh.

"I want to hold your hand, but I can't take the one I got off the wheel."

"I know, darling. It's not so bad."

They focused then on the night, on their headlamps marking the edge between what they could see and what they couldn't. "I trust us," Maire whispered, "We'll figure it out." Her soft voice curled like smoke along the glass of the windshield and drifted into Franklin's ear.

It was midnight when they followed Willow's directions up a half-frozen driveway. One lantern flickered from the steps of a small house. An old woman stood wrapped in a wool blanket. "She always knows," Jesse roused himself. He leaned heavily on a cane. Gramma glanced at his bandaged leg and grunted.

The old woman's eyes in the weak lamplight were almost the same dark as the night, but Maire felt the strength of her scrutiny. The *Hmmm* tingled in her mind. "May I meet Natoyii's cousin?" Maire pulled back the shawl that covered Flora in her arms. "I see why he says her hair is on fire. You are welcome, granddaughter." She turned her inscrutable gaze on Franklin. "Hello again, Bear Heart." Maire watched her husband nod deeply, a bow of deference. They followed her inside.

"I made you frybread and honey," Ruth Otter Woman, gestured them to sit. "This is BB's and my house. You will sleep here tonight."

A short while later, Maire changed Flora's diaper and placed the toddler between them in bed. "She called you Bear Heart?" she whispered.

"I can't speak it yet," Franklin whispered back.

"I can wait." The baby fussed. Maire put her to breast though she was mostly weaned. The threesome spooned together. It was the second night after the cave.

39
Soldier from the War Returning

OCTOBER 28, 1943: *Heavy rains mire Allied advances in Italy. The grueling campaign costs 31,880 Allied lives, with 188,550 missing and wounded. U.S. Marines land on Bougainville, Solomon Islands where the battle will last the duration of the war.*

"I LOVE YOU," SHE HAD SAID. Hand on his chest. Finger to his lips. Flora was napping in the backseat, wrapped in the shawl. They'd be home in an hour. They'd be waiting.

Before leaving the reservation, with Jesse limping and leaning heavily on Franklin's shoulder, Gramma Josie had beckoned them outside where they stood shivering at the flap to her lodge. "I speak where only the wind can hear," she said. "You carry a secret. You carry a killing. What you make of your lives is linked to how you carry this death." Wind swirled around the lodge skirt. She looked at Franklin, "Creator's medicine has cleansed the war in you." She looked at Maire, "Creator's medicine has cut the cord between you and the evil that chased you." She turned to Jesse and Willow, "This story happened on white land. Here, you speak it only to the fire." She ducked under the flap of her lodge and emerged with her medicine bag. One by one she cleansed and painted them in a holy way. "Pay attention. Help each other. When you need to speak of this, hold your council under the Sky. Ask your ancestors for help and do what they say."

The Beekeeper's Question

Mid-morning, Maire left him by the tracks, down by the river. Not the greatest part of town, but handy for his deception. "I love you, too," he said. He shouldered his duffel and walked up Lower River Road until he found a barber shop accustomed to serving rough men.

The owner wanted to talk, but Franklin gave him as little as he could. "Going home, clean me up for my family." The old barber wouldn't take two bits, so Franklin put it on the counter. "Give the next guy a free shave and cut. Helps a man feel like himself again." His head felt exposed to the raw wind, his cheeks naked to the day. He wasn't sure he felt like himself, but maybe. He smelled of Brylcreem and aftershave.

He cut over to Upper River Road looking for a diner. Now he was hungry. Now he was tired. He wanted to be unremarkable, unrememberable, though with one arm, a hook, and his battle-ragged uniform, he supposed that might not be possible. Had to get off his feet, think things through, get ready for re-entering and not leaving.

A neon sign was blinking at him: Missouri River Diner. He slid into the last booth, set his duffel beside himself, telltale green canvas. "Coffee, if you got it. Eggs and bacon." He glanced at the girl in her waitress uniform, checkered dress, stained apron that hadn't been white in a while. Her hair needed washing, roots growing out, little lacy thing tangled into it with bobby pins. Civilian life, cheap end of town, middle of a war.

"Got a ration book?" she asked. "You got to tear out stamps."

Franklin hadn't thought of that. "No book. I'm just out, heading home."

"Well, in that case, soldier, (she looked around—the diner was nearly empty, and the cook was on the phone) I'll give you anything you want. Where you been?" she asked.

"North Africa." She looked him over for the oddity he was.

"My boyfriend's in the Pacific. Never could figure out quite where. He just said hot, buggy, sand, and jungle, bullets, and big guns. Sounds like hell to me. You from here?"

christina baldwin

"Out of town a ways."

"My guy is from Pigeon River." Franklin's heart skipped a nervous beat. "He's MIA. His pa comes in here and we tell each other he's gonna be all right. Suspect we're lying." Tears were springing into her eyes. "Good to see you, though, someone who has lived through it. Someone headed home." She noticed his wooden and metal wrist with the hook sticking out his sleeve. "Oh Jeez, your arm. Let me get you breakfast before I make a mess of myself." She brought him coffee. She brought out a plate of eggs, four pieces of bacon, some toast. More than he'd planned to eat. Made him sleepier. "You look tired," she said. "We don't get a crowd until noon whistle at the warehouse. You can rest awhile before you hit the road."

"Thank you, but don't let me scare off other customers." Franklin barely finished his sentence before he slid half down onto his duffel and fell asleep with his hand cradling the precious cup of chilling coffee.

He jerked awake with the hard contours of the prosthesis hurting his ribs and opened his eyes to see Homer Torgerson sitting across the table reading *The Tribune*. "Well, I'll be. That really you, Frank Cooper?" Homer scratched at stubble on his chin. "Stella said there was a soldier boy in here might need a ride. Looked you over, my heart near stopped, but I couldn't be sure till you sat up. It is you though, in't it?"

"Yessir," Franklin reminded himself to sound military. "It's me. Well, most of me." He hefted his hook onto the table. "Medical discharge," he watched Homer's eyes. "On my way home after rehab."

"Yah, Stella said. Too bad. Albert still on a ship. Ronnie missing..."

"Yah, Stella said. Sure sorry, Homer; hard on you, Milly, and Susan."

"I came into town to pick up this Irish guy. Said he wanted work. Said he knew your missus from back there." Homer was slapping the newspaper on his thigh. Franklin couldn't read his tone. "He sure was interested in finding you Coopers. Now I can't find him."

"Yah, well drifters drift. That's their nature." Franklin stared his old neighbor down.

Homer scratched his head. "I dunno. There was something mighty determined about him. And something scary. I'd had a few beers. Didn't want him in the truck with me at night."

"Maybe he already hitched out, beat you home." Franklin hoped he sounded a little bit helpful and a lot uninterested.

Homer puzzled onward. "He was big. Arms thick as a lady's leg, hands like bear paws. Gonna look him over in daylight, maybe keep him through the winter, do the hardest stuff."

This was a train of thought Franklin desperately wanted to derail. He reached inside his jacket and under his shirt, unfastened the buckles that held the leather and metal arm to his shoulder and slid the whole contraption off onto the table. Homer's eyes near bugged out. "Jesus, Cooper that's quite a stunt. That hook thing work?" Just what Franklin wanted, distraction.

"Thing's heavy, straps rub the skin in your armpit, and I'm still mastering the little pinchers. It ain't exactly pretty." He gave Homer a hangdog look. "Thinking to arrive with just an empty sleeve, so I don't scare Maire."

Homer gulped three times. "Yup, good idea." His eyes were rimmed in white.

Franklin laid the arm out on the table. "Your boys could have one of these. Or a leg. Lots of guys are missing legs." Franklin had to admit he was enjoying Homer's discomfort. "Those islands are booby-trapped with landmines. Or if his ship goes down Al might get shark bit, hanging out there in the ocean waiting for rescue. Don't mean to worry you, but you got to be prepared. No one comes home the same as they left."

Homer folded the newspaper, trying to recover himself. "Well, I just hope they both come home, yah know."

"Me too, Homer. Your boys, my friends." He truly meant it. "Maire wrote that Ralph's not coming back. That's a rough one." In the wave of emotion, Franklin felt himself tightening like a violin string. His legs were jumpy. This was the moment he would have run out of Froggy's with Preacher Boy at his heels, loping across landscape until exhausted. All he had now to calm himself was a deep breath, and another. He swirled the dredges of the coffee. Homer looked ready to run himself. Franklin opened the duffel and stuffed the arm inside, breaking them free from ruminations. "Can you help me close this up?" Pondering the whereabouts of an Irish drifter long forgotten.

"Give you a ride?" Homer grabbed the duffel, "I paid your breakfast." He hefted the dirty canvas bag in the back of the pick-up where it bounced around with farm tools, feed sacks, and whatever Milly had wanted from town. Homer nestled the duffel in amongst a dozen pumpkins. "For the grade school kids. Halloween in a few days."

Franklin nodded, "That's good of you. Guess I have my costume figured out for the next few years—Captain Hook." Okay, he scolded himself, knock it off.

"You coming home," the rancher scratched his head, "is it a total surprise? Your pa been sick. You know? Heart trouble."

"Maire wrote."

"Well, I was thinking you don't want the shock to kill him."

"They know I'm discharged and heading this way."

"Good, 'cuz I don't want to be party to no homicide, what you call a complice?" He spread his hands in the space between them. "Headline in the *Tribune*, 'Soldier's Surprise Kills Father.'" Homer's laugh had an edge to it that made Franklin's skin crawl. "Hop in. I'll fill you in on the valley."

Franklin opened the passenger truck door, slid onto the seat. The movement was not hard to manage, long as he had nothing in his one hand, like a baby. The inside of the cab smelled of straw, cow manure, and Homer himself. Franklin hugged the door, leaving a gap between them big enough to hold the secret that would always linger there, along with whatever other secrets were about to accumulate.

The day remained nondescript gray as they followed the river road to Vaughn Junction. "Well, you wanna talk about the war?" Homer asked as they cleared the city and veered into the muted landscape.

"Nope, definitely not," Franklin tried to keep the tension out of his voice.

"Okay then," the old rancher harrumphed. "How'd you lose your arm?"

"Uh…in the war which I don't want to talk about." He paused and decided to take it down a beat. "Why do people do that, Homer? Hi there, why don't you tell me about the worst day of your life, especially the part that's gonna haunt you for years to come. Buy you a beer in exchange for your nightmares." He watched his words register. Point taken.

"Folks do that same with me," Homer said. "Think if they buy me a beer I can tell 'em how bad it is to have a son missing in the fight." He smiled ruefully, "If they buy me two, I do. Buy me three and I end up cryin'. Guess folks like to see somebody miserable, long as it's not them."

"Exactly." Franklin turned to watch him driving. "Your boys come home, don't ask 'em first thing what they've been through, okay? They'll talk. Just give 'em time to figure out how to be back here and say it."

Homer nodded. "If you don't want to talk about your war, I'll tell you about the bit of war we got going on here." (That awkward grunting laugh again.) "First off, your brother Jesse turned Injun. He showed up here last winter with a squaw and a half-breed kid."

Franklin bit his lip and looked out the window to hide his flash of anger. "Not yet," he mouthed to his reflection.

Homer droned on. "Come spring he brings down a bunch of reservation boys, gonna put them in the sugar beet fields alongside our own. Everybody out of school planting, then they 'sposed to come back for thinning. Don't like mixing races. Not natural, and he obviously don't care since he married one. I suggested they go home…," Homer smiled to himself in a disconcerting way, "but Doc got her ire up, so we had a community meeting in the church. Sheriff came. Folks stood against me. Don't see much of your pa since then. Well, he got to stay loyal to his own kin, I understand that. I mind my own business. Hard to run things around here with most the boys gone, but I ain't gonna hire Injuns." Through the reflection in the window glass, Franklin saw Homer glance at him. "You know this stuff?"

"Bits and pieces. Maire's letters."

"Just want you to know, despite our differences, Jesse helped me save a dozen head of cattle from bloat. And I rescued your gal when some unknown suspect set a bee yard on fire. She was out there all alone, middle of the night, 'cause the Rev had a heart attack." Franklin nodded. "All happened around the same time, so kinda confusing, but that next Sunday I heard he was laid up in town. Probably why she was out there trying to manage a fire line. Virgil and me saw smoke and drove over to help. We still got to hang together most ways we can."

"Thank you, Homer. I appreciate that." He unclenched his jaw. They turned west at Vaughn onto highway 89. When the road split north toward Browning, images of Josie Shines the Light and her family, of Jesse, Willow, and Drum floated in his mind. How they had stood in the cold morning singing a protection song as he and Maire drove away. The Old Woman had helped him. She didn't have to. He was a white man. A stranger. He had searched her eyes in the morning light. "Medicine goes where it's needed," she told him. "*Pita*, the eagles heard your call. I answered."

The Beekeeper's Question

"I don't know how to thank you…"

"Thank Spirit in how you live your life." Her words flowed into his hollowed-out places. Bear Heart: The name had opened his mind.

Homer turned south, heading to Pigeon River. The modern landscape splayed out before them in a grid of homestead lines, irrigation ditches, railroad tracks. Boxy grain elevators and church spires poked the sky and clustered farm buildings invoked a litany of names Franklin had known all his life. But something much older lay just below the plowed surface: a wilder land, a freer people, and the symbiosis of bison and grass that sustained a culture ten thousand years long.

His parents had arrived only thirty-three years ago. Homer's grandfather had come fifty years ago when the state was raw. Homer always spoke a hardscrabble story, as though hardship made their land claim more valid. Franklin had kissed Susan in ninth grade; maybe she thought he'd marry her after that. A lot goes unsaid, and what remains unsaid piles up inside a person and between persons. We're going to undo that kind of silence, he thought. Maire and me. All those nights of story. He smiled to himself.

"What you grinnin' at?" Homer took one hand off the wheel, slapped his seed-cap up and down on his head, nervous habit of a rural man trying to make talk in confined space.

"Smilin' cuz I'm headed home. I'm going to see my wife, my baby, my father. Smilin' cuz I'm nervous," he admitted. "I got a lot to figure out."

"Well, that you do, Cooper. You can't be much of a beekeeper with one arm, sorry to say. 'Least your pa got Jesse and the Irish girl." Homer's slapping seed cap made Franklin jumpy. "I got my situation settled, better'n women or Injuns. I got me genuine German POWs, courtesy of the U.S. Army. Pennies an hour, drive 'em back to the Fort at night, government providing room and board. Costs us farmers near to nothing."

Franklin flinched so hard his shoulder hit the side of the door, "Cost you nothing?!?!" The truck swerved in Homer's hands. "You think there's no cost to those POWs!? *I* brought you those gen-u-ine Germans. I chased their sorry asses across a thousand miles of desert until they were near pushed into the sea in Tunisia, probably a place you cannot even find on the map. Trapped and outnumbered, they threw down their guns, raised their hands, and surrendered. Besting them cost thousands of American lives, tens of thousands wounded. I've seen men with three limbs gone, men blinded, burned, tore apart with shrapnel. You call that free labor?"

Homer was looking at him sideways with the whites of his eyes showing as the injured valley boy he thought he know became an angry man he didn't know. Good. Franklin wanted to instill a touch of fear in the rancher. He, Franklin Cooper, was to be dealt with as a man, a man who could match tempers and take care of things, a man not afraid to get angry, and a man in control of his anger. He wanted Torgerson to back up and back down, to never think he could humiliate the Cooper men—not Leo, not Boyd, not Jesse, not him. No longer lying filthy and traumatized in the shrub brush overlooking the fort, he was restrained and disciplined, in possession of himself. Homer clenched his hands white-knuckled to the wheel.

In a voice deliberately steely Franklin went on, "The U.S. and British armies, who follow the rules of warfare, suddenly had more than 250,000 prisoners on our hands. Couldn't drive them into the desert. Couldn't drown them in the Mediterranean. We needed them out of the way and out of the war so we could invade Sicily and Italy without having to fight them all over again. So, while I'm laid up in a British rehab hospital, the Army shipped them stateside to be scattered across the continent, housed in government facilities, and put to common labor. But don't-you-ever-say they come to you at no cost!"

The Beekeeper's Question

The two men drove in silence, their ragged breathing echoing in the truck's cab. They passed JC Adams' stone barn, fortress of another type, and a line of cottonwoods, marking the riverbank. Nearly to town, Homer finally spoke, "Guessing you don't exactly want to see them again."

"Never would be too soon," Franklin muttered. "I'll stick with my brother. Stick with the people he trusts and whatever relations he brings into our family." Franklin took a breath; he understood the trade they were engaged in. He had to give Homer something in return. "Jerries are tough. You want to work them, they'll work. This is better duty than anything going on out there in the real war."

Homer grunted. "Sliced my shin last winter when I was feeding stock. Rather have some POWs to do the heavy lifting, haul out bales, chop the water hole open." He sounded like he was gearing up again.

Franklin had jumped an invisible divide—from one of the boys to one of the men. He would take his place differently. "Let this valley war go, Torgerson. For the sake of your sons, make a peace for them to come home to." He waited to see if Homer would acquiesce.

They had reached the town and Homer swerved into the church parking lot, brought the truck to a halt, turned off the engine. He kept both hands on the wheel and stared straight ahead. "About my boys..." he choked up, cleared his throat. "Do you think... I mean you've been in it... is there really any chance they're coming back?" His face looked as grey as the afternoon light, stubble grizzled with age and strain. Franklin took pity on the man.

"I don't know so much about the Pacific war. It's Navy and Marine action. Long as Al's boat don't eat a torpedo, he should be okay. Stella said Ronnie disappeared at Guadalcanal. No body, no dog tags, no telegram. There's your hope. There's your chance. Battle is chaos, but guys keep track of each other, rip tags off the dead when we must, give 'em to a commanding officer, make sure word gets back to those at home. Everybody wants to be counted, dead or alive." He watched Homer's face. There seemed to be something new in it, like he was listening, not just waiting to get in the next word. Franklin turned to him, reached out and put his sleeved stump on the old rancher's shoulder. Homer shuddered. "They won't come home as boys, Homer. They'll be men who have lived through hell. Ronnie will have survived conditions even I don't want to imagine. They'll have nightmares and terror. They'll be angry in ways that don't make sense. They'll do and say things that make you scared for them. And it will take them awhile to find their way, just like it's gonna take me awhile."

Homer's expression was going through all kinds of contortions. Finally, he spoke in croaking anguish. "If they make it, my boys, or one of them, will you still be their friend?"

Franklin patted Homer's shoulder with his stump. "'Course I will, Homer. 'Course I will." And then Franklin struck the bargain, "You and my pa got differences, and you may not approve who Jesse married, but we been living alongside each other a long time. We still got a town and a valley to live in, that's more than a lot of people got these days. I didn't survive all that fightin' to come home and find my neighbors at war. We're the lucky ones, we're safe." Franklin shivered to think how close that had come to not being true. "I don't want to have to turn around and check if you're sneaking up on my family with some kind of meanness. You understand?" Squirming under the discomfort of the stump pressing his shoulder, Homer nodded. "Good," Franklin said, "There's a lot going bad in the world right now, neighborliness is one thing that must not change."

He took Homer's twitching as a promise and opened the truck door. "Thanks for the ride. I'll walk from here. Want to show up on my own two feet. Let you go deliver those pumpkins." He slid out of the cab, closed the door with a little thump on the side of the old

The Beekeeper's Question

truck, hefted his duffel, and headed into the long block home. He didn't turn around when Homer started up the pickup and spun his tires in the pot-holed church lot. They had a deal. He would trust Torgerson. Neighborliness, the thing that must not change.

Franklin straightened himself to full height and walked down the center of the gravel lane. He hoped Gertie was looking out the store window. He hoped Belle turned around as she unlocked the saloon. He imagined Caleb and Ethel Pocket peeking between curtains, biting their lips to call back tears, seeing that Leo, Maire, and Flora were about to have the reunion that they would never know. Franklin Cooper was alive, the first soldier from the war returning. He walked a path that others would follow. He sensed the responsibility. He paused, took a breath, the exhale clouded around his head. He shook out the tension and reached the end of the block. Stepping onto the Cooper homestead in daylight, he walked between the honey house and the farmhouse and around to the kitchen door.

The chill of late autumn blew at his back pushing him inside. The smell of hot biscuits wafting to greet him. He set down the duffel. The bark of the dog, scent of soap and wet fur, announcing his arrival. The sight of his daughter hitting her spoon on the highchair tray calling out, "mamamama." The delight in his wife's face turning from the stove, saying, "Welcome back, *mo chroi*." He had only to step over the threshold.

"Love you," she had said. Yes, that was why he had come in, and would come in again, be tested and flee, and then return again and again to this threshold. His war was done. Broin was dead. Froggy's was gone. There was a bear in his heart and no place else to go except into the "Yes" that would become his life.

Yes.
No matter what.
Yes.

Epilogue
Telling the Bees

OCTOBER 1946: *The Nuremburg War Trials conclude and convicted Nazi leaders are executed by hanging. The St. Louis Cardinals win the World Series. The United Nations convenes in Flushing Meadows, NY.*

MAIRE DROVE THE FLATBED WITH EASE, despite her large belly. The baby rolled and kicked inside the tiny skep of her womb. The thermometer on the side of the house had read 72 degrees, and Maire headed out to enjoy the sight of bees flickering in the last days of autumn warmth. She turned the truck onto the bench, into a view that still took her breath away. Leo's bee bonnet, stained and sweat-ringed, lay beside her on the seat.

Monday, a week ago, she had summoned Franklin back from university classes in Missoula to keep watch as his father's heart inexorably weakened. "Go rest," Leo had whispered. "My ticker and I are in God's care." She had kissed his waxy brow, smiled into his tired eyes. A few hours later, the dog's howl awakened them. They had jumped up and turned on the lamp. The old man was gone, his mouth a hole of not breathing, hands curved atop the blanket. Around his closed eyes, peace resided. After days of hand-holding and tender declarations, Leo Cooper had slipped away with only the dog to witness. Preacher Boy stood on his hind legs, front paws on his master's pillow. He raised his head, howled again.

"Yes, Boy, I see." Maire knelt alongside the dog. Franklin's hand caressed her hair. The baby kicked. The *Hmmm* rang in her ears. Honoring tears rolled down her cheeks.

Jesse came bounding down the attic stairs. "He sneaked off on us," Franklin said.

Jesse stood sentry at his father's feet. He'd been sleeping in the attic the preceding week, ever since they'd sent word it was time to pray. He arrived the next morning, followed shortly by Willow, Drum, and all their relations. "Dying is a family affair. He's my father, Willow's father-in-law, Gramma's counterpart. We come. Everybody helps."

Uncle Stanley and the Sons of War were camped up at Doc's cabin. BB and Darrell took over the barn and constructed a coffin—wooden planks, trimmed and oiled. Doc sat by the bed and Josie sat by Doc. Leo had three more sleeps left to his life.

Aunt Aggie took on the kitchen, making meals, washing dishes. Ethel Pocket tied on an apron and ventured across the street. "Might as well be useful." Church women brought casseroles and fresh bread. Joy and sorrow seasoned the soup.

When the saloon opened, Homer rested his elbows on the bar and lamented to Belle, "Jesus said 'Give me your tired, your poor, your huddled masses,' so if the Rev wants to die with a bunch of Indians hovering around, I guess that's his right."

Belle set out a bowl of peanuts. "You're quoting the Statue of Liberty, Homer, but you got the right idea."

And then, it was done. The exhale that did not return. The women washed and dressed Leo's body. The men hefted him into the box. Flora peeked in and announced, "Grumpa's dead sleeping," Her fourth birthday coming in a week—funeral followed by party. Leo would think that perfect.

Drum put his arm around her, "But we only night sleep, Flory, cuz we're live people."

The Beekeeper's Question

Wednesday morning, the sons and farmers slid the coffin onto the old flatbed and drove Leo up the block to lie in the sanctuary of his own church. Bill left the door unlocked and folks came and went, sitting with their pastor, saying private goodbyes. The young women of the Thursday Club kept a sideboard going with cookies, apples, and a plug-in coffee pot, newly acquired. The supply preacher arrived, hung out at Gertie's, shaking people's hands, getting in the way. "I've been on preaching rotation in Browning," he announced, "Blackfeet are either Methodist or Catholic."

Doc stomped to the cash register, looked him in the eye, "Round here, Blackfeet are family. They'll be at the service." People took a breath and practiced the acceptance Leo had modeled for them.

Thursday afternoon, Boyd arrived from Seattle, driving into the honey yard in a brand-new Chevrolet Fleetmaster sedan. Maroon. White wall tires. The car drew most the attention as he jumped around to help his wife, Mariko, and their year-old son out the passenger side. Gertie was in the kitchen delivering cans of Spam. "Boyd was always the favored son, but it's going to take something for folks to let a Jap into church with the Pockets and Torgersons."

Ethel Pocket emerged from the cellar with a basket of canned goods. "Shut your mouth, Gertie. We won. They lost. No amount of hating gonna bring back Ralph." They watched Doc pull the young doctor into a happy-tears hug. "Poor girl, probably terrified." She untied her apron, "Going out to introduce myself. Somebody got to set a tone."

Friday noon, the Cooper sons, their wives, and children filed into the front pew. Sunday regulars and assorted valley folks quickly filled middle rows. Strangers arrived from Great Falls and Helena, president of the Western Beekeepers Association, board of the local bank, even the sheriff. The church hadn't been this full since the night of "the Indian fight," and some arrived with similar curiosity.

Josie escorted Doc forward, but the other Blackfeet sat quietly in back pews, respectful guardians of ceremony. "I been up front," Darrell reminded Jesse. "With all those *makóyi* eyes boring into my neck." The supply minister offered a eulogy about the early years of Methodist mission, Leo's influence, on and on. What Leo had done far away was not their interest. People's thoughts were swimming with what he did here, how Rev Leo had shepherded them. Each son spoke a few words. Doc stood last.

She wore a suit of warm brown wool with a cream blouse a bit untucked at her waist. "I met Leo and Charlotte Cooper the moment I stepped off the train on a hot August afternoon in 1910. I was struggling with luggage and a long skirt. I tripped on the step of the train car and was headed for a nasty fall." She smiled at the memory. "But Leo and Charlotte each reached out a strong arm and caught me. We steadied ourselves and said hello and that's how we stayed—holding each other up, helping each other carry our roles in this valley. The three of us. Then the two of us. Always friends." Her voice quavered. "Methodist or not, he tended us. In parlors and on porches, he listened and advised. He challenged us. And while he seemed mostly right, he wasn't always right. Leo was a decent man who did his best. He wanted us to do the same. As we lay him to rest, I hope we carry on, like his beloved bees, working to make sweetness out of life's bitter requirements." She tucked in her blouse and sat down.

In honor of Charlotte, Gladys played Dubussy's "Claire de Lune." The Blackfeet men filed out and lined the church steps. The pallbearers—Boyd, Jesse, Franklin on the left, Bill, Caleb, (and to some surprise) Homer, on the right—carried the coffin down the center aisle, between the honor guard of Piikuni warriors, and onto the cemetery cart.

The supply minister stood over the lowered box, sprinkled dirt. "Into Thy hands, Lord, we commend your faithful servant,

The Beekeeper's Question

Leo Cooper. May he be welcomed into the company of saints and anointed with the Balm of Gilead. May he rest in peace until we meet again in glory. In the name of the Father, Son, and Holy Ghost."

Josie Shines the Light stood at the grave foot. "*Nato'kssin Napiiki.* Thank you, grandfather. You were a chief among your people and a friend to my people. In the school years, you were the white man we had prayed for. Your bones are welcome to rest in *Niitawahsin.*"

Jesse placed a tin of honey atop the coffin. Willow laid sweetgrass. Maire laid sunflowers. The people said, "Amen." The young men shoveled the old man into ground.

A few days after the funeral, Maire had heard her Nana's voice, "*Bees part of the family. They got to mourn, or they die of grief. Go sing 'em the truth. Dinna need be fancy.*"

So it was, that Maire found herself driving into late autumn sunshine. Hive by hive, yard by yard, she knocked on the wooden tops, set Leo's bonnet to rest, and sang the ditty she'd composed on her way out of town. "*I come with sad tidings to say, Leo your keeper has gone far away. Death carries him now to the far golden shore, a heaven of honey his reward ever more.*" She tapped on the next box and the next, each time laying out the bonnet, each time singing. "*Do not be afraid of the winter that comes, I am here in all weather to tend to the combs. I honor the sisters, the queen, and the drones, and vow to tend faithfully your sweet honey homes.*"

The bees flew around her, drifting in motes of sunlight. "He has gone to the Great Flowering," she told them.

"*He has become the Dræn, and you become the keeper.*" The air was a flutter. "*What is your question?*" the *Hmmm* inquired.

Leo had studied order. *What was order now?* Maire rested her hands on her pregnant belly and closed her eyes. *Into what kind of world was she birthing this child?*

Surrender in Europe, surrender in Japan; a bomb that could destroy whole cities in seconds; a radio announcer said fifty-five million people had died. *How can the human heart comprehend such disaster?* So many young men, like Franklin and Ronnie, were haunted by what the war had required—the amputated arm, the twisted leg, the tortured mind. Young widows, like Hazel, braving onward in her apartment in Portland, Bonnie starting kindergarten. "We're turning into city girls," she'd written, "See you next summer." By summer, Maire would have the baby. By summer, she and Jesse would be training farmers' sons and Blackfeet boys to work the bees. She wanted the question to carry her beyond the war without denying the war. *What were the lessons they must never forget?*

Maire spun slowly, taking in the landscape of buttes and hills, far mountains, close-in fields and grazing land. She would spend her life here, far from the graves of her own ancestors, yet carrying Nana's guiding whisper. She would be a Montana woman, a beekeeper, a professor's wife. They would raise children as Leo and Charlotte and Doc had raised the Cooper boys—to think, to question, to imagine themselves beyond. She thought of Annenberg's library, how books had saved her, prepared her. *What stories would come now? What ideas would lead the way?*

A few months ago, Maire had raised a hive frame and found the bees making a chain of their bodies between sections of comb. That evening she described the phenomenon to Leo. "Ah, that's called festooning, a living garland of bees attached head-to-toe." He'd become a frail man, confined to porch and rocking chair, still thoughtful. "Beekeepers don't know why bees festoon, but it must have purpose. Everything does."

She couldn't get the image out of her mind. Insight suddenly lit her thoughts. "Leo!" she summoned his name into the brightly buzzing day, "Festooning is order combined with connection. Order without connection is fascism. Connection without order is chaos. This is what bees show us. This is Unity, their secret in plain sight."

The buzzing of D-above-middle-C intensified. *"Question?"* asked the *Hmmm*, *"wee are waiting…"*

Maire's whole body was vibrating. Earth below. Sky above. *She* was a festoon. "That's what people are," she called into the world, "We link mind and matter, work and dreams. We make the story." A question formed deep in her thorax, *"How do I be a living connector among my people?"*

Her words floated in the sun-warmed air. *"Hmmm,"* said the *Hmmm*.

She felt the whir of tiny wings. "Just to be clear," she informed them. "My question is a hive box. Many other questions reside inside it, but this is the bottom board on which I stand." Drifting crumbs of pollen anointed her skin. She breathed in grief and comfort from grief. She clutched Leo's bonnet. "I miss him," she whispered.

"All is one," said the *Hmmm*. Maire MacDonnell Cooper whirled in a golden tornado of tiny bodies on the threshold of a world becoming.

Acknowledgments

Acknowledgments traditionally start with professional connection and end with family. I am starting with family. My beloved partner, Ann Linnea, has listened to variations of this story since 2012, encouraging, editing, critiquing with her own authorly skills. She graciously accommodated these characters cohabiting our life and honored my need for uncountable hours of research, reading, and writing. My father, Leo Baldwin, who lived nearby for the last dozen years of his ninety-eight-year life, served as an invaluable consultant on beekeeping and rural Montana in a time before I was born. My sister, Becky Dougherty, intrepid family archivist and historian, supported me with Montana details and images. My brother, Carl Baldwin, US Army/ Vietnam, helped research Franklin's journey through the war (along with Robert Cabot, Age 100, US Army Signal Corps/ WW2, and Michael Orange, US Marine Corps/ Vietnam who honed my understanding of battle trauma). My brother, Eric Baldwin, for many years the "best one-handed drummer in Anchorage." inspired my understanding of Franklin's capabilities. And my knowledge of Debussy in the parlor and women in the kitchen, I learned from my mother, Connie McGregor.

As mentioned in The Author's Note, this story (and my grandfather's homestead parcel) stands on the traditional territory of the Blackfoot Confederacy. I am humbled and grateful for the introduction to a member of the tribe who would mentor me from ignorance to the beginning of understanding. Her willingness to educate me in the realities of Blackfeet life and to trust me to respectfully portray the fictional Shines the Light family was essential to the story. I would not have proceeded without this tutoring.

I acknowledge the generations of the Blackfeet Nation (Amskapi Piikuni). My heart is broken open to the real history between us. I vow to use my writing and outreach to raise white awareness and foster reckoning and restitution.

I have been a teacher of writing most of my adult life and am blessed with a sisterhood that listened, encouraged, and helped to craft, especially "The Queens" Joanna Powell Colbert, Gretchen Staebler, and Janis Hall; The Blue Couch Cafe, Deb Lund and Kate Stivers; also, Kelly Anderson, Sarah MacDougall, and dozens of beta readers. Thank you, thank you—partner, parents, siblings, friends, ancestors—you put honey in my heart.

Special gratitude to my literary agent, Meredith Bernstein, who has supported my writing from beginning to end. Her dedication to this story amid huge shifts in the industry made the book better and better. Thank you to Beth Farrell, Sea Script Company Book Publishing, for stepping in with decades of art and skill to bring this project to launch.

A book is crafted evidence of long, private dedication to writing alone in a chair. For further explorations of the backstory, bibliography, discussion guide, and deeper dives into the issues and themes raised here, please visit www.christinabaldwin.com.

CHRISTINA BALDWIN is a pioneer in the fields of personal writing and story. Her fascination began as an avid girl reader, and as a journal writer who, at age fourteen, constructed a tiny "secret annex" in her family's basement to hide her diary. She became an early teacher in the field of journal writing, from church halls to national conferences, and has helped thousands of students claim their lives in story. Her titles related to this work are: *One to One*, *Life's Companion*, *The Seven Whispers*, and *Storycatcher*.

In the process of discovery that goes on in writing classes and retreats, she and her partner, Ann Linnea, reached into their Celtic/Nordic heritages to reimagine societal beginnings as "the common first culture of circle." For twenty-five years, they taught modernized skills of circle practice across North America and around the world. Her titles related to this work are: *Calling the Circle* and *The Circle Way* (with Linnea).

She continues her lifework through her online presence and personal appearances, blogging, and additional writing. Her website: www.christinabaldwin.com, is dedicated to discussion guides, videos, podcasts, and ongoing writing about issues raised in her books. She and Ann live on an island north of Seattle, Washington, held by trees, surrounded by salt water, with a view of mountains, and in a community of friends.

Christina Baldwin books and eBooks
available at:
Amazon.com

To contact Christina:
christinabaldwin.com

Facebook

Printed in Great Britain
by Amazon